GOODNESS, GRACE

AND ME

GOODNESS, GRACE

AND ME

Julie Houston

Contents

About the Author

Julie Houston started writing when a child in her class told her she had the biggest tits he'd ever seen! Her horror turned to uncontrollable hysterics when he added, "My last teacher's were nowhere as big and always in red - never in green!" She knew she just had to get it down in writing and 'Goodness, Grace and Me' was the result. She was taken on by agent Anne Williams at KHLA in London and Bristol and, whilst she still teaches part time, (and still finds ten-year-old kids hugely funny) she is working on the sequel which she hopes will continue to make people laugh. Julie lives in West Yorkshire, where her novels are set, with a long-suffering husband, two bolshy teenagers of her own and a mad Cockapoo called Lincoln. She is a teacher and magistrate and loves nothing more than dancing round the kitchen practising her Gangnam Style moves while polishing her granite.

You can contact Julie at:
joolshouston2002@yahoo.co.uk

Twitter: @juliehouston2

Julie Houston on Facebook at:
http:www.facebook.com/Julie.houston.

Acknowledgements

There are several people to whom I'd like to say a big thank you. Firstly to Fiona Woodhead and Janet Winch at Wooldale Junior School who, over the years, have made me laugh out loud with their one-liners and who read the very first draft and said they loved it. Others who encouraged me in the early days were Jayne James, Lynda Hulme and Janet Wills, but particularly Janet who, at the very start of *every* book club meeting says 'How's the book going, Jools? When can we get our hands on it?' Loyalty indeed! Thanks to Clare Brandstrom who, when faced with me polishing my granite rather than drinking the proffered wine, coined the phrase, 'Compulsive Granite Disorder' the original title of 'Goodness, Grace and Me' and for sharing her hilarious stories of barking mad and randy au pairs.

I'd like to thank my agent, Anne Williams at KHLA, for believing in me and my book, for taking me on and doing such a good job in editing the MS before hauling it round the publishers. Thanks to Susanne Hillen for doing such a brilliant job with the copy editing and Aimee Fry at Author Works for the design of the front cover and the website.

Finally, one big thank-you to Nigel, Ben and Georgia. For just being you.

1993

'Lust,' Grace scoffed as I pointed out the man with whom I intended spending the rest of my life. 'Pure unadulterated, don't kid yourself it's anything else but, lust.'

'The One,' I countered, secure in the knowledge that indeed he was.

I recognised him instantly of course. Not from any prior knowledge, but from a deep instinctive belief that here was the man I'd been waiting for. A feeling, almost of relief, that my search was over.

And I could have missed him, for heaven's sake. Gone home for the weekend as I so often did in that first term of my second year at university. Or spent the Saturday evening in the laundrette without the indignity of queuing, bulging black bin liner in hand, until a washer came free.

But I didn't miss him. Sat with Grace and me, but not actually speaking to us, was Michael, my boyfriend from home. He'd travelled down from Yorkshire as he had every other weekend for the last year or so, and the reason he was in a deep sulk was not only the presence of Grace, my best friend from the age of eleven with whom I now shared a student house, but because I wanted out of the relationship – and he knew it.

My eyes, restlessly travelling the room, had been arrested in their journey by another pair, holding their gaze for what seemed an eternity. Flushed, I'd looked away, seeking my drink in order to give my hands – and eyes – something to do. And then started that *glorious* game which has only two players. And which ignores everything around it, but concentrates solely on the meeting of eyes, again and again, the winner being the one whose lingering glance lingers longest.

The contest was hotting up nicely, and I would have said my last glance, accompanied by a slightly wry, almost flirtatious smile had me in the lead, when Nuala, one of the other girls in our house bounded into the bar. She came over, spilling Noilly Prat and Irish conviviality in equal measures as she pushed her way through to where we were sitting. Catching sight of Michael, she frowned. Like Grace, she didn't approve of Michael, couldn't see the point in conducting a weekend-only relationship with someone who, it had to be said, appeared to spend the time he was with me either trying to persuade me to get engaged or in a deep sulk.

'Hi, Michael. How *are* you?' Nuala said carelessly. Not being remotely interested in Michael's health she turned her back on him and, in the act of squeezing her ample behind into the space between us, proceeded to alienate him even further.

'What's *your man* doing here?' she hissed, loud enough for him to hear. 'I thought you said he'd finally got the message when you went home last weekend.'

'Obviously not,' Grace complained, leaning over me in order to speak to Nuala. 'He turned up a couple of hours ago, and rather than spend an evening arguing with him at the house, she's brought him down here where there's safety in numbers. I thought the plan was a night out on the town, didn't you? And what do we find? *Him,*' she nodded towards Michael, 'still in situ. And *her,*' here she gave me a nudge, 'mooning over some other man.'

'Do you mind, you two, not speaking about me as if I wasn't here?' I'd lost eye contact with the man across the room and was desperate to get it back.

'Harriet, you are being a total *eejit*. Do you want us to tell him to bugger off, or what? Come on. Grace and I are off into town without you if you're going to stop here with that boring little fart.' Nuala was beginning to get cross. Downing the remains of her glass in one practised move she turned to leave and then instantly sat down again. 'Jesus, Mother of God, don't look now, but there is the most divine man looking in my direction. Don't look. *Don't look!*'

2

'Actually, it's *me* he's looking at,' I hissed back, giving her a poke in the ribs for good measure.

'Shame on you,' Nuala said. 'You're practically engaged to this lovely man here,' and, turning to Michael, she patted his knee encouragingly while taking another surreptitious glance across at *The One.*

Michael might have been thick-skinned (or possibly just thick – I don't really recall) but all this whispering and giggling between Grace, Nuala and myself was too much. With as much dignity as he could muster, he stood up and, like Captain Oates of the Antarctic going to his untimely death, made his exit from the union bar with the words, 'I'm going now – and I shall be gone some time.'

Nick and I had met up every evening for a week. I loved everything about him: loved his voice – the way he said 'barth' and 'clarss' rather than the 'bath' and 'class' with the flattened vowels that I'd been accustomed to hearing and using back home. I loved his dark blonde hair that he was forever pushing back out of his amazing eyes. I loved that he was over six-foot tall and seemingly unaware of the female glances he attracted wherever he went. But, most of all, I loved being kissed by Nick.

In fact Nick didn't kiss me at all until our second date and even that was a brotherly sort of kiss on the cheek as he dropped me off home at the end of the evening. When he did finally kiss me properly we were tucked into the corner of an Irish bar buzzing with noise, and I had to lean forward to catch what he was saying. As I moved towards him he brought up his hand to my hair and simply kissed the corner of my open mouth. And I was intoxicated: not from the alcohol, but from a clear, absolute certainty that everything was as it should be. The anticipation of what was to come was almost unbearable and I wanted to freeze-frame everything, absorb all that was going on around me because I knew this was it. He was *The One.*

I was in love, lust – call it what you like. I felt feverish, unable to sleep, going to lectures as normal, but unable to concentrate. Every part of me just wanted to drown in those chocolate-brown eyes, so when, at the end of one evening, he'd kissed me on the cheek and

3

said he'd call me, I was frantic to know *when*.

When I'd not heard from him for six days (and this included a very long weekend where I'd hardly moved from the hall phone, willing it to ring and then snarling at the astonished callers when it did) I had to find out why he'd not been in touch. Disregarding advice from all the females in our shared house to play it cool, I decided to call round at the house I knew he shared with two other blokes from his course. This was conveniently close to the university library so I figured it wouldn't seem untoward if I just happened to drop in, say I'd been to the library, and was there a coffee on offer? So, armed with a pile of books as my alibi, I set off.

I was so nervous I nearly came home, but I really was desperate to see him. All the way there, shifting my books from one arm to the other, I rehearsed the nonchalant speech I'd deliver as soon as he opened his front door. Except he didn't. Open his front door that is.

'Yeah?' A rather ugly, sallow-faced guy, bearded and obviously just out of the shower, answered my timid knock on the peeling, sludge-coloured door.

'I was just passing,' I gabbled, 'and wondered if Nick was around?'

'Well he's around. But rather *busy* if you get my drift.' He leered at me, showing uneven, discoloured teeth.

I felt as if I'd been winded, as if all the breath had been squeezed out of me, as I stood there, my eyes fixed on those revolting teeth in a vain attempt to dislodge the image of Nick doing God knows what – with God knows whom – from my brain.

'Any message?' The teeth seemed to have a life of their own as I continued to stare at them in fascination.

'Er, no thanks. It's fine. It doesn't matter. I just called round on the off chance.' I was gabbling again, and couldn't seem to make the necessary connection between brain and feet in order to actually walk away. The teeth, asymmetrical as the fallen, crumbling tombstones found in the graveyard backing on to our student house, protruded even further as their owner grinned an all-knowing gesture of disbelief at my risible 'off chance' claim. My feet finally engaged and turned in the direction of the garden gate.

'Should have brought my brolly,' I muttered to myself as raindrops began to fall onto the books that, now redundant from their former shallow pretext, were clutched to my chest as an armour-plated comfort blanket. It was only with the realisation that the rain was falling at a much higher temperature than one could expect from a chilly autumn evening that it hit me that I was crying, great big fat tears dripping messily from my nose and onto my hands and books.

'Oh my God. Get out the gin. Hattie's back.' Nuala, just about to draw the moth-eaten rags that passed for sitting-room curtains, had witnessed the last few steps of my return home. Grace and Sara (our fourth housemate), whose sole intention for this Monday evening had been a post-boozy weekend soap-fest, left the sofa, with its Nutella and half-eaten Pringles, and joined Nuala to witness the journey's end of their very own soap character.

'You wouldn't listen to your Auntie Sara would you? If you will go chasing after men who've promised to ring and who then don't, well, you're just asking for trouble.' Sara unbuttoned my jacket while Grace relieved my cramped arms of the books and Nuala returned from the kitchen with the bottle of gin.

'He didn't *promise* to ring,' I sobbed. 'He just *said* he'd call me.'

'Yeah, six days ago,' Sara said caustically, retrieving the jar of Nutella from the sofa and digging out a huge spoonful.

'So what did he say to you?', demanded Nuala, handing me a gin the size of which guaranteed a hangover by the end of the evening, never mind the next day.

'Nothing – I didn't get to speak to him. He was 'otherwise engaged' to quote the sniggering flatmate from hell.' I winced, as much from the memory of myself rooted to his front door step in embarrassed silence as from the huge slug of neat gin that was now burning its way down my throat. 'Jesus, Nuala, haven't we any tonic or orange to put in this gin?'

'Never mind the technicalities of the drink, Hat. What do you think your man was up to? Having a shower? Having his tea?' Nuala probed the possibilities, hopefully.

'Having Anna Fitzgerald more likely,' sighed Sara.

'Oh God. I knew he was too good to be true,' I howled. 'Who the hell is Anna Fitzgerald and why didn't you tell me about her?'

'Anna Fitzgerald is that gorgeous, upmarket blonde who zooms around the university campus in a little red sports job and who, I'm afraid, Hattie, has been going out with Nick Westmoreland since the first year.' Sara had the grace to look a little shamefaced with this admission. How could she have kept this vital information from me?

'I can't believe you let her rave on about Nick, let her go out and meet him when you knew he was involved with someone else.' Grace, always my champion when the chips were down, glared at Sara before snatching the jar of Nutella from her hand.

'Hang on a minute,' Sara protested, 'don't shoot the messenger, Grace, it's not my fault he led her up the garden path.' And then turning to me said, 'For heaven's sake, Harriet, you've only been seeing him for a couple of weeks. And furthermore, *I* didn't know Anna Fitzgerald's boyfriend was the same bloke you've been lusting over.' Sara was beginning to get angry herself now.

'So when did you realise?'

'Not until this afternoon when I saw them together in the library. I was with Becky Patterson and she spent the entire time telling me how she'd fancied Nick Westmoreland since she'd seen him at the Freshers' ball last year but hadn't been able to have a crack at him because he was always with Anna Fitzgerald. As soon as she said his name I realised *your* Nick and the one sitting across from me with Anna were one and the same. *That's* why I kicked up such a fuss about your little plan to just drop in on him this evening. *That's* why I told you to play it cool and not go hunting him down. Sorry Hattie, but he's well involved. Mind you, you were right about one thing.'

'What's that?' I asked, starting to cry again.

'He *is* bloody gorgeous.'

Nuala, recalling Nick from that first sight of him in the union bar, shook her head sadly. 'Gorgeous,' she repeated. 'An absolute ride. A total gobshite of course, but an absolute ride nevertheless.'

'Well, at least one good thing has come out of all this,' said Nuala, as she and Grace tucked me into bed with Keith, my teddy bear, and a cup of hot chocolate.

'What's that?' I asked again. My crying had subsided into occasional little hiccups and my head was beginning to ache.

'You might not have got Nick Westmoreland, but at least you haven't got that boring little fart, Michael, either.'

I reasoned that I could either hibernate for the next few years or I could face the world. So the next morning I showered, took several Paracetamol, put on my favourite jeans and the crimson cashmere sweater passed on to me by my big sister Diana and, with an extra layer of bright-red lipstick, did just that. Thank goodness I'd stepped out with hair washed and head held high. Grace and I had a nine o'clock lecture so we made our way to the Education block, cutting a swathe through what I considered to be ridiculously overeager students waiting impatiently for the library to open.

'Harriet?' Nick, looking pale, but undoubtedly still sublime, pushed his way through a chattering group of girls from where he'd been leaning against the gum-decorated wall outside the Education faculty.

'Hello, Nick.' Calm or what? Grace, for once at a loss for words, gave me a meaningful look and then made her way to the lecture theatre, leaving me face to face with the man who was about to complete the job, started last night while he bedded his long-term girlfriend, of breaking my heart.

'Can we go for a coffee?' he asked, taking my arm.

'I've a lecture to go to,' I said, moving towards the steps.

'I've been here since half-past eight, hoping you had a nine o'clock lecture. I really need to talk to you.'

Oh God. Here it comes, I thought. The 'I-should-have-told-you-about-Anna' routine.

'Look, you obviously know I called round last night,' I said, looking somewhere in the region of his chest. I knew if I'd looked into those wonderful eyes I'd have been lost, started blubbing, or buried my nose into his neck just to smell him, or something equally awful. 'I didn't realise you were involved with someone else or I'd never have agreed to go out with you. You really don't need to explain anything to me. I must go or I'll miss this lecture, and psychology isn't my strong point.'

Nick took my arm again and said, 'Harriet, please just come with me for a coffee. One missed lecture isn't going to ruin your career.'

I nodded and without another word we walked off the campus and across the busy main road to a quiet little Italian coffee place I didn't even know existed. As Nick stood at the counter ordering the coffees, I took in every aspect of him, from the dark-blonde hair curled on to the blue-striped shirt collar, down to the frayed bottoms of his faded jeans where they skimmed his somewhat weathered desert boots. How was I to sit there, listening to his apologies, when all I wanted was to wrap my arms around him, lose myself in his eyes, his voice, his smile?

But he wasn't smiling as he stirred his coffee. 'Harriet, I'm really sorry about this,' he said miserably.

'Just tell me how you managed to see me nearly every evening for over a week without your girlfriend finding out?'

'She's doing a languages degree and is spending the year in France.'

'France? How come you were with her yesterday then?'

'She was back in England for her brother's wedding. He got married at the weekend and I was invited. That's why I didn't get in touch with you. I knew Anna was on her way back to her parents for the week, and I knew I needed to sort out in my own mind how I felt about her. We've been together a long time, you know.'

When I didn't say anything – couldn't say anything – Nick sighed loudly. 'Look Harriet, it doesn't make me feel very good to know that I'm involved with someone else but came on to you.'

Was there a hint in that last sentence – 'am involved' – as in the *present* tense?

'When I first saw you in the union bar,' Nick went on, 'I knew I had to get to know you. The week I spent with you was wonderful.'

Oops, definitely another hint – 'was wonderful' – as in the *past* tense.

'But why didn't you tell me you were involved with someone?'

'I suppose I was afraid you wouldn't agree to see me again.' Nick took my hand. 'The last time I saw you I knew Anna would be back in the country the day after that. I wanted to sort it all out with her before I got in touch with you again. I was really honest with her. After the wedding I told her I'd met someone else and she seemed to take it OK. Even told me she'd met someone else herself in France.'

'Well she would wouldn't she?'

'Would she?' Nick seemed surprised at this.

'Of course. The poor girl's pride had been dented. So if it was all sorted how come you were cosily ensconced in the library with her yesterday?' Damn! I hadn't meant to let slip that I knew about that. He'd think I'd had my spies out on him.

Nick didn't appear to take much notice of this and went on, 'I got back from staying with her parents on Sunday evening and planned to get in touch with you last night. I was in the library yesterday afternoon catching up with a couple of assignments when she just suddenly appeared. Said we needed to talk and how she couldn't go back to France leaving it like this. I spent all afternoon and evening with her, trying to calm her down as she became increasingly hysterical.'

When I didn't say anything Nick sighed and went on, 'Harriet, it wasn't my intention to hurt her *or* lie to you.'

'Well no,' I acquiesced, 'I don't suppose it was. So where is she now?' I turned to the open door, half expecting her to come through it and lay claim to Nick once more.

'About one this morning I finally called her friend who came to pick her up. She's taken her to the airport this morning. Her plane leaves about ten o'clock.'

There didn't seem much point in going to what was left of my lecture. Instead, Nick and I went back to his room in his shared house. Everyone else, including the goofy letch from the previous evening, was out, thank goodness.

While Nick made more coffee, which neither of us wanted, I nervously prowled his room picking up books and reading blurbs in which I had no interest.

'Have you read this one?' I asked as Nick came into his room from the kitchen.

'Um, yes.' Nick put down the mugs on the table.

'And, um, any good?'

'Harriet? Will you please put down the sodding books and come here?'

Nick unwrapped the scarf from around my neck and slowly unbuttoned each fastening on my jacket, lifting my long hair from the nape of my neck before letting the coat fall on to the floor. Still holding my hair in his fingers, he kissed the skin on my neck and I was lost.

Making love was a revelation. I marvelled at his body, hard and tanned and lithe. I traced every sinew, every blonde hair and made it mine. His warm hands stroking my back under the softness of my cashmere sweater was a heady combination, and as he pulled it over my head, kissing me slowly as my breasts struggled for freedom, I felt truly beautiful. When he entered me I felt as if I'd come home, and when, after making sure I came first, he gave himself up to his own climax, he bit his lip to stop himself from crying out loud.

And so this is where, almost twenty years ago, in 1993, the *Nick* bit of the story starts. It was fortuitous that Grace, who had been with me at every other momentous happening since the age of eleven, should have been with me on *that* evening in the union bar.

And that, for the first time, also since the age of eleven, when Grace and I first set eyes on 'Little Miss Goodness', I'd once again fallen utterly, and irrevocably, in love.

Chapter 1

'So, this David Henderson. Tell me something about him, and why he's invited someone he only met last night to his house for dinner.'

I closed my eyes and leaned back against the car headrest, soothed by the steady hum of tyres on wet road and the Mozart clarinet concerto that always reminded me of school speech days long gone.

When Nick didn't respond I turned my head towards him, and opened one eye.

'Nick?'

'What?'

'David Henderson? Why has he invited us for dinner when you only met him last night?'

'I didn't say I'd only met him last night.' Nick had the grace to look uncomfortable if not downright shifty.

'Yes you did,' I retaliated, sitting up properly now. 'Yesterday morning you said you were having a meeting and dinner with some businessman Brian Thornton was going to introduce you to. You didn't say you already knew him.'

'What difference does it make, Harriet, whether I met him last night or a month or so ago?' He was irritable, obviously tense about the evening ahead.

I knew it shouldn't make any difference, but it did. The knowledge that Nick had been what I could only think of as, well, *plotting,* with this man, made me uneasy. Glancing over at Nick, I could see that, irritable and stressed as he was, he was also animated, full of unspent energy. This was the old Nick, the one I'd not seen for years. Not since the months straight after University when he'd taken all that life had to offer, grabbing it with both hands and started his ascent to the top with his new textiles company. For fourteen years the business could do no wrong as Nick took on more and more people and the company expanded. He gained the respect, not only of other newcomers to the business, but also of the old West Yorkshire mill owners who, struggling with new technology and obsolete premises, very often turned to him for advice. Within a year of marrying we were able to leave our tiny rented flat and move into the old farmhouse we now lived in. Once the children were born, and decisions needed making about education, we were in a position to go private, despite my dad's mantra to 'remember your roots, Harriet'. To quote some corny seventies pop song, 'we had it all.'

And then, quite shockingly, the business had failed, one of the very first victims of a recession that would continue, unleashed and out of control, leaving devastation in its path. It had started slowly at first with a couple of bad debts which, though annoying, weren't enough to rock the boat or stop us having what would, it turned out, be our last wonderful holiday in Barbados. Because Nick's business, The Pennine Clothing Company, had been so successful in such a short time, he had been able to pay off most of the start-up loans within a few years. But there had been one loan outstanding, and when the banks became jittery and demanded larger, faster repayments at exactly the same time as Nick's three biggest customers all went bust, the death knell on the business was sounded – loud and very clear.

Which is why, apparently, we were now on our way to have dinner with someone who Nick reckoned could be the answer to his prayers. What those prayers entailed was anyone's guess.

'You'll really like David,' Nick now said, in an effort to mollify me. 'And Mandy is great too.'

'Mandy?'

'David's wife. You'll really like her. She's wonderful. Very supportive. Good dress sense.'

His wife? He knew his *wife* too? And when had he ever noticed anyone's dress sense? The unease I'd been feeling over the last couple of weeks began to intensify and I could feel my stomach start to churn.

'Nick,' I spoke slowly. 'What are you up to with this David Henderson?' And then, as an awful thought hit me, 'Oh, please don't tell me you've already handed in your notice at Wells Trading?'

'Don't be ridiculous, Hat, of course I haven't. I might hate the damned place but it has kept a roof over our heads for the last two years. Look, we're nearly here. Just relax, put a smile on your face for God's sake will you, and make an effort to be civil – for my sake?'

I can only ever sulk for a maximum of five minutes, by which time I've usually had enough of giving the cold-shoulder treatment and need to start talking again. Life is just too short to spend it in silence. The sulking gene, rife throughout my mother's side of the family, seemed to have mutated and come to a natural standstill with Aunt Zilla, my mum's youngest sister. She once kept a sulk going for almost two months, only communicating with my Uncle Maurice through her sons – my cousins. It became a family joke; my dad even opened a book and took bets as to how long Uncle Maurice would be in Coventry for this time. With the odds at twenty to one for a two months' silence, my Granny Morgan scooped the winning bet and, obviously still on a gambling high, blew it all on an orgy of slot machines one wet, Sunday afternoon in Blackpool.

I adjusted the mirror to check that my lippy was still in place and to try out the little pout I'd been practising the last few weeks.

'What on earth's the matter with your lips?' Nick asked nervously, peering at me as we crunched onto the drive in front of one of the most beautiful houses I'd ever seen. A *25 Beautiful Homes* junky, I was about to overdose.

'Just putting on my pout to impress,' I said airily as we got out of the car. 'My God, Nick, who are these people? They must be billionaires.'

'Well, millionaires at least,' Nick agreed and then, catching sight of my foolproof 'pout to impress the rich and famous,' laughed out loud. 'Stop it, you idiot,' he grinned. 'You look like Donald Duck.' Straightening his tie and stroking my bottom in the way he knew I loved, we walked up the steps to a door that, for sheer size and grandeur, would have given Buckingham Palace a run for its money. 'Behave yourself!'

Unfortunately, not only did being likened to Donald Duck make me laugh, but I now had it in my head that the Hendersons were about to metamorphose into the Queen and the Duke of Edinburgh and I was going to have to curtsy. By the time the huge polished door opened I was having a serious fit of the giggles.

Now some women laugh delicately. A feminine, tinkling little titter that in no way compromises their standing in society, their carefully applied make-up, or their knickers. Unfortunately I am not, and never have been, one of said women. When I laugh, I roar. I snort. Tears amalgamate with snot and I am, in a word, a liability.

With tears coursing down my cheeks and legs desperately crossed, I clung to Nick, hysterical with laughter.

'For God's sake, Hattie, think of something to take your mind off it!' Nick hissed. 'Think of the little boy who stopped Holland flooding by putting his finger in the hole in the dyke.'

This was the worst vision Nick could have suggested. As the door opened, an appraising pair of brown eyes took one look at me practically on my knees, mascara running down my flushed face and gabbling hysterically about 'Dutch lesbians,' before turning to Nick for explanation.

I reckoned I could do one of three things: apologise calmly to David Henderson and then go home and kill myself. Or pretend I was a mad wife in the style of Mrs Rochester, and wait for *Nick* to kill me, or thirdly … I didn't need a third option. The sight of David Henderson's wife appearing behind her husband in an obvious desire to find out what all the commotion was about had the same effect on my hysterics as a sudden shock on hiccups.

'I'm sorry,' laughed Nick heartily. Too heartily. The bray hanging in the air while the couple at the door tried to make sense of what was in front of them gave every indication that Nick could count donkeys among his ancestors.

'Harriet was just, er, recounting the joke one of the children in her class told her today,' Nick continued desperately.

'Well, Harriet,' said David Henderson kissing my cheek, 'you must share it with us all over dinner. Lovely to meet you at last.' *At last?* 'Do come in. This is Mandy.'

'We have met,' I muttered, as all three looked at me in surprise.

'We have?' Mandy peered at me, looking me up and down as if I were a particularly strange specimen she'd been asked to identify in an A-level biology exam. 'I don't ... I'm sorry ...'

She tailed off when, sighting a downstairs' cloakroom ahead, I interrupted with, 'Look, do you mind if I just nip to your loo?' and made a dash for it.

Shame the Alice Cooper look wasn't the height of fashion that season. A black rivulet of mascara had descended down each cheek, one finishing somewhere around my left ear, the other merging with the 'Crimson Dawn' lipstick that must have departed company with my lips on the Hendersons' steps.

Blimey! No wonder Mandy Henderson, aka 'Little Miss Goodness', hadn't recognised me. Giving thanks to God that my pants were only *slightly* damp, and I'd had the good sense to stick a spare lipstick and mascara into my handbag, I set about repairing my ravaged face and composure. The huge Victorian-style washbasin in which I rinsed my hands was set into a block of exquisitely polished granite marred only by the droplets of water that had escaped my ablutions. Glancing round almost guiltily, I used one of the wonderfully soft and scented hand towels to return the granite to its former unblemished glory. There, that was better. The granite was pristine once more and I began to relax.

'You silly bitch,' I chastised my reflection in the mirror and, taking a deep breath, followed the direction of voices to a ravishingly elegant sitting room. Immensely tall windows were swathed from head to toe in cream, the superfluous silk pooling onto the cream carpet so it was difficult to tell where one finished and the other began. The walls, not to be outdone, were also clad in cream silk with the exception of the long back wall, so sated with books it almost groaned, standing to attention over a grand piano as black and shiny as a large, dignified beetle.

'Ah, Harriet, there you are. Champagne?' David Henderson left the group of men where he'd been holding court, and came over to where I stood admiring what I guessed were leather-bound first editions. 'Do you read?'

Stifling the impulse to say, 'Yes, since the age of five,' I smiled and took the proffered glass. 'You have a fantastic collection here.'

'My father was an avid collector, if not a great reader. I think he probably bought them in the same way that he accumulated his wine cellar – the enjoyment was in the acquisition rather than in the actual drinking of the wine.'

I raised my eyebrows, as much at the thought of anyone buying a bottle of wine and preferring to look at it rather than drink it as the champagne bubbles which were going up my nose.

'So, don't tell me,' I said, 'You've got a wine cellar to match this library of books?'

He smiled. 'That's where my father and I differed. While his books tend to remain pretty static, his wine portfolio is fairly quickly diminishing. Having said that, I'm not a total philistine. I do sit down some evenings when I have time and lose myself in one of his books. So, tell me, where do you think you know Mandy from?'

'Amanda and I were at school together. I was a grubby-kneed third-former at Midhope Grammar when she was head girl.'

'Really? Mind you, if she was so much older than you it's no wonder she didn't appear to remember you. You always remember the people in the classes above you at school, don't you, but never the ones below?' As David filled up my glass I didn't like to remind him that my own mother very probably wouldn't have claimed kin with the giggling, squirming jelly that had taken root on his doorstep earlier that evening.

There were twelve of us for dinner and as David, remembering his duty as host, led me to where Nick and a group of five others stood talking by the fireplace, Amanda reappeared presumably from carrying out some task in the kitchen.

'Mandy,' he called as she hovered at the edge of a circle of four women, 'Harriet says she was at school with you – that's how she knows you.'

'Was she? Good God! Harriet Burton!' Mandy enunciated each syllable in the upper-class drawl that took me back twenty-five years.

'Oh, you remember her?' David confirmed, pleased. 'I'm amazed. Can't say I remember anyone more than a year below me – unless they were in the rugger team of course.'

Amanda walked over and kissed me on the cheek before saying, 'How could I ever forget Harriet? You really look very much the same as you did when you were at school.'

'Oh gosh,' I twittered nervously, 'I think I've moved on a bit since the days of spots and inky fingers.'

'Do you ever see your partner-in-crime these days?' she asked pleasantly. We both knew she was referring to Grace.

'Grace? Yes, I see her every day – I've actually been working with her for the past two years. We both teach at Stanhope Junior near Farsley.'

The look of disbelief tempered with amazement that traversed Amanda's face was the self-same expression regularly bestowed upon Grace and me in response to the many excuses we manufactured as to why we were without our berets, running in the corridor or hiding in the loo in preference to freezing our fourteen-year-old tushes off in the playground.

'Amazing.' Amanda looked me up and down, taking in every aspect of the thirty-eight- year-old woman that that fourteen-year-old had become. 'Both of you teachers? And how amazing that you're married to Nicky.'

Nicky? You had to be on pretty intimate terms to call my husband Nicky. Said it reminded him of a dog's name, and had always much preferred the more down-to-earth Nick. I began to get the feeling, glancing over to *Nicky* and then back at *Mandy*, that I might have to do some serious calling to heel.

The Hendersons' dining room was every bit as stylish as the room we had just departed. Classically understated, the huge oval table was a work of art, each of the twelve place settings a masterpiece of gleaming cutlery, cut glass and crisp cream linen. Amanda obviously had no truck with elaborate, silver candelabra; instead there were lone red candles, each one adrift in a jasmine-scented lake contained in receptacles reflecting the mellow hues of autumn. The last of the Floribunda roses, blowsy as ageing call girls, flaunted their all in shades of scarlet and brass, while a wooden bowl of orchard apples, flushed with their own success, made an original centrepiece to the table. The overall impression was one of falling leaves and *Harvest Home*. I could almost smell garden bonfires burning, and the words of Ted Hughes' poem, 'October Dawn', danced around in my brain, looking for release.

October is marigold, and yet
A glass half full of wine left out
To the dark heaven all night, by dawn ...

By dawn what? For the life of me I couldn't remember what happened with the dawning of, well, dawn.

I closed and screwed up my eyes in a bid to remember the lines I'd last recited in A-level English class.

'Are you alright?' The voice to my right held misgiving rather than concern.

'What? Oh sorry, I was just trying to remember the words of a poem. The colours on the table reminded me of a poem about October.'

He laughed and said, 'Thank goodness for that. I thought you'd had too much champagne and were going to be sick.'

'No, don't worry. It's my turn to drive tonight. I've had my allotted units, and I'm now on water.' I held up my glass of sparkling Perrier as added proof I wasn't about to vomit over him. I held out my hand. 'Hi, I'm Harriet. We weren't introduced in the sitting room.'

'Mike Rawlinson. Hello. How do you know David and Mandy?'

'I didn't until this evening. At least I didn't know David. Mandy, I now realise, I was actually at school with. She was head girl when I was in the third form. We're here because my husband, Nick, met

David through business.' If I didn't acknowledge the fact that Nick was intent on becoming *part* of David Henderson's business, I could forget about it for a while. No such luck, it seemed.

'Ah, I wondered which of these guests was David's latest protégé.' If I hadn't sneaked a quick look at Mike Rawlinson and seen otherwise, I would have wagered the last fiver in my pocket that his tanned face held a sneer rather than the perfect smile he actually proffered.

'Protégé?' I asked nervously. 'What exactly are David's protégés? How many has he got?'

'Oh you *know*,' he answered as he accepted the breadbasket doing its journey around the table. He took one of the warm, fragrant rolls and broke off a piece, buttered it lavishly and popped it into his large mouth.

'No, I'm sorry, I really *don't* know and why do you assume that Nick is the latest one?' I didn't like this man with his cavernous mouth and large white teeth. It was a bit like sitting next to a contemptuous shark.

Mike Rawlinson took a sip of wine and leaned into me. 'Look,' he smirked. 'Just look around you. David is a very wealthy, very clever man. He's made enough to sit back on his laurels and enjoy the fruits of his labour. But he's driven. He'll always want more, so he homes in on those who he feels may be of use to him in his next project.'

'Which is what?' I asked.

'No idea,' Mike said. 'He usually has several ideas kicking around in that complex head of his, and he certainly won't let the fact businesses are failing daily put him off. Tough economic times will probably spur him on further. If your husband is ambitious and determined and not afraid to take risks then he'll make a success of whatever David has in mind for him.'

Risks? Oh shit. I didn't do risks. I did security: a roof over our heads, and bank balances in a nice soothing black colour rather than the devilish red that had characterised our morning mail when Nick's business was crumbling.

'And if he doesn't?' I realised I'd been holding my breath.

'Doesn't what?'

'Doesn't make a success of it?'

'Then he'll chew him up and spit him back out right where he found him.'

'And you're sure about this, are you?' I asked.

'Does Pinocchio have wooden balls?' He smirked once more and I turned away from him and looked over to where Nick was deep in conversation with Amanda. He looked animated, alive, full of the same restless energy he'd had when I first met him and throughout the early years of our marriage when he'd been building up and making a success of The Pennine Clothing Company. Amanda was laughing at something he'd just said and was leaning towards him, her hair almost touching his shoulder – surely for far longer than was absolutely necessary – and I felt the hairs rise slightly on the nape of my neck. It had been a long time since I'd just sat and looked objectively at this man to whom I'd been married for over fifteen years. We never seemed to have time these days to just *sit*, never mind sit and look at each other. Nick hadn't altered much at all, really. He was still tall and chunky with dirty-blonde hair that lightened in the sun, and his eyes were the same melted pools of Galaxy-chocolate that I'd wanted to drown in the first time I met him. He loosened his tie slightly, revealing that lovely hollow at his collarbone, and I knew that if I were to go over there right now and press my face against it, the faint citron tang of Dior would be lingering on his still-tanned skin.

I loved him, every tiny little bit of him.

Amanda now touched Nick's hand, fleetingly but with an intimacy that set my heart racing, before rising and leaving the table. This was ridiculous. I was a grown woman, and yet Amanda Goodners was having the same mesmerising, almost hypnotic effect on me now as she'd had when Grace and I had adored her at the age of eleven. The same effect, I could see, that she was having upon my husband.

Chapter 2

'Good-looking man, your husband.' Mike Rawlinson had followed my gaze across the table to where Nick was in the process of topping up the now absent Amanda's wine glass.

'I think so,' I said shortly, wishing I could be rescued from this patronising marine-life on my right. I turned towards the man on my left to whom I'd been chatting earlier in the sitting room, but he was in the middle of telling what appeared to be a long and complicated joke to the people around him.

'Yup,' the Great White continued, drawing out the word as he leaned right into me once more. I *really* wished he'd stop doing that. I couldn't compete with those teeth, but if his leg pressed against mine just one more time I'd give it a bloody good kick. 'I can see he fits the Henderson bill exactly – and not just with *Mr* H, if you get my drift. I don't think you'll be seeing much of your husband over the next few months.'

When I didn't reply, Mike Rawlinson moved in even closer. His breath smelt of stale wine and bad digestion and I recoiled slightly, as much to remove myself from these fumes as from his insinuations. 'I mean, could any man resist the delicious Mandy?' he drawled. 'Look at that face, that mouth, those tits. I think you'll find, Harriet, you'll be spending a few evenings alone in the weeks to come. Now, if that's the case and you need a little comfort …'

I extricated my leg from Mike Rawlinson's, turning my back on him and, hearing what I assumed to be a joke-teller's punchline, joined in with the laughter emanating from the guests on my left. My laughter seemed to go on longer and louder than anyone else's, but what the hell, I was in, a fully paid-up member of the joke-telling crowd, rescued from Mike Rawlinson's insinuations, and the only currency needed had been to laugh like a drain at a joke I hadn't even heard.

I spent the next fifteen minutes or so swapping jokes and making small talk with the Tony Blair lookalike on my left, only interrupted by mouthfuls of the most divine food I think I've ever eaten. It was so sensational I found myself gazing wistfully at the barely touched plate of the Prada-clad anorexic seated on David Henderson's left. She must have felt my eyes upon her because she suddenly turned in my direction and barked, 'So, Harriet, I believe you teach?' Her words were so clipped as to be almost non-existent, the vowels presumably swallowed instead of the delicious food.

'Yes, that's right,' I smiled.

'St Andrew's or Beldon House?' she asked, naming the two most expensive and prestigious private schools in the area.

'Stanhope Junior in Farsley actually,' I said politely, moving to one side slightly as one of Amanda's little helpers for the evening laid a plate of pink, succulent lamb in front of me.

'You teach in the *state* system?' If I'd told her I worked as a pole dancer in the newly opened Girls R Us in Brandon, the notoriously sleazy area just outside Midhope town centre, I don't think she could have looked any more astonished.

'Gracious, you are brave aren't you?'

'Brave?'

Ignoring her food in favour of a very large glass of wine, she took a huge glug and went on, 'Well, one reads such *stories* about *state* education. Are they true?'

The phrase, 'Get a life, Lollipop Head,' sprang to mind, but to my horror I heard myself saying, 'Tell you what, Suzy, why don't you come and find out for yourself?'

'How do you mean?'

'Well, we have a new head teacher. He only started with us a couple of weeks ago and he's determined to have an open-door policy. He's always happy to have parents and visitors in the classroom.' Quite the opposite of Harold Parkin, our previous head, who had been equally determined to 'Keep the buggers out.' 'Come and spend an afternoon with us instead of believing all you read in the papers.'

'Do you know, I'd really like to do that.'

I don't think I'd ever seen such a tiny person consume so much alcohol. Another full glass went down, her eyes gleamed and I could see that she was filled with a missionary zeal to see how the other half lived. 'Farsley's on the way to my gym,' she said, her voice slurred. 'I could pop in and see you after my advanced step class. Do you have a card with your phone number?'

Oh God! Grace and Valerie Westwood, my deputy, would have a field day if Suzy actually turned up, never mind the kids who wouldn't understand a word she was saying.

''Fraid not,' I smiled, reaching into my bag for pen and an old used envelope. 'State school wages don't run to such luxuries.'

The evening seemed interminable, and was not made any easier by my lack of alcohol intake as everyone around me seemed intent on getting as much down their necks as was possible.

I sipped my water and looked over to where Amanda was now talking to a rather voluptuous redhead seated to her left. There was no doubt about it, Amanda was still as beautiful as when I used to crane my neck to see her as she sat on the prefects' bench in assembly. There was a sheen about her that reminded me of whipped egg white when it achieves that glossy look, as meringue ready for piping. Her hair, still ash-blonde but now with different coloured lowlights, fell to her shoulders in a fashionably straight curtain. Her breasts, displayed to full advantage in a stunning copper-coloured dress, were high and tanned but there was nothing of the leathery handbag about them. A smattering of freckles across both her décolletage and the bridge of her nose gave an air of youthful dewy freshness to her whole countenance, and the few lines that the years had added around her eyes did not detract from her overall beauty. She was one sassy lady.

Amanda continued chatting to the redhead, but I could see her attention was wandering. Even as she smiled and made small talk, her eyes would constantly move away, coming to rest again and again on my husband and, when Nick moved to refill her water glass, she laid her hand on his arm once more but now kept it there in a gesture of possession.

She must have become conscious of my gaze because she suddenly broke off mid sentence, turning those cool, appraising, almost navy-blue eyes in my direction and raising quizzical eyebrows as she did so. Flustered at having been caught blatantly gawping, I was relieved when Tony Blair tapped my arm in order to attract my attention.

As I dutifully sent on the large decanter of port that had arrived in front of me, Amanda insisted we all change places. Thank God she hadn't suggested we leave the men to their port and business deals and retire elsewhere. Modern woman she might be, but I bet some of her mother's ideas on good form still lingered. It was well after eleven and I began to worry about Jennifer, the sixteen-year-old babysitter. Liberty and Kit, my two elder offspring, had both escaped babysitting duties and, with my mother-in-law away for the weekend, I'd had to draft in the daughter of a school colleague to take care of five-year-old India. I was trying to catch Nick's eye as Amanda came round the table and seated herself in Mike Rawlinson's vacated chair.

'Now then, Harriet, you do know about the Midhope Grammar School get-together, don't you?'

Did I? I vaguely remembered a letter about some reunion arriving a month or so ago, but hadn't given it another thought. I'd more than likely tossed it into the dresser drawer where it would stay amongst the bits of Lego, rubber bands and India's art work until the drawer no longer closed, heralding a major clear-out.

'I think something did come in the post, Amanda, but I have to say I didn't really take much notice of it. Reunions are not really my thing.'

The look she gave me was reminiscent of twenty-five years ago. I might as well have said going out into the wet playground wasn't my thing.

'Oh, but you must come. It's the school's 100-year anniversary in a couple of weeks. Sally Davies, Andrea Collins and I are helping to organise it, and the head teacher there at the moment has given us permission to meet actually in the school rather than in the hotel or pub that we've had to use in the past.'

The thought of going back to what had been Midhope Grammar and meeting up with old girls, and presumably staff too, was actually quite exciting, but I was only going to go if I could persuade Grace to come too. Amanda reached into the drawer of a bureau behind her back, and fished out replicas of the letter I now recognised as having received just a couple of weeks ago.

'Leave it with me,' I said, putting the letters into my bag and simultaneously pushing back my chair. 'Actually, Amanda, we really must be making a move. I told the babysitter we wouldn't be too late.'

She crossed one elegant leg over the other before asking, 'How many children do you have?'

'Three. Liberty is fifteen, Kit almost fourteen and India is five. The elder two are staying with friends and I've left the little one with a new babysitter.'

'You're lucky still having them all at home. We've just got the one, Sebastian. He's twenty-three now and has found it difficult to settle down to the idea of working for a living. He finished university, but has had wanderlust ever since. He's travelled to Europe, South America and has even been involved with some project in the Antarctic. He's been in New Zealand for the last six months, but he's actually on his way home at the moment.' Her face softened as she spoke of her only child.

'What's he been doing out there?' I asked, genuinely interested.

'David's brother owns a sheep farm on the South Island and Seb has been there since last March, having an absolute ball by all accounts. He's coming back via Australia, Fiji and Thailand, and is back in Midhope in a couple of weeks. I can't wait for him to come home.'

Her excitement was palpable, but tinged with sadness. 'I say home,' she went on, 'but I can't see it will be long before he's off again.'

'What did he study at university?' I asked.

'Law, same as me. Both of us studied law at Oxford.'

'Did you ever use your law degree?' I was curious about what Amanda had been up to since coming back to Midhope.

'I didn't finish Oxford. I was married and had Seb when I was nineteen. I transferred to Leeds to finish my degree when he started school, and now I help David out whenever I can. I'm really hoping that Sebastian will do articles and settle down once he gets home.'

I glanced at my watch again, and jumped up. 'Sorry we've to leave so early, but I'm afraid tonight it was a choice between a get-home-early-babysitter or no babysitter at all.' I still had to drive Jennifer to the other side of town once we'd got home.

Suzy seemed to have disappeared – possibly under the table. As Nick and I made our goodbyes, The Great White shark waved a dessert fork in my direction, presumably as a gesture of farewell. Whatever its intention, it gave a whole new meaning to the phrase, 'Prick with Fork!'

Nick closed his eyes and stretched himself out full length on the passenger seat as I manoeuvred the car between what must have been a half million pounds worth of upmarket wheels parked in the drive.

'Well, I think that went pretty well,' he grinned. He was the metaphorical cat that had landed the cream. Any minute now he'd be purring.

'So what did you think?' he demanded as he buckled himself in to his seat belt.

'What did I think about what?' Normally there was nothing I enjoyed more after an evening out than a good old dissection of who'd been there and who'd said what, but seeing Amanda Goodners again after all these years had made me irritable, if not nervous.

'Well, David, Mandy, the house?'

'I thought David was charming, but I wouldn't trust him as far as *our* house. Amanda, well of course I have the advantage over you on this one, seeing I've known her for years. You do know who she is don't you?'

'What do you mean, 'who she is'?' Nick, still in self-congratulatory mode, merely opened one eye as he stretched his six-foot frame even further into the car seat.

'Your Mandy,' I hissed, 'is Amanda. You know, Amanda, my brother John's Amanda?'

'Amanda as in 'never mention that woman's name in my hearing ever again'?' Nick's eyes, both now fully open, were in perfect synchronisation with his dropped jaw.

'The very same,' I said grimly as I finally exited the Henderson's protracted driveway and turned on to the meandering country lane down which their house was hidden.

'Phew.' Rendered speechless for a full thirty seconds, this was the only word Nick could come up with to break the silence in the car. 'But what about the house? What did you think of that?' he gabbled in a valiant attempt to get Team Henderson back in the good books.

What could I say except the truth, that it was the most divine house I had ever seen.

'And that's what I want for *you* – for us, the kids.' Nick looked almost fierce. 'If Pennine Clothing Company hadn't gone pear-shaped when it did, we'd have moved on and be in a house like that by now.'

'But it did,' I said gently. 'And we've survived haven't we? We live in a beautiful house of our own. A bit in need of a general makeover I grant you but, for heaven's sake, Nick, we really shouldn't be complaining about the house we've got.' Compared to the tiny council house I'd grown up in it really was a palace. And I loved it.

Nick sat up and banged the car door with his fist. Golly, he was getting het up.

'Hat, I don't want you to have to share your house with my mother.' Well, he had a point there. Losing my study and playroom to incorporate a granny flat for Nick's mother Sylvia after my father-in-law died hadn't been my idea of fun either. It had been a question of having Sylvia move in with us and share the mortgage or downsize to a much smaller place.

'I don't want you to have to teach those horrible children when you should be, well, when you should be spending your days having lunch out and shopping.'

'Hey, steady on,' I protested. 'What century are you living in? I happen to quite like my job.' Well, some of the time anyway.

'Harriet, I don't want you to have to work if you don't want to. But at the moment we just can't survive without your wage as well as mine.'

Nick had hit the nail squarely on its head.

'Exactly!' I said as calmly as I could. 'We can't survive without your wage. So how can you think about throwing it all in at Wells Trading and risking everything by joining up with someone you know nothing about?'

Nick was genuinely puzzled. 'I know lots about David Henderson. He has brilliant business acumen – made an absolute fortune. Mind you, I don't imagine he suffers fools gladly – you wouldn't want to get on the wrong side of him. You should be very impressed he's interested in what I might be able to do for him.'

We'd stopped at a red light, so I turned to Nick and said, 'The man next to me at dinner seemed to know all about David Henderson's business deals. Gave me the impression it was all a bit shady and you should watch your back.' I'd unconsciously lowered my voice.

Nick laughed. 'God, Harriet, you are so bloody melodramatic.'

Melodramatic? Moi? We'd soon see who was being melo-dramatic when he was being fed to the fishes.

'What are you so worried about?' Nick's question echoed that of Grace from the night before. Myself and Grace, my best friend and confidante, had shared every moment of celebration as well as despair since we'd met on the first day at grammar school over twenty-five years earlier. Last night I'd poured out all my anxieties about Nick's restlessness to her over a bottle of wine in my kitchen. Nick now yawned widely, running his hands through his hair before nudging me. 'And you're speeding, by the way.'

My stomach churned as my foot hit the brake and I recalled, once more, the horror of the unexpected collapse of Nick's company two years ago. 'I'm worried about you giving up your job, investing any money we don't actually have in a business which could, I'm sorry, Nick, which could fail again.' I knew my voice was getting louder, could feel myself becoming agitated. It was the stuff of my nightmares. I took a deep breath, trying to talk to Nick logically and calmly, wanting him to see my point of view. 'And when it did fail, finding ourselves without a roof over our heads, the kids unable to go to their schools any more, and me having to work at Stanhope Junior until I'm eighty. And there's your mother. Where would she go if we had to downsize? You can't make a granny flat out of the two-up, two-down that we'd have to move to if we couldn't pay the mortgage on our place every month.' It all came out in a rush. I was tired and I was frightened and I didn't want to discuss this anymore.

Particularly since Amanda Goodners seemed to be a big part of the equation.

My immediate thought on entering the darkened sitting room was that a very pink pig had somehow found its way in and was gyrating wildly on our Persian rug. My second was, how would I ever be able to look Margaret Walker in the eye at school on Monday knowing that sixteen-year-old Jennifer had been having sex on my Persian rug under the pretext of babysitting my daughter? Some sixth sense must have told the owner of the buttocks that they were under shocked scrutiny, for they came to a sudden standstill. The grandfather clock in the far corner of the room, a wedding present from a great-aunt of Nick's, had stopped at nine forty-five, presumably aiding and abetting Jennifer and the boy – boyfriend? – in their illicit romp.

I honestly didn't know what stance to take. Should I act the Victorian guardian, telling them to get out and never darken my door again? Or should I be all matey matey, asking if the Earth had moved for both of them and offering them a post-jump cigarette? I did neither. I told Jennifer I was going into the kitchen to make a cup of tea and suggested they both get dressed.

'What's the matter?' Nick, returning from upstairs where he'd been checking on India and finding some cash to give to Jennifer, caught sight of my face as I filled the kettle at the tap.

'Sex in the sitting room,' I muttered hoarsely, nodding in the direction from where I'd just come.

'What, this minute? I'm game, you little hussy, but don't you have to take the babysitter home first?' Nick started nuzzling the back of my neck, and I had to bat him off.

'The *babysitter* has been having sex in the sitting room,' I hissed.

'The *babysitter?* Who with?' Nick looked round in genuine astonishment, as if any number of sexual partners were about to manifest themselves in our kitchen. I began to giggle.

'Shhh!' I whispered. 'I'm going to have to go back in there and sort them out. Make the tea will you?'

Jennifer, looking very pale, was sitting alone on the sofa with her coat buttoned up to the neck. She looked very young and vulnerable. Of the boy there was no sight.

'Is he your boyfriend, Jennifer? Does your mum know you're sleeping with him?'

'Oh God, no! She'd kill me. You won't tell her will you? She doesn't think I'm seeing him any more – she can't stand him. Thinks he isn't good enough for me because he left school last summer instead of doing A levels, and hasn't got a job yet.'

'Where is he now?' I asked. 'Has he left you to face the music by yourself? That's not very brave of him, is it?'

'He doesn't live very far from here. He's gone home. Look, Mrs Westmoreland, I'm really sorry about this. I know I should have asked you if James could come round, but I didn't want Mum to know I was still seeing him. He literally only came round an hour ago. I didn't realise it was as late as this.'

Obviously. 'Listen Jennifer, you're so young. I mean I know it's nothing to do with me, but are you practising safe sex? Are you using contraception?'

Jennifer blushed. 'This was the first time we did it tonight. James didn't have anything on him, but he said it would be alright because he'd wrap it in food wrap.' She looked apologetic as she said 'I hope you don't mind, but we found some in your kitchen.'

Food wrap? He'd actually wrapped his dick in food wrap? For one awful moment I had a vision of his willy basting in tinfoil like a barbecued sausage, until I realised she must mean cling film.

She was almost in tears now as she stuttered, in a rush, 'I mean, I've never really seen a ... you know a condom. I was in hospital having my in-growing toenail seen to when they did that thing with a condom on a banana in Sex Education at school, but James said cling film was just as good as one.'

Holy Moses. And we think that kids today are sophisticated? 'Come on, Jennifer, let's get you home.'

I was bushed, and desperately wanted my bed. Thank God it was Saturday in the morning.

As we drove back, almost in the direction we'd come from an hour earlier, Jennifer huddled lower and lower into her seat until she was almost in a foetal position.

'Will you tell my mum about this, Mrs Westmoreland?' she asked from the depths of her coat.

'Jennifer, it really is nothing to do with me.'

Apart from losing your virginity to an apparent waster, while using less than satisfactory contraception, in *my house* I wanted to add. Losing one's virginity is hardly the best sex one ever has; losing it to a roll of Sainsbury's cling film can't have ranked high on experiences to be repeated in a hurry.

'Jennifer, can I just ask you one very personal question?' I wanted to put my mind at rest about any possible pregnancy.

She nodded bleakly.

'When was your last period?'

'Um, a couple of weeks ago. But I don't think he actually, you know, came.' I could sense her blushes without actually seeing them. 'You arrived home before that,' she added.

Well, Halleluiah and thank The Lord for small mercies.

I dropped Jennifer off, noting that an upstairs light was still on in what was presumably her mother's bedroom. I hoped Margaret wouldn't quiz the girl about her babysitting until the morning by which time Jennifer would have had time to compose herself or could avoid her mother by staying in bed until lunchtime.

It was almost one-thirty by the time I drove through Netherfields, a residential area just out of Midhope town centre. I made the decision to cut through a narrow street of tall Georgian houses many of which, although retaining much of their former glory of long-gone halcyon days, were now living a second, interim life as upmarket apartments. The black taxi cab that I'd followed for the last half a mile or so drew up outside one of the more elegant houses, forcing me to stop while the two occupants alighted and the man paid the driver. As they turned towards me, I saw that the man was Dan, Grace's husband, and the Titian-haired beauty with him was not, by any stretch of the imagination, my best friend.

Chapter 3

Being an inveterate list writer, I had usually compartmentalised Saturday on to an A4-sized sheet of paper long before Ulysses, next door's mentally defective cockerel, woke us with his discordant, strident rasp. The morning following the Hendersons' dinner party, having no paper to hand, I mentally organised the day ahead as follows:

1.　Go see Dad re my new garden.
2.　Have sex
3.　Ring Grace!!!!!!!!!!!!!

I didn't seem to be able to get any further than number three because the thought of ringing Grace after what I'd seen last night obscured all other thoughts. Why didn't I just leave Grace alone and hear what she had to say at school on Monday? If there was a problem, *she'd* ring *me* before then. When I'd seen her at school on Friday she'd been fine. No hint that Dan might be up to anything. She had mentioned that Dan was away and would be back on Saturday. More than likely he'd returned to Midhope earlier than anticipated, and had been in the process of dropping a work colleague off before heading for home and Grace. All these arguments were going through my head as I lay beside Nick, unable to get back to sleep. I looked at my watch. It was only seven o'clock. I considered waking Nick with a little morning delight and, in the process, being able to cross number two off my list, but I could hear India on the prowl and knew that within minutes she would launch herself squarely between the two of us.

For the next hour or so, while I went through mundane but necessary Saturday morning chores, my heart did little flips as I considered, and reconsidered what to do re Grace. This was my best friend, and I didn't want to be humping around illicit knowledge about her husband. By nine o'clock I was dialling her number. On the pretext of telling her about last night's dinner with Amanda I hoped to catch her still in bed, or doing whatever childless women do on a Saturday morning. When no reply was forthcoming, I tried her mobile. I was just about to give up when someone, or possibly *something* answered. Heavy breathing, very reminiscent of that which had accompanied the request for my knicker colour one morning at two o'clock many years ago, was all I could make out at first. Then Grace's voice pleading, 'Enough, for God's sake, Max, enough.'

Max? Who the hell was Max? Had Grace found out about Dan last night, and was already endorsing her revenge with a new, and obviously very active, lover?

'Grace?' I asked. 'Is that you?'

'Who's that? Max, enough I said. Really, enough now, I'm on the phone.'

'Where are you, and who the hell is Max?'

'Oh, Hattie? Is that you? I'm out on Thornfield Hill with Max.'

'Max *who*?' I demanded. I could hear the wind intent on stripping the first leaves from the trees up on Thornfield Hill, a godforsaken place very near to Grace's house.

'Max, next door's new dog. He's a rescue Dalmatian, and between you and me he's really too much of a handful for Beryl and Stan. I offered to take him out to run off some of his energy, but to be quite honest it's me that's knackered. He's still as fresh as a daisy. Bloody dog, come here! Come here! Right, I've got him now. What are you up to, ringing so early on a Saturday morning?'

'Oh,' I said, postponing the moment when I would have to ask about Dan. 'I just wanted to tell you whose house we were at last night.'

'And? Whose? Anyone I know?' I could hear Grace's breathing begin to slow down as she readied herself for gossip.

'Amanda Goodners and her husband.'

'Ohmigodno! Not Amanda Goodners! You actually had dinner with 'Little Miss Goodness'? What does she look like? Is she fat and ugly? Did she remember you? Did she ask about me? Did you ask her if she was still giving blow jobs down by the cut?' Grace started giggling.

For someone who two minutes ago was breathless, her recovery rate was spectacular. Must be all those hours she put in at the gym.

'Grace, she's as gorgeous as ever. Their house is to die for – I nearly did when I saw it – and yes, she did ask about you. In fact, there's some Midhope Grammar reunion in a couple of weeks. She wants us both to go.'

'You must be joking. You can count me out. I'm not going to any reunion. Best day of my life when I left that nunnery. And the last person I want to see after all these years is Amanda Goodners.'

'I'll talk to you later about it.' I was disappointed; thought Grace would have enjoyed the prospect of a trip down memory lane. 'So what are you up to the rest of the day?'

'Well, as soon as I've taken this animal back home,' she panted with the effort of holding Max, 'I'm going to get ready for Dan coming home – going to make myself really gorgeous to make up for being so bloody awful about this baby business. And, Hattie, I've had such a good idea.' Grace's voice rose in excitement and, before I could ask her what it was, she went on, 'We're going to adopt. It's about time I got on with life. If we can't have babies of our own, well then we'll just have to have someone else's. I'm going to tell Dan as soon as he gets home. You know, wine, lovely meal, the full works and then hit him with it.'

'Oh,' I said, the sudden vision of Dan with the gorgeous redhead reducing me to monosyllables.

Immediately on the defensive, Grace snapped, 'Oh, I suppose you're going to be like everyone else when it comes to adoption? You know, my cousin's friend adopted a baby last year and *it* hasn't turned out to be a drug-taking delinquent.'

'A drug-taking delinquent? At six months old?'

Ignoring my last question, Grace tutted and said, 'Well, whenever

I've broached the subject of adoption with anyone, particularly my mother, they all look horrified and regale me with tales of adopted children who have gone off the rails and brought heartache to their new families.'

'Rubbish,' I countered furiously. 'I know lots of adopted children who have grown into fine, upstanding members of the community!'

'You do?' asked Grace eagerly. 'Who?'

'Well, there's um, there's ...' I tailed off. I couldn't for the life of me think of anyone I knew who'd been adopted. 'I know. Mrs. Bealby, our geography teacher at Midhope Grammar. She was adopted as a child. I remember her telling us, for some reason, in one of her lessons.'

Even over the phone I could imagine Grace's face. 'Big-bottomed Brenda Bealby! A fine upstanding member of the community? She was a sadist – and as mad as a hatter. She once made me trace every single map of the world out of those great big atlases we used to have. Blimey, Hat, can't you come up with anyone better than Brenda Bealby?'

I couldn't.

'Well, I think adoption is a great idea,' I lied. 'So is Dan back home now?' I forced the question, hyperventilating a little as I tried to keep my voice normal.

'No, he phoned me last night from his hotel in London. Said he'd be back home this afternoon sometime. Seeing to a few things this morning before he sets off.'

And I could well imagine *who* he was 'seeing to.' Did I tell Grace I'd seen her husband with another woman when he was supposed to be still in London? I did not want this responsibility. It was going to be bad enough keeping *Jennifer's* little transgression from her mother, but this was something else.

I felt tainted by these underhand goings-on, and decided I needed fresh, clean air in my lungs so, after dropping India off at her birthday party, I drove straight to Dad's allotment. I knew I'd find him there, pruning the last of the roses or making a bonfire of the autumn leaves. He did have a bonfire on the go, and the acrid smoke it was generating was so thick he didn't see my approach. He was standing, slightly stooped, feeding a mixture of dead vegetation and dry wood into the rapacious mouth of the fire. When he sensed my presence, he left what he was doing and, picking up a dirty mug, came towards where I stood by his shed.

'Alright, love? Are you by yourself?' He looked around in the hope that I would have Kit or India with me. He adored all his grandchildren, but India, being the youngest and the last, was particularly revered.

'Just me, Dad,' I said as I breathed in his smell. The same, almost pungent, smell of flat cap, corduroy jacket and freshly dug earth he seemed to have always carried. 'All the kids are out socialising so I thought I'd come and pick your brains on how I'm going to do this garden of mine.'

I'd tried to tell him my plans on the phone, but he was becoming increasingly hard of hearing with every passing year and it was always debateable as to whether he'd fully grasped what I was trying to tell him. Hating his disability, he would pretend to have heard rather than admit to his deafness.

'How's Mum?' I asked now, as we made our way down through the adjoining plots towards the overgrown path that ran behind their house.

'Oh, you know, love. Much the same. Keeps on insisting she's told me things and then gets on me case when I've no idea what she's talking about. She apparently booked a holiday t' th' Isle of Man a couple of months ago, and only told me about it yesterday.'

'To go when?' I asked in surprise.

'Next Friday.'

'Blimey, that's short notice. Are you going?'

'Well, it looks like it. I don't mind Douglas – we went there for our honeymoon you know – but I do worry about what else she's bin up to. For all I know it could be Douglas next week and a trip up t' Nile week after.'

I giggled, but squeezed his hand in sympathy. I had an awful feeling this could be the beginning of some sort of dementia. She'd been behaving rather oddly for the last year.

Very little had changed in Mum and Dad's house since I'd left to go to university twenty years previously and I hadn't really lived there since. The curtains were different but the pink, three-piece Dralon suite was still the one of my childhood. Dad's snooker trophies still held pride of place in the corner cabinet along with the sherry and bottle of advocaat that he would dilute with lemonade for my elder sister Diana and me at Christmas, adding a cherry apiece in order to make Snowballs.

Mum was washing up at the sink as we walked down the garden path, and on seeing us she wiped her hands and came to open the door.

'Hi,' I said giving her a kiss. 'I hear you're off to Douglas next week.'

'No we're not. Your dad's got it wrong again,' she snapped, glaring at him. 'We're going to the Isle of Man. We'll be able to sit on the beach and get a nice tan.'

'But, Mum,' I said gently, 'it's the middle of October. You'll need to wrap up warm if you're going to the Isle of Man.'

'Whatever,' she said dismissively, sounding like Liberty. 'Now then, have you seen our Patricia lately?'

Patricia? Who the hell was Patricia?

'Do you mean Diana?' I asked, glancing at Dad for help. He just shrugged his shoulders.

'Yes, Diana. She's not been to see us for ages.'

'Keturah, love, she was here yesterday. She called in on her way home from work and brought you your magazine.' Dad raised his eyebrows at me.

'Well, it wasn't the one I like. I don't know why she bothers.' Mum sniffed and looked me up and down as if assessing what *I* might have brought her.

'I'm hoping Dad can help me sort out a little garden,' I said, sitting down and changing the subject. 'I want to live 'the Good Life,' Mum, you know, make a herb garden and grow some easy vegetables. Maybe rhubarb and strawberries?' I glanced at Dad for approval.

'What do you want to go to all that bother for with all the money your Nick earns? Get yourself down to Sainsbury's and buy the stuff. Better than off the allotment any day – comes without the dirt and slugs.'

I realised she was doing two things here: making out that Dad's allotment, and as such Dad himself, was a waste of space, and having a dig at me because financially, despite my not having a bean at the moment, I was better off than she'd ever been. She was becoming as caustic as the soda she regularly used to unblock her sink. When had she metamorphosed from the loving, caring, slightly scatterbrained mum of my childhood into the irascible old woman that stood before me now?

My mum had always hated her name, Keturah, especially as a teenager in the fifties when, apparently, she'd tried to modernise it by shortening it to 'Kat'. She'd longed, she always said, to be called something like Lana or Rita, after Hollywood movie stars, but, despite her pleas to shorten and update her name, very few people had taken it on board and she'd simply had to put up with the biblical-sounding name that was handed down through the generations. Despite having spent much of her adult life at loggerheads with my Granny Morgan, part of Mum seemed to shrivel and die when Granny had finally shrugged off her mortal coil four years ago at the age of ninety-seven. Like a couple of twittering sparrows, they'd spent years warily circling each other, one of them occasionally giving the other a quick, triumphant peck. With her mother gone, she'd appeared to lose direction, to lose sight of who she was, where she'd come from and, more importantly, where she was going.

'Listen, love, I'll pop over to your place tomorrow morning,' Dad now interrupted my thoughts, 'and you can show me what you want to do. I don't mind giving you a few tips.'

Mum pursed her lips before nodding in my direction and stating, 'Well, make sure she pays you, Kenneth. Tell her your hourly rate.'

Trouble was, I don't think she was joking.

'Mum, I'm starving, what is there to eat?' Kit had his hands on the shopping almost before I'd staggered in from the car.

'Is that all I am to you? Food?' I panted, trying to disentangle tight white polythene from my stiff fingers which looked, after carrying so many bags, slightly gangrenous.

'Not at all,' he grinned, grabbing a sesame-encrusted French stick before cutting himself a piece of cheese the size of a door wedge. 'You're pretty good at muddy football boots and French homework too – don't undersell yourself, Mother!'

Kit paused only to finish his mouthful and then went on, more gloomily, 'Talking of French, can you give me a hand, Mum? I've got a French test on Monday and I've absolutely no idea what it's on about. Old Juan goes mad if you don't get it all right.'

'Juan? I didn't know Mr Kerr was Spanish. Kerr doesn't sound a very Spanish name does it?' I mused. 'I must say he must be very clever if he's Spanish and teaches French too. You should listen more, Kit. He'll teach you a lot.'

'Mum, for heaven's sake!'

I turned to see both Liberty and Nick shaking their heads.

'What?'

'Mum, just think about it. Juan? Kerr?' Libby raised her eyebrows pityingly while Nick laughed out loud and patted my head. Very condescending, I thought.

'And I'm working my socks off just to keep him at a school where he learns things like that?' I tutted. 'Right,' I went on, ignoring the Everest of dishes that was waiting dispiritedly by the dishwasher ready to be loaded, 'from now on, just call me Harriet Titchmore. Bring on The Good Life!'

Stopping only to grab the potting shed keys from amongst its fellows in the dresser drawer, I breezed out into the garden leaving Kit muttering, 'Harriet Tits More? Who the bloody hell's Harriet Tits More?' into his cheese sandwich. I was instantly reminded of the very similar response I'd given to my mother's question about Patricia a couple of hours earlier, but pushed it to the back of my mind. I didn't want to think about anything unpleasant just at that moment, and knowing that my lovely old mum was acting a bit strange wasn't a happy thought.

I was going to live The Good Life. We might have very little money just now, but people from miles around would flock to gaze in wonder at my serried ranks of green beans, flawless strawberries, scarlet and rude with fecundity, and a veritable cornucopia of Brussels' sprouts. Ah, *season of mellow fruitfulness*. Yesterday's rain had, as if by magic, cleared away completely, leaving a perfect, warm day. Ralph-Next-Door already had a bonfire lit, sending a pungent trail of wood smoke spiralling lazily skywards and I breathed it in, intoxicated by its musky odour and the fact I was free for a couple of hours to do just what *I* wanted. And if I just didn't *think* about what might happen if Nick carried on this crazy idea with David Henderson, didn't *think* about the very obvious chemistry I'd witnessed between Nick and 'Little Miss Goodness', I could stop the panic that threatened to overwhelm me if I dwelt too long upon it.

Shit! One fingernail down as I struggled with the potting shed lock. Swearing under my breath, and then aloud and more profusely as the key refused to turn, I contemplated returning to the house to seek help from Nick. No way! This garden was *my* baby and, as with all my children, its birth depended on my labour alone. Swearing and panting at the door in much the same way as I had at the midwives who'd attended my three labours, I was interrupted by Ralph's pale, moon-like face appearing over our dividing garden wall. Hoping he hadn't been privy to the whole litany of swear words (there was one that I blushed to hear, never mind use) I was more than relieved when he offered to come over and use his superior masculine force on the door.

Yesss!! I was in business. Armed with more metalwork than the hardware shop in the village, I shuffled down to the flat, sunny patch at the bottom of the garden that I'd had my eye on for weeks.

Three hours later, I surveyed my efforts with more than a modicum of satisfaction.

True, the string that I'd used to stake out an area roughly fifteen metres square had the distinct appearance of a dog's back leg. True, I'd screamed out loud and jumped up from my knees, disturbing Ralph for the second time that afternoon, when the cold feeling on my leg which I'd assumed to be the edge of the garden fork, turned out to be a worm of unbelievable proportion stretched nonchalantly across my ankle. And true, five more fingernails had met the same fate as the first. But what the hell. I was a gardener extraordinaire.

Now for the bonfire. Having been a fully paid-up member of the gardening fraternity for only a couple of hours, I obviously didn't have a great deal of garden rubbish to dispose of, but if both my dad and Ralph thought it mandatory to be a pyromaniac as they went along, who was I to argue? Not wanting to be left out, I scouted around for fallen leaves, dead branches and any other garden litter that I could utilise. After ten minutes spent scouring the immediate vicinity I had a mound no bigger than a couple of inches high, consisting mainly of leaves that, as a result of yesterday's rain, were as damp as, well, as a damp squib. In frustration I shaded my eyes against the lengthening shadows and scanned farther afield. Up in the very top corner of the garden was Nick's compost heap (not Nick's own *personal* compost you understand – he is quite house-trained) a rusting water butt, and – hey ho – a very substantial pile of garden litter.

It was like being back on one of the Bonfire Night raiding expeditions I'd carried out as a child. With Diana and her mates in charge, I was allowed to tag along behind them as they descended onto the neighbouring Westfield Estate rec which lay low behind the run-down woollen mills whose Victorian outline still dominated the November late afternoon gloom. Like scavenging rats we would break cover, making a dash for the neatly built bonfire, intent on seizing anything that could be extricated and filched away without too much difficulty. The same deliciously potent brew of guilt and excitement now urged me on as I set off to raid Nick's abandoned pile. He really was quite an anorak when it came to the garden, whereas I was more than happy to haphazardly fling a few dozen packets of wild-flower seeds every spring and hope for a vestige of summer blooms a few months later. His garden bonfires, very much like his cooking, were indicative of his precise and determined nature. If he was going to do a job, then he was going to do it well or not bother. A feat of engineering that would have won the admiration of German car designers, Nick's present bonfire had not yet realised the necessary dimensions that would signal its readiness for setting ablaze.

With one measured pull, I released a couple of armfuls of dry branches that had once graced the elderly apple trees that grew in the small orchard adjoining our garden. Several wheelbarrow trips later and I'd transferred about half the pile to mine. If he remonstrated with me later, as I knew he would, I could always say he'd promised, in front of witnesses 'with all his worldly goods to me endow.'

It wasn't much of a fire; it smouldered sulkily for a while, reminding me of Darren Slater in my class when asked to do anything that might involve his having to put pen to paper or tax his brain. Completely absorbed with my fire, I neither heard nor saw Libby until she shook my arm.

'Mum, I've been shouting for you for ages. Dad wants to know if he's cooking tonight.'

'Hello, darling, I don't seem to have seen you all weekend. How was your evening at Beth's?'

'Fine,' she said dismissively, obviously not willing to divulge anything. 'Does Dad know you've nicked his bonfire?'

'What makes you think it's his?' I asked nervously.

'Well, the fact that this morning he was putting the finishing touches to it after he picked up Kit and me, and the fact that it's now half the size it was, is really a bit of a giveaway.'

'Yes, well don't you dare tell him it was me. I can always pretend that those kids from down the estate have been engaged in an early chumping raid.'

'What's it worth?' Libby asked, grinning.

'A fiver.' I declared firmly. 'Final offer, take it or leave it.'

'Done!' she affirmed, and we giggled, shaking hands on the deal. It wasn't often I had my elder daughter on my side against her father and, despite knowing it was financial gain rather than maternal loyalty that manipulated her thinking, it felt good.

Liberty idly kicked some stray dead leaves on to my somewhat depressed bonfire and demanded again whether Nick was to cook.

'Yep, tell him to start one of his specials, and I'll be up in a minute. I just want to tidy up here a little.' I was ready for a long soak and a large gin.

Ten minutes later I was steaming in a hot tub while India, never one to miss a soak en famille, was stripping off her kit and getting ready to join me. Thank goodness I'd married a man who could cook.

'Mummy, when will *I* get bosoms?' India was surveying my partially submerged chest with detached curiosity.

'When you're a big girl, darling.' My eyes were closed, and I felt wonderfully relaxed after an afternoon spent at one with nature.

'And when will *I* get bosoms?'

I opened one eye to find Nick standing over me, gin and tonic in one hand, leering lasciviously like a dirty old man.

'Silly man,' India giggled, 'men don't get bosoms.'

'They do if they're lucky,' said Nick, eyeing mine meaningfully.

'You're on my list of jobs to do,' I said, taking the gin and spilling some of it down my naked front. 'You're definitely on my list!'

I watched Nick's retreating back as he went back downstairs to start supper and smiled at my reflection in the mirror, piling my hair up on my head while simultaneously hoisting up my bosom – no mean feat – and relished the idea of sex with my husband. The afternoon spent in the sunshine and fresh air (or perhaps it was the effects of the huge gin and tonic) had given my skin a warm glow – and for some reason made me feel particularly horny.

I'd put 'Have Sex' on my Saturday morning list because, quite frankly, I *wasn't* having it. I didn't mean, *I* wasn't having it, but Nick *was.* I meant both of us weren't having it. With each other. Nick had been getting home incredibly late for months – this David Henderson thing had obviously been occupying him for a lot longer than I'd imagined – or we were both so knackered once we'd rolled into bed, that even one round of rumpy pumpy wasn't generally on the bedtime menu.

A sudden vision of 'Little Miss Goodness', and the possessive way she'd called Nick *Nicky* had me sitting bolt upright in the bath. Were Nick's recent late nights out a result of business talks with *Mr*

Henderson or knee-touching dinners with *Mrs?* Though I'd never once doubted Nick, that was before throwing Amanda Goodners into the equation. She seduced people, young and old, male or female. I knew. Both John, my brother, and I had been there.

Leaving India blowing bubbles in the now cooling bath water, I hurriedly towelled myself dry, headed for the bedroom and began searching. Searching for the red – no, one could surely describe it only as scarlet – basque that Grace had given me last Christmas and which, to my shame, I'd tossed into my knicker drawer and never retrieved. Ah, there it was. Realising I'd have to grease myself all over just to get the damned thing on, I liberally rubbed 'Aromatics' body lotion onto every inch of skin and set to work.

So where was the actual bra bit? Surely not these flimsy scraps of lace that looked like half-doilies peeping out from a plate of my mum's home-made cherry buns?

'Ooh, you look like one of those rudey ladies in Kit's comic.' India, skipping into the bedroom, came to a sudden standstill, mesmerised. 'And your *botty's* hanging down!'

Oh please, not too much, I prayed, twisting round in order to see the offending body part while making a mental note to see Kit re his 'comics'.

Ten minutes later, thanks to India's little fingers doing up the hooks and eyes, I was ready. Trussed up like a scarlet chicken, I was having trouble breathing, but the anticipation of a few hours with my lovely, lovely husband couldn't keep me from smiling.

Chapter 4

'Hat, we need to talk.'

Half asleep in a post-coital stupor, I glanced at my alarm clock. Almost midnight. The last thing I needed was a showdown about Nick's decision to sell his soul to David Henderson. Or did he want to talk to me about something else? *Someone* else, even? Was the sex we'd just had a parting gift before he told me he was in love with Amanda? Playing for time I feigned sleep.

'Can you smell burning?' Nick shook me roughly, sat bolt upright and sniffed the air like a cartoon dog.

'Hey, ah knows we just had some 'haat sex',' I affected a Deep South American accent, 'but ah never set the bed on fire befooah.'

Naked, and still sniffing, Nick hopped out of bed and went towards the open window.

'Fucking hell, Hattie, the potting shed's on fire.' And he was off, like Seb Coe at the Olympics – only slightly more demented and about one hundred percent more naked – down the stairs to the front door and out into the garden, grabbing and tugging at the hosepipe which hadn't been reeled back in very successfully after being used for car washing by Kit a couple of weeks previously.

Bored after an hour of trying to earn enough money to buy a new PlayStation game, Kit had obviously unceremoniously dumped the heap of twisted green rubber, where it had lain like an exhausted and defeated snake in a misjudged Houdini-type trick. Oops! Kit was going to be in trouble. Nick was, if anything, even more of an anorak over his usually neatly coiled garden hose than his bonfires. And no prizes for guessing who was going to be in trouble, big time, for setting the garden shed on fire. Unable to divest myself of the scarlet basque – I'd kept it on in the anticipation of seconds before breakfast – and unable to find any jeans or sweater, I set off just as I was and ran down to the bottom of the garden to join Nick, noticing as I went how much the wind had got up since my afternoon's gardening session.

The more we pulled at the hose, the more stubbornly it refused to budge. The next minute two huge fire tenders raced through the garden gates, blue lights flashing, sirens blaring and proceeded to spill what appeared to be the entire Midhope Fire Brigade onto our drive.

'You looked to be having trouble,' shouted Ralph-Next-Door, peering over the garden fence and averting his gaze from Nick's jiggling genitalia, 'so I dialled 999.'

'Thanks Ralph,' I gasped. 'I can't think how it can have started.' I needed to bluff my way out of this one.

'It'll be that garden bonfire you lit this afternoon. Obviously flared up again with this wind.'

Thank you Ralph and Goodnight!

I didn't have time to gauge Nick's reaction to Ralph's tale-telling before more blue flashing lights and sirens made their way through the garden gates. This time a panda car raced up the drive, parking itself neatly next to the fire engines.

'Mr Westmoreland?' a slim, very attractive WPC who made no attempt to avert *her* eyes from my husband's nether regions joined us by the sulking hosepipe. 'We've had a call from your alarm company to say your alarm has gone off.'

'Oh shit, I'm sorry. Well, as you can see for yourself we're *not* being burgled. We obviously forgot to turn it off before dashing downstairs – it's got a five minute delayed action on it. Not much good anyway. You can't even hear it down here.' Nick crossed his legs, trying desperately to cover his bits with a strategically placed hand.

'Mum, the alarm's going off,' shouted a frantic Libby from the safety of the front door. And then, stating the blindingly obvious, added 'And the potting shed's on fire and Dad hasn't got any clothes on.'

As Liberty was joined at the door by Kit and India who, just to confirm it, shouted, 'Daddy, you've no clothes on,' the unlit, shadowed drive became blue once more as another cop car hurtled towards us.

'Had a report of a naked man in your garden, sir,' said the older of the two uniformed policemen now walking towards us. The younger one, who clearly had the hots for the WPC in the first panda car, was trying very hard to appear nonchalant and grown up, but couldn't help sneaking surreptitious glances at where she now stood lounging against the side of her car watching the fire and chatting with her partner. This must be better than mopping up drunks as the clubs closed, and they seemed in no hurry to move off now that they'd established our family silver was still in situ.

Nick, looking decidedly chilly, sighed heavily before saying, with great irony, 'Well, yes, I am that man – obviously.'

Before he could offer any reasonable explanation as to why he was standing naked in his own garden while his garden shed burned, two things happened simultaneously, bringing what can only be described as an arresting quarter of an hour to an even more impressive conclusion.

The two boxes of fireworks bought by my dad a few weeks ago in readiness for Guy Fawkes night, and stored down in the garden shed where they'd be out of sight and reach of an inquisitive five-year-old, joined forces with the plastic container of lawn mower petrol, blowing off what remained of the potting shed roof. A whole rainbow of flashes and sparks from several Roman Candles, Rockets and Golden Rains lit up the night sky accompanied by a succession of triumphantly loud bangs and crashes.

From his vantage point above the garden fence a thoroughly overexcited and pyjama-ed Ralph shouted 'Get down,' and, falling off his upturned water butt, proceeded to do just that as yet another car, civilian this time, swept up the drive towards us.

Grace, stopping only to pay the open-mouthed taxi driver, walked calmly over to where we stood and, surveying one naked man, one scarlet basque-attired rudey lady and various others in uniform, announced, 'If I'd known you were having a swingers' fancy dress bonfire party I'd have got here earlier.'

'Dan's gone,' Grace said, explaining her presence twenty minutes later as the last of the emergency services departed and we made our way back up to the house.

'Yes,' I sighed.

'What do you mean, "yes"?' Grace asked, stopping in her tracks and turning towards me for explanation.

'Well, I don't assume your turning up here at one in the morning is just a social call.' The events of the last hour made my retort sharper than I'd intended.

'Look, I'll go if it's not *convenient,*' she said, her voice breaking as she turned and began to walk back down the drive.

Although she was certainly not drunk, I could smell the alcohol on her breath as I grabbed her arm and hauled her back in the direction we were going. I was relieved that she'd had the good sense to order a taxi rather than drive herself here.

'Don't be silly. Come on. Let's get inside.' I linked my arm with hers and drew her into the sitting room where the remains of a fire still glowed dully in the grate. Throwing some more wood onto the embers, I pushed her down onto the settee and went to make us tea. Nick was already in the kitchen, now in a towelling robe, and waiting for the kettle to boil. Specks of soot freckled his face and dried blood from a cut on his hand combined to give him an air of vulnerability.

'I'm sorry,' I whispered, burying my face in the warmth of his robe. It smelled of aftershave and smoke.

'How could you have been so bloody stupid as to light a fire and then leave it?' The combination of shock, cold, and embarrassment at being viewed in the buff by all and sundry, had made him angrier than I'd seen him for a long time.

'I just wanted to be a real gardener. I'll pay for it all,' I added, hoping that might calm him down.

'Harriet, you haven't *got* any money to pay for it,' he snapped, stirring his mug viciously so that its contents slopped over on to the granite worktop.

Stung into self-defence I snapped back, 'And whose bloody fault is that?' and instantly wished I hadn't.

'I'm going back to bed,' Nick said coldly, pushing me away. 'Make sure you lock up – we can do without burglars. Although,' he said as an afterthought as he reached the door, 'I'm sure no self-respecting thief would look twice at what *we've* got.'

Oh bugger!

I still had Grace in the next room to sort out. She was sitting, dry-eyed, perfectly still as she stared into the fire. I knew nothing about first aid and wondered if I should have added several teaspoons of sugar to her tea to counteract shock.

'I didn't know where else to go,' she said, still intent on the flames in the sitting-room fire but accepting the tea that she now cupped in her two hands, gaining comfort from its warmth. 'As he was getting a few things together, all I could think was, now I'll never have a baby. They'll never let me adopt one by myself.' She lifted her head pitifully, but still didn't cry.

'What happened?' I asked, stroking her hand and gently removing the cup from her grasp, where it threatened to spill and burn. I don't think she'd have noticed if it had.

Grace sighed a couple of times before turning to me. 'He said he had to put some distance between us for a while. That he couldn't carry on like this any longer – this whole baby thing was destroying us.'

Oh yeah? And the messing about with the redhead wasn't?

'He saw you last night, you know. Recognised the number plate as they got out of the taxi. Looked in the car and saw it was you.' Grace smiled. 'I assume that's why you rang me this morning when I was out with Max?'

'Yes. I'm really sorry, Grace. I just didn't know whether to tell you or not.'

'Well I suppose that knowing you were party to his little affair meant that he'd realised he'd have to come clean sooner or later. But I'd spent a good five minutes as soon as he got in the door this afternoon bombarding him with my plans for adoption. I was so excited, you see. Thought that this would be the answer to it all. It was only when I saw the look of utter despair on his face that I realised we were going nowhere. He actually said, "Grace, how can we even think about caring for another human being when we can't even care about ourselves?" ' Grace's voice faltered as she said this but she continued 'I told him, "*I* care. *I* care about us!" '

'And what did he say?' I had an awful feeling I knew the answer.

'That all I *really* cared about was trying to get pregnant. That I'd become *obsessed* with having a baby. That I'd reduced him to a penis and a pair of testicles.'

'So, where's he gone? To her?'

Grace stood up and looked around for her coat. 'He says not. Says he's going to stay in the company flat. You know they have one in that newly converted mill just outside Midhope. They use it for corporate entertainment. Apparently, because of this bloody recession, no one is being entertained there at the moment. Look, can I ring for a taxi? I've left my mobile at home.'

'Grace, you're in no state to go home by yourself. Stay here.'

Grace made a wry grin. 'No offence, but I'm not sure I can cope with your Laura Ashley spare room. Honestly, I'd rather go home. After all I'm going to have to get used to being by myself.'

'He'll be back,' I said, giving her a hug. 'Just give him some time and space. And at least he hasn't actually shacked up with this woman. Have you any idea who she is?'

'Camilla,' Grace said bleakly. 'Her name is Camilla. Arrived a couple of months ago from the Australian office. I told Dan to bring her over for supper as she didn't know anyone. She's petite, with that gorgeous deep-red colour of hair. She was good company, very confident and very bright and, oh bloody hell, Hattie, very young.'

'How young?' I asked carefully.

'Young enough for her to think the world owes her a living, young enough to wear her hair in one long shiny auburn plait down her back, and bloody young enough not to be kept awake at night by the ticking.'

'Ticking?' I was puzzled. 'I thought she was in finance like Dan. You didn't say she was a teacher too!'

'No, ticking. *Ticking*. You know, tick tock biological clock?

We've been trying for two years – two bloody years, Hattie!'

'I know you have, Grace.'

Grace sniffed, 'He's just so fed up with the person I've become. I'm a woman obsessed and I get on his case all the time. I think it would have been better if they could have pointed a finger at one of us and said, "It's your fault – you're to blame. Your sperm is just weak little tiddlers." Or "Your eggs are past their sell-by date." But they say everything is in working order. They just tell us to go away, relax and enjoy each other. It's very difficult to enjoy each other when you're geared up to making sure you have sex at the right time, or I'm checking to make sure the temperature of Dan's bath water is not too high because it might boil the little beggars, or I'm buying him underpants two sizes too big so that they're not too tight which might suffocate them.'

I tried not to laugh, but it didn't matter because Grace had started giggling too, hiccuping through her tears.

'I don't really *want* to hear this,' said Grace through gritted teeth as a rhythmic ticking outside on the drive announced her taxi, 'but I need to know. Was he kissing her last night when you saw them together? Did he look happy? I mean, what were they actually *doing*?'

'It really all happened so quickly, Grace. One minute they were on the pavement and the next I was driving around them, frantically looking through my mirror to confirm that it was Dan that I'd seen.'

'But you managed to get a good look at her, did you? She's beautiful isn't she?' whispered Grace almost wistfully.

'She looked totally ordinary to me,' I lied, remembering the ravishing redhead who had stepped from the taxi alongside Daniel.

'Thanks, Hat,' she said as she went down the steps into the cold autumn night air, 'but we both know that's not true.'

I was so bone-weary when I finally fell into bed that all I wanted to do was become one with it. Wanted it to envelop me and not release me until I'd caught up with a whole load of sleep. Nick was either asleep or pretending to be, and turned over away from me as I moved towards him. I knew that my jibe about whose fault it was that we were broke had really gone home, and I wanted to kick myself for lashing out at him like that. In the years since we'd gone from being pretty wealthy to just making ends meet, I'd never once blamed Nick for our change in circumstances although I knew he constantly castigated himself for it. I'd always been able to jolly him along, tell him I'd gone back to my roots where I'd never had much materially but had always been happy.

I turned again and then sat up to look at Nick who was now definitely asleep. I thought back to last night at the Hendersons' and how animated he'd been about David Henderson's achievements. But at the end of the day, both Nick and I had OK jobs. We'd be fine: always a little short of the readies, maybe, as we tried to maintain this house and the kids' private education, but we'd be fine.

Rather than counting sheep, which steadfastly refused to run in my direction, I took to counting garden tools like those that had perished in the potting shed fire, and my last thought was that tomorrow I'd have to *make* Nick understand that giving up a perfectly good job in these dark days of economic turbulence in order to throw his lot in with David and Amanda Henderson was just not on. No way, Pedro.

Chapter 5

Nick very rarely stayed in bed on Sunday mornings and this particular one was no exception. What *was* different was the absence of tea, toast and the *Sunday Times*, which he habitually brought up to me on his return from a run or an hour down at the gym. This had started soon after we were married, but then he'd always jumped back into bed with me. Once Liberty had been born, and particularly if I'd spent much of the night wandering the house trying to get her back to sleep, he'd take her downstairs and give her breakfast while I caught up on my sleep. Wonderful man that he was, he insisted on my breakfasting in bed, luxuriating in strong, freshly ground coffee and, for a special treat, blueberry muffins or croissants.

Sylvia, Nick's mother, had come to live with us almost two years ago. Faced with the choice of selling this house or having the newly widowed Sylvia move in with us, we opted for the latter, altering the nicest part of the house to accommodate her and her decrepit dachshund, Bertie. Hearing Bertie barking maniacally as he ran on his little legs after the balls India threw for him, I realised that Sylvia must have returned from her weekend away. Hardly a weekend, then, if she'd returned so soon. I rolled out of bed, smelling the lingering odour of acrid smoke in my hair, and headed for the window.

The whole family, including Libby who, as far as I could remember, hadn't seen the light of day on a Sunday morning for years, and Sylvia who, I thought savagely and unfairly, couldn't keep her nose out of anything, was down at the incident scene looking like extras from *Midsomer Murders*.

'But, what was she *doing* lighting a fire in the middle of the garden? And so near to the shed?' Sylvia's clipped vowels floated up and through the open window. She was probably, even now, mentally adding pyromania to my ever-increasing list of misdemeanours. They included, in no particular order: my being from the North, being working class, voting Labour and ensnaring her son who, after all, could have married Anna Fitzgerald, a District judge's daughter from Epsom.

Kit, I assumed, had had a dressing-down about the tangled and useless hosepipe and was, as a result, even more on my side.

'She was competing with Somebody Tits More,' he said stoutly, defending my honour against his father and grandmother who, combined, were a force to be reckoned with.

'Yes, well, her competitive spirit didn't stop her from nicking my bonfire and rebuilding it down here – right next to the shed.' Nick was being unusually self-righteous.

'Oh get over it, you pompous arse,' I muttered, slamming the window with such force that a blackbird, in the middle of a solo rendition in the eaves above, took to the air with an offended 'chuck, chuck.'

Feeling martyrish I showered and, grabbing a cup of coffee, made my way to the tiny alcove at the top of the stairs that now masqueraded as our study. I thought longingly of the huge room we'd turned into a combined study and playroom just after India was born but which was now Sylvia's granny flat. It was the sunniest room in the house, south-facing and with French windows that opened directly on to the garden allowing the scents of lavender and honeysuckle to drift in on a summer breeze.

I knew I should feel grateful that Sylvia's moving in had allowed us to hang on to our home when the business collapsed, but this morning I felt nothing but resentment for her presence. Maybe we *would* have been better downsizing when we knew we'd hit rock-bottom, I mused, as I found the file on the computer containing the school English policy I had to update and hand in by the next morning. I sighed, acknowledging that, until India was older, I needed and relied upon Sylvia far more than she needed us. She gave her time freely, taking India to and from school and looking after her if she was ill or when her school holidays differed from my own; and Sylvia was not averse to doing a load of washing or giving the house a quick Hoover every now and again. She might drive me bats occasionally but I never underestimated what she did for us, or took her for granted.

But I did *resent* her. I resented the fact that she was now living, albeit separately, in my house. And at times like this, when I knew I'd been pretty stupid lighting a fire and leaving it to the elements, I resented the fact that my stupidity was being discussed with Nick.

Temper and tiredness and lack of breakfast (damned if I was going to show my face in the kitchen) persuaded me that the policy would have to do just as it was without adding the extras that I knew were expected.

'How many people will read the bloody thing anyway?' I challenged the computer, and pressed the print key just as my big sister, Diana, walked in to my little alcove carrying her own cup of coffee and a handful of Sylvia's flapjack.

'Hello, you little firebug. Hiding in here out of Nick's way?' And she laughed through a mouthful of cake, almost spilling her coffee on the pristine document that lay like foot-stepped virgin snow in the tray of the printer.

'If *you've* come to have a go at me too, you can f-off right now,' I snapped, ignoring her as she laughed again, scattering crumbs onto the computer keys. '*And* you're eating Sylvia's flapjack, you traitor,' I added, my mouth salivating at the sight and smell of Sylvia's syrupy confection.

'I think it's hilarious,' she chortled. 'The kids told me all about your early bonfire party with Nick in the altogether.'

'Yeah, well, Nick is being totally over the top about it. And bloody Sylvia is sucking up to him, egging him on. She loves it when he's fallen out with me and she can step into the breach and hold his outraged hand.'

'Actually, they were all beginning to see the funny side and wondering where you'd got to.'

'How did you know I was here?' I asked.

'I didn't. I've been here a while looking for you.'

'Oh? What's up? Not like you to be around on a Sunday morning. I thought you'd be out walking with Marcus.' Diana, now well into her forties, single and more than happy with her lot, had dangled the adoring Marcus on a string for years. He loved her but had to accept he was, and probably never would be anything other than, just one amongst her many men friends.

'Couldn't cope with him today,' Diana said, yawning widely apparently at the very thought of him, 'so I thought I'd come and see you playing happy families with your brood.'

'We're *always* happy aren't we, Hat?' Nick shouted as he came up the stairs bringing with him a bacon sandwich that he set in front of me. As I've said before, I can never hold a grudge for too long, especially when I know that it was my fault that my family almost ended up as toast, and the smell of a peace offering is working its way up my nose. And this surely wasn't a husband in love with another woman?

'I'm taking the kids out for a walk,' Nick said as I devoured the sandwich. 'Do you want to come? I thought we might grab a pub lunch over at Upper Clawson.'

'What time is it now?' I asked, hesitating. 'And can we afford lunch out?' The thought of donning wellies and shuffling through the falling leaves was really tempting, but I knew I still had some school work to do and there was a pile of ironing that had been sitting, accusingly, in the corner of the kitchen for days. If it grew any bigger I'd need a slab of Kendal Mint Cake before I launched myself at it.

Nick glanced at his watch. 'I think we've got enough to cover lunch. We need a treat after last night's little surprise. It's nearly midday, so we need to get off if we're going. Mum says she'll do any ironing you might have if we take Bertie for a walk with us,' he added, almost reading my mind.

There are times when I just love my mother-in-law.

Ten minutes later we were all wading our way across a boggy field, avoiding (unsuccessfully, in India and Bertie's case) ancient and not so ancient lacy cowpats. A herd of brown and white cows whose breed I couldn't for the life of me recall, gazed balefully at us from their vantage point against a broken-down dry-stone wall, assessing our progress across a parallel footpath out of eyes even more beautiful than Nick's. One did put her head down warningly as Bertie, thoroughly overexcited at being out with so many of us, grew brave and made a detour towards them. Within seconds he was back in our midst, his short legs paddling ten to the dozen as he endeavoured to keep up, his sausage tummy skimming the wet grass.

Liberty, plugged in to her iPod, had taken the lead, her constantly active fingers the only indication that she was being brought up to date on the Saturday night events of her friends by text. What would she write about *her* Saturday night, I wondered, as I moved to catch up with Nick and Diana who were deep in conversation several yards ahead. Probably something along the lines of *'Crzy mthr nrly set hse on fire last nite. Dad stark bollk nkd in grdn. Crzy deserted godmthr arrived in taxi in middle of nite to join in wth fun.'*

Talking of Grace, I needed to ring her – make sure she was OK – but realised I'd left my mobile at home. Damn! I'd have to ring her once we returned from our walk. I waited until India and Bertie, both panting, both with tired little legs, caught me up and I rallied them forward, promising Sunday lunch just around the corner.

'Don't fib, Mummy, I know it's not round the corner. There's loads of corners to get round yet, and my wellies are hurting me.' India's lip began to tremble as Bertie flashed me a wall-eyed, mutinous glare.

'Nick, can you give India a piggyback?' I called. 'She's had it.'

'Don't think I'm giving that excuse for a dog a leg up,' Diana shouted back as Nick hoisted India on to his shoulders.

Up to me then, as usual. I took off my pashmina, a birthday present from Grace a couple of years back, fashioned a papoose and tied Bertie on to my back, leaving his back legs dangling around my waist and his nose on a level with my shoulder.

'You certainly aren't going to win friends and influence people with that breath,' I muttered to Bertie, turning my head and squashing him a bit further over to one side, before drawing level with Diana where she stood waiting on a rocky outcrop, convulsed with laughter at the sight of me like a disgruntled Quasimodo, struggling up the hill towards her.

'I had Christine on the phone yesterday,' said Diana, once we were on level ground again, and Bertie and I had settled into a fairly steady, rhythmic pace.

'Oh yes? What did *she* want?' Christine was our sister-in-law who'd been married to our elder brother John since getting pregnant at the age of eighteen and, without mincing words, a right royal pain in the butt. Diana and I, perhaps unfairly, had never forgiven Christine for ensnaring John at his most vulnerable. Though maybe it was Amanda Goodners we should never have forgiven.

'You know what she's like. Always got her nose where it's not wanted. She wanted to know if either of us had been to see "Mother" lately.'

The way Christine had hijacked our mother on to her side after years of making snide comments about her was a constant source of irritation to Diana and me, and her use of the handle "Mother" when referring to her *mother-in-law* grated on my nerves in much the same way that references in "Mother and Baby" magazines to "Baby" made me want to screw them up and toss them in the nearest bin.

'What was she implying?' I asked. 'That she's the only one who cares about her and that we don't spend enough time round there?'

'Yup. I got the whole lecture about how we don't go and see her enough; how we just don't know how many years they have left, and how it's our duty to spend more time with her.'

'Bloody cheek of the woman. I go and see Mum and Dad because I *want* to see them, not out of any sense of filial duty.' I was seething, as much from knowing that my sister-in-law had, in reality, got a point – I didn't go and see them as much as I should now that I was working full time – as from her acerbic comments.

'Apparently Christine's round there most days, helping her with her ironing, doing her shopping and even taking round food parcels.' Diana paused to give Bertie a lift further up my back.

'Food parcels? What do you mean by food parcels? How do you know Christine is taking stuff round for them? Did she tell you?' I was so put out by Christine apparently treating *my* parents as if they were on their last legs that I spat out a volley of questions without waiting for a response to any of them.

Diana laughed. 'Calm down. You'll make the dog travel sick waving your arms around like that. Of course she didn't come straight out with what she'd been doing – that's not her style is it? She just let it slip how she couldn't get used to cooking smaller quantities now that Hollie has left home, and how much "Mother" and "Dad" seemed to appreciate it when she took any "little leftovers" round for their tea. "You know how partial 'Dad' is to my lasagne," she told me, smugly.'

'News to me,' I said rudely. 'Since when has "Dad" ever eaten anything other than liver and onions or cow heel and oxtail?' A dyed-in-the-wool Yorkshireman, my father had always looked upon any food with a hint of "foreign" as downright suspicious.

'I know. I can't believe Mum and Dad want to be babied like this – they've always been totally independent. Anyway, after I'd had all this from her, Christine then began to hint that she thought Mum might be losing it a bit.'

I was instantly alert, and looked across at Diana as we made our final descent from the moorland down onto the main road where the welcoming gabled end of the pub could be seen just a few hundred yards away.

'What did she mean – losing it a bit?' I asked.

'Well, you know, not quite as with it as she used to be. I think Christine's talking rubbish. OK, maybe Mum's memory isn't as good as it used to be, but she is seventy-four now.'

'I went round yesterday morning, you know,' I now said, 'and I have to say I think Christine might have a point.'

'Oh?'

'Did you know Mum has booked a holiday for her and Dad to go to the Isle of Man? Trouble is, she only told Dad about it a couple of days ago and they're off next Friday.'

'Nothing sinister about that. She probably wanted it to be a romantic surprise – after all, they did go there for their honeymoon.'

I shook my head. 'No, I don't think so. She said they weren't going to the Isle of Man – they were going to Douglas.'

'Douglas *is* the Isle of Man isn't it?' asked Diana looking puzzled.

'Exactly! Mum also asked me if I'd seen "Our Patricia" lately.'

'Patricia who? We don't have any relatives called Patricia do we?'

'Not that I know of. I think she actually meant you.'

'Me? Since when has my own mother forgotten my name?'

'Since yesterday, apparently,' I replied, bringing a relieved and wriggling Bertie back down to earth on the floor of the Public Bar of The Coach and Horses before joining the rest of my family.

Chapter 6

Nick and the others had forged ahead and were already seated at a table in the corner of what used to be the tap room, hoovering up crisps while engrossed in the bar meal menu that offered everything from home-cooked Sunday roast to curry.

'Come on, Mum,' called Kit, 'I'm starving.'

'Well, what a surprise,' I grinned, taking a slurp of Nick's lager to quench my immediate thirst before moving to the bar to order drinks for Diana and myself.

I loved this place. High up on the Pennines, it had long been a stopping-off point for travellers who, for whatever reason, were intent on crossing the border from God's Own County into Lancashire.

Nick had disappeared from the tap room when I returned from the bar for a second time with water for the dog; we'd all forgotten about poor old panting Bertie in our eagerness to get food and drink down our own necks. I could see Nick through the window, leaning against the car park wall, talking animatedly while continually running his hand through his thick blonde hair. Whoever he was talking to, I had a feeling it wasn't merely good manners that had taken him outside. Diana raised her eyebrows but said nothing as I finally sat down to peruse the menu. For weeks she'd been party to my fears about Nick wanting to throw in his job, and, perhaps at the memory of Mum's face when we were kids and very little money was coming into the house, she more than anyone knew how I felt about it. What Diana didn't know, because I hadn't told her yet, was the way Nick had been looking at Amanda on Friday night. The same way, I realised with a jolt, that he'd looked at me all those years ago in the university bar. Suddenly my mouth was dry, my appetite gone.

We had all ordered and were just about to start eating our meal when Nick reappeared, breezing in but not quite meeting my eye.

'Where've you been, Daddy?' asked India plaintively, offering him one of the picked out mushrooms that lay around her plate like discarded slugs. 'I've saved you my mushrooms.'

'Thanks, darling,' he said, glad that someone was on his side.

Diana, who was very good at diffusing situations and should really have been a diplomat at the United Nations rather than the social worker that she was, launched into a tale about her cat, Hector.

Just as she was coming to the punchline, Nick's mobile went off again. We all jumped and I looked meaningfully at Nick. Couldn't we even have Sunday lunch together without the Hendersons edging in on us?

Nick leapt up once more, walking swiftly towards the door as he answered the call, then turned and handed his mobile to me.

'It's Mum. Your Dad's at the house – says you arranged to meet him there when you called round yesterday?'

Shit! I'd forgotten all about asking Dad to come round to give me advice on my garden.

'Hi Sylvia,' I said, taking Nick's mobile and trying to think on my feet. 'We're a good hour's walk away from getting home. Could you ask my dad to hang on until we get there?'

'Why don't I come and pick you up?' Sylvia's strident voice came down the phone. 'I'm sure Bertie and India would be grateful for a lift back as well. Then Nick and Diana can walk back with Liberty and Kit.'

There she was, organising my life again. I knew I was being unfair – keeping a conversation going between my Dad and Sylvia would be hard for both of them. Dad's deafness and Sylvia's clipped vowels normally rendered him nodding in agreement to anything she said, while Dad's broad Yorkshire accent often had Sylvia utterly perplexed.

'Actually, I wouldn't mind a lift back,' said Diana swiftly

finishing her meal and screwing up her paper napkin before tossing it onto the table. 'I really could do with seeing Dad after what you were saying about poor old Mum earlier, and I hadn't *intended* coming out for lunch. I've a lot to do at home. Why don't I grab a lift with Sylvia, India and the dog and you walk back with the others?'

'Because Dad's come round specially to see my garden.'

'Look, I'll take him down to your plot – I assume it's that newly dug patch by what remains of the potting shed – and I can ask him about Mum. He'll be more than happy down in your garden by himself once I've gone.'

The lure of apple crumble, coffee and another hour's walking before the Sunday afternoon ritual of school work, uniforms and kit bags was too tempting to resist. In the end, both Kit and Liberty, pleading homework, piled into the back seat of Sylvia's car alongside Diana, India and Bertie for the ride home.

'You'll be pleased to know I think we're fully insured for the potting shed,' Nick said after the waitress, who couldn't have been any older than Libby, had cleared away our plates and taken our order for pudding. 'I pulled the policy this morning and we should be OK.'

'They even insure stupidity?' I asked ruefully.

'Yes, even that,' laughed Nick.

'I bet sometimes you wish you'd married Anna though don't you?' I sighed, looking down at my wedding ring.

'Anna? What's she got to do with this?' asked Nick in surprise.

'Well, I bet she wouldn't have pinched your bonfire and set your shed on fire.'

'No, I don't suppose she would. But then again, she wouldn't have dreamed of doing her own garden. She'd have had a gardener to do that.'

'So you don't think Anna would have hung around, once your business went down the pan, if you'd have been married to her instead of me?'

'I doubt it. She'd have been off, back to Daddy, the minute the shit hit the fan.'

'So, really, what you're saying is that *I've* been a good and faithful wife all these years?'

Nick patted my hand. 'Absolutely. Although, I have to say, last night's little shenanigans blotted your copybook somewhat.'

'So,' I persisted, 'you reckon I've done the very best I possibly could, even when times have been bad?'

'None better. Just improve your Yorkshire puddings so we can eat them rather than play Frisbee with them and you'll be the perfect wife.'

I paused to stir the coffee that had been sitting, untouched, in front of me for the last five minutes before hitting Nick with my *coup de grâce*.

'So, if what you say is right, if you feel I've done all I can to get us through the bad bits, why then are you wanting to do something which, in this bloody recession, will quite possibly really sink us into the mire?'

Nick said nothing. Instead he stood and, without looking at me, made his way across to the main bar where he paid the bill for our meal.

'Come on, let's go,' he said, passing me my coat and muddy pashmina before putting his arms into his own jacket. 'It's a long walk back, and if you want to see your dad before he goes, we'll have to get a move on.'

Outside, a cold wind was blowing – harbinger of the winter that was inevitably just around the corner – making me shiver and dig my hands deep into my pockets. On cold days like this Nick would normally reach for my hand, pushing it into his own pocket, keeping it warm. Instead he set off at a cracking pace back down the road that led to the edge of the Pennine hills.

Once we had climbed back onto the moorland, Nick slowed down and said,

'Hattie, I'm handing in my notice at Wells Trading tomorrow. I've accepted David Henderson's offer and I'm going into business with him.'

'You've accepted his offer without consulting me?' I stopped walking and turned into the wind in order to face him. 'How could you?' I shouted wildly. 'There are people out there who'd *kill* for a decent job like yours. Are you totally mad or just slightly deranged?'

'Harriet, I've been trying to consult you for *weeks*. Every time I've tried to tell you anything about what I want to do, you've blanked me. You haven't wanted to hear what I've had to say, so you just haven't listened.'

As I tried to splutter my defence, Nick went on, 'On Thursday when I came home I needed to sit you down and tell you about the meeting I'd had with David and a couple of others but you were too busy gossiping with Grace. Last night in bed, when I tried to talk to you, you pretended to be asleep.'

'I bloody well was asleep. Haven't you been married to me long enough to know when I'm asleep and when I'm not?' Fear made my voice strident, shrewish.

Nick grabbed my hand but, feeling my resistance, dropped it again and took both my shoulders instead. Not a Nick gesture at all. It was as if by forcing me to be physically close, he could make me listen to what he wanted to say.

'I have to do this, Harriet. I'm fed up with working for someone else, I'm fed up with not earning enough money to have the life that I want us to have and I'm bored rigid with the actual job that I'm doing at Wells Trading. I want the buzz of working for myself again.'

'But that's just it – you wouldn't be working for yourself. You'd be working for David Henderson.'

And Amanda.

'Not exactly. David believes in me. He knows what happened with Pennine Clothing Company – knows that it was circumstances rather than my poor business acumen that forced me to quit. He's taking a chance on setting me up again.'

'And what, exactly, is in it for your *Fairy Godmother*? Now that David Henderson has waved his magic wand, what does *he* get out of it? And don't tell me it's altruism, because if you believe that then we're doomed from the start.'

'Little ray of sunshine you are, aren't you?' Nick shook his head despairingly, and then went on, 'David will obviously get a share of the profits. He will be a main shareholder. The more money I make, the more money he makes.'

'And what if you don't *make* any money? What if it all goes pear-shaped again? If you hadn't noticed, because of all your swanning around with David Henderson and his bloody wife, there's a sodding great recession on. A business is far more likely to crash now than it was two years ago. What then, Nick? What *then?*' I wanted to cry with frustration. I stopped suddenly, mid-stride, as I recalled Mike Rawlinson's sneering face from Friday evening. 'Nick, I don't believe David Henderson is willing to risk investing in a new business without some sort of financial surety from you. No one in their right mind would just pump money into something these days, willy-nilly. Look at banks. They never just give people money without them putting money up front themselves, or offering their home as collateral.' I stopped again. 'Nick, please don't tell me you've put up the house as surety.'

'Oh for heaven's sake, Hat. How could I do that, even if I was stupid enough to consider it? You own the house with me. How could I start offering the house as surety without you knowing?'

He had a point there, I conceded.

'So, how much?'

Nick hesitated. 'Fifty.'

'Fifty pounds?'

There was a long silence before Nick sighed and said, 'Fifty grand.'

'Fifty thousand pounds?' I said, in horror. 'But Nick, we haven't got *one* thousand pounds never mind *fifty*.'

Nick had the grace to look shamefaced. '*We* haven't got fifty thousand pounds, Harriet, as I'm only too aware. If *we* had fifty thousand pounds I wouldn't be worrying about the hole in the roof, about the tyres on your car, about Libby's university fees in three years. If *we* had fifty thousand pounds, I wouldn't care that the council tax is probably going to rocket next year, that the bathroom needs decorating or that we don't entertain as much as we used to because it's just too damned expensive.'

'So, Nick, if *we* haven't got fifty thousand pounds – who the fuck has?' There was an icy feeling in the pit of my stomach as if I'd just swallowed an oversized ice cube.

'Mum's lending it to me.'

'Oh, Nick, no! Please, please don't tell me this. Please don't tell me you've been discussing all this with your mother without consulting me.'

'Harriet, she wants to do this. I'm her only son for heaven's sake. And if I had consulted you, you would have reacted in just the same way as you're doing now.'

'But where's your mother getting fifty thousand pounds from? I thought that once she'd sold up and contributed towards the flat conversion, she was just about as broke as we are.'

'Well I know Dad wasn't able to leave her much. There was some capital that keeps the kids in school – you know he always wanted them to stay where they were – and of course he was able to leave her his pension, small though it is. The lump sum from the house sale provides the interest that she lives off. We've done some sums, and she can live, for the moment, fairly comfortably on what remains of that. Mum is totally behind me, encouraging me, which is more than I can say for you,'

'But you *can't* take it, Nick,' I said, trying to ignore his last dig. 'It's not fair. Your mum will have so much less to live on. You know what interest rates are like at the moment. How is she going to manage? And what happens if this deal with David Henderson is all a con? You'd be without a job again and we *would* have to sell the house this time, but this time Sylvia would have to actually *live* with us – in a smaller house.' I could feel hysteria rising and I was beginning to walk faster. 'She'd be totally dependent on us. In my kitchen. In my face.'

The weak October sun had slid behind a bank of increasingly grey clouds and the wind up here on the hills was no longer playful but sneaky, loitering for a while around my legs before giving me a furtive, underhand push forward. Nick tried to slow me down by putting out a restraining hand but I was in no mood for coercion. As the first drops of rain began to fall I doubled my pace, wanting to be home, away from Nick and his plans.

'Slow down, Harriet, and talk to me. You're doing it again – refusing to listen and consider what I'm saying.' Despite his regular visits to the gym Nick was beginning to breathe more rapidly, while I was giving every impression of being in training for a power-walking marathon. Anger, it appeared, had given rocket fuel to my legs.

'For heaven's sake, slow down will you?' he shouted again, his open Barbour jacket flapping in the wind like an out of control kite. 'I can't discuss this while you're walking at this pace. What are you so afraid of?'

'You really want to know what I'm frightened of?' I shouted to the elements. 'Well I'll tell you. I don't want to have to pick up the pieces again when your new business falls on its backside. I don't want to have to live, and I mean *really* live with your mother when we can no longer afford the mortgage because *you* don't have a job.'

And I'm frightened of Amanda Goodners. Frightened of how she'll seduce you, draw you in. Because that's what she does.

I finally stopped the manic speed at which I was moving and slowed back down to a walking pace so that Nick was able to catch up with me. Taking my hand and holding it tight so that I couldn't bolt again like an unbroken horse, he said, 'You know as well as I do that teachers never lose their job. Your jobs are for life.'

'Well maybe, Nick, just maybe I don't want my bloody job for life.' And when Nick made no reply, I went on, 'It seems you've made your mind up without even considering me and the kids.' I suddenly felt defeated and, as the rain began to fall in earnest, I realised my worst fears had manifested themselves: I was going to have to be responsible, on my teacher's wage, for making sure all the bills were paid while Nick made a success of this venture and kept David Henderson happy. That I could cope with. Was more than happy to do it for however long it took until we were solvent again. But what if it *didn't* work? That didn't even bear thinking about.

'How long?' I asked as we joined the road that led through our village towards home.

'How long for what?' Nick fell into line beside me after being forced to walk in single file along the grass verge for the previous mile.

I sighed. 'How long before you know if you're up and running? How long before we know that it's going to be a success, before you'll be able to help keep our heads above water once more?'

'I'll need to give a month's notice – I may actually get away with two weeks – and then it should be all systems go. I'll hopefully be making my first trip in about a month's time. After that, well, I hope we should be making a profit within the first year.'

I stopped and stared at Nick as the rain made rivulets down his waxed jacket and fell silently onto the tarmacked road. 'Your first trip where?'

'Harriet, I've been telling you this for weeks. David has contacts with the Italian textile industry. We'll be importing Italian men's designer wear. I'll need to be over there quite a bit to source the goods, to decide which Italian textile factories we can work with.'

'So not only am I now in charge of this family financially, I shall in effect be a single mother for much of the time while you're 'Living La Dolce Vita', whooping it up in Milan and Rome?'

'Harriet, you supported me wholeheartedly when I set up Pennine Clothing – you were right behind me all the way. What's the difference now?'

'How about three children at private school, and a rambling house that's got a bloody great mortgage and very probably dry rot as well? How about a mother-in-law that *I* am now solely financially responsible for? How about the fact that the world is in a recession? How many fucking differences do you want?'

'Can you not try to look on the positive side and raise a modicum of enthusiasm for this new venture, Harriet?' Nick pleaded as he let us both into the house.

Feeling sick with terror at the thought of losing everything, I could only shake my head numbly. I should have known, seeing Amanda Goodners in action once more the other evening, that there was nothing but trouble ahead.

Chapter 7

So, you must be thinking, what exactly is the rap with this Amanda Goodners woman?

I met both Grace and Amanda on the very same day. The first time I saw her I was eleven, terrified and desperately wishing I'd failed my eleven-plus so I'd have no reason to be sitting cross-legged in Midhope Grammar School's cavernous assembly hall. It was the first day of term, my new grey woollen tunic scratched uncomfortably and I was waiting, along with all the other new intake of girls, to be called to join my new class. Not for me the comfort of a friendly face. I had known no one except the third-former whose newsagent father supplied my Granny Morgan with the *News of the World* each Sunday and who had been persuaded, rather unwillingly it seemed to me, to accompany me on the school bus that first morning.

A blonde angel sat on the fifth-form benches at the side of the hall. Our eyes met, the angel bestowed a smile and I was hooked. My terror at knowing no one in a new school was momentarily eased by that one look, and while she was there I felt safe, secure. When my name was eventually called it seemed to hang in the air unclaimed, like a long-lost soul, and certainly not belonging to me. I had hesitated slightly, looking back once more for the angel, before joining the line of girls who were to make up one of the four parallel classes named after illustrious, long-dead women.

Homesick for my junior school and the friends who, knowing their rightful place, had gone off cheerfully to the local comprehensive, I had followed the Pankhurst form teacher along corridors that smelt of polish and long-ago school dinners, and some other odour that I couldn't pinpoint but was, by its very nature, overwhelmingly female. Once in the form room, I had panicked, moving into what seemed the only remaining vacant double desk. When a pale, myopic giant named Cynthia slid, spectre-like, into the seat beside me, my heart had plummeted further still.

Rescue had come from the pigtailed moppet to my left. Nudging my arm, Grace had leaned over whispering, 'I wouldn't sit next to Silent Cynthia if I were you. She was at my junior school. You won't have any fun with her!'

Doubting that fun could ever be on the agenda at this new school, I moved gratefully across the aisle to sit by Grace, cementing a friendship that would span decades.

Throughout that first miserable year as a grammar-school girl I would search Amanda out in the corridor, in assembly and in the lunch queue and for some reason be comforted by her presence. She would walk past me on the way to the senior common room surrounded by a crowd of girls eager to be in the shadow of her aura. Just one look in my direction was enough to put the unfathomable intricacies of French and trigonometry, over which I sobbed regularly, firmly in their place. I was besotted.

Every autumn the second-year girls at Midhope Grammar were expected to take part in a house drama competition produced by our Lower Sixth house prefect. Before rising to the dizzy heights of head girl in the Upper Sixth, Amanda had been Pankhurst House junior prefect. It was 1987, and she was just seventeen, tall, blonde and stylish, glowing from a six-week sojourn to the family villa in Tuscany.

Grace and I were twelve, Badger and Rat respectively in Amanda's production of 'Toad of Toad Hall', and in love. We never admitted to each other that she was the object of our desires, and while it certainly wasn't sexual, we tried to grow our hair like her, found ourselves emulating the way she spoke, and generally followed her around like devoted puppies.

Despite the fact that my alter ego, Rat, jumped up at the wrong moment to deliver the words 'I object' in the courtroom scene, and Silent Cynthia the class geek vomited backstage – not very silently – into Toad's abandoned trilby hat, Pankhurst House won the drama cup for the first time in many years.

Our reward, although not in heaven, was, to our twelve-year-old selves, just as impressive. Amanda's father, probably the last of his breed of Northern mill owners, invited us home for tea. Mr Goodners was God, Amanda our guardian angel, and the gates to the Goodners' pile the entrance to Paradise.

I'm a little hazy as to why only Grace, Serena Todd, Marilyn Baxter and myself were invited, but after taking off our costumes and make-up and being granted permission from our mothers who were in the audience, we climbed into Frank Goodners' Rolls-Royce and off we went.

Nothing could have prepared me for the sudden realisation that here was a world vastly different from my own. The entire downstairs of our council house would have fitted into the Goodners' kitchen – with room to spare. While Grace and the other girls were at ease with the whole situation – Grace's father was one of the town's most prominent solicitors and he and Grace's mother moved in the same social circles as the Goodners – I spent the two hours that we were there in mortal terror of being exposed as an impostor: the girl from the Woodglade Estate on the other side of town who must have wandered in off the street by mistake. Mrs Goodners probably thought people from our estate didn't venture forth to this neck of the woods unless they were one of the band of cleaning women, earning a few quid while their husbands were on the dole, who regularly made the trip on the No. 21 bus. Or kids intent on a bit of breaking and entering, making the trip in knocked-off cars.

While Amanda's father was bluff, red-faced and jolly, with a voice that didn't quite deny his northern roots, Mary Goodners was a product of the southern counties, educated at Cheltenham Ladies' College and thereafter somewhere in Switzerland. I'm sure if Mrs Goodners had had her way, Amanda, too, would have been bundled off to boarding school at the age of eleven, but Amanda was an only child, adored by her daddy and, at his insistence, kept at home where he could delight in her very existence on a daily basis.

After we'd romped around the grounds, where we marvelled at a tennis court with which not even John McEnroe could have found fault, and tried the almost ripe purple figs in a glasshouse that, to me, was on a par with the one in our local park, we were called in for tea.

Whenever I look back to that afternoon, I can never understand why Mary Goodners went to such lengths over tea. A glass of juice and a crumpet in the kitchen would have been more than gratefully received by four hungry twelve-year-olds, but the trolley over which Amanda's mother presided in the sitting room was laden with fare more suited to tea at the Ritz.

I remember being so shy I could hardly eat. I couldn't quite work out how to balance my plate as well as the cup of weak, fragrant tea that my dad, if he'd been there, would have referred to as 'gnat's piss'. Even Grace was subdued, on her best behaviour, and I think that was Mary Goodners' intention. It may have been the eighties, the workers no longer doffed their flat caps to 'the missus', and the servants had been whittled down to one 'daily', but she was sure as hell not going to let us forget her status as mill owner's wife.

On the journey home, I was the last to be dropped off by Amanda's father. It had been an unusually warm September that year, and quite a number of the local kids were still out, swooping around the estate on bikes, unconsciously imitating the gathering swallows that within weeks would be gone. Any credibility I might still have had about being one of them, despite my ascent to the Grammar School, was finally and irrevocably squashed at the sight of Frank Goodners' Rolls-Royce drawing up in front of our garden that evening. I walked the gauntlet of a score of eyes, flagrant or hidden behind net curtains, and I felt myself to be different.

My adoration of Amanda continued throughout that year. I would try to catch a glimpse of her in assembly as she sat with the other sixth-formers in their hallowed positions behind the teachers. A smile bestowed as we moved from one lesson to the next along the corridor would fill me with a glow far superior to that resulting from the porridge forced upon me by my mother at breakfast now that the winter mornings were here.

Eighteen months later and Amanda was half way through her final year at school and head girl. Grace and I were fourteen-year-old rebels at the mercy of our hormones as was anyone brave enough or daft enough to cross us. My poor mother, who, having given birth to me relatively late in life, had her own hormones to contend with, came second only to those in authority at school. Being grammar school girls, and knowing that any defiance towards staff would end ultimately in expulsion, our militancy was of the cowardly variety, as we vented our adolescent insolence on the foot soldiers that policed the corridors and cloakrooms rather than the generals in charge of the battle.

Amanda, once our darling, took her responsibilities very seriously indeed and had, to us, now crossed over to the side of authority. Grace, always passionately loyal to those she loved, felt particularly let down by what she regarded as Amanda's traitorous change of allegiance, and renamed her 'Little Miss Goodness'. She then went out of her way to goad Amanda into confrontation. She would wear her beret pinned to the back of her head so that, when Amanda demanded to know why she wasn't wearing it, Grace was able to turn in mock surprise and assure her that indeed she was. Lip gloss, mascara, chewing gum and, eventually, cigarettes were all confiscated, but it was the incident in the games shed that tolled the death knell on our former adoration.

Being in the dusty shed at lunchtime, instead of braving the north wind that regularly blew off the Pennine hills and swept across the playground, was an offence in itself, but with its racks of hockey sticks and ancient shin pads and its profuse atmosphere of sweat, dust and linseed oil, the shed was a haven in which Grace, myself and our gang of four others would regularly find refuge.

This particular lunchtime we were huddled into a corner, our duffle coats a barrier against the draughts that threatened to permeate our bones, engrossed in a game of 'Consequences'.

At the very moment that Grace opened the multi-folded scrap of paper, the shed door opened to reveal Amanda with a posse of senior prefects. My eyes met Amanda's cool, measured stare as, simultaneously, my warning toe failed to marry with any part of Grace's anatomy.

'Right, listen to this,' Grace guffawed as she quickly scanned the paper before standing to read. 'Are you ready?'

'Mr Hardcastle met Amanda Goodners down by the canal. He said: 'I know what you want darlin'!' She said: 'It's a blow job for you, Randy Pants!' And the consequence was: A flock of little piglets.'

'A *flock* of piglets? Pigs don't come in *flocks* do they?' continued Grace. 'I bet you wrote that, Hattie!' Even at fourteen she would argue the toss over details that she felt weren't quite right.

'We didn't quite catch all that, Grace.' Amanda's voice was pure steel. 'Please read it again. I'm particularly riveted by my response to Mr Hardcastle.'

Grace turned, her face ashen, the scrap of incriminating paper a tight ball in her sweaty hand.

'Oh come on, Grace. I've never known you lost for words before. I'd very much like to hear again what I apparently said to our school caretaker.'

Grace remained rooted to the spot while the rest of us dealt with the situation in our own particular way. Sarah Armitage was blinking madly, the whole of her facial features convulsed in a bizarre Saint Vitus Dance, while Clare Hargreaves was staring intently at a spot on the floor a few inches from her feet. My fingernails were gouging a valley into the palm of each hand as I held them imprisoned in my coat pockets.

Grace seemed to shake herself, sighing slightly before opening the crumpled paper. With her eyes fixed on the paper, the slight tremor of her hand the only indication that she was about to seal her fate, Grace spoke the words that would condemn the six of us as profane, grubby-minded miscreants.

Almost twenty-five years on the ructions that were caused by this little lunchtime incident hardly seem credible, but the fall out was far reaching. We were hauled in front of Miss Seddon, the ageing despot whose demise as head teacher would come about only with the extinguishing of the town's Grammar Schools a few years later, and made to hand over the incriminating piece of crumpled paper. Not only had our smutty little game insulted and degraded our head girl and school caretaker (who unfortunately happened to be a snooker-playing friend of my dad down at the British Legion) , we had also shown a flagrant disregard for school rules by being found in a place that was strictly out of bounds. This was the icing on the cake for Amanda as far as our behaviour was concerned. As we stood, condemned, in the dock of Miss Seddon's study, Amanda unburdened herself with a litany of our misdemeanours over the previous six months, and sentence was passed.

We were excluded from the premises for a week and given a warning, both verbally and via the letter that was posted home, as to our future conduct in school.

'Oh and just one more thing, Grace.' Amanda's voice was triumphant as she caught up with us on the way back to the classroom to collect our things. 'Keep your grubby little adolescent mitts off Jonathon Farrell. Get back to the nursery where you belong and stay there until you're old enough to play with the big boys.'

Ah, so that's what this was all about. I'd warned Grace she was crackers to flirt with Amanda's gorgeous boyfriend, but she would take no heed and, to be fair, he had come on to her, even snogged her once against the wall of Studio 89 coffee bar in town. The dangerous thrill of a two-minute encounter with the enemy's boyfriend must have been immense.

'But what exactly had you written?' my mum had asked, perplexed as to how such a game, resurrected each Christmas by Granny Morgan after the Queen's Speech, could possibly have led to such disgrace.

Giving the honest answer, 'our head girl was fellating Dad's snooker partner down by the canal', was never on the cards, not least because I doubted my mum knew what a blow job was. Mind you, I was fairly much in the dark myself as to the intricacies involved in the whole ghastly sounding procedure, believing it to be largely a product of Sarah Armitage's overactive imagination. I spent the week banished to my room, ashamed to meet my mum's hurt eyes, and avoiding my Dad's all-knowing ones. Diana thought my fall from grace was a hoot, constantly expanding on the fact that she, and my brother John, might only have got as far as the local comp, but *they'd* never brought such disgrace to the family.

The whole tawdry incident might have been forgotten, or passed into the annals of school history to be resurrected as 'Do you remember ...?' over a glass of wine on a girls' night out, had Amanda not moved in on my brother, John and, in his words, 'ruined my life for ever.'

Chapter 8

Two things happened during the week that followed Nick's declaration he was quitting his job. Firstly, Wells Trading, the company just outside Midhope that had employed Nick since the demise of The Pennine Clothing Company, decided that if he was handing in his notice and leaving them, he could jolly well go right now without further ado. By that Monday evening Nick had been ordered to clear his desk, been escorted from the premises by security – presumably to prevent his taking anything that might assist in a new venture – and was now officially out of work.

While I cringed at the thought of him being escorted off site like a criminal in full view of all the other rubber-necking employees, Nick was more than delighted that he'd not actually had to work his month's notice.

He spent the next few days in cahoots with David Henderson, and by Thursday he'd left on the first of his fact-finding trips to Milan.

The second thing to happen was that changelings came in the middle of the night, spirited away Kit, and left one of their own in his place: that's the only explanation for Kit's rapid descent into teenage hell. He looked remarkably the same, apart from hair that seemed to have grown several inches overnight, and a school uniform, bought only a month ago for the new term, that now appeared to have shrunk in the wash. With a week to go until his fourteenth birthday, he'd metamorphosed into a monosyllabic, grunting adolescent.

The signs had been there, I suppose, but with my full attention given over to Nick and *his* madness, I'd chosen to ignore them. I felt bereft. Not only had Nick deserted me for David Henderson and

Italy, Kit seemed intent on getting on with new ventures that certainly didn't include his mother, but certainly *did* include the opposite sex. He was suddenly spending an inordinate amount of time in his room playing music that sounded alien to my (eighties-music-loving) ears, and communicating relentlessly with all and sundry on Facebook.

I had little experience of this. Liberty, at fifteen, was too disdainful of spots, greasy hair and puppy fat to have ever embraced the adolescent stereotype that her brother appeared to have taken on with remarkable speed and gusto. To be fair, his hair, the same dirty-blonde as Nick's, was washed too often in the shower (hogged morning and night) to be anything other than floppily clean and shiny and, while I'd noticed that several of his friends seemed to have outgrown their faces, leaving their noses and lips at odds with the rest of their features, Kit had managed to keep everything in proportion.

Grace, who'd come with India and me to watch Kit play rugby for the school team on the Saturday morning following Nick's departure for Italy, commented as such as twenty-two or so fourteen-year-old boys fought for the ball on the frost-hardened playing field.

'Why is it that these privately educated boys have long, flowing locks, while the kids we teach all seem to have number one buzz cuts?'

I pondered this. 'Maybe it's just that the boys who leave us at eleven start to let *their* grow hair when they get to High School? I don't know.'

'Well, they all look so much more attractive than the fourteen-year-old boys we came across when we were their age. Don't you remember how the boys from the Boys' Grammar School all had suppurating blackheads and cheese-and-onion breath? The boys here are demi-gods compared to the ones in our day.'

'Probably something to do with the tan they all still have from exotic holidays with Mummy and Daddy,' I laughed. 'Does wonders for spots. And I bet half these boys go to their mothers' hair salons and get highlights for their hair. Having a gorgeous, well-groomed teenage son is as much a designer accessory as the latest Chloe handbag,' I added as I turned to make sure India was still in hailing distance. Over by the touchline stood a gaggle of teenage girls, their shiny GHD straightened hair and incredibly skinny jeans tucked into flat, fleecy boots lending them a uniformity they'd probably spent hours trying to achieve. Nothing worse than being out of place amongst your teenage peers.

'I hate to tell you this but I think your son is one of the main attractions on the pitch,' Grace commented idly as she turned her attention to the girls on the touchline.

'What makes you think that?' I asked, squinting to get a better look.

'"Go, Kit!' on their home-made banner is a bit of a giveaway,' she laughed.

'These girls are so forward,' I exclaimed. 'Kit's constantly on his mobile, receiving texts from them. I've threatened him with no birthday money if he brings the damned thing to the dinner table once more. It's very disconcerting when we're enjoying a nice shepherd's pie and there's a relentless bleeping and buzzing coming from his groin.'

'His groin?' Grace laughed, the first I'd heard from her for what seemed a long while.

'He keeps the phone in his trouser pocket hoping we won't notice the constant activity going on down there. One girl rang at ten-thirty on the landline the other evening when Kit was in the shower. I told the little hussy he was fast asleep in bed.'

Grace laughed again. 'I bet he loved you for that.'

I handed Grace a beaker of coffee from the flask I'd brought with me, and she curled her leather-clad hands around its heat while stamping her feet in order to bring back some warmth. We did seem to be having a very early cold snap. If it carried on like this I wouldn't be able to do much to my new garden. My dad had been up to dig around and straighten out my plot a little during the week, but the ground was very hard and progress had been slow.

The insurance people were due to pay a visit to assess damage and loss after our fire and I'd already had a lovely evening poring over gardening catalogues in order to choose a new potting shed and replacements for the garden tools that had gone up in smoke. I reckoned that if we were going to have a new shed, we might as well have a proper job – one in which I could actually potter. Maybe even have a comfy chair down there so I could escape and read my book in peace.

'Dan's not coming back, you know,' Grace suddenly said as she continued to watch the scrum in the middle of which Kit appeared to be coming off rather badly.

'Have you seen him?' I asked as I refilled her coffee mug.

'He actually took me out for dinner last night. We were very civilised and we talked about what we both wanted.'

'And? What is it that *he* wants?'

'A stress-free life away from me, I reckon. Says he loves me, but can't live *with* me at the moment. Says I don't realise how much *he's* suffered with not being able to become a father. I suppose I never really looked at it that way. Anyway, he's going to carry on living at the corporate flat for the moment.' Grace paused before adding, 'And just for the record he's going to carry on seeing Camilla.'

'Oh, wonderful,' I said. 'I'm sorry, Grace, but I think he's being an absolute shit. He wants his mistress *and* his wife and he's making out that you're the baddy in all this. He's basically saying that you've become neurotic and that *you've* driven him into the arms of another woman. And just to even it all up a little more you're supposed to feel sorry for him because you've not been able to produce a baby. If he were that bothered he'd be here with you, holding your hand and trying to work out what to do next. Oh, and by the way, 'he still loves you!' Typical male – blaming anybody but himself for having an itch in his boxers!'

Grace opened her mouth to defend Dan, but then saw my face, thought better of it and sighed, 'Yeah, yeah, you're right.'

The whistle to signal the end of the match sounded from the far end of the pitch and Kit and his team trooped off towards the changing rooms. Having spent much of the game talking to Grace, I wasn't quite sure who'd actually won, but from the way Kit's team walked with their heads down, I assumed they hadn't.

In the car on the way home Kit, who with a nod and a grunt had confirmed his team's defeat, turned to me and said, 'I've been invited to a party tonight. Can I go?'

'I don't see why not. Whose is it, where is it and who's going?' I replied.

'Some girl's over near Blackbrough.'

'Blackbrough? Oh, Kit, that's miles away.' This was the trouble with your kids going to school with children from all over the county – you spent your weekends doing nothing but ferrying, like an unpaid taxi driver, from one end of it to the other.

'What time does it start and what time do you need picking up? Remember there's only me doing the taxi driving this weekend with Dad still in Italy.'

'Well, it starts about six o'clock and finishes at twelve.'

'Midnight? But it's an hour's journey there and an hour back. I really don't fancy doing that at that time of night. And what am I supposed to do with India?'

'I actually meant twelve o'clock tomorrow.'

'What, stay there all night? No way, Buster. You're thirteen years old for heaven's sake.'

Kit tutted and rolled his eyes. 'Fourteen next week, Mum. Everyone's going.'

'And what sort of parents allow their thirteen-year-old daughter to have an all-night party? With boys?' And alcohol, drugs and sex, I added, silently, for good measure.

'I suppose you think there's going to be alcohol, drugs and sex there,' Kit tutted again.

'No, I wasn't thinking that, Kit.' I lied. 'Who is this girl, and if you've been invited where's the invitation? And where do you all propose sleeping?'

'She's called Tara, no one gives invitations anymore and her mum and dad will be there. And I suppose we'll sleep wherever we can.'

'No way,' I repeated, more firmly this time. 'You are far too young to be gadding about and sleeping out all night. Do you know

I was eighteen before I went to an all-night party and even then I had to tell your Granny Keturah I was staying at a friend's house for the night because I knew there was no way she would have let me go.

'Mum, it's a *sleepover*. I've been going to sleepover parties since I was nine or ten. You wouldn't have thought twice about it if it was at Joe's house and all the people who were going were just my mates from my class. What difference does it make because there are girls there?'

I don't know why it did make a difference, but it *did*. And he wasn't going.

'You're so *tight*, Mum,' Kit exploded as we drove down the track to our house. This was reiterated by the slamming of his car door and his stomping into the house through the kitchen door.

Where was my beautiful boy? And where was my bloody husband when I needed him to back me up? This being a single parent lark was definitely *not* cricket.

While I'm not the tidiest of human beings, the state of the kitchen, as India and I followed in Kit's wake, appalled even me.

The breakfast things remained where they'd been left on the table after our hurried departure for Kit's rugby match earlier that morning. A bowl of saturated cornflakes, drowned in an overenthusiastic pouring of milk, lay testament to India's unsteady hand with the six-pint plastic milk carton. Adhering tenaciously to the hundreds of multicoloured beads and sequins that had lain undisturbed on the floor since India had dropped her 'craft box', as she called it, two days previously was a sticky trail of golden syrup. A Nutella-laden knife, balanced precariously on a half-empty glass of breakfast juice, lay surrounded by the detritus of several croissants for which the chocolate spread had obviously been intended, and the remains of Kit's full English breakfast, which I'd cooked to salve my conscience for not having the time to cook him breakfasts on schooldays, lay resplendent in a congealed greasy mess of red and orange.

With our chief dishwasher-filler away (Nick said *I* filled the dishwasher like I did the car boot when we were going on holiday – badly), no one else in the family had thought to take on the responsibility of dishwasher monitor, so dirty dishes from a backlog of meals had formed an uneasy gridlock on the already overcrowded work surface.

The week's ironing, hanging on precariously to the sides of the wash basket, rose in a reproachful tumescence on top of the ironing board which I'd set up in a fit of optimism last night, only to abandon it to a glass of wine and Ian Rankin after processing two handkerchiefs and a pair of pants.

If a new glossy magazine calling itself *25 Most Disgusting Kitchens* should ever break through on to the newsagents' shelves, ours would have had no problem in being one of the first contenders to appear in all its dirty, undisciplined glory.

Liberty wandered down the stairs and into the kitchen, waving her newly French- manicured nails before her.

'You look in a mood,' she said, glancing over to where I stood, arms folded, against the grease-smattered Aga. 'What's up?'

Without waiting for a reply to what was obviously only a rhetorical enquiry she went on, 'You've had five phone calls: Grandad, Auntie Christine, Dad, Uncle John and some posh-sounding woman called Mandy. They all want you to ring them back. I've written down the phone numbers somewhere. Libby glanced round in an effort to locate the piece of paper. 'It's somewhere round here, but this kitchen is such a tip it could be anywhere.'

That's when I exploded. 'Right, you stay right there. Don't move.' Striding to the stairs I bellowed, 'Kit, India, down here this minute. Now. This instant.'

Still wearing an expression of mutinous dislike, Kit slunk into the kitchen and slouched onto the one chair that had managed to escape the plethora of dirty rugby gear, Bratz dolls' paraphernalia, and school bags regurgitating books, pencil cases, artwork and pencil shavings. India, dressed in my long-abandoned wedding dress and shoes, shuffled into the kitchen and joined the elder two for my prolonged rant.

'It may have escaped your notice, but this house is, as you so rightly point out Liberty, a tip. It may also have escaped your notice that I work full time, I am, at present, a single parent and you three do absolutely nothing to help around here. So,' I paused for effect, 'each one of you will abandon whatever you were thinking of doing for the next hour or so and contribute to your keep.'

'That's gay,' Kit muttered, as India began to protest that this was her wedding day and her husband-to-be was waiting for her so that they could become man and wife.

'If he really loves you he'll wait an hour,' I snapped, and proceeded to allocate jobs. It was about time that Liberty did her share of the ironing. After all, the majority of the stuff in the basket belonged to her.

With much muttering under the breath from Kit, heavy sighs and rolling of eyes from Liberty and continued protests from India that her fiancé would go off with Adriana Saxton if she wasn't at the church on time, we set to and blitzed not only the kitchen but the sitting room and downstairs loo. Admittedly, I did most of the hard graft but I lightened the proceedings by blasting out T.Rex's 'I Love to Boogie', so that Kit even forgot that he was a fully paid-up member of the moody brigade and jitterbugged round the furniture with the Hoover.

After an hour or so, and with the promise of tuna-melt panini for lunch, I sent the kids upstairs to see to their bedrooms and made the first of the five return phone calls to the numbers on Liberty's list.

Nick had rung home on Thursday, once he'd arrived in Italy, but I'd not had a word from him since. Ringing him was to be my treat after the other three, so I resisted the idea of phoning him first and dialled my sister-in-law.

'Harriet, you're there now. Where've you been?' Christine sounded a bit uptight, to say the least.

'Kit's rugby match. What's up? You sound a bit stressed.'

'Have you spoken to your father?'

'Dad? He's in The Isle Of Man. Liberty said he rang here this morning and I was going to ring him after I'd spoken to you.' I was suddenly filled with dread. 'What's the matter? Is anything wrong?'

'Mother's gone missing.'

'Missing? What do you mean missing? When did she go missing?'

'Dad rang me this morning about eleven o'clock.' Christine, ever the drama queen, paused for effect and even the knowledge that my mum seemed to have disappeared didn't prevent the now familiar feeling of irritation that she'd somehow hijacked my mum and dad. Why hadn't Dad rung me first, or Diana? And if he'd rung my brother John why the hell wasn't *he* dealing with this apparent crisis instead of letting Christine handle it as per usual? 'Apparently he decided to go out for a quick walk to buy a paper and said he'd see Mother down in the dining-room for breakfast. When he got back, ten minutes later, the girl who was serving breakfast said Mother had arrived at their usual table, but after sitting down had immediately got up again and left the dining room. No one has seen her since.'

I glanced at the kitchen clock. It was now nearly one o'clock. Knowing that my mum and dad, like many elderly people, were early risers, I reckoned she must have wandered off – I didn't like to use the word missing – about five hours ago.

'Have you spoken to him since he first rang?' I now asked.

'Harriet, I've been in *constant* contact with Dad for the last two hours. With both you and Diana not being available, I've been the one who has jollied him along, telling him she'll have just wandered off for a walk and not realised the time.'

I gritted my teeth. She was loving this.

'Christine, put John on. He rang me earlier so maybe he knows something.' I couldn't bear listening to her smarmy, patronising voice any longer.

'He's been out playing golf since early this morning, and has turned his mobile off. You know what bad form it is to have your mobile ringing in the middle of a game.'

No, Christine, I don't know.

'Well he's tried to ring me this morning,' I said. 'He must have got wind of this somehow.' My brother very rarely rang. In fact, thinking about it, I'd not seen him or been in touch for ages. I quickly made a decision.

'Listen, Christine, I'm going to ring my dad myself and see what's going on. I'll update you if there's any news.'

'Oh, I'm sure Dad will do that. He knows how worried I've been.'

I rang the number that my father had left, and a hotel receptionist answered it immediately. I explained who I was and she put me straight on to dad who must have been there, in reception, with her.

'Dad, what's going on?' Mindful of his deafness, I had to enunciate every little word, my voice at full volume.

'It's alright, love. She's back. Came back about half an hour ago. The hotel was just about to contact the police for me, when in she walked as if nothing had happened. Couldn't understand why we were all worried about her. In fact, she got cross with me. Said I was making a fuss about nothing.'

'But where had she *been*, Dad?' Relief that my mum had turned up, apparently safe and well, didn't stop me sounding sharp.

'Ay, lass, I can't figure her out. Said she'd been to Patricia's.'

That name again. 'Has she said who Patricia is? Do we have any long-lost cousins called Patricia and living in the Isle of Man?'

'Nay, I don't know. Only Patricia I've ever known is that lass you used to go to infant school with. We took her to Blackpool that time and she was sick in the car. Do you remember?'

'Vaguely. Dad, can I have a word with Mum? Is she there?' Lurking at the back of my mind was the fear that had been with me for a while and which I'd tried to push under the carpet – the fear that my mum had dementia of some kind. I needed to speak to her to reassure myself about her state of mind.

'No, she's up in the room having a bit of a lie-down,' Dad sighed audibly. 'I think all the excitement of this morning has worn her out. I've come down to reception to get out of her way. Give her a chance to sleep.'

'Dad, do you think there's something, well, wrong with mum?'

'Eh?' I could visualise my father straining to hear, the receptionist glancing irritably at him as the call went on, leaving her without her phone.

'Something wrong with her, Dad. Do you think?' I shouted.

'Well, it's not normal behaviour is it? Wandering off without telling anyone and looking for someone who doesn't exist.' Dad sighed again.

'When are you coming home?' I asked, feeling helpless.

'Not until next Thursday. I daren't let her out of my sight in case she wanders off again.'

'Has she done anything else strange?' I now asked.

'What like?'

'Well, anything out of the ordinary?'

'At our age, lass, we do a lot of things out of th'ordinary,' Dad chuckled. 'I'll let her have a sleep and then take her out for tea somewhere. A walk by the sea and a couple of light ales this evening and she'll be right as rain.'

I had a feeling Dad wasn't facing up to things. As soon as they returned next week, I'd get Diana to come with me and we'd go and see Mum together and have a chat with her. Telling Dad he had to ring *Diana* or *me* if anything untoward happened during the rest of their stay in the Isle of Man, I put the phone down and got on with making lunch.

We were only halfway through eating when the phone rang again.

'Leave it,' I ordered, as India rose to answer it. 'We're eating. The answer machine will pick up.'

'Where are you all? Why haven't you returned my call?' Nick's voice, sounding incredibly jolly, floated across the kitchen and, to a man, we all jumped up and raced to grab the receiver.

'Hi, Dad,' shouted Libby, who, having pipped us all to the post, was now talking ten to the dozen while holding off India who was desperate to speak to her daddy. After the two girls had flirted shamelessly over the phone with their father, and Kit had answered whatever Nick was asking with monosyllabic grunts, it was my turn. Taking the phone into the sitting room so that I could indulge in my own bit of flirting with my absent lover – being suspicious and jealous, I'd decided, wasn't going to make Nick want me more – I collapsed onto the sofa, sitting down for the first time that day.

'Hi, my darling. How's it going?'

'Really good. Italy is a fabulous place. How come we never managed a holiday here?'

'What's the weather like?' Why do the English always ask this? Why wasn't I asking him if he was missing me?

'It's actually very warm. Short-sleeve weather. Got a bit of a tan.' Nick sounded very relaxed. Too relaxed. Shouldn't he be sweating with finding new business, not with sitting in the sun?

'So, what are you actually *doing* out there?' I asked, a tiny modicum of resentment seeping in at the thought of him in balmy Italy while I was keeping the home fires burning, working my socks off and looking after *his* kids in the middle of a particularly cold and miserable week in an English autumn.

'Things are going well. I've had several meetings with David's contacts and one particularly seems very interested in doing business. He makes the most fantastic menswear and is looking to set up a manufacturing outlet in Yorkshire. You know, the original home of the textile industry, and all that?'

'Why?'

'What do you mean, "why"?'

'Well, forgive me if I've got the wrong end of the stick,' I said, 'but isn't Italy having a worse time of it than we are?'

'That's just the point,' Nick said excitedly. 'I know the pound isn't overly healthy at the moment but the Euro in Italy is even worse. The Italians are looking for investment from us, from Germany, and perhaps even Russia. It's a lot more complicated than I can explain right now.'

'Germany and Russia? What are you getting into, Nick?'

'Look, don't worry. I trust David and his business plan. It's up to me to check out the actual clothing. Is it the best on offer or do I need to look elsewhere?'

'What, like Russia? You're not off to bloody Russia now are you?' My heart plummeted.

Nick laughed. 'No. Well, not for the moment anyhow. I'm just trying to find the very best men's Italian designer-wear in the country. I'm having dinner with another manufacturer tomorrow evening, actually at his home, so that should be interesting.'

'When are you coming home?' I knew I sounded a bit peevish, but I thought he was supposed to be on a business trip, not actually *enjoying* himself for heaven's sake!

'Well, today's Saturday,' I could almost hear him mentally ticking off the days, 'so I reckon I should be home mid-week. How are the kids?'

'Kit's hit adolescence big style.'

'I thought he sounded a bit moronic. Well it had to happen. We've had it pretty easy with Liberty. Too much to expect that we should get off so lightly with both of them.'

'Suppose,' I said, and then remembering Grace added, 'Daniel's not coming home to Grace, you know.'

'Really? Oh well, give her my love. I'm going to have to go now, Harriet. Signor Buttoni, my contact has just arrived. Take care.' And he rang off. Just like that. Without saying he loved me, and without telling me how desperately he was missing me. Signor Buttoni? Sounded like a bottled sauce for pasta – or the Mafia.

Just as I put the phone down on Nick, John, my brother, appeared through the kitchen door. Whenever I saw him I always marvelled anew at what a good-looking man I had for a brother. Over six-foot tall and with dark, almost black wavy hair, he often reminded me of a particularly handsome cowboy. You could imagine him lying beside his horse, hat pulled down over his sleepy blue eyes, a cigarette hanging from his full lips. Not that, as far as I knew, he'd ever been anywhere near a horse. Since he was a tiny boy his passion had only ever been cars. There was always an old banger which he'd tinker with, do up and sell on, before buying another. His passion became his job and, having become a car mechanic straight after school, he now owned and ran Midhope's most prestigious, upmarket car garage. In place of the old bangers, John now drove only the sleekest, sportiest and probably most expensive of motors.

I had certainly never been as close to John as I was to Diana, partly because he was seven years older than me and partly because I'd never particularly got on with his wife, Christine. It meant we really didn't see as much of each other as perhaps we would have done.

'Hello, stranger,' I now said, giving him a kiss. 'Don't worry, we've sorted the problem. Mum's turned up, thank goodness.'

'Mum? What do you mean, turned up? Where's she been?'

'She went missing for a few hours in the Isle of Man. You mean you didn't know? I assumed that's why you're here.'

John glanced towards the now deserted lunch table. 'Where are the kids? I need to talk to you, Hat.'

'They've eaten and gone back to their rooms,' I said, surprised at the tone of his voice. 'What's up?'

John sat down amongst the debris of tuna-melt paninis, empty yoghurt cartons, and spilt orange juice. He appeared distressed. Agitated even.

'I've just come from the golf club.'

'Yes, Christine said you were there. We tried to get in touch with you.'

John appeared not to hear me, but went on, 'Steve Ruscoe, one of the members, came up to me in the bar and told me about Nick going into business with David Henderson.'

'Ah.'

'Ah? Ah? Is that all you can say? Ah? Do you know who his wife is?'

I went to fill the kettle before sitting down at the table with John.

'John, I'm perfectly aware that Amanda Goodners is David Henderson's wife. We had dinner with them last week.'

'You knew? You had dinner with them but didn't think to tell *me*?'

'Well, no. I'm having enough on trying to get *my* head round the fact that Amanda bloody Goodners appears to be back in my life. I thought it best to keep it from *you* as long as I could. It is all in the past, you know, John. I mean, I realise she hurt you terribly, but it was a long time ago when you were both very young.'

John scowled furiously, his fists clenching and unclenching repeatedly. 'I can't believe you're letting Nick anywhere near her. She'll have taken one look at him and been determined to have him. Nick is a very attractive bloke, Hat. We all know that.'

John got up from the table and began to pace the room. 'I

wouldn't be surprised if she hasn't set this all up herself. I bet she met Nick somewhere and persuaded David Henderson to take him on.'

I took a deep breath. 'John, calm down. You're not being rational. Look, I agree with you that Amanda always gets what she wants,' I shivered slightly at the very thought, 'but I don't for one minute think *she* was behind getting Nick into her husband's business.'

'You don't know what she's like,' John almost shouted, looking me straight in the eye.

'Yes, I do. You know I do.' When John didn't reply, I got up from the table, scooped coffee into the percolator and poured on boiling water before finding a couple of mugs and setting them down before him. 'Look, John, you and I both know that Amanda Goodners is the most beautiful and therefore most dangerous woman on the planet. But you've moved on from her. You haven't seen her in years and it's about time you got over her and let her go, for heaven's sake.'

John looked down at his coffee for a long time before saying, quietly, 'Did she mention me?'

'No, why should she?' I retorted, exasperated. 'Do you know, John, I'm not sure she ever even knew you were my brother. She was so big in our lives – for me at school and for you when you fell so hard for her – but I don't for one minute think those feelings were ever reciprocated.'

John's eyes, as he raised them to mine were so haunted, I reached for his hand. 'John, this is ridiculous, it's twenty-five years ago. You can't still have feelings for her.'

He laughed but without mirth. 'I never got over her, Hat, and I never will. And if you think it finished all those years ago you're more naïve than I thought. Amanda has never been out of my life. She has the ability, just when I think I'm back on track, to reappear and it starts all over again.'

I stared at my brother in disbelief. 'What are you saying? That you still see her?'

'Oh, Hat, you really don't know do you? I might not see her for years, and then she'll ring me or she'll send me a funny little note or she'll be waiting by my car in the car park as if she's never been away. Or she isn't married with a son. She dangles me on a string, Hat, and the minute I show my feelings again, she's off.'

I felt sick. 'Does David Henderson know about this?'

'God no, I shouldn't think so. She's like a drug, I can't give her up.'

'And where, in this sordid little affair, are you at the moment?' I was beginning to feel angry now. Angry at Little Miss Goodness for messing with my brother's head, but also for John, for his weakness, for all the wasted years. And much as I wasn't Christine's most avid fan, I hated the idea that I was now party to something of which she obviously wasn't aware.

'I've not seen her for nearly six months. I was just beginning to get my head round it once more when I hear Nick's teamed up with her husband. I'm telling you now, Harriet, you have got to get Nick out of there. He won't stand a chance once she moves in on him.'

Although this was the very thing that had been skittering through my brain since the night of the Hendersons' dinner party, I wasn't prepared to have John think Nick was such a pushover. He was married to me, for heaven's sake. He loved me. No one could come between us.

'This is stupid, John. Just because *you* can't resist Amanda Goodners, there's no reason why Nick should be the same. And anyway, I don't imagine Nick will be seeing much of her. He's in Italy at the moment. She's at home in Midhope – she rang here this morning apparently.'

Hearing Libby coming, singing down the stairs, John stood up to go. 'Well, you now know what's been going on, Harriet. I'm not proud of myself, but there it is. You know as well as I do what Amanda is like. If I were you I'd be on that phone telling Nick to get out of this deal as soon as he possibly can.'

As if I haven't tried, I thought, grimly, as I watched John drive off. And you're *not* me and your whole security *isn't*, as from a couple of weeks ago, connected to that woman and her husband. My mood didn't lighten when, on closing the kitchen door, the phone rang and Amanda Henderson's distinct voice sounded, immediately taking me back twenty-five years to when I was a schoolgirl.

'Ah, Harriet. You're home now. How are you?' Her assurance that I would know straight away who was speaking without any introduction did nothing to make me feel any better.

'Hello, Amanda. I'm fine.' I couldn't get my head around calling her 'Mandy.' 'I was going to call you back, but I've been busy.' I didn't expand on this – there was no way I was going to let Amanda Goodners know that my mother was apparently going doolally in a two-star hotel on the Isle of Man. Or that John had left me totally stunned by what he'd just told me about her.

'Don't worry. I just wanted to ask you if you'd had any more thoughts about this Midhope Grammar reunion before I fly off to Italy. My flight is at five, and I really need to get back to Sally Davies – you remember Sally? – with the final numbers.'

'Italy? You're going out to Italy?' My heart was suddenly hammering frighteningly in my chest.

'Yes, I'm meeting Nicky out there. Didn't he tell you? Typical man.' She laughed comfortably. 'This is where I help David with his business ventures. I speak a few languages, for my sins, and my law training helps with the small print in contracts. You'd be amazed how often our contacts think they can get away with murder because their contracts are not written in English. Anyway, Harriet, can I put you down on the twentieth?'

'Put me down?' I asked in surprise, my head still full of terrifying thoughts about *Mandy* and *Nicky*, together, in Italy. What was I, an unwanted moggy that had to be got out of the way so that these two could make hay together while the Italian sun shone?

'Yes, put you down for the Midhope Grammar School 100th-year reunion.' Amanda was beginning to sound a trifle impatient. 'Now, I'm expecting you and Grace to join us. Clare Hargreaves and Sarah Armitage were your year weren't they? They're going to be there.' Amanda knew perfectly well these two were my year – they'd been with Grace and me in the 'games shed affair' and I didn't think for one moment that Amanda would have forgotten this.

'I can't actually see Grace coming,' I said, struggling to bring myself back to the present from my schoolgirl past, and away from possible scenarios involving Amanda and my husband in the future.

'Well, that's up to her. It would have been very interesting to meet up with her again after all these years.' She paused before saying, 'So, Harriet, it's actually next Friday evening at the school itself at seven-thirty.'

I made a decision. My social life was pretty nonexistent at the moment, and it *would* be interesting to see people I'd last clapped eyes on twenty years ago. Not only that, what do they say about keeping your friends close but your enemies closer? At least if she was with me then she couldn't be with my brother. Or my husband.

'I'll be there, Amanda. You can *put me down.*'

'Oh, goodo. Now, any message for Nicky?' she trilled.

What could I possibly say that could be carried via Amanda to my husband?

'No, no message, Amanda,' I said and hung up the receiver.

Chapter 9

Never one to do anything by half measures, Grace took on her new status as single girl in need of a social life with extraordinary gusto. Attempting to hide her hurt and fury over Dan's affair and his subsequent behaviour towards her, Grace threw herself into a manic round of visits to the gym, training for the London Marathon, and job searching for promotion. This, coupled with a determination to go out and socialise as often as possible, meant she was able to fill much of the time she would otherwise have spent at home brooding over Dan's defection and the constant sadness caused by her infertility.

While there was little I could do to help with the former – no way was she persuading *me* to pound the pavements in a sweaty tracksuit – it appeared I was to be roped in to help with the latter. On the morning of Nick's intended return from Italy, Grace appeared in my classroom and thrust a ticket under my nose.

'Here we are, this is what we're doing tonight,' she said, grinning as I warily tried to make sense of what she'd handed to me.

'Sing-a-long-a-Sound Of Music'? Grace, I don't think so. I've no babysitter, and Nick's due back some time this evening.'

'All sorted,' she said triumphantly in the tone of voice I knew from many years' experience meant she would brook no argument.

I glanced at the classroom clock. I had ten minutes until the kids came in for morning school and I still had a pile of unmarked maths books in front of me. 'Go on,' I groaned, 'hit me with it.'

'I've just spoken to your wonderful mother-in-law and she totally agrees with me that you're looking a little tired and overworked and could do with a night out at the theatre. She's more than happy to sit in with the kids while you gain a little culture.'

'My *wonderful* mother-in-law, as you so succinctly put it, will be overjoyed at the thought of being in *my* sitting room to welcome back *my* husband and to find out before I do just what has been happening in Italy.' It still very much rankled that Sylvia had given Nick the wherewithal to be in Italy in the first place, and she knew it. She'd been pussyfooting around me ever since Nick broke the news to me that she'd given him what amounted to a huge slice of her life savings.

'Oh give the poor woman a break,' Grace said, impatiently. 'Most people would kill for a mother-in-law like yours. Now, Sylvia and I have sorted out the housekeeping, as it were, between us so it's just a matter of dropping off at the fancy dress hire shop on your way home.'

'Why? Don't tell me you've organised a fancy dress party for me to go to as well?' This really was going too far. The only reason I was going along with her plan for a night out was my childish need for Nick to realise that he wasn't the only one who could have a good time on his own. Although I was desperate to see him, it wouldn't do him any harm to come home to find me not there. I could do, 'getting on with my own life' as well as the next woman. Alright, as well as Amanda.

'Do you not know what 'Sing-a-long-a-Sound of Music' is?' Grace asked in amusement.

'Of course I know what the "Sound of Music" is,' I said huffily. 'I assume this is what Valerie Westwood has been rehearsing for the last few weeks. Mind you, she's kept it quiet. She's normally practising her words and touting tickets long before the first night.'

'No, you daft thing. This is a sort of spoof. The audience all get dressed up as something to do with the "Sound of Music" – like being a nun, or one of the Von Trapp family or Maria herself – and then we go along and watch the film.'

'Why?'

'Why?' Grace repeated, starting to laugh at the expression on my face. 'Well, we go and sing along with all the songs and heckle the baddies and cheer the goodies.'

'Dressed as a *brown paper package tied up with string*?' I said in disbelief.

'Hey, that's a good idea. I hadn't thought about that one.'

'So what *had* you thought about?' I was curious to know what she intended going as even if I was damned if she was getting me to go along with her on this whole debacle.

'Not sure yet, but there are plenty of nuns' habits available at that fancy dress place on your way home. I've just rung them and asked them to put one aside for you.'

'You've certainly done your homework,' I said and then catching sight of Darren Slater who was skulking in the cloakroom rather than freezing his tush off out in the playground and no doubt taking in all our conversation, I shouted, 'and I hope you've done yours too, Darren Slater.'

'So, I'll pick you up about seven. We want to get a good seat. All the better to hiss at the countess.'

I shook my head incredulously. I might, secretly, be a bit tense at the thought of Nick's return home that day – I knew I'd have to quiz him into the ground about Amanda's presence with him in Italy– but I didn't really want to let on to Grace just how twitchy I was feeling about the whole thing. Better to pretend everything was fine. Maybe I could even relax and believe my own lovely dream, of Nick arriving home, sweeping me up the stairs and tumbling me into bed with the words, 'My darling, Harriet, no one compares to you. How you could even think I could be tempted by another woman when you are all woman to me?' Or something along those lines.

'Well?' Grace interrupted my vision of Nick handing me the single red rose he just happened to have about his half-naked self, 'Are you up for it, or not?'

'I don't believe you're expecting me to dress up in a nun's outfit and sit in that fleapit of a theatre, booing and hissing when I could be at home lying in wait for my long-gone husband, ready to tear the clothes off his fit, tanned body the minute he walks in the door.'

Grace did waver for a moment. 'Well, put like that you might just have a point. But there again, I bet you've always wanted to sing and yodel along with a lonely goatherd.'

'Always. Top of my list of things to do. Right, I'll come with you on one condition.'

'Ok. What is it?'

'You have to come with *me* to Amanda Goodners' school reunion thingy tomorrow night.'

'No problem,' said Grace airily. 'I'd already decided I wanted to go. Didn't I tell you?'

'No! You said definitely no way were you spending an evening with people we didn't even like when we were *fifteen*. You said we'd more than likely *despise* them now.'

'Did I really say that? How short-sighted of me. Now that I'm on a quest to get out and meet new people it sounds like a great idea. Count me in.'

'But they're *not* new people,' I said in exasperation at her unexpected volte-face. 'They're old people plus an extra twenty-five years.'

'Brilliant. I shall look forward to it immensely. And because you've been such a good pal all these years, and especially tonight in coming with me dressed in your nun's habit rather than hanging around in your best suspenders and high heels waiting for that wonderful husband of yours' – she paused for effect – 'you can come and get ready at my house tomorrow and you can borrow my new Max Mara jersey clingy dress that I've not even worn yet.'

'Can I really? Wow!'

'Absolutely,' said Grace magnanimously, 'for you are my very best pal in the whole of the world.'

'Very best *pushover* in the whole of the world,' I muttered irritably to myself that evening as I struggled with my wimple in front of the dressing table mirror. It just wouldn't *sit* properly at all. Every time I thought I'd got it right, it fell to one side giving the general impression of my being a cross-eyed, mentally defective penguin.

I had our part of the house completely to myself, Sylvia having offered to give tea to the children in her flat and then take them all to the cinema. She really *was* bending over backwards to be helpful at the moment.

I assumed that Kit and Liberty would plump for one showing while Sylvia and India would watch something more suitable for five-year-olds. That said, the two elder children were usually more than happy to watch a *Shrek* or *Toy Story*-type film, and Sylvia usually fell asleep after the first ten minutes or so no matter what she was watching.

Nick had phoned earlier, leaving a message to say he'd be home around ten o'clock. When I'd tried to phone him back on his mobile there'd been no reply, and I assumed he must have already got on the plane.

Grace was late. I gave my wimple another tug and adjusted my suspenders. I'd thought I might as well kill two birds with one stone, as it were, in hopeful anticipation of a night of passion with my husband on his return, as well as a night of goatherd yodelling. It really was a very strange feeling seeing my features defined quite differently from usual by the black and white starched material, knowing that, underneath the incredibly heavy fabric, I was wearing underwear of which any high-class whore would be proud.

'Hattie, I'm running late. Could you save us some time by meeting me at the top of your lane in ten minutes? ' Grace called from her mobile.

'Dressed like this?' I started to say, but she'd rung off and there was nothing for it but to gather my bag, my habit and my dignity and dash up the darkened lane that led to the main road.

With the excess habit gathered haphazardly into one hand for ease of movement, and my wimple held centrally with the other, I staggered up the tree-lined lane. It was a beautiful evening, sharply cold and with a full moon already sailing to the west like an extravagant silver cheese. Ever since Nick, who'd once spent a summer with relatives in America, had told me how Americans look for the *rabbit* in the moon rather than the *man* in the moon, I'd looked out for it whenever there was a full moon in the heavens. I stopped for a few seconds to hoist up my frock and decipher the rabbit, which was lying on its side. A sudden rustle of leaves and a sneeze that appeared to come from the middle of the bush ahead of me rooted me to the spot, heart hammering in my chest. This was a fairly lonely lane; there was no reason to be on it unless en route either to our house, Ralph-Next-Door's house, or the Melvilles' Farm which made up the little hamlet where we lived. I stood stock still now, unwilling to carry on up the lane past the bush where the sneeze appeared to have originated. There was another rustle of leaves and the bush gave the impression of parting. A dark figure stepped out and gave a little start at the same time as an involuntary scream escaped my lips.

'Jesus, Ralph, what on earth are you doing lurking in the bushes?' I squeaked, relief flooding over me like a warm shower.

'Who's that?' Ralph answered, peering through the dark from his position just to the left of the bush.

'It's me, Harriet. Who the hell did you think it was?'

'A bloody nun, that's who the hell I thought it was.'

'It's me. I'm off to the theatre.'

'Dressed like a bloody nun?'

'Yes. Ralph, what are you doing in that bush?'

There was a silence for a while before he answered, 'Call of nature, Harriet. Got caught short. You know how it is.'

'Right. Well, I must be off,' I said breezily and then added, 'bless you, my son,' as I hurried past him to meet Grace.

Bless you, my son? I repeated out loud, tittering to myself as I huffed and puffed up the rest of the lane. Wasn't that what the Archbishop of Canterbury said to his genuflecting flock? Not the words of a lowly nun, surely? I was getting serious giggles now and had to remind myself that I'd spent a hell of a lot of time putting on several layers of Liberty's new mascara, nicked while she was out of the house, in addition to the lovely new knickers I'd bought in hopeful anticipation of Nick's return. So busy was I trying to control my giggles, my habit and my wayward wimple that it wasn't until I reached the main road that ran adjacent to our lane that it suddenly occurred to me that there was no rational explanation for Ralph taking a leak in the bush when he had a couple of perfectly good loos at home. And no explanation, as far as I could see, as to why he should have a pair of *binoculars* hanging round his neck.

Grace drew up just as I was beginning to shiver, musing: what did *authentic* nuns wear under their black habits? Did their frocks traditionally come under the same genre as Scottish kilts so they wore nothing? Or maybe they suffered hair knickers and bras to go with their hair shirts?

'Get in, Sister, we're late,' Grace shouted from the depths of her warm car.

'Don't I know it,' I grumbled, hauling myself and yards of fabric into her car. 'Oh thanks *very* much,' I added as I saw how she was dressed. 'You order me the habit from hell and get yourself tarted up to look gorgeous.'

Grace was dressed as the archetypal female German Officer – the dream of every man who has ever had fantasies about women in uniform. She wore a very short and tight-fitting skirt and the jacket was tailored and figure hugging. Her black, seamed stockings were elegantly placed in killer black stilettos, and she'd obviously spent a great deal of time on her make-up as well as her hair which she'd swept up into a severe, chestnut chignon under a peaked cap. She looked like Madame Sin does Adolf Hitler.

'Where's your German Shepherd?' I asked.

'Um, I did consider asking Beryl and Stan if I could borrow their Dalmatian, but reckoned he'd get thoroughly overexcited once the singing got under way,' she said seriously through red-painted lips.

'I've just come across Ralph-Next-Door lurking in the bushes along our lane,' I now said as we hurtled along country lanes trying to make up lost time.

'Have you? What was he up to?'

'I dunno. Very strange, but he said he was taking a leak. He nearly scared me to death.'

'He's got a dog hasn't he? He was probably taking it out for a walk and needed to pee. It is a bit parky out there this evening.' Grace pulled into the theatre car park with a good five minutes to spare.

'Well that's what I thought at first, but Shep *wasn't* with him, *and* he had a pair of binoculars round his neck.' The more I thought about it, the stranger it seemed. 'I mean, you just *don't* hide in bushes with a pair of binoculars unless you're either a burglar or a Peeping Tom do you?'

'Oh, *I* don't know,' said Grace looking in the car mirror and adding more lip gloss, clearly not overly interested in the strange nocturnal habits of my neighbours. 'Hey, look at Ray over there,' she laughed, pointing to what could only be described as a grotesquely tangerined sunflower.

'Ray? Ray who? Do you know him?'

Grace laughed again, 'No, *Ray*. Ray, a Drop of Golden Sun. Get it?'

I groaned. I could see I was in for a wing-dinger of an evening.

And I was. It was really good fun. Best evening I'd had in ages. We sang along at the top of our voices, we booed and hissed the German baddies and the Countess and we cheered every time Julie Andrews made an appearance, which, given that she was the star of the show, was rather a lot.

I glanced across at Grace several times during the film and she too seemed to be genuinely enjoying herself. I'd been worried that the almost feverish air she'd been sporting for the last few days could, at any time, dissipate, leaving her empty and vulnerable as the events of the past month really kicked in.

'I can't see Nick's car,' said Grace as she drove up our drive. 'Do you reckon he's not back yet?'

'I hope he is,' I said looking at my watch. It was eleven o'clock. 'His car is in the garage. Sylvia took him to the airport last week and he said he'd get the train and taxi back from Manchester Airport. It's actually quicker than driving now that the Trans-Pennine train goes right into Terminal 1. Come on in and have a quick coffee.'

'No, I'll leave you two lovebirds to your reunion,' she said almost wistfully.

I suddenly couldn't bear the thought of her going home all alone, dressed in her Nazi uniform with no one there waiting to show it off to as she walked into her empty house.

'Come on,' I said firmly. 'It'll be a laugh. Nick's no idea what we've been up to this evening.'

'Two minutes then,' Grace agreed, switching off the engine and putting off for a little while the moment when she'd have to accept all over again that Dan wasn't going to be at home, waiting for her to come in.

A light was shining under the closed sitting-room door and I motioned Grace to be quiet as I flicked the switch from the hallway, plunging the room into darkness. Opening the sitting-room door we caught Nick as he rose from his favourite chair, the light from the wood-burning stove illuminating his way as he stumbled towards us looking for the light switch.

Giggling helplessly, Grace grabbed him in an all-embracing clinch, forcing him back into the chair as she whispered in a low, guttural accent, 'Don't move, my darling. Ve 'ave vays ov making you talk. You 'ave been a very naughty boy ent you must be punished.'

The sitting-room light snapped back on as Nick walked in, a look of utter incredulity on his face. He was carrying a tray laden with a cafetière and my best Emma Bridgewater mugs.

'Hello, Grace,' said Amanda coolly, giving Grace a long hard stare as she followed in Nick's wake, the Belgian chocolate biscuits I'd hidden from the kids at the back of the kitchen cupboard in her hand, 'I see you've met my husband.'

'How were we supposed to know you had the Hendersons in tow?' I demanded of Nick twenty minutes later. 'There was no car in the drive to warn us. I assumed you were at home by yourself after catching the train from Manchester.'

'David had arranged to meet Mandy off the flight and obviously offered me a lift home. I invited them in, not only for a coffee but because Mandy wanted to have a word with you about some do you're both going to tomorrow, apparently. There were also still loads of things I needed to iron out about what we've sorted in Italy.'

'So where was David's car? We might have acted with a little more decorum if we'd known you had *visitors*.' Actually, if Grace had had any idea that the first sight Little Miss Goodness would have of her after twenty-five years was dressed as a Nazi tart she'd have been back down our drive before you could say 'Auf Wiedersehen, Pet.'

'David's car was round the back,' Nick explained as he loaded the empty coffee cups back on to the tray. He looked exhausted, the slight tan he'd acquired failing to mask the lines around his eyes and the tension in his shoulders. 'He overshot the drive and ended up round the side and stayed there rather than reversing.'

'And why was *Mandy* in the kitchen with you?' Just what had those two been up to in the kitchen while David Henderson was left alone to be assaulted by marauding nuns and Nazis? As I recalled how stunning she'd looked in a brown suede tightly fitting dress with dark brown suede boots, I heard my tone become peevish. 'Since when do you need help making a cup of coffee?'

'What is this, Harriet? Why the third degree over a cup of coffee?' Nick said crossly as he made his way into the kitchen, me still in my nun's habit, albeit *sans* wimple, worrying at him like a terrier with a rag doll.

'Well, she must have been in my kitchen cupboard,' I went on. 'In all our married life *you've* never known where I've hidden the chocolate biscuits.'

'Harriet, I've *always* known where you've hidden them. Inside the blue Tupperware box labelled, "Bones' Cat Biscuits".'

'Really? You've always known?' I was momentarily nonplussed. If he'd kept this from me what else was he capable of hiding?

'Look, I'm dead on my feet. It's not been all beer and skittles, you know, this trip to Italy.'

'Hey, don't look at me for sympathy.' I said, following him doggedly up the stairs. 'It was your idea to jack it all in and swan off leaving me a single parent and chief breadwinner. I've had to cope with a son who's apparently suddenly Midhope's answer to Casanova, a mother who has taken to wandering round the streets of the Isle of Man, and a perverted neighbour who hides in bushes and jumps out at nuns with a pair of binoculars round his neck.'

'Tell me all about it in the morning,' Nick said, pecking me on the cheek and falling into bed, leaving me grinding my teeth and twanging my unappreciated suspenders in frustration.

Chapter 10

It never ceases to amaze me how evocative sounds and scents, but particularly scents can be. The pungent scent of 'Opium' perfume immediately takes me back to 1989. I'm fifteen, The Bangles are belting out 'Walk Like an Egyptian' and Grace and I are drinking Lutomer Riesling in her bedroom, deciding what to wear for some party or other that we've been invited to.

Even though they'd split up years before we were both still big into Wham! – Grace favoured Andrew Ridgley, even before his nose op., while there was only ever George Michael for me. Dressed in our vivid blue jump suits, the trouser legs rolled up to reveal an ankle chain, the sleeves pushed up beyond the elbow and the waists cinched in with wide leather belts, we'd add another layer of mascara and eyeliner to our already sooty eyes and jump around Grace's room to 'Wake me up before you go-go'. Or we'd wear our five-year-old Frankie goes to Hollywood 'Relax' T-shirts over black footless tights, secured around our middles with a huge black plastic belt and topped with denim jackets studded with very tasteful rhinestones. Frilly socks worn with high heels completed that particular choice eighties ensemble. Hair was big as were our shoulders, our blue eyeliner matched our blue plastic button earrings and we thought we were the proverbial dog's bollocks.

It was Friday evening, half term had officially begun, and I was once again in Grace's bedroom, getting dolled up for the much-lauded Midhope Grammar reunion and breathing in the smell of Opium as Grace, in an effort to recreate 'getting ready' sessions of yesteryear, sprayed the scent around the room. I'd left the kids to

Nick – and, presumably, Sylvia – and made good my defection for the evening.

'Phew, how old is this Opium?' I asked, sneezing as the fumes found their way up my nose.

'Very,' Grace admitted, as she scrabbled in the bottom of her wardrobe for something. 'Right, here we are,' she said, placing a 1984 Compilation CD on her CD player. 'I don't seem to have anything later than 1984 but this should still bring back some memories.'

'Ninety-nine red balloons,' sang a soulful Nena whose German accent maybe Grace should have noted last night prior to jumping on, and whispering in the ear of, David Henderson.

'No Lutomer Riesling or Liebfraumilch?' I asked as Grace returned from the kitchen with two glasses of cold Australian Sauvignon Blanc.

'Hardly. One has to draw the line at retro somewhere,' she smiled. 'Anyway, they're German aren't they, and I don't want anything to do with anything German tonight.' Her tone was flippant, but I knew that, in her present vulnerable state, feeling exposed, she'd been highly embarrassed by the events of last night. With Dan at her side she'd have laughed it off, even thoroughly enjoyed the whole debacle, but her emotions were too raw to have enjoyed making a spectacle of herself in front of someone she'd never met before. *And* in front of Little Miss Goodness.

'So, what did you think of David Henderson?' I ventured, reading her thoughts as she sipped her wine.

'I think he's probably the type of man I would find extremely attractive had I not been too embarrassed to take a second look. Once I'd nibbled his ear and to all intents and purposes rotated my bum in his groin, the last thing I was going to do was actually meet his eyes,' she said ruefully.

'How do you think I felt?' I laughed, in an effort to make her feel better. 'The first time I met him I was a gibbering wreck on his doorstep, and the second time I'm dressed as a bloody nun.'

'That's true,' she conceded. 'Nick must think we're a real pair of head-bangers. There he is, trying to be all grown-up with his cafetière and Belgian biscuits, showing the Hendersons what a suave, cool business man he is, and his wife and best mate ruin it all for him, acting like a pair of overgrown, giggling schoolgirls.'

'Hmm, unfortunately the last time Amanda saw us both together, that's what we both were. Bet she thinks we haven't changed a bit. *She* still looks pretty good though, don't you think?'

'Stunning,' Grace agreed. 'But then, she would wouldn't she? She was gorgeous at seventeen, and hasn't changed much since then.'

'Do you think she fancies Nick?' I asked airing the thought that had been uppermost in my mind since our dinner at the Hendersons'.

'Bound to. Who wouldn't? And do I think Nick fancies Amanda? Again, the same answer – Bound to. Who wouldn't?' And then seeing my face, she added hastily, 'But of course, you and I both know there's never been anyone else for Nick since that Saturday night in the university union bar.'

'Yes, but I would have said that about Dan and you, and look what happened.'

Grace snorted derisively. 'Daniel has always had a roving eye, if never, as far as I'm aware, until now that is, extending it to roving hands.'

'Really?' I was shocked. 'You never said.'

'Well, you don't do you? It's a matter of pride. I'd have been embarrassed to tell you every time Daniel looked at another woman. One has to pretend everything is hunky-dory even if you think maybe it's not.'

'Ooh, I hate this,' I interrupted, as a new track started on the CD. 'I spent the whole evening fighting off Simona Kennedy's brother at her sixteenth birthday party, and every time this track came on he grabbed me, pressing his hot sweaty hands on to my bum.'

'Not surprised. It's Chaka Khan's "I Feel For You", Grace laughed squinting at the CD sleeve.

'Yeah, well, he certainly felt for me, the little pervert. He was only thirteen.'

'Same age as Kit,' Grace pointed out. 'Mind you, *he* doesn't look like a sweaty groper. He seems far more grown-up.'

'Hmm,' I agreed. 'That's what worries me. He's fourteen this week, and suddenly my little boy isn't so little any more. I caught him with a copy of *Loaded* the other day.'

'Pretty harmless stuff isn't it?' Grace called back from the depths of her immense wardrobe of designer clothes. 'Right, Hat, we are going to slay them tonight. We're going to show them that we're still young, gorgeous, and now sophisticated, women of the world. Here's the dress I promised you.'

'Are you sure?' I breathed, as she handed me a brand new Max Mara grey jersey dress, the labels still attached. I flinched when I saw the price. 'This is far too expensive a dress to let me have first shot at,' I said, handing it back.

'Oh rubbish, get it on,' she said. 'Think of it as a reward for all the times you've been there for me lately.' She turned away, slightly embarrassed, busying herself with tidying the room of the clutter of glasses, clothes and make-up. A very different room from Grace's bedroom of 1989, this one was essentially feminine and, like anything to do with Grace, very tasteful. I noticed she'd deliberately positioned her pillows in the middle of the bed, moving them from the side she'd always favoured before Dan had left.

The room, very much like the Hendersons' sitting room I'd coveted a couple of weeks ago, was predominately cream. It was a rich, buttery cream reminding me of the clotted cream we'd eaten with raspberries on our one trip to Devon many moons ago. Heavy, cream damask material sporting a gold leaf hung at the windows and was also pleated and gathered at the bed head. A large easy chair, covered in a gold chintzy material, stood in front of French windows which opened onto a balcony resplendent with pot plants. In my new role as Head Gardener, I recognised that many of these plants should have been brought inside now that autumn was well and truly under way. Knowing that Grace had no interest whatsoever in anything horticultural, I surmised that she wasn't the only one to be suffering because of Dan's defection.

I moved over to the long cheval mirror in order to get a good view of myself in Grace's dress. It fitted like a kid glove, the jersey material obligingly accommodating the hills and troughs of my body.

'Oh wow!' Grace exclaimed, turning round from where she'd been putting on yet another CD. 'You look absolutely fantastic. It fits you much better than me.'

'Hardly,' I said. Grace's gym-toned body could give mine a run for its money any day of the week. 'Mind you, it does look fantastic doesn't it?'

'Absolutely. Look at your boobs. How voluptuous are they?'

'Time of the month. I'm due a period any day.'

'And your stomach's so flat. God, three children and you've still not got any flab on you.' Grace said admiringly and without rancour.

'Oh oh, problem,' I wailed. 'I've forgotten to bring any shoes. I've only got my flatties I've been wearing for school all day.'

'There's a pair of grey suede high heels somewhere. You could probably just squeeze into them. They're really too big for me.' She looked round as if they were about to appear by magic. 'Damn, where did I put them at the end of last winter? I know, go and have a look down in the bottom, spare bedroom. There's a big wardrobe down there where I put all the stuff I know I shan't wear any more. They're in an L.K. Bennett box. Go and have a root round while I have a quick shower.'

This spare bedroom, unlike the rest of the house, had not been decorated since Grace and Dan had moved in five years ago, and I realised with a slight pang that this was the room Grace would have been waiting to paint in a soft pink or blue, for the baby that had never arrived. It had an air of abandonment about it, the walls still wearing the dated wallpaper chosen by the previous owners many years before.

I pulled the left-hand mirrored wardrobe door back on its runners and stared in confusion. Instead of the no longer needed clothes waiting patiently, at Grace's whim, for their disposal to charity shops that I'd expected, I found a bank of shelves jam-packed with just about all the things needed to fuel what was obviously an addiction. Pornography, vodka, a whole hydroponics system of cannabis plants, even heroin I could probably have coped with, but row upon row of fluffy bunnies, tiny bootees, and little designer outfits in white, blue and pink was just something else. Dismayed, I hurriedly shut the wardrobe door, feeling as guilty as if I'd been reading Grace's private diary, and pulled the right-hand door open to continue my search for the elusive shoes. Right at the back, hidden by long coats and other abandoned footwear, was the distinctive white, L.K. Bennett shoebox. Grabbing it, I composed my features, and with a cheery, 'found them, let's hope they fit,' made my way back to Grace's bedroom where she was just emerging from the shower.

Although a little tight, the shoes were a perfect match for the dress and twenty minutes later we were both ready for the off. Grace looked fabulous. The extra time spent in the gym and pounding the local pavements had certainly paid off. She was slim, toned and, in contrast to her tarty outfit of the previous evening, was stylishly dressed in cream and chocolate brown. Her chestnut hair fell silkily to her collar and she had spent an inordinate amount of time outlining and defining her brown eyes so that they appeared huge. Although she hadn't said anything, I knew her efforts had been largely directed at showing Amanda Goodners just how stunning she could look when not dressed as a Hitler lookalike.

It had been twenty years since our final days at Midhope Grammar and, while the original early Victorian building was essentially the same, two new glass and concrete extensions had been added, creating updated accommodation for the two thousand or so co-ed comprehensive school students who were now educated here.

'I hope there's going to be people here we'll know,' I whispered to Grace as we made our way down what had once been known as 'G' corridor, following a group of women ahead who seemed to know where they were going.

'There'd better be. I can't see me spending all evening making small talk with Amanda, discussing whether she's had much action down by the canal lately.'

'Shh,' I giggled, as Amanda herself came into view standing, with some of those who'd been prefects when she was head girl, at the entrance to what I presumed was still the Great Hall, welcoming people and handing out name tags.

'Trust Amanda to be so bloody efficient. Far more fun to see if we can guess who people are twenty years on,' grumbled Grace.

Amanda turned towards us, giving Grace a particularly hard, almost searching, stare. What *was* she looking at? Then she relaxed and said breezily, 'Hello, you two. Good to see you again.'

'Does she mean after twenty years? Or after seeing us groping her husband in the dark?' Grace said in my ear, as we walked towards a makeshift bar being tended by more of Amanda's cronies.

'Shh,' I giggled again. '*Please* don't make me laugh. I don't want to be reunited with all this lot while snorting like a mentally defective hyena.'

'Grace, Hattie. Over here! We've got a bottle!' An excited shout accompanied by a prolonged bout of bottle waving from a table in the centre of the hall had heads turning in every direction, craning to see what the noise was all about.

'Oh, my God, they're *all* there,' laughed Grace incredulously as we made our way forward to where Sarah Armitage was waving her arms, beckoning us over to join them.

'Amanda said she hoped you were both coming,' said Sarah excitedly. 'We've saved seats for you. Come on, sit down, have a drink. Tell us everything. You both look fantastic!'

Around the table were eight of our former classmates: girls with whom we'd shared so much in our formative, adolescent years, but with whom, other than with fairly irregular Christmas cards, we'd not really kept in touch. There had been the occasional twenty-first birthday celebration, a couple of engagement parties, and we'd both been invited to Sarah's wedding – she was the first of us to marry, getting hitched to the boy from the Boys' Grammar who she'd met when she was just fourteen. But as the years had gone by, and several of the gang had moved away from the area, Grace and I had lost touch with the rest of them.

The whole 'games shed affair' contingent was out in force as Grace and I joined Sarah, Clare Hargreaves, Sally Wise, and

Rebecca Martin. The other four at the table were friends who, had it not been for netball practice, would probably have been with us in the games shed and condemned along with us to a week's exclusion from school.

'So, are you still married to Alan, Sarah?' Grace and I asked simultaneously as we poured wine and settled down as well as we could on the grey plastic chairs which didn't seem to have altered since our young bottoms had sat on them nearly a quarter of a century before. I bet if I'd looked hard enough I'd have found the one with 'I love George Michael' carved with a bent compass onto its underneath – the result of half an hour's boredom while Mr 'Mad' McGregor, the maths teacher we'd inherited from North of the Border, worked himself up into a right Scottish lather, shouting that we, the bottom maths group girls, would 'niver in this werrld parrs yi exams. Y'arr awl second clarrs citizens – gid fer nethins.'

'Am I still married to that little *twerp*?' Sarah asked in mock horror. 'You have to be joking. We got married far too young. I put up with three years of his fumbling in bed. Towards the end, I knew I could *not* put up with it any longer. Foreplay, to Alan, was cleaning his teeth and folding his Y-fronts ready for the next day. After I'd very nicely suggested we might be a little more adventurous – you have to realise we'd had no experience apart from what we'd had with each other – he then spent the next few months twiddling my right nipple – only ever my *right* one, as if he were tuning into *Radio Luxembourg*, before diving on as usual. One Saturday night, he'd twiddled away, this way and that for at least ten minutes, so I said, very politely, that I didn't think that that particular combination was going to open the safe, got out of bed, packed a case and went back home to my mum.'

The rest of the table, obviously having heard this tale before, egged Sarah on to tell us more as Grace and I, hysterical with laughter, shook our heads and wiped our eyes in disbelief.

'Talk about "Shitty Shitty Bang Bang!" It really was dreadful. Thank goodness we didn't have any children, or I might still be with him, gazing at the ceiling of a Saturday night, planning what we were having for tea the next day while he got on with his ritual twirling,' Sarah laughed. 'Instead, I made up for lost time, had a whale of a time with men who *did* know what they were doing, and finally met Richard who I married nearly eight years ago. Not only is he brilliant in the sack, I also happen to love him very much indeed.'

'So where did you meet him?' I asked.

Sarah guffawed. 'He came to do my electrics – and stayed to do my plumbing!'

'Any children now?' asked Grace, once the alcohol-fuelled laughter had died down. An innocent enough question, but only I knew the answer she was looking for. She always felt happier with those who, like herself, hadn't, for whatever reason, produced any offspring. I just think it made her feel better about herself if there were others in the same boat.

'Four,' Sarah laughed, unaware that, where Grace was concerned, this was the worst possible response. Pulling a face of anguish, she continued, 'Can you imagine? We went into overdrive somewhat and had one after another. Mind you, I wouldn't swap them for the world, even though I've ended up the size I am.' She patted her large bottom ruefully. '*And*,' she said emphatically, 'I shall encourage all my four to *sleep around* a bit before they settle down with one person. A bit of experience counts for everything.'

I needed to steer the conversation away from babies and children, but once Sarah had set the ball rolling as it were, everyone else seemed to leap in with tales of their own.

'Well, I don't know how you manage with four,' said Rebecca Martin who, out of all in this particular group, had probably aged the least. 'I have my work cut out with two.'

She'd always been a real Alpha female, into all sports at school and, by the look of her now, still obviously working out. I remembered seeing an article about her in the 'Midhope Examiner' – 'Local business woman sets new Iron-woman record' – and feeling exhausted just reading about how she'd swum, cycled and run what seemed, to me, a ridiculous amount of miles in an impossibly small amount of time, in order to achieve this goal.

'What's your business, Rebecca?' I now asked her. 'I saw the bit in the paper about your being a "local business woman".'

'The "Iron-woman" article, you mean? I've actually set up a new business since then. I sold out on the one I had, designing knitwear.'

'Knitwear?' laughed Grace. 'I didn't even know you could knit!'

'Ah, you see, all that hanging about sports grounds and travelling to and from competitions meant I needed something to do to alleviate the boredom while I was waiting, so I took up knitting. And then I began designing sweaters, and soon I had a whole load of outworkers around the country making up my designs by hand. They used to sell for a fortune. I actually had some selling in Harvey Nicks in Leeds.'

'So, why give it up?' I asked curiously.

'Fashion changes all the time. And I got bored with it. You know me. I always needed a new challenge, even when we were at school. Still do. Problem is, I get bored with husbands too. They begin to irritate me after a while, so I ditch them.'

'How many have you had?' I asked, beginning to feel very staid, as a one-man woman, in the light of Grace's, Sarah's, and now Rebecca's marriages.

'The third moved out about a year ago. Trouble is, I keep on having to pay them out, and so I'm constantly working every hour God sends. This new business I'm just getting up and running takes me all over the country. I only made it tonight by the skin of my teeth.' Rebecca sighed and knocked back what remained of her wine.

'So, how do you manage? With the kids, I mean. How old are they?' Grace asked.

'Isobel is eight and Frances seven. They both belong to my first husband, but unfortunately he's gone back to live in America. I say unfortunately, only because it would take some of the childcare worries off me if he were around. Apart from that, I really couldn't wait to see the back of him.'

'Sounds like you need a wife,' Clare Hargreaves said sympathetically.

'Well, I certainly don't need another husband. I've had a whole stream of au pairs and live-in nannies, but they're either too soft, too homesick, or too randy.'

'Too randy?'

'Yep. Had a new girl from Croatia. First evening with us, we took her along to a neighbour's barbecue. She was a quiet little thing from a tiny catholic village, and when she disappeared I was afraid the whole thing was a bit too much for her. When I eventually found her she was on her knees in the back bedroom.' When I asked the kids if they'd seen her, Frances said she was on her knees in the back bedroom.

'Praying?' Clare asked.

'Giving blow jobs to our neighbour's son, home from university, and all his mates.'

'Was she charging them?' I asked, fascinated.

'No, enjoying herself I gather. Must be a traditional Croatian method of introducing yourself,' Rebecca laughed.

'You mean a hand job as opposed to a handshake?' Sarah chortled.

'Anyway, I decided we needed a bit of discipline after that. The girls were playing up and, because I'd been watching a programme about that "zero tolerance" police chief guy up in the north-east, I said to Helga – our new girl from Germany – that she wasn't to tolerate any bad behaviour. The next morning, Isobel decides she's not going to eat the porridge that I'd made – she wants Weetabix instead. Whereupon Helga, still dressed in a huge furry dressing gown and what must have been size eleven slippers, descends upon poor Isobel like some Germanic devil, slapping spoonfuls of porridge into her dish and shouting, in her best broken English, "zero tolerance, zero tolerance" with every spoonful. I fully expected to hear the music from "The Valkyries" as she whirled around, sloshing porridge all over my kitchen. I tell you, they're all mad. It's them that need looking after.'

I knew Grace was beginning to feel sorry for these two little girls. 'So, how do you manage now?' I asked.

'Got a lovely Nanny-Granny. She's sixty, loves the girls and doesn't stand any nonsense from them. She plays games like "Guggenheim" with them and the cupboard is always full of home-made cakes. She bullies me and makes me eat my broccoli, and tells me what she thinks of any men I bring home. We call her Mrs Doubtfire, even to her face, and she loves it.'

'And do you?' Grace asked.

'Do I what? Call her Mrs Doubtfire?' Rebecca seemed puzzled.

' No. Do you still have time for *men*?'

'Absolutely. But you can forget any idea about marriage. I mean, why buy the whole pig when you just fancy a sausage!'

The time simply flew by as we caught up with twenty years of births, marriages, occupations, adulterous affairs, places we'd travelled to and deaths. Apart from Sarah who, with four young children, didn't have the time or inclination to hold down a full-time job, the majority of women around our table were professional, university graduates who, like myself, juggled the commitments of family and work either through the desire to 'have it all' or through the necessity of paying off the mortgage each month.

Every so often, one of us would go up to the makeshift bar for more wine and be waylaid by more faces from our past. I spent a good ten minutes chatting to someone who'd grabbed me in a bear hug and explained that though she'd never married I wasn't to think she was gay. Unable to ascertain who the hell she *was* – her name tag had twisted round after the constant hugging of old schoolmates – never mind her sexual orientation, I made my way back to our table.

'Don't look now, Grace,' I said, as she immediately turned right round in the direction from where I'd just come, 'but who *is* that at the bar, the one with the bright orange top. She just accosted me.'

'Dunno,' said Grace, 'unless it's Barbara Richmond.'

'It is,' Sarah confirmed. 'She's head of the Flying Squad in Midhope. Goes round smashing down doors and arresting people. She's been having an affair with my cousin Rose for years.'

'Girls, girls, can I have your attention?' Amanda was up on the stage surrounded by her former prefects, smiling and tapping on her glass for quiet.

'She's still so beautiful, isn't she?' Rebecca Martin whispered. 'I idolised her when I was thirteen. Had the biggest crush ever on her.'

'Even you?' I asked, in surprise. I knew how Grace and I had felt about her, but didn't realise the adoration we felt was widespread.

'And me,' admitted Sarah. 'I used to love assemblies, even when we had to sing forty-nine verses of "Fight the Good Fight", just so I could see how she'd done her hair, or try and catch her eye so that I could smile at her.'

'Beautiful,' Clare agreed, sighing, 'but very, very ruthless. Amanda always knew what she wanted and she certainly made sure she got it. She had Old Ma Seddon wrapped round her little finger. I don't think we'd ever have been excluded from school for that week if Amanda hadn't persuaded Miss Seddon to do so.'

I turned to face the stage and Amanda. She was wearing a very tight, ruched red dress which clung in all the right places. Her full mouth, also crimson, was a work of art and her hair, usually a sleek, blonde curtain, was pinned up in a tousled pile on top of her head. She breathed charm and allure from every pore and I felt defeated. How could I blame John for still wanting her after all this time; the women in the room from hanging on to her every word; my husband for falling under her spell? Between them she and her husband held all the cards as to whether I was going to end up in a back to back in Wigton – Midhope's notorious sink area – sharing my kitchen and the rest of my life with my mother-in-law; toiling away day after day until I could get my state pension, Nick having to pay his mother back the money he'd borrowed from her out of his meagre job-seeker's allowance. I felt quite panicky and gulped back a huge slug of wine in order to make me feel better.

'Steady on,' said Grace, slapping me on the back. 'Are you alright?'

'Fine,' I said, coughing as the too-big mouthful of wine tried to find somewhere to go.

' ... so let's raise our glasses and show our appreciation for Midhope Girls' Grammar School in the time-honoured way. Miss Rhodes, over to you.' Amanda raised her glass, we all stood, raised our own glasses and dutifully shouted, 'Midhope Girls' Grammar

School' as the familiar, introductory notes of the school song rang out from the ancient piano situated on the left of the foot of the stage.

'Fuck me, not the fucking school song,' Sarah Armitage whispered in a too loud aside to the rest of our table. 'I never knew the words when we actually *were* at school. I certainly can't remember them now. And that can't be Ratty Rhodes Amanda's managed to exhume. I thought she'd croaked when we were in the sixth form.'

I don't know if it was that last gulp of wine, the look of absolute horror on Sarah's face or the notion of Amanda digging up Miss Rhodes from her resting place in the local cemetery for the sole purpose of playing the school song just one more time, but I began to giggle uncontrollably.

'Oh no,' whispered Grace, giggling herself. 'Don't make her laugh.'

'She doesn't still snort like a walrus when she laughs does she?' asked Rebecca, wide-eyed, and as Grace nodded in affirmation, began to cackle herself.

Soon, our whole table was affected. Infectious as measles, the tittering and chortling spread amongst us until we were in the grip of uncontrollable laughter, tears rolling down cheeks, shoulders heaving, my buttocks and pelvic floor clenched to dizzying new heights of tightness. Thank goodness I'd been for a pee the last time I'd gone to the bar.

As the desiccated old fossil who'd once ruled the roost in Midhope Grammar School's music department brought the school song to a triumphant end, Grace wiped the mascara from below her eyes, took a long drink from her glass and said, 'Girls, I think we're in trouble again.'

Chapter 11

Now that we were all best friends again, we were in no mood to go home. The lugubrious-looking caretaker who'd been hanging around in the corridor, breathing heavily as he leaned on his broom for the last ten minutes in the hope that we'd all get lost so that he could polish his floor, lock up and drink the cocoa that was even now gathering a skin, began to give us beseeching looks while glancing meaningfully at the ancient hall clock.

'Who's for *"Jimmy's?"*' asked Sarah Armitage suddenly, draining her glass and looking round our table expectantly.

'*"Jimmy's?"* as in *"Jimmy's"* nightclub?' Grace asked, pulling a face.

'Yep, unless you know some gorgeous *man* called Jimmy who'd give us a drink and let us carrying on talking,' said Sarah, putting on her jacket. 'Come on, it'll be a laugh. We can't any of us drive home, apart from Clare, who for some reason has never liked the taste of alcohol, so we may as well leave our cars here, grab some taxis and head into town.'

And with that, she jumped on to the stage, smiled sweetly at Amanda who was helping Miss Rhodes into her cardigan, and took hold of the microphone.

'Listen, everyone, some of us are going to carry on with our reunion down at Jimmy's. Anyone fancy coming? I think there's actually an "Eighties' Night" on so we won't feel too much out of place.'

Various murmurs of assent, particularly from those who'd been in our year and below, meant she seemed to be in business.

'No slinking off, Amanda,' Sarah now called. 'Are you coming with us?'

'I don't think so,' Amanda laughed, shaking her head and indicating, by means of gestures, that she was still responsible for Miss Rhodes.

'Come on, Amanda. We need you to keep us all in order. How about it, Miss Rhodes? Do you fancy a bit of a knees-up?'

'Oh, my God,' said Grace, in dismay, 'She's off her trolley. A nonagenarian in Jimmy's on a Friday night? That's all we bloody need.'

'God, I hope Sarah is right about it being an eighties' night,' I said, half an hour later, as Grace, Rebecca and I clambered out of the taxi in front of Jimmy's, Midhope's longest running nightclub. 'Could you see Miss Rhodes boogieing on down to 'House' or 'Rap' or whatever it is people dance to these days?'

'She's not actually coming with us is she?' Grace said grimly as she searched the queue in front of Jimmy's. 'If she is, I'm off. And if I see any of my ex-pupils in there I'm going straight home too.'

Laughing, Rebecca and I took hold of Grace's arms, bundled her past the two mesomorphic bouncers on the door and made straight for the loos where we repaired the damage to our make-up caused by the laughing fit in the school hall.

Having commandeered a number of tables and chairs, and thus established a safe haven to which we could retreat if and when necessary, Sarah and Clare and a couple of others from our table were already on the surprisingly spacious wooden floor, dancing round their handbags while Culture Club confirmed that we were, indeed, in the required decade.

From Phil Collins and Lionel Richie to The Thomson Twins, from Howard Jones to Spandau Ballet and Duran Duran, the music belted out non-stop. Even Grace began to relax and enjoy herself, resurrecting the dance moves we thought we'd forgotten years ago, and joining in with 'Relax, Don't do it' from Frankie Goes to Hollywood.

I was amazed to see Amanda on her feet, shaking her blonde hair, jiggling her pert behind and dancing, if a little out of rhythm, with gusto. Miss Rhodes, chaperoned by Amanda's prefects and nursing a sweet sherry in one corner of the club, appeared animated, nodding her head to the music and generally giving the impression of being totally at home with her surroundings.

'Oh shit,' I mouthed to the others, nodding in her direction. 'What if she has a cardiac arrest? I can't remember the procedure for resuscitation, can you?'

'Or resurrection,' Rebecca shouted back over the music. 'Don't worry, if she goes now, she'll die a happy woman.'

By one in the morning, only a hard core of the original crowd remained. One of Amanda's cronies had finally persuaded Miss Rhodes to call it a night, and she'd been taken home.

'Night-night, girls,' she'd waved on her way out, her Crimplene frock somehow caught up in her enormous cream plastic handbag. 'Behave yourselves now. Don't be too late going to bed.' No doubt her bunions would give her jip in the morning, but she'd left with a smile on her face, determined to do it all again next year.

The rest of us, including Amanda who, to my surprise, had seemed determined to stay the course, had all had far too much to drink. We were at the stage of believing that dancing with our arms overhead while yelling 'woo-hoo' was seriously cool. Every time a different record came on that took us back to our youth one of us would get thoroughly overexcited, shouting, 'Oh I just love this record. It reminds me of when I used to go out with John/ Peter/Michael/first time I had a snog/ that holiday we went on to Majorca.'

Rebecca, who'd been knocking back alcopops like some let-loose fourteen-year-old, had overestimated the tenacity of her stiletto heels and, after a particularly vigorous stamping of her feet, was now in the process of swinging a broken-heeled shoe above her head as she hopped about on one foot. Even Clare, with no alcohol to fuel her emotions, must have told every one of us, including Amanda, how much she 'luurrved' us at least ten times each while Sarah, who'd been engaged in some very energetic dancing with a Robbie Coltrane lookalike, was rendered speechless when, after escorting her back to our table, he complimented her by patting her bottom and saying, 'Eh, you don't sweat much fer a fat lass, do you?'

'You seemed to be getting on well with *him*,' I said to Rebecca, indicating the guy she'd been deep in conversation with a few minutes before. He'd appeared to be doing most of the talking, whispering intently into her ear. 'He reminds me of someone. Who is it?' I looked over to the bar area where he now stood, trying to think who he looked like.

'Brian Cox?' Rebecca asked. 'You know, *Professor* Brian Cox?'

'God, yes, that's right,' I said excitedly. 'It's just like him.'

'The thing is, I've got a bit of a thing for Brian Cox. It's all that brainpower, and the fact that he was once in a rock band. But mainly it's his voice. I just have to watch him on TV in that tight black T-shirt and jeans saying, "black holes" or "particle physics" and I feel ridiculously randy.' Rebecca looked slightly embarrassed. 'So when he came over to me I asked him if he wouldn't mind whispering something, you know, Brian Cox-ish into my ear.'

Grace and I laughed. 'And did he?'

'Well , yes. He started with "the moon" and "Jupiter" and built up to "asteroid belt" and "relativity". He needs to flatten his vowels a bit more – too Yorkshire rather than Mancunian – but I'm meeting him next week, hopefully for some "quantum mechanics".'

Grace and I nodded sagely. We'd both been through the Brian Cox syndrome and knew exactly where she was coming from.

'Oy, Mrs Stevens!' came the cry from the bar where a gang of youths, all similarly attired in short-sleeved, open-necked shirts worn outside their trousers, stood, bottled lager in hand, surveying the room for talent.

'I knew there'd be someone here I used to teach,' Grace said irritably, peering through the dark in an attempt to put a name to the voice. 'I've no idea who it is – they all look the same to me with their short-cropped hair and identical shirts.' And then as the owner of the voice, grin all over his face, pushed through the crowd towards her, Grace laughed delightedly.

'My goodness, Chubby Tingley. Well, you've grown a bit since you were eleven years old.'

'I should hope so. I don't think they'd have let me in here if I hadn't.'

'So how old are you now? No, don't tell me. You must be, oh golly, seventeen?'

'Eighteen next week,' Chubby said proudly. 'What you doing in here, Miss?'

'My old school reunion. The school I actually *went* to. Not the one I used to teach in. And this is my friend, Mrs Westmoreland,' Grace said, pulling me forwards to be introduced.

'It's all right, Chubby, you can call me Harriet,' I laughed, thinking what a lovely face young Chubby had. 'So were you actually in Grace's class?'

'Grace? Oh you mean Mrs Stevens! Yep, best teacher I ever had. I was a real little bugger until I went into her class, but she wouldn't let me get away with anything. She used to make me laugh if I was about to get up to something. It sort of made me stop wanting to mess about.'

'Don't you believe it,' Grace laughed, in turn. 'You still had your moments.'

'Yeah, do you remember when I tried to superglue the hamster's paws to its exercise wheel and you stapled me to the wall through my jumper?'

'Those were the days,' said Grace wistfully. 'Couldn't get away with it now. We'd be up for child cruelty. Irrelevant that I was trying to show you how the hamster would have felt if you'd succeeded.'

'Come and have a dance, Miss. And then I can tell all the lads at football who were in your class that I've seen you and had a dance with you.'

'We really should be going shouldn't we, Harriet?' Grace looked at me meaningfully.

'All the time in the world, Mrs Stevens,' I said airily. 'I'm going to get another drink.'

Glaring at me, Grace reluctantly followed Chubby onto the dance floor, which was slowly emptying of people. I stood with the others, watching Grace cringe with embarrassment as Chubby put her through her paces.

'My God, his hips need their own postcode,' Rebecca sniggered, as Chubby's legs gyrated this way and that to Michael Jackson's 'Beat it.' Never once taking his eyes from his favourite teacher, and occasionally thrusting his nether regions towards her, à la Jackson, Chubby obviously thought he was set up for the rest of the night.

I could see that Grace didn't quite know what to do and where to look. Should she throw caution to the wind and 'bump and grind' along with Chubby? She stepped and hopped daintily on the spot, a fixed smile on her face, every now and then turning to where we stood to fix us with a glare.

'Rightio, you ravers,' the ageing DJ shouted over the music, 'we're going even further back in time. Never mind the eighties. In fact, fuck the eighties. It's rock and roll that we want. It's Rockabilly that we need.' And with one, not overly fluid, movement he did a sort of scissors jump from his turntables and was on the dance floor.

He must have been sixty, if he was a day, but he couldn't half move. As Little Richard's 'Lucille' belted out, he grabbed Grace from Chubby and spun her round before taking her two hands and jiving her around the floor. I honestly saw the whites of Grace's eyes as, mouth open in a single 'O' of protest, she disappeared over his shoulder only to reappear between his splayed drainpipe-trousered legs.

A crowd, consisting almost entirely of weekend Teddy boys reliving their youth, gathered, egging Eddie the DJ on to ever more amazing feats of rock and roll while Chubby, rendered both speechless and motionless by the kidnap of his former teacher and dance partner, looked on helplessly.

'You're going to have to get in there and save her,' I hissed as a collective 'woah' went round the room as Grace disappeared round Eddie's back once more.

'No chance,' Chubby said, taking a swig of lager. 'There's no chance. I've seen Eddie in action before. There's no escape.'

'We're gonna *rock*-around-the-*clock*-tonight,' the crowd yelled as Bill Haley made his appearance over the speakers and Grace simultaneously made hers between Eddie's legs once more. Thank God she was wearing trousers. Rebecca, just back from the loo, stared in amazement at the scene in front of her. Whooping with excitement, she kicked off her remaining good shoe, grabbed the hand of the nearest foot-tapping member of rent-a-crowd and joined the other two, centre stage.

'Whose *fucking* idea was this *fucking* nightclub?' Grace managed to snarl in my direction from her upside down position over Eddie's shoulder.

'Hey, I didn't know teachers swore,' Chubby said, shocked.

As Bill Haley sang the final notes —'Doop doopy doop doopy doop doopy doop doopy dooooop doopy bedoop'— Grace executed a final twirl and landed back at my, and Chubby's, feet.

'Do not say a word, Harriet. Not one single word.'

And with that she gathered up her Mulberry bag, her drink and what was left of her dignity and, head held high, walked in the direction of the Ladies.

Amanda was still sitting with Sally Davies and Andrea Collins. She said something to the pair of them and they all turned to watch as Grace reappeared, face freshly made-up and hair restored to its pre-jiving state. No doubt Amanda had related last night's little episode to them both, and they'd thoroughly enjoyed Grace's discomfiture on the dance floor.

'Ok, time to go,' I said, steering a still obviously shell-shocked Grace back towards the table next to Amanda's where the girls, my unfinished drink and handbag waited. I was suddenly fed up with Amanda's superior, cool gaze. Those navy-blue eyes of hers were as unfathomable as the deep, but they didn't miss a trick.

'Right, are we off?' I asked, at the same moment as Rebecca dug me in the ribs.

'Look at that,' she breathed. 'Just get an eyeful of that would you?'

We all turned in the direction she was gazing. At the bar, waiting to be served, dark eyes surveying the crowd as if looking for someone, stood Enrique Iglesias. Well, obviously it wasn't *the*

Enrique Iglesias – I mean, I doubt that the real Mr Iglesias had ever *heard* of Midhope, never mind visited its seedy nightclubs of a Friday night. But this man, with his olive tan, his dark eyebrows and his designer stubble was Enrique down to a T. No, I tell a lie. At around six foot three, his very obvious six-pack outlined beneath a white T-shirt and well-scuffed brown leather jacket, he was even more stunning. His eyes continued to search the room and then, without warning, he suddenly left the bar, slowly making his way towards our table.

'He's coming over,' Rebecca squeaked, unconsciously shaking back her hair and wetting her lips.

'Oh for heaven's sake, get a grip, Rebecca,' Sarah said, watching as he came towards us. 'I've got *knickers* older than him!'

Grace seemed transfixed, her eyes never leaving his for a second. He came right up to her, gave her a slow sexy smile and then carried on to where Amanda was sitting, oblivious to his approach.

'My God, Amanda's pulled,' Rebecca hissed. 'Would you believe it? The bitch has pulled!'

Amanda turned in surprise as Enrique laid a gentle hand on her shoulder and then, losing all her usual composure, jumped up, knocking over her chair in the process as she threw her arms around him, burying her face in his shoulder.

'Blimey,' Sarah said in surprise, 'She doesn't hang around does she?'

'How did you know I was here?' Amanda said, half laughing, half crying, taking his hand as he righted her overturned chair. 'Everyone, this is my son, Sebastian. I've not seen him for nearly six months.' And she grabbed him again, kissing his face, while he grinned down at her in adoration.

'Can we give anyone a lift?' Sebastian Henderson asked ten minutes later, gazing unblinkingly at Grace.

She still hadn't said a word apart from a muttered, 'Hi,' in response to Amanda's introduction. She reminded me of the terrified rabbit I'd once held hypnotised in my car headlights. Even when I'd actually jumped out and tried to shoo it away, the silly thing had still remained in the road, rooted to the spot.

'Well Clare, who very sensibly has not been drinking all evening, is the right direction for Rebecca, Harriet and myself. So, the only one who *is* going your way is probably Grace,' said Sarah.

'No, really, I'll get a taxi,' Grace protested. 'I really don't want to put anyone out. I'll ask the guy on the door to get me one.'

'Do they do that these days?' asked Sarah in surprise.

'Well, whatever,' said Grace in some embarrassment as she realised she was at the centre of attention. 'I've got my phone. There really is no problem.'

'Oh come on, Grace,' said Amanda, almost impatiently. We go right through your village. Seb's got David's car so he can squeeze us all in. Mind you,' she added, turning once more to her son, 'I'm surprised you're not on your bike. I'd have thought that would have been first on your list once you got home.'

Sebastian grinned showing a set of perfect white teeth. 'When Dad told me you'd rung home to say you were down here, I just fancied surprising you. I couldn't see you coming home with me on the back of my bike.'

'I would think a bike is the *last* mode of transport *you'd* choose, Amanda,' I said rather cattily. It still rankled that I didn't know what she'd been up to with Nick in Italy, and too much wine had loosened my tongue.

'I'm sure you're absolutely right, Harriet,' she said sweetly, 'but Seb's bike is a Harley-Davidson. I have to say that travelling at high speed on the back of it is one of the most exhilarating experiences I've ever had.'

Having been put well and truly in my place, I'd suddenly had enough and wanted to be home. I was beginning to feel hung-over and bad-tempered; I'd had too much to drink and it had been a long night.

Rebecca, Sarah and I followed Clare up to the large underground car park a couple of streets away from Jimmy's. It had been the only available place to leave her car and now, footsore and with drizzle seeping determinedly into our clothes, the walk uphill seemed interminable. Grace's borrowed shoes were pinching my toes and Rebecca had abandoned *her* broken shoe in the overflowing bin outside Macdonald's where it sat, demoralised, amongst the greasy remains of innumerable Friday night takeaways.

'Who'd have thought Amanda would have produced such an amazing specimen as Sebastian,' Rebecca panted, alternating hopping on her one remaining shoe and walking in her stocking foot along the pavement.

'Why ever not?' Clare asked, in some surprise. 'Stunning women invariably produce stunning sons.'

'Yes, but she's so blond and blue-eyed. Sebastian is dark and brown-eyed.'

'He has his father's colouring,' I said.

'Oh? Have you met him?' All three turned expectantly towards me.

For some reason, I didn't really want to get into a full explanation of our present relationship with the Hendersons, so I shrugged it off with, 'Nick's in the same line of business as David.'

'Wow,' said Sarah, obviously impressed. 'My mum knows Amanda's cleaning lady, and she says their house is to die for. Says they must be loaded. Does that mean you are too?'

'If only,' I said, wishing I hadn't got myself into this conversation. The last thing I wanted was for it to get back to Amanda via Sarah's cleaning lady friend, or anyone else for that matter, that I'd been telling everyone we were their new best friends.

Luckily Rebecca, screaming a load of profanities as her stockinged foot stepped neatly into a puddle, diverted further attention from any possible relationship there might be between Nick and David Henderson.

Ten minutes later, with Clare concentrating on exiting the warren-like car park, and both Sarah and Rebecca falling almost immediately into a drunken stupor, I relaxed into the car seat, mulling over the events of the evening and particularly Grace's reaction on meeting Sebastian Henderson. I felt uneasy. Having Amanda and David Henderson, virtually uninvited, in my life was bad enough. Bringing the gorgeous Sebastian into the equation was, I feared, a potential recipe for disaster.

Chapter 12

'My very eccentric mother just shot Uncle Norman's pig,' I said, spilling scalding tea down the front of Nick's pyjamas as I climbed back into bed. Nick, thank the Lord, wasn't wearing them at the time – I was. I could never have married a man who wore pyjamas in bed, but I felt it totally acceptable to be wearing them myself. A present from his mother many Christmases ago, I regularly dug them out from the bottom of my wardrobe once the nights started getting chilly.

'What?' Nick muttered from the depths of his pillow, turning to look at his watch, which, as always, had been neatly laid on his bedside table the night before.

'My very eccentric mother just shot Uncle Norman's pig,' I repeated, plumping up my own pillows and luxuriating in the fact that it was Saturday morning and half term stretched, like the Sahara desert, endlessly into the distance. I reached for Nick, so glad to have him home again after his week in Italy.

'Jeeze,' Nick muttered again, turning now to look at me with sleep-filled eyes. 'I know you said she was going a bit, but you never said she was capable of this. Where the hell did she get the gun from?' And then, after a pause, 'which is your Uncle Norman? Is he the one that ran off with the barmaid from The Black Bull? The one that your mother doesn't talk about?'

'What? Oh don't be ridiculous, Nick. I've been lying here for ages trying to remember the mnemonic for the names of the planets in our solar system. It suddenly came to me as I was waiting for the kettle to boil, downstairs. I was just trying it out so I'd remember it when I got back to school. We're doing Planet Earth and the whole solar system when we go back next week.'

'Well, you'll soon have to change your little mnemonic,' Nick said, reaching over for my tea. 'Pluto is about to be made defunct.'

'You're joking. How inconsiderate is that?' I fumed.

'Don't panic. You just have your very eccentric mother shooting Uncle Norman himself rather than his pig.'

'Suppose,' I said, suddenly bored with the whole damned thing. I don't know why I was even thinking about school when I was free from it for a week and I had my husband to myself for once.

'So what time did you get in last night?' Nick asked. 'How was it?'

'Late and Different,' I replied, answering both questions in one sentence. 'Got a bit of a hangover. In fact, I don't think I feel very well at all.' I didn't, I now realised.

'You're getting to be a little pisshead lately,' Nick said, with the superiority of one who hadn't had anything to drink the previous evening. 'I blame Grace. She was fairly much on the straight and narrow until Daniel went off with his Australian bit. Now she's got you jumping out on unsuspecting men while dressed as a nun, and having you out until all hours at the seediest places in town.'

'Mandy stayed the course,' I said, glancing at Nick for any reaction her name might evoke.

There didn't appear to be any apart from a simple, 'Oh?'

'Her son turned up out of the blue,' I continued. 'Back from somewhere. I can't remember where.'

'New Zealand,' said Nick. 'David's brother lives out there and Sebastian's been working with him.'

'For someone who never normally notices or remembers any detail about anyone,' I said scathingly, 'you certainly seem to know enough about Young Sebastian.'

'Probably because Mandy talked non-stop about him all the time we were in Italy. From what I gather, he is the main reason she and David are still together.'

'What do you mean?' I asked sharply. 'Did she tell you that?'

Nick shrugged. 'I get the impression from what she said that she and David would probably not still be together if it wasn't for

Sebastian. She says David is away from home a lot, and feels maybe they've drifted apart somewhat, but didn't want Sebastian being the victim of a broken home.'

I snorted. 'Sounds to me she was telling you this for a reason.'

'What sort of reason?'

'Oh don't be so naïve,' I said. 'She fancies you. She was just letting you know that "her husband doesn't understand her" so that if you were up for a bit, it would be fine by her.' Fired up, I reckoned now would be as good a time as any to tell Nick about John still having contact with Amanda. More than just contact if John was to be believed. I'd hardly seen Nick since he'd come home and hadn't yet told him about my brother's apparent on-going affair with Amanda.

Before Nick could defend either himself or Amanda, or I had the chance to break the news about John, the telephone on his side of the bed began to ring.

'Who? Oh hello, Kenneth, you're ringing early. Is everything alright?' Nick shouted into the receiver aware, as always, of my dad's deafness. There was a long silence as Nick tried to work out exactly what Dad was ringing up about at seven-thirty on a Saturday morning. I looked out across the garden and down to the fields beyond. It was only just coming light, a heavy mist wrapping itself, like a smug grey cat, around the still, silent trees.

'Hang on, Kenneth, I'll just put Harriet on,' Nick shouted, handing the phone to me while indicating, by a shrug of his shoulders, that he couldn't quite make out what Dad wanted.

'Are you ok, Dad?' I found myself shouting.

'Your mum's acting a bit queer, love.' Dad sounded tired and distressed. 'She's talking to your Granny Morgan, arguing with her, like.'

'Dad, Granny Morgan's been dead for the last four years.'

'*I* know that, love and *you* know that. Problem is, your *mother* appears to have forgotten.'

'Where is she?'

'Who?'

Blimey, I could see this was going to be hard work. 'Mum,' I shouted. 'Where's Mum at the moment?'

'In the kitchen. She's cleaning out the cupboard under the sink and talking to her mother.'

'How do you know it's Granny Morgan she's supposed to be talking to?' I asked. 'Maybe it's the postman or the milkman?'

'Don't be daft, love. She doesn't call the milkman *or* the postman "mother."'

'Well, what's she saying to her?'

'She's really cross with her,' Dad said. 'She gave me t' fright of me life when she started. She's shouting and carrying on. Having a real go at her.'

'Dad,' I said gently, but loud enough for him to hear me, 'how can Mum be having a go at her when Granny Morgan's not there?'

Nick was shaking his head in disbelief. I think, in truth, he'd always thought my family a strange lot, with their northern working-class way of doing things. The fact that my mother was now on her hands and knees, cleaning out cupboards and talking to my long-dead grandmother all before eight o'clock on a Saturday morning simply confirmed his suspicions.

'Ay, I don't know, lass,' Dad was saying now. 'She obviously thinks she's still alive.'

'Look, Dad, don't you worry. I'm going to call Diana and we'll both come round as soon as we can.' I put the phone down. There was something obviously very wrong with poor Mum and we needed to sort it out.

'Nick, you're going to have to do some shopping for India's birthday party tomorrow. I don't know how long I'm going to be over at Mum and Dad's and I haven't even thought about a cake or games or party bags.'

'You know that Kit has also invited a load of people over tomorrow, don't you?' Nick asked, not quite meeting my eyes as he did so.

'You are joking? Who gave him permission to do that? Oh great, Nick, thanks very much indeed. You do realise the last thing that Kit and his mates want is potted-meat sandwiches and Blind Man's Buff?'

Born exactly eight years and one day apart, this time of year had always been hectic as we celebrated both Kit and India's birthdays. Although I'd warned Kit that we really wouldn't be celebrating his birthday with a party, I was dreading to think what he had in mind this year now that he was officially a moody grunter.

'I have to tell you, Hat, I think potted meat and Blind Man's Buff isn't exactly on India's wish list either. She was talking about a pink limo, and having her party at "Little Miss Cute" when I was putting her to bed last night.'

'She can dream on,' I said grimly. 'I can't bear the sight of little girls dressed up as if they were off to one of those dreadful American pageants.' 'Little Miss Cute' specialised in parties where 'tweenies' had their hair styled and nails manicured until they were grotesque parodies of their mothers.

Nick put up his hands in protest. 'Hey, don't shoot the messenger. I'm only telling you what she told me last night. I'm sure whatever you're laying on for her will be fine.'

This was, unfortunately, the problem. Apart from supervising the sending out of invitations, which India had insisted on doing herself, laboriously writing each one while her tongue hung out with the effort of concentrating, I'd not done a thing towards it. Gone were the days when I'd spend hours planning party themes and creating novelty cakes that kept me up into the early hours. They always took a lot longer than I'd anticipated, and there was invariably a twiddly bit that broke and needed remaking.

For Kit's sixth birthday I'd transformed what was now Sylvia's flat into a veritable rain forest. Snakes hung drunkenly from verdant branches brought in from the garden, and huge, showy butterflies flapped their florid paper wings as they hung, circling giddily, from a makeshift mobile. Kit's cake was the *pièce de resistance* that year. I'd spent days creating double-sided sugar-paste animals that marched and trumpeted purposefully around the edge of the cake in their pairs. On the actual morning of the party I'd got a bit caught up in the excitement of it all and went out to hire a costume, suggesting Grace, as Godmother and all-round party good egg, might like to do the same. I ended up looking very much like a dumpy cartoon character in a moth-eaten lion's outfit that smelled as if the previous owner had actually died in it. Grace, of course, arrived sleek and beautiful in a black panther costume that had all the dads hot under the collar and more than happy to accept a second glass of wine rather than dumping their offspring and beetling off for a couple of hours' respite with Saturday afternoon football, as was the norm.

Since I'd been back working full time the kids were lucky if I had time to actually bake a cake, let alone decorate the damned thing. If they were really lucky, it was a ready-decorated birthday cake from Sainsbury's, which, according to Liberty, was what they'd really been after all along.

Jumping out of bed for the second time that morning, I realised I really was quite hungover. I felt sick and the room was beginning to spin a little. I glanced longingly back to the bed where Nick appeared to think *he* could stay a little longer. Sod that for a game of soldiers. If I was up, after working every second God had sent this last week, then I didn't see why he should stay in bed after a week messing around in Italy with Little Miss Goodness.

Pulling off all the bedclothes and shouting, 'Get up, there's a party to be organised,' I fled into the shower in the hope that the hot water might bring me round.

It didn't. And neither did the mug of strong coffee that I attempted to get down my neck twenty minutes later. Leaving Nick with full instructions to sort out the kids as well as India's birthday party, I rubbed on some foundation and bright pink lipstick in a vain attempt to hide my death-like pallor, and drove over to Mum and Dad's.

Diana's car was already parked on the road outside their house and so, God forbid, was Christine's.

'Bloody hell, you look rough,' Diana said as I walked into the kitchen where she was making tea.

'I feel it,' I groaned. 'I really am going to have to stop drinking. I used to be able to drink whatever I wanted without feeling like I'd died and ended up in hell the next morning.'

'It's your age,' Diana said cheerfully. 'I should stick to cocoa from now on if I were you.'

'What's Caring Christine doing here?' I asked, nodding towards the living room where I could hear my sister-in-law's voice, no doubt talking to Mum as if she were a child.

'Dad rang her, apparently, and she was round here like a shot.'

Christine closed the kitchen door carefully behind her as she joined us in the kitchen shaking her head, a concerned smile etched onto her face. As per usual she was loving the drama of it all and I wanted to slap her face and muss up her perfectly highlighted blonde bob. Always a huge monarchist, Christine had been devastated when Princess Diana had died in that car crash and seemed to think it her mission in life to carry on where Diana had left off. With her blue-striped shirt collar set at a jaunty angle against her squeakily clean neck, and the vertical crease of her immaculate chinos a perfect perpendicular to her cream tasselled brogues, she certainly seemed to be succeeding.

'I'm so glad you're both here now. Dad rang me in a bit of a panic and I came straight over.'

'So did we,' said Diana brusquely, making a point of not offering Christine any tea.

'Yes, well, the thing is I do feel this has gone on long enough. Poor old Dad is at his wits' end.'

'What, exactly, has gone on long enough, Christine?' I asked, still feeling a bit dizzy and wishing I could sit down, but refusing to be put at a disadvantage .You had to look Christine in the eye – a bit like you might a cat with a superiority complex – or she'd have the upper hand.

'Harriet, you *know* what's been going on with Mother,' Christine tinkled, a condescending little smile hovering around her lips. 'She keeps wandering off, and now she thinks her mother has returned from the dead. She needs help, maybe a *rest* somewhere.'

'By *rest* I assume you mean some sort of hospital?' I said angrily.

'Or even a *home*,' she added smoothly, glancing towards Diana for confirmation. Diana gave none, but stood quietly at the kitchen table, drinking her tea.

'I mean, it might only be for a little while,' Christine went on hurriedly, little pinpricks of colour now highlighting her perfectly Max Factored complexion. 'There are some really *caring* places where Mother would be with people like herself. There are lots of activities that she could get involved in. She'd be able to watch TV and play cards and I believe there are things like bingo and even line dancing for the more able.' She trailed off as she saw Diana's face.

'You are a very *silly* woman, Christine,' Diana now said, evenly. 'You were a very *silly* girl when, despite all the sex education and contraceptives freely available, you still managed to get yourself up the duff at the age of eighteen. You've continued to be a very *silly* woman throughout your marriage to my poor, *silly* brother who, I might add, should be here, himself, this morning. Now, will you please keep your very clean, but particularly *silly* nose out of *my*, not *your*, mother's business, and *fuck off*.'

'Where's Patricia gone?' Mum asked as the back door slammed behind Christine, and Diana and I took in tea and biscuits to our parents who were sitting side by side on the pink Dralon sofa. Dad was stroking Mum's hand, a look of utter bafflement on his increasingly lined face.

'Mum, who's Patricia?' Diana asked gently, taking her other hand.

For a moment Mum seemed confused, unable to work out the question, let alone the answer. Then she gave a crafty cackle. 'Ah, you don't think you're going to catch me out again, do you? That's for me to know and you to find out,' and she tapped the side of her nose with one finger.

'Was Granny Morgan here this morning?' I asked, feeling rather foolish. 'Dad seemed to think you were talking to her.'

Mum gave me such a look of incredulity, I wished I'd kept my mouth shut. 'Your Granny Morgan, Harriet, has been dead these last four years. Did no one tell you?'

'Of course,' I said. 'How silly of me. Did you see Patricia when you were on holiday last week?'

Mum leaned towards me, away from Dad, and said in a confidential whisper, 'I looked, Harriet, I really did. But she'd gone again. Where do you think they took her?'

'I don't know. Where do *you* think?' I whispered back.

Looking incredibly sad, Mum shook her head, but said nothing.

'Are you going to come to India's birthday party tomorrow, Mum?' I now asked once it was clear that she wasn't going to expand further on the mysterious Patricia.

'Is that mother-in-law of yours going to be there?' she asked.

'Sylvia lives with us now, Mum. You know that.'

'Don't ever let her tell you what to do,' Mum said sharply. 'You tell her it's none of her business.'

'Ok,' I laughed, surprised. 'I'll bear that in mind. So are you coming? You've not seen India for a few weeks.'

'We'll be there, Kenneth, won't we?' Mum said, looking at Dad. 'But, don't you go telling your Granny Morgan about it. I'm not speaking to her.'

Once we'd rung the local surgery and made an appointment for Dad and Diana to have a chat with Mum's doctor the following week, we cleared up the tea things and made our way down the garden path to our respective cars.

'So do you think you'll have John on to you about the way you spoke to Christine? You were a bit over the top, you know,' I said as Diana made to unlock her car door.

'Doubt it. I think he probably agrees with me that his wife is a particularly silly woman,' Diana grinned. 'He's far too idle to get off his backside or the golf course with the sole purpose of driving over to me in order to defend his wife's honour.'

'Well actually, Di, he did just that last week.' John had sworn me to secrecy over his on-off thing with Amanda, but there was no way I was keeping this from Diana.

Diana turned, key in hand, and laughed out loud. 'What? John came over to defend Christine's honour? From whom?'

'Shh!' I didn't want the whole neighbourhood knowing John's business, and there was already a woman in the next-door garden who seemed more intent on eavesdropping than deadheading her autumn roses. 'No, nothing to do with Christine. John's found out about Nick and David Henderson and basically came round to warn Nick off him. With Nick away in Italy, I got the brunt of it.'

'What does John know about David Henderson, apart from his being married to Amanda Goodners?' Diana asked, puzzled.

'Absolutely nothing, I should think. He was actually trying to make sure Nick had nothing to do with Amanda.'

Diana frowned in disbelief. 'What, you mean John had had such a bad time with her he was coming round to warn Nick what a terrible person she is?'

'Well, not quite as altruistic as that. Basically, Di, John is still in love with her and can't bear the thought she might make a play for Nick.'

'Oh for God's sake. It's about time John grew up. He hasn't seen her for years,' Di snorted in derision.

I hesitated. 'That's where you're wrong, Di, and that's why I can believe Amanda would have no qualms about getting Nick, if that's what she wants. Being married to David hasn't stopped her from keeping John on a string all these years.'

'Well more fool him,' Diana retorted angrily, once I'd told her of John's confession only a week earlier. 'And don't you go thinking Nick is of the same ilk as John. Nick is straight as a die – John has had living with Christine all these years to warp him.'

For once I sprang to my sister-in-law's defence. 'Don't go blaming Christine for this,' I snapped. 'Have you forgotten that awful summer when John first met Amanda?'

How could we forget?

My brother John had married Caring Christine on the rebound. From Amanda Goodners.

He'd gone into town as usual with his mates one warm, June evening and there, in all her blonde glory, was Little Miss Goodness celebrating, with the same posse of prefects who followed her everywhere, finishing her A levels. John is still a good-looking man, but at the age of fourteen even I could see that my big twenty-year-old brother, with his almost Italian good looks, was quite devastatingly attractive. My mother despaired at the number of heartbroken girls – Christine included – that hung around our doorstep in need of mopping up after being abandoned by John in what can only be described as a totally cavalier manner.

One idle glance across the heaving, smoke-filled bar and John was a lost cause. With the same beguiling smile that she'd deigned to bestow on my eleven-year-old self, Amanda cast a net at her intended victim and John swam in. For almost four months, until she went off to Oxford, John was her willing slave. They were out almost every night, and I know John spent an absolute fortune taking her out to restaurants in Manchester and Leeds and paying for weekends away in the Dales and the Lake District. His Mini was traded in for a little blue Spitfire and he would roar off, hood down, obsessed with this new woman in his life. At the time, we knew nothing of the identity of the girl – John was far too embarrassed to bring Midhope's wealthiest mill owner's only daughter home to our council house – only that by turns he was, depending on Amanda's treatment of him, either ecstatic or despairing.

Apparently, and I only learned of this many years later, Amanda openly spoke of my brother as her 'bit of rough.' Perhaps she'd been reading *'Room at the Top'* and got carried away by the sheer novelty of it all, but John was out of his depth, heading for a fall.

And fall he did.

Big time.

Amanda played with him, sucked him dry, and threw him right back where she'd found him, refusing to answer any of his phone calls or letters once she left for university. It didn't surprise me a bit once I learned who was the cause of John's despair, but it was Mum's reaction to the affair that we didn't understand. Instead of berating John, telling him he'd at last got his come-uppance for all the hearts he'd broken in the past, she spent weeks just listening to him as he raved about Amanda, sat in his room as he paced the floor, and physically held him back every time he threatened to go round to the Goodners' house or drive down to Oxford. Our whole household was in a state, all of us caught up in the sheer drama and misery of John's broken heart.

Christine, waiting patiently in the wings while the whole sorry Amanda drama was played out, bided her time, made her well calculated entrance and emerged triumphant. By Christmas of that year she was pregnant, and by Easter she and John were married.

'You know, I do sometimes forget that Christine can't have it that easy living with John,' Diana now said as she finally opened her car door and got in. 'He really is a sod, isn't he? I bet he really makes her feel second best. Do you reckon she knows he's still in love with Amanda?'

I sighed, still wanting to talk, not really wanting to go home. 'It wouldn't surprise me. She'll put up with it. She knew the score when she married him.'

'Well with any luck she'll keep a low profile for a while, particularly where poor old Mum is concerned. I mean, can you imagine Mum dressed in rhinestones and a cowboy hat, line dancing with the rest of the inmates?'

'Hardly,' I grimaced. 'So why do you think she's got such a bee in her bonnet about this Patricia? Dad's certainly never heard of her.'

'Dunno. Maybe it's someone she was at school with – I seem to remember her talking about a friend called Pat. Maybe it's her.' Diana shrugged her shoulders. 'Right. I'm off into town to buy birthday presents for your two. Any ideas?'

'Something pink for India? And a packet of condoms for Kit? That should do nicely, thank you very much.'

'Fine. Take it as sorted.'

'I *was* joking, you know,' I said nervously.

'Oh, you mean she's no longer into pink? Something in a different colour then?'

'You know exactly what I mean. I wouldn't put it past you to buy Kit just that.'

'You can't be too careful,' Diana shook her head sagely. 'Look what John brought into the family at the age of twenty-one by not being prepared. You don't want to end up with some daughter-in-law who'll persuade Kit to put you into a home where the highlight of your week will be doing the "Birdie Song" with all the other residents of a Saturday evening, do you?'

'He's *fourteen*,' I said laughing.

'Yes, and we all know what is constantly on fourteen-year-old boys' minds. And it certainly isn't Lego!'

When I arrived home, I couldn't, for a moment, quite work out what was different about the garden. Still feeling slightly hungover after the excesses of the previous evening, my sole aim was a large mug of Earl Grey and ten minutes on the sofa with the latest edition of *25 Beautiful Homes*. I knew, though, I'd only be setting myself up for an afternoon of discontent as I faced the fact that our lovely house was badly in need, not only of decoration, but of major structural repairs. Only this morning Liberty had pointed out a huge damp patch in her bedroom that, like an unchecked tumour, appeared to be growing at an alarming rate. The knowledge that fifty thousand pounds of our money – alright, Sylvia's money, but money that could have been used for some essential decoration – was now lining David Henderson's pockets didn't bear thinking about.

I stepped back and took a proper look through the window at what had fleetingly caught my eye as I'd reached, automatically, for the kettle.

This wasn't just any old potting shed. This was the crème de la crème of potting sheds. It stood where the original, burned out version had once stood, majestically surveying its kingdom, haughty in the knowledge, like a top supermodel, that it had nothing to fear from any inferior being.

Forgetting my still fragile state, I whooped down the garden to where Nick and Kit were helping a couple of well-tattooed lackeys to place windows and doors.

'Big enough for you?' Nick grinned, hammering a couple of nails into the shed's side.

'It's beautiful,' I breathed. 'It's what I've always wanted. But how can we afford it?'

'Insurance. I told you they'd agreed to pay up in full. I have to say I'm amazed they've been so quick about it. We thought we'd surprise you. They sent the cheque last week, Mum supervised the laying of the flags for its foundations yesterday while you were at work, and Jez and Daz here have been working on it all morning.'

When I was a little girl, the one thing I'd coveted above all else was the Wendy house belonging to Sharon Gillespie who'd lived three doors down from us. She'd been given it on her seventh birthday and had actually hosted her birthday party in it. I had thought it the most beautiful thing I'd ever seen. It had a little flight of stairs with a carved wooden handrail that led to a minute bedroom above the main downstairs room. Sharon's mother had sewn curtains in a poppy-decorated fabric and they'd hung jauntily at the diamond-leaded windows on either side of the bright green door. I had longed for my own wooden house just like this one but money was short and, despite writing a myriad of letters to Santa, it soon became obvious that he never received them.

Standing now, more than thirty years later, in front of my new potting shed, I felt a rush of love for Nick. He'd heard the sad tale of my longing for a little house just like Sharon Gillespie's Wendy house many times over the years, and had obviously gone out of his way to track down a potting shed that he knew might compensate for my deprived childhood.

I stepped inside, intoxicated by the smell of new wood and creosote. I was already planning bookshelves and a rug. A couple of easy chairs that had seen better days and were now languishing in the loft would be perfect after I'd tarted them up with some new throws and cushions.

'Don't forget all the garden stuff has got to fit in,' Nick warned, reading my mind. 'I know exactly what you're thinking, but at the end of the day it *is* a garden shed.'

'Couldn't we maybe just partition off part of it in order to create a little den for me?' I asked hopefully.

'I don't see why not. I've asked Bill, the electrician from Wells Trading, to pop over next week. He's going to see if he can run a cable from the house so that we can have electricity down here.'

'So I can have a kettle?'

'Yes and a little fridge for your Sauvignon Blanc,' Nick grinned, my enthusiasm clearly infectious.

'I can invite you down for a drink and then seduce you amongst the plant cuttings,' I said, desperately hoping for a reaction from Nick that would convince me he was still mine. I had an awful feeling that if Kit, Jez and Daz hadn't been there I might have whipped off his trousers and had him up against the still wet creosote.

'Yes, well, you're going to have to get a bit further on with your garden if you're thinking of taking cuttings. You've only spent a couple of afternoons down here so far.'

'That's because I'm so busy working and bringing up your children single-handed.' I replied, stung into petulance once more. I really was going to have to stop this sulky attitude. It wasn't at all becoming.

I hadn't realised just how much I'd missed my little haven that was now Sylvia's flat. Although technically the kids' playroom, it had been where I'd ended up most days once the children had gone off to school and nursery in the days before I'd had to go back to work. With the French windows flung open onto the garden, I'd spend my time at the computer writing; or I'd take my coffee down there and catch up with the Sunday supplements, or spend a good hour with whatever novel I'd been reading and been unable to put down. I'd spent the winter before Nick's business collapsed rereading the novels of Thomas Hardy, the occasional, insomniac squirrel chasing across the frosty lawn my only distraction.

Sometimes, before India was born, I'd get the older children off to school and just sit, basking in the view down the garden and across the fields beyond, watching the blackbirds and robins making tracks in the snow in winter, unable to believe that all this was mine. I'd never spent any length of time alone: I'd shared a bedroom with Diana until she left home just before I went to university. Then there were flatmates and Nick, and then the children. With the kids at school, and a cleaner to crack off the majority of the housework, I relished each day of solitude. Looking back, it was an idyllic time but, like many love affairs, short-lived.

The new potting shed promised a place that I could call my own, away from the mundane realities of school and housework. The door from the shed opened out onto exactly the same view as the playroom but, from here, you felt to be firmly ensconced *in* the view rather than looking down upon it. Perfection.

'Thanks, my darling,' I said, hugging him so tightly that the nails hanging from his mouth nearly shot down his throat. 'Thank you so much.'

Chapter 13

When Nick's company first began to crash three years or so ago, I would wake in the night and find that he was no longer in bed. Where his body had lain would be quite cold and I'd know, with a sinking feeling in the pit of my stomach, that he'd been up for hours, unable to sleep, wandering from room to room and sometimes even out into the garden, desperately worried about what was going to become of us – the mortgage, the school fees, the bills that seemed to be coming in at an alarming rate.

Once Nick had accepted the inevitable and creditors had been paid, we found that we just managed with my return to teaching and Nick's new job, and his nocturnal wanderings had eventually ceased as we began to pick up the pieces and get on with our new life.

Waking at three in the morning, I knew instantly, without having to feel, that Nick's side of the bed was empty. I sat up immediately, praying that he'd just popped to the loo, but knowing in my heart that he'd been gone for a while.

'Oh dear God, not again,' I muttered, searching on the floor for my abandoned dressing gown.

I found him at the kitchen table, hunched over the laptop that had been vital to this new venture. A glass of milk lay abandoned and he was frowning at the screen as his hand raked constantly through his thick blonde hair.

'Nick, do you know what time it is?' I asked gently, stroking his hair and arresting the fingers that he'd entwined there.

'There's just something I need to figure out,' he said. 'It's all so new and I need to know that I'm on the right lines with all this.'

'Nick, I know you through and through. You wouldn't be down here worrying if you thought everything was going ok. Talk to me. Tell me what's wrong.'

'No, honestly, Hat. It'll be fine. Things have moved on so much since Pennine Clothing was up and running. Everything is more cut-throat. Everyone is wanting a bite of the cherry and I can't afford to miss a trick.' He sighed, rubbing his hand across his face where a hint of black stubble was just beginning to show.

He looked desperately tired but still managed to exude the allure that had drawn me to him in the first place. It's not many men that can carry designer stubble – most manage to end up looking like something from 'Care in the Community' – but my husband, along with George Michael of course, wears his five o'clock shadow like a true sex god.

'Are you beginning to regret throwing your lot in with David Henderson?' I asked, holding my breath in fear of an answer I didn't want to hear. I needed Nick to be confident about what he'd started. He seemed to me to be on the first step of a roller-coaster ride and I didn't want to hear him saying that he'd made a mistake; that he was suddenly afraid of heights and needed to get off. This was one journey he was going to have to sit tight and get on with.

Nick reached out for me, nuzzling his face into my neck and stroking my hair as he pulled me on to his lap.

'No, I had to do this. I just hate the fact that so much of the running of the house and everything else is on your shoulders.' He paused. 'And I can't understand this sodding Italian legal jargon.'

Now here was the dilemma. Did I a) encourage Nick to get help from Amanda in the hope that her knowledge of both Italian and the law would help Nick to succeed with this new venture? And I'd still have my house. But maybe not my husband. Or did I b) shout, swear and dig my heels in assuring him that if I caught her dainty little backside anywhere near his, professionally or otherwise, they'd both have me to answer to?

I took a deep breath. 'Can't Mandy help you?'

'Yes, very likely.'

'Well, give her a ring in the morning. Just forget about all this until then.'

And with that compromise I was able to persuade him back to bed.

We were woken, only a few hours later, by a thoroughly overexcited six-year-old, bouncing on our bed and demanding presents.

'Happy birthday, darling. Goodness me, six years old. You *are* getting to be an old lady!'

'You're the old lady,' she giggled, bouncing on the bed while simultaneously scanning the room for any signs of booty, a feat that was beginning to make me feel dizzy. This damned hangover seemed to be hanging on indefinitely.

Putting her out of her misery, I reached down to where a cache of birthday presents was waiting and settled down to watch her divest them of their wrappings.

Once she had satisfied her lust for material gain, India turned her attention to the coming afternoon's birthday party.

'What are we actually *doing* at my birthday party this afternoon?' she asked, looking up momentarily from the task of undressing a rather randy-looking Bratz doll. It was no wonder those fourteen-year-old girls had dressed and behaved as they had on the rugby touchline last week if they'd been subjected to role models like these when they were six years old.

'Doing?' I asked, playing for time. I'd no idea what we were doing apart from, hopefully, tiring out twenty little girls with a lethal cocktail of marmite and jam sandwiches and 'The Farmer Wants a Wife.'

'Yes, what are we actually *doing*?' echoed Nick as he dressed one of the dolls in killer high heels and a black tasselled bra. 'Do you fancy a get up like this?' he asked hopefully.

Ignoring his last question and smiling sweetly, I said, 'You're games master, Buster. You decide.'

'Me?' Nick looked terrified. 'I've got work to do. Didn't we agree last night that I should speak to Mandy today and sort a few things out, maybe ask her if she wouldn't mind popping over?

Anyway, you're the one that knows all about children and how to keep them under control.'

Well, that was debateable for a start. And my suggestion that Amanda come over and help Nick out with his work was only made in the early hours of the morning in order to make Nick feel better and come back to bed. I'd been hoping he'd forgotten all about it. The last person I needed in my house when I was trying to be party planner of the year was Little Miss Goodness.

'We're going to have a good old-fashioned children's party with games and proper party food,' I said firmly. 'There won't be a children's entertainer in sight – apart from you, Nick – nor a chicken nugget nor a burger. I'll write you a list of all the games we're going to play. Meanwhile, I shall be organising the marmite sandwiches and jelly.'

Nick groaned. 'I need to clear my head. I'm off for a run,' he said, getting out of bed.

'Excellent,' I enthused, removing several bits of unidentifiable plastic from where they'd lodged beneath my bottom before handing them back to India. 'Games masters need to set a good example. Off you go. Oh, and Nick, seeing *you* agreed to Kit having friends over as well today, maybe *you* can come up with some idea of how you're going to entertain them as well?'

'No problem. We'll stick them all in the newly erected potting shed with a pile of *'Loaded'* magazines and a crate of Red Bull and leave them to fend for themselves.'

Pleased with himself for coming up with this solution, Nick was out of the door leaving me to clear up the post-present unwrapping debris, muttering to anyone who cared to listen that it wouldn't be just the bloody potting shed that would be newly erected if we went along with his suggestion for Kit and his mates.

By mid-afternoon the sitting room was awash with balloons of various size and hue. A number of vulgar Day-Glo jellies were in the fridge under strict orders to set – I'd totally forgotten to make them until an hour previously – and the dining-room table was piled high with sandwiches and crisps. The whole spread was a celebration of 1970s kitsch complete with sausages on sticks, named flags atop the sliced white bread sandwiches and even a cheese and pineapple hedgehog which, rather top heavy, had made several bids for freedom by lurching drunkenly off the table. The yummy-mummy food police would have a field day once they realised there wasn't an organic or wholemeal bit of food to be seen anywhere.

A 'Pin-the-Tail-on-the-Donkey', drawn hurriedly and not very artistically by a bored Liberty who had been press ganged into the task, hung jauntily on the wall, uncannily resembling a rather lecherous, cross-eyed Prince Charles. Just as I was putting six candles onto the home-made - ok Sainsbury's - birthday cake, Grace arrived laden with gifts and champagne.

"I thought you might need this," she said, handing me the bottle.

"Do I ever," I sighed gratefully. "Shall we have a glass now?"

"Absolutely," she replied, taking two white plastic cups from the pile.

"Make that another. Diana's just arrived," I said, catching sight of her car as it came down the lane.

"Are you taking in asylum-seekers?" Diana asked, as she ushered Mum and Dad into the sitting room where India was already holding court with two friends who'd arrived early.

"Asylum-Seekers?"

'You seem to have acquired a stonking great edifice in your garden.'

'My new potting shed,' I said proudly. 'I'm going to make a den down there just for me. When the trials of family life get too much, I shall bugger off down the garden with my pipe.'

'Pipe?'

'Well, the equivalent, whatever it is. A glass of wine and *Okay* magazine probably.'

'So,' I asked, turning to Grace. 'How was the lift home?'

'Lift home?' If I hadn't known better, I'd have sworn she flushed.

'Yes, the lift? On Friday night?'

'It got me home, as one would expect from a lift.'

'And what did you think of the lovely Enrique?'

'Enrique?'

'You didn't think he was the image of Enrique Iglesias?'

'Was he? I didn't notice.' Grace's eyes didn't quite meet my own.

'Who are we talking about?' asked Diana, helping herself to a second cup of fizz. 'Hey, don't tell anyone else we've got this. We don't want to share it. Pretend it's fizzy water.'

'We're talking about Amanda Goodners' son, Sebastian. He turned up on Friday night and gave Grace a lift home.'

'Bloody hell, Grace, keep well clear of him if he's anything like his mother,' Diana said.

'And?' I prompted, ignoring Diana. While I totally agreed with her sentiment, I wanted to know what Grace had thought of him.

'And nothing,' Grace protested. 'He happened to give me a lift home – along with his mother and her prefect cronies – because it was on their way home. Now, I think you'll find you've got a queue of little girls in the garden wondering if there's a party on offer.'

She was right. Diana and I had been so interested in the story of the return of the prodigal son we hadn't acknowledged the insistent ringing of the front door bell. Sylvia, however, had, and was now ushering in a gaggle of shy little girls, while yet more could be heard through the open door, crunching their way up the gravel drive, carrying presents and expectations of a good time ahead.

'Oh shit, here we go,' I groaned and, plastering a smile on my face, went to take over from Sylvia as chief host.

The majority of mothers were dressed as if for a party of their own, or at least as though they were doing lunch with friends. Fully made-up, hair streaked and straightened, there wasn't one in a baggy tracksuit or leggings and T-shirt. All of them dedicated gym bunnies, they were toned and slim and obviously fit enough to carry the huge regulation Mulberry or Chloe handbags that went everywhere with them.

'What sort of party is this?' came the petulant voice of Adriana Saxton who, depending on how she got out of bed on a particular morning, was either India's declared best friend or, more usually, her worst enemy. I couldn't bear the child – or her manipulative mother – and tried as much as I could to wean India away from her influence.

'What sort of party would you like it to be, Adriana?' I asked sweetly. Maybe she could give me some sort of clue as to which particular party genre direction we were heading in because, for the life of me, I still didn't have a damned clue.

'Well, I'm bored with clown parties, swimming, and cinema parties. I've been to two parties at 'Wacky Warehouse' already this month, so I'm very pleased India decided against that. Sophie's was 'Laser Quest' and Matilda's was Pot-Decorating. *I'm* having 'Little Miss Cute' when it's my party next month and we're getting there by limo – it will be the best party ever – so it will be interesting to see what India's having.' Adriana drew breath for all of two seconds before launching, once more, into the breach. 'I thought she was really mean at school on Friday when she wouldn't tell us the theme of her party. She said it was going to be a surprise.'

Well it was certainly going to be that. The theme, as this precocious little brat had so succinctly put it, was still one hell of a surprise to me too.

It very quickly dawned on me that two hours of party games was *not* going to go down too well with these sophisticated little madams. As uber-socialite Ms Saxton prepared to launch once more into party themes she'd experienced, and who knows, maybe even enjoyed, I silenced her with my best teacher glare and prepared for action.

Ushering the whole gaggle of them into the sitting room was easy. Getting rid of the mothers was not. But eventually I was able to turn to Diana and Grace who, having downed the remains of the champagne, appeared to have forgotten their responsibilities as aunt and godmother.

'Right, I have a cunning plan. It'll either go down a storm or India will end up a social outcast at the age of six. Can you two keep this lot occupied for fifteen minutes with Pin the Tail on the Donkey? Mum and Sylvia are in there in case you need back-up.'

Grabbing Dad and shouting for Libby and her two mates who were firmly ensconced in the kitchen with the omnibus edition of

EastEnders, I dashed to the garage where I hoped the contents of the ancient, worm-ridden cupboard would lend substance to my plan. If this didn't work India would never speak to me again. She'd be relegated from the premier division of alpha females in her class and be forced to go around with Elizabeth and Aditi, both new girls who hadn't quite yet made the grade.

Twenty minutes later we were sorted.

'Ok, girls,' I said grandly, 'we are having a *gardening party!*'

Total silence. I didn't dare meet India's eyes in case they were full of unshed tears.

Little Ms Saxton, who apparently had the same aspirations to royalty as my sister-in-law, was the first to speak.

'A garden party? Like the Queen has at Buckingham Palace?' Adriana turned to peer down the garden as if expecting to see the Duke of Edinburgh lurking amongst the Leylandii.

'Yes, absolutely, Adriana.' I needed to get this little witch on my side or it would be curtains for India. 'Now, this is what we're going to do ...'

Mindful of the designer gear that most of them were dressed in, I'd issued each one with a black bin liner cut with holes for head and arms and found enough old pairs of wellies and trainers in the garage cupboard – abandoned by my three over the years – to set up a shop. With the twenty little girls split up into groups of four, they moved between four activities, each one led by an adult. Dad, assigned head gardener to my new plot, showed his little group how to dig and plant out the masses of spring bulbs he'd bought for me as a present for my new garden. My four, paintbrush in hand and with tongue hanging out in studied concentration, had the job of painting the new potting-shed doors, while Grace and Diana, with two groups at any one time between them, were refereeing a sort of mini-rounders' tournament. Liberty and her two school friends, sitting in the conservatory, were more than happy to paint the nails and braid the hair of each girl once it was their turn to move inside.

After twenty minutes with each group, I would shout, 'all change' and the party guests would move on to the next activity. I started to relax once I heard shouts of excitement and laughter coming from the girls and saw that India was smiling. Little Ms Saxton threw herself into each pursuit with abandon and, at one juncture, could be heard saying to India, 'No wonder you kept your party theme a secret. This is *so* original!' If India had had any idea whatsoever about the meaning of 'original' she might have been tempted to agree with her; but as her vocabulary was that of an average six-year-old, it was enough that her friends seemed to be more than enjoying themselves.

At the end of almost two hours, with the shadows lengthening over the garden, we all trooped back into the house. Admittedly, those girls who had had their beauty treatments *before* digging and painting needed a bit of a retouch once they'd washed their hands, but Liberty, taking on the role of adored big sister, was more than happy to go round with the nail varnish.

Sylvia, getting into the party spirit, had unearthed her precious lead-crystal wine goblets and brought them over from her flat, filling each one with fizzy lemonade and a cocktail cherry on a stick. With a snow white, starched napkin over her arm, she handed a drink to each girl while thanking her most graciously for coming to the garden party.

'Is that the Queen?' asked one little tot of Adriana, obviously under the assumption that if anyone knew her identity it would be Ms Saxton.

'Don't be silly, of course it isn't,' Adriana answered, before grudgingly adding, 'but I think she must be a very close relative.'

So where had 'Le games master extraordinaire' been hiding all this time? Once I'd rounded up the last party guest and handed it thankfully to its parent with many an apology for the state of its dress (the bin liners hadn't totally afforded the protection I'd hoped) I went in search of my errant husband. The obvious success of the afternoon – I overheard at least two little girls saying they wanted 'garden parties' for *their* birthday celebrations – had put me on a magnanimous high and I was ready to forgive his defection.

I slipped upstairs, following the sound of voices. Nick and Amanda were seated at the new laptop he'd set up in front of our ancient computer, on the table in the upstairs recess that now acted as our study. I paused, my chest tightening at their togetherness in attempting to overcome whatever problem had caused Nick's insomnia. Their two blonde heads were virtually as one in their mutually concentrated effort over the laptop screen, and I felt inextricably excluded. And frightened.

Nick jumped – guiltily I thought – as he took his eyes from the laptop screen and acknowledged my presence with a too-hearty smile, while Amanda continued to scroll down, unaware that I'd joined them at the top of the stairs.

'Right, I've got it, Nicky darling,' she said triumphantly. 'Here's your missing link. You wouldn't have been able to make any contact with the people in Milan without this address.' Realising Nick's attention had wavered, Amanda looked up at him and then round to where I was standing a couple of feet away.

'Oh, hello Harriet,' she said coolly, as if I were the guest.

'I hadn't realised *you* were here,' I said, almost childishly. After all these years she still had the wherewithal to make me feel awkward. Even in my own house. 'I didn't see your car come up the drive when we were all out in the garden.'

'No, you wouldn't have. When Nicky rang to ask if I'd come over, I decided to grab a lift with David part of the way, and then walk the rest. I wanted to explore these wonderful country lanes. David had a meeting with a client down in Midhope, so he dropped me off in Monkton village and I walked the rest.' She proffered her trainer-clad feet as evidence and I felt even more resentment as I acknowledged that, even in walking shoes and jeans, she still had the ability to make me feel like a country bumpkin – or the kid from the council estate who'd ventured onto her turf once more.

'You missed all of India's party,' I said, turning to Nick, unable to keep the petulance from my voice.

'Oh God. I'm sorry, Hat. I thought this would only take a minute.' He trailed off lamely, then, obviously feeling cornered, came out fighting. 'I had to sort this out, Harriet. It would have been impossible to make any progress if I hadn't. In fact, there would have been no point in my going back to Italy this week if I hadn't been able to sort out this contact.'

'Italy? You're off to Italy again? This week?' I breathed.

'I told you it was on the cards,' Nick said curtly, plainly embarrassed that we were having this discussion in front of Amanda. She, apparently, was not, giving him a sympathetic look that spoke volumes.

'Well, can I just remind you that Kit and his mates are *your* responsibility? I think I can hear some of them arriving now.' And so saying, I turned and retreated without another word. I was wild. Wilder than wild. In fact as wild as a wildebeest in the wilderness. How dare Nick miss his daughter's birthday party? He was being sucked in by Amanda, seduced by the same Goodners' charm that had fascinated and enthralled not only the girls and staff at Midhope Grammar, but also my poor brother over twenty-five years ago.

I stomped downstairs, the good humour I'd generated at the success of India's party now totally evaporated, and went in search of the others. India had taken root on the sitting-room sofa with Sylvia, both engrossed in one of the new DVDs she'd been given as a birthday present. Diana, my mother-in-law informed me, had taken my parents home.

'Granny Keturah was over in Granny Sylvia's flat, looking for Patricia,' India said, through a mouthful of birthday chocolate, without once looking up from the television screen. 'She seemed a bit strange. Who's Patricia?'

Oh my God. Of course! Amanda and Mum, together, in the same house. Had Amanda been introduced to anyone at the party? I doubted it. Too eager to get her mitts on Nick to be interested in overexcited kids and wandering Grannies. I bet she'd snuck up my stairs, revelling in the fact that she was going to get my husband to herself. Meeting my mother for the first time wouldn't have caused Amanda any worries – I still wasn't convinced she was aware that I was John's sister. Mind you, I suppose even if Mum was still in possession of all her marbles – and after yesterday's little episode I feared she no longer was – there was no reason why Mum would associate Mandy Henderson, Nick's new boss's wife, with Amanda Goodners. She'd never met her, after all.

'Patricia, Mum? Who's Patricia?', India insisted, as I had an awful vision of Mum, armed with the cheese and pineapple hedgehog or whatever weapon came to hand, stalking Amanda through the house as she sought a final revenge for what Amanda had done to John.

'Oh just someone she used to know, years ago,' I said, too brightly, as Sylvia looked at me, eyebrows raised. 'Where's Grace?'

'Gone for a ride on a motorbike,' said India.

'A motorbike? Whose motorbike?'

'A very attractive young man's motorbike,' Sylvia laughed. 'If this arthritis in my knee hadn't stopped me riding pillion, I'd have been up there in the queue waiting my turn. I think he must belong to that delightful young woman who is helping Nick with his computer. She *is* a poppet isn't she?'

'Isn't she just?' I said with a saccharine smile.

'She brought me this.' India, momentarily distracted from the screen and chocolate, fished down the side of the sofa, bringing up the most divine, midnight-blue jacket I'd ever seen. 'It's from Italy,' India crowed proudly. 'And there's a scarf and hat to go with it.'

So, not content with seducing adults, she was now bewitching vulnerable grannies and defenceless children.

And what the hell was Enrique Iglesias doing here? What was it with these Hendersons? Didn't they have a fucking home to go to?

I made my way to the kitchen where the sad remnants of the party feast stared balefully up at me from under, as well as on, the table. Half-eaten sandwiches – the Queen would surely have insisted *her* guests eat up their crusts – curled up in protest at their relinquishment, lay wantonly abandoned. Even Bones, always an indiscriminate and insatiable forager of food, had turned his nose up at the remains of the potted-meat sandwiches and was making his way disdainfully out of the room, tail held stiffly aloft, in search of something more to his liking.

Sweeping the whole mess into a black bin liner, I made my way to the freezer in search of pizza. While fourteen-year-old boys are probably no more discriminating in their eating preferences than

Bones, I accepted that I really could not serve Kit's friends a birthday tea of leftovers.

I felt tired and defeated. Everyone seemed to be having a lot more *fun* than me. I was just chief-cook and bottle-washer while everyone else seemed to be getting on with their lives. Most of all I hated the waspish and petulant person I seemed to be turning in to. I was never like this before Amanda had arrived back in my life.

'Who's the dude on the bike?' Kit asked as he came into the kitchen followed by the five boys he'd invited over to help celebrate his birthday.

'Mandy Henderson's son, Sebastian. He must have come to pick up his mother.'

'Well he's obviously changed his mind and *picked up* Grace first. As in *picked up*,' Kit tittered, to the accompaniment of sniggering adolescents. 'And that Mandy's a bit fit. I wouldn't trust Dad upstairs with her if I were you.' More guffaws from the hormonally saturated five.

'Pizza alright for you lot?' I asked. 'Or would a bucket of cold water suffice?'

'Can we eat it in the new shed? Sort of camp out?' asked Kit. 'We can take some music and torches down there and be out of your way. There are some new batteries somewhere that I can put into the CD player.'

Now that was tempting. 'I don't see why not,' I said, 'but you'll need something warm on. There's no heating down there, you know. Give me ten minutes to sort some food out for you.'

'Have you any idea where the binoculars are?' asked Kit as the boys left the kitchen in search of drinks.

'Binoculars?' I asked, surprised. 'What on earth do you want binoculars for?'

Kit hesitated for just a fraction before saying smoothly, 'I think I saw a heron the other day. I'd like to see it close up if it comes back into the garden.'

'Since when have you been interested in birds?' I asked in amazement. More explosive laughter drifted out from the utility room where the boys were filling a carrier bag with coke and crisps.

'Since Bella Sinclair started going on our bus,' sniggered Tom Prestcott. Tom had been at school with Kit since infant days and, while friendships came and went, Tom and Kit seemed fairly constant in their regard for one another.

'Since I saw the heron a couple of days ago,' Kit retorted with some dignity. 'I believe this is going to my new hobby. I might even spend half term researching birds.'

'Well, it doesn't look as if you'll have to visit the library to find books,' I sniffed, indicating with a nod the copy of *'Nuts'* that was poking out of the back pocket of Tom's over-long jeans and resting artistically on the waist band of his (clearly new) Calvin Klein boxers.

'So where do you think the binoculars might be?' Kit asked again, amidst the ensuing laughter.

'Bottom of my wardrobe, I think. I'll get them for you.'

Was it my imagination or were Nick and Amanda now sitting even closer together than before? I couldn't quite make out where Amanda's blue denim shirt ended and Nick's started. For a mad second I contemplated leaping in between them, grabbing Nick and shouting, 'Mine, I think you'll find, Amanda!'

Instead, I retrieved the binoculars from their usual habitat amongst my shoes, quickly painted on a layer of bright-red lipstick and sailed past them back to the waiting boys.

Chapter 14

'Hi, Harriet. Good to meet you again.' Sebastian Henderson extended a leather-clad hand and grinned down at me as I manoeuvred myself out from under the kitchen table after spotting and retrieving the rather sorry-looking pineapple and cheese hedgehog. It had obviously made a final bid for freedom while we were all out in the garden, and wedged itself, rather squashily, against a chair leg. Reversing has never been my strong point and I'd managed to somehow entangle Sebastian's foot beneath my bottom. Emerging puce-faced from my exertions on all fours, I marvelled anew at the sheer beauty of this twenty-three-year-old. While he may have had his father's colouring, there was no doubt who his mother was: Amanda's high cheekbones and large, almond eyes were uncannily reflected in Sebastian's own features.

'Fabulous house you've got here,' he said, gazing round.

'Needs a huge amount of work doing on it, I'm afraid,' I sighed, seeing the shabbiness of the kitchen as if for the first time through a newcomer's eyes.

'And your garden has so much potential,' he went on, moving over to the window and taking in the view down the garden and to the farmland beyond. Now late October, the nights were drawing in but the farms and tiny cottages down the valley were still visible as were the wreaths of wood smoke ascending silently from the chimneys silhouetted greyly against the trees.

'Time. We just haven't got the time to do what is needed,' I said wistfully, joining Sebastian at the window. My little plot, its newly turned dark earth making it stand out in that part of the garden, seemed to gaze back reproachfully, demanding more attention than

I was able, because of all my other commitments, to give to it.

'I'd love to get my hands on that banking down there.' Sebastian nodded towards a neglected piece of garden that had lain, untouched, certainly since we moved in about ten years ago. It had probably been ignored even by its previous owners, an elderly couple who, realising the amount of work that needed doing to both the house and garden after years of neglect, were happy to downsize to a new-build semi near their son in Sussex.

'Help yourself,' I laughed. 'It's all yours.'

'Really?'

I glanced curiously at Sebastian. He seemed animated. Why would this gorgeous, bright young man who was about to launch himself into the world of the law want to spend time digging my garden?

'You'd really come and tackle that bit of wilderness out there?' I asked. 'I thought you were back from New Zealand to start law college?'

'Well, yes I am, but the course doesn't start until January. I really intended staying out in Christchurch until Christmas and then coming back ready to move to London in January, but then I got a bit fed up with sheep – they're pretty boring creatures – and decided to have a couple of months at home.'

Hmm. Sheep, my Aunt Fanny! I bet there was some female out there who he was a bit fed up with. Some poor girl who was saving up her pennies and poring over maps of England, planning her trip to see her errant lover.

'I've realised I really like being out in the fresh air – I've felt a bit cooped up since I got home – so I'd be more than happy to attack that banking of yours.'

'Well it's all yours, but I'm afraid I can't pay you anything for doing it,' I said, embarrassed at having to reveal my lack of funds, but knowing I had to lay my cards on the table now rather than in a few weeks when Sebastian might expect a wage packet.

Sebastian looked put out. 'I don't want any money. I'm more than happy to be out in the fresh air rather than at home kicking my heels until January. I'll go and have a quick look at the garden on my way out and then start on it this week if that's OK with you. Is Mum ready to go?' He raised an enquiring eyebrow at me as he turned finally from his gaze over the garden. With a pang, I realised that Amanda and Nick must still be ensconced together over the laptop.

'I'll go and give her a shout. Tell her you want to be off,' I said, throwing the balding hedgehog into the overflowing black rubbish bag. 'Where's Grace, by the way? Did you drop her off at home?'

'Yes.'

Nothing more. No explanation as to why Grace had abandoned her god-daughter's birthday party without saying goodbye. There would have to be some serious phone calling to do later on this evening.

'Hi, my darling. Are you waiting for me?' Amanda breezed into the kitchen, totally unfazed by the fact that she'd been virtually wrapped round my husband all afternoon. Nick, following in her wake and conscious of my present mood, was not quite as self-assured and was steadfastly refusing to meet my eye.

'Sebastian has offered to come and work in my garden,' I said pointedly, putting emphasis on the word *my*. 'Isn't that great of him?'

For a split second, Amanda's navy eyes narrowed slightly and then her composure returned. 'You keep him occupied and out of trouble, Harriet,' she trilled condescendingly. 'He needs something to do before he goes to London in the New Year. A bit of digging will be great. Right, Sebastian, do you have the spare helmet? I'll just pop next door and say my goodbyes to Sylvia. What a *lovely* lady she is. We've had *such* a chat this afternoon. She knows the Henderson-Smythes, from Epsom – Penelope was my mother's bridesmaid. You are so lucky to have such a saint on hand twenty-four hours a day, Harriet. I'll be in touch, Nicky.'

And with that she was off – game, set and bloody match to Mandy. Sebastian, grinning widely at my obviously dropped jaw, kissed me lightly on the cheek and went to start up his bike.

'I'll go and open a bottle of wine, shall I?' Nick said, hastily backing out of the kitchen.

'You'll be lucky,' I shouted, as he began to search in vain through the various cupboards in the utility room. 'We drank the last bottle a couple of days ago.'

'We always have a bottle somewhere,' Nick shouted back.

'Not any more. Can't afford it. I think there's a bottle of Dad's home-made rhubarb wine that's been hanging about for a few years. Should have quite a kick to it by now.'

Nick came back into the kitchen. 'You trying to make a point here?' he asked.

'A point?'

'Yes. A point.'

'And the point being?'

'That now I'm working for myself we haven't a bean?'

'We haven't. Not even a tin of baked beans. Kit ate the last one as a snack before he went to bed last night.'

'Shall I pop down to the Co-op? It should be still open shouldn't it?'

'Well, you can, but spending money on wine isn't a good idea when we're broke, you know. India had my last pound to buy a poppy.' I knew I was being a dog in the manger but Amanda's presence plus the after-effects of midday drinking had made me irritable.

'Poppies already? We haven't had Bonfire Night yet have we?' Nick smirked, attempting to lighten the atmosphere, before adding, 'Oops, of course. Had that a couple of Saturdays ago, I believe.'

'Oh, we are a wit, aren't we?' I had a sudden urge to kick Nick's shins.

'I really could do with a drink,' Nick went on, looking round as if hoping a bottle would magically materialise in front of him. 'I spent all my ready cash on things for the party yesterday. Come on, Hat. You're being very overdramatic, you know. We're not that broke. Hasn't India had any birthday money? I'm sure she wouldn't mind subbing her poor old dad with a fiver until I can get to the hole in the wall in the morning.'

'Don't even think about it,' I said, petulantly. 'And don't go begging to your mother either. And how long have you been having an affair with Amanda Goodners?'

My God, where did that come from?

'Amanda Goodners? Who the hell's Amanda Goodners? Oh Mandy! *Mandy?* What sort of question is that?'

'An uncomfortably direct one going by your reaction to it,' I said, suddenly feeling curiously detached. Maybe the word was defeated.

'I shall treat that with the contempt it deserves, Harriet. For heaven's sake, what's the matter with you? When have I had time to have an affair? Lighten up, can't you? This whole thing with Mandy, you and Grace and now your brother is really beginning to wind me up. Just leave the poor woman alone, will you? Now, I'm going to find, by whatever means it takes, enough cash to buy myself – yes *myself*, Harriet – a bottle of wine from the Co-op. I'm then going to lay down on the sofa and drink it all and get *very* drunk.' And with that he made his exit.

'I know my Shakespeare,' I yelled after him. 'I know *'Macbeth'*. "Methinks he doth protesteth too much.'''

India decided she wanted to spend what was left of her birthday with Bertie, so Sylvia said she would put up the camp bed in her little sitting room and India could bunk down there for the night.

'I'm going on a sleepover,' she announced. 'I need to pack my bag.'

'I'm off as well, Mum,' Liberty said, poking her head around the kitchen door.

'Where are *you* going?' I asked, surprised. My whole family seemed to be deserting me.

'I told you. I'm off to Beth's. Her dad is dropping us off at the cinema, and then I'm staying over. He's here now.'

Had she told me? I really couldn't remember. 'Well, have you got your toothbrush and some clean pants? And don't forget: 'May I?' and 'Please' and 'Thank you.' Oh, and make sure you eat all your crusts.'

'Mum, I'm not five years old,' Liberty sighed as Beth giggled from the other side of the kitchen door.

'Have you got some money?' I asked, praying that she wasn't

after a sub too.

'Don't worry, Mrs Westmoreland,' Beth called. 'Dad's treating us. We'll have to go or we'll miss the start of the movie. My mum says she'll bring Libby home tomorrow.'

Well, thank heavens for Bethany's father. I really would have had to raid India's piggy bank if Liberty had demanded money for the cinema. This was getting silly. When was payday? Was I going to have to go to one of those loan sharks and then spend the rest of my life hiding behind the front door, sending India to tell the man on the doorstep that Mummy wasn't home right now? Or could I make enough to keep the wolf from the door by putting my fake Mulberry Bayswater handbag back for sale on eBay pretending it was genuine? Or was that fraud? My head was beginning to spin. Perhaps I needed another drink or to talk to Grace. Or both.

I decided I definitely needed both. I unearthed Dad's rhubarb wine from the cellar, poured myself a large glass and, ignoring Nick who had just walked past me to the sitting room, a plastic Co-op carrier bag in tow, dialled Grace's number.

'You went without saying goodbye,' I said, as she picked up the phone.

'I had the chance of a lift home, and seeing as I'd drunk almost a bottle of champagne it was either that or your spare room.' Grace sounded defensive.

'You sound defensive,' I said, grimacing slightly as the rhubarb wine hit the back of my throat.

'Defensive? Why should I be defensive?'

'Ah ha! *Macbeth* again.'

'Macbeth?'

'Yes, you know – "Methinks the lady doth protesteth too much."'

'It's *Hamlet*. And the actual quote is, "The lady doth protest too much, methinks".'

'And does she?' I asked, ignoring the put-down. I was sure she was wrong anyway.

'Does who do what?'

'Oh stop trying to be clever Grace, and just tell me what you're up to with Enrique.' I was getting thoroughly confused. The rhubarb wine was obviously stronger than I had anticipated.

There was a long pause. 'What do you mean, "up to" exactly?' she finally asked.

'Alright, in plain English, are you anticipating a game of "hide the sausage" with the lovely Sebastian?'

'Hide the *sausage*?' In spite of herself Grace began to laugh. 'Where do you come up with such drivel?'

'Hey, don't get all superior with me, Buster. I'm drinking my dad's rhubarb wine, my daughter on her sixth birthday prefers the company of a squint-eyed dog to her mother, my son is down the garden up to no good with a pair of binoculars, and my husband is bankrupt and in the middle of an affair with your potential lover's mother.' And to my horror I began to cry.

'Hat? Don't! Don't be so bloody silly. I'm sure Nick isn't having an affair with Little Miss Goodness. And as for me and Enrique Iglesias, well both he *and* his sausage are fourteen years younger than me, so I don't think there's anything going on there.'

Ah ha! Wistful, I thought, drunkenly. I can definitely hear wist in her voice.

I sniffed and drank more of the wine. It was nice to think that my dad had lovingly grown what I was now drinking. Probably been peed on by all the local cats though. This thought made me giggle.

'There,' Grace exclaimed, laughing too. 'Told you it was laughable.'

'No, I'm not laughing at that. I'm thinking of the cat pee that must have gone into this wine.'

'Cat pee?'

'So why is it so laughable that my husband is having an affair with Little Miss Goodness?' I demanded, bored of feline urine conversation. 'Don't you think he's good enough for so gorgeous a woman?'

'It's ludicrous because he's never looked at anyone but you. That's why, you ridiculous person.'

'Ha!' I said, triumphantly. 'Isn't that what we said about *your* husband? And look what he was up to, all along.'

'Harriet,' Grace said patiently, 'go and make yourself some

coffee and sober up and then go and talk to Nick, right now.'

'I would,' I said, 'but I think he's laid out, very drunk in the sitting room. Besides which, I think I'm going to be sick.'

And I was. Slamming the phone down, I hotfooted it to the downstairs loo where I was violently ill, retching several times in a way I hadn't since I'd been pregnant with India.

Oh my God. Pregnant? Pregnant! Rinsing my mouth with cold water, I racked my brains as to when I'd last had a period. When Grace had complimented me on the voluptuousness of my boobs in her clingy Max Mara dress on the evening of the Midhope Grammar reunion, I'd just assumed they were as a result of an impending period. And they probably were, I told myself firmly. I'd been sick because I'd eaten very little except potted-meat sandwiches, and drunk Dad's ancient cat-pee wine.

The very thought had me scurrying for the loo once more.

Shaky, but feeling a good deal better, I made my way upstairs. A hot bath and an early night was what I needed. It seemed a very long time since this morning's present opening session.

The daisy-strewn wallpaper that I'd insisted, against all advice, we hang in our bathroom many moons ago had finally given up the will to live. Clouds of pernicious, shower-generated steam had drifted around our bathroom silently over the years, working their insidious way through even the most tenacious roll of wall-hanging, with ruinous results. I'd attempted to patch it up with the children's Pritt sticks and even something from B & Q, but now, as I walked through the door, I was greeted by not one, but two, peeling pieces, arching their backs down the wall in a final dance of death. This was all I needed. Sod it! The drunk downstairs would have to do something about it.

Kit had obviously been the perpetrator of the crime – his abandoned boxers and three-day-old socks testament to the fact that he'd used our bathroom for a too hot and too long shower. Gingerly picking up his different articles of underwear, I threw them into the already overflowing wash basket where they were soon joined by my own.

My breasts, no longer encumbered by my greying M&S bra,

stared back at me from the bathroom mirror. They looked huge, each one veined in a veritable motorway network of blue, resembling nothing more than the colossal Blue Stilton cheese which appeared every Christmas along with the assorted nuts and tangerines.

In the days when we could afford Christmas, of course. As far as I knew we were up to our overdraft limit on our joint account. Things were just so expensive these days and teenaged boys in particular ate so much. It seemed I only just filled the fridge before it was empty once more and Kit was bemoaning the fact that there was nothing to eat. Focusing on the inescapable fact that Christmas was but a mere eight weeks or so away, and that I'd have to do a hell of a lot of carol singing just to buy a turkey, meant I didn't have to acknowledge, for the moment anyway, that my breasts looked very, very pregnant.

Did they have Christmas in the local Poor House, I mused? A vision of me holding India's hand as we struggled through a snowstorm towards a Christmas soup kitchen, Liberty and Kit bringing up the rear with the few possessions we'd managed to hide from the bailiffs, sent two big tears rolling down my cheeks and onto my bosoms which, as I dared to look into the mirror for a second glance, seemed to be inflating and becoming more cheese-like by the minute. Self-pity really had a good grip now as I visualised Nick spending *his* Christmas frolicking in Italy with Amanda while I was forced to protect not only myself and my children but also Sylvia and Bertie from a revenge-seeking David Henderson. Well sod that for a game of soldiers. If Nick was off spending Christmas in Italy with his mistress, he could take his mother and her bloody geriatric dog as well. That would soon cramp his style.

I wallowed in the bath and self-pity for a good half-hour before covering up the evidence of a possible pregnancy with a voluminous, winceyette nightie and, hugging India's Rudolph the Reindeer hot-water bottle, gratefully sank into bed.

I glanced at Granny Morgan's alarm clock, which seemed to have been behaving itself of late. Blimey, nine o'clock already. I knew I should go down the garden and see what Kit and his mates were up to, but the soporific effects of the warm, scented bath together with any alcohol that had evaded being thrown up, meant my eyes were closed within minutes.

A frantic hammering on the front door had me sitting up in bed, my heartbeat echoing the banging from downstairs. Disorientated, I jumped out of bed and, after dashing along the corridor in bare feet, hung over the banister to work out what was going on. The sonorous boom of the grandfather clock at the bottom of the stairs belted out the first of eleven bells, drowning Nick's expletives as he struggled (drunkenly, I presumed) to fit the correct key in the lock in order to open the door and find out what was going on.

'Mr Westmoreland?' A woman's voice, deep and authoritative reached my ears.

'Yes?'

'We have your son here. Kit is it?'

'What do you mean, "You have him here?" He lives here. He's been in the garden shed celebrating his birthday.'

'The shed? Funny place to celebrate a child's birthday isn't it? At eleven o'clock at night?'

Shit, what was going on? Nick didn't sound to be any the wiser despite being one to one with this woman, whoever she was. Going back into the bedroom, I grabbed my dressing gown and ran down the stairs. Nick, dishevelled and bleary-eyed and looking not unlike the *Big Issue* hawkers who regularly patrolled their patches in Midhope Town Centre, was obviously finding it difficult to work out just what was going on.

'Ah, *Mrs* Westmoreland, I presume?' The woman turned her attention from Nick to myself. 'Oh, Harriet? Well I didn't know you lived out here.'

Standing just inside our front door, wrapped up against the late October night's chill in a huge purple parka-type coat, was Barbara Richmond, last seen only two nights previously partying at Midhope Grammar School reunion. What the hell was she doing here? I began to wonder if the rhubarb Dad had grown for his wine had somehow come in contact with those clever little magic mushroom things and I was actually hallucinating.

Alarm bells began to ring as I recalled Sarah's description of her from Friday evening. What was it she'd said Barbara did for a living? Wasn't she head of some police department and was 'always going round bashing down doors?' Good job Nick had opened our front door in time then. The last thing we could afford right now was a new front door.

I realised both Nick and this purple-parka-ed policewoman were looking at me – waiting for a reaction, I presumed.

'What on earth is going on?' I spoke as calmly as possible, fastening my dressing-gown cord tightly around my middle.

'Would it be a good idea if we actually came in?' Barbara asked.

'We? How many of you are there?' I looked towards the still open door, fully expecting the combined might of the Midhope Flying Squad ready to burst forth at any moment.

'There's just myself, and a couple of my men – and the boys, of course. I need to let my DCs get back down there, so could the boys perhaps go and watch some TV or something while the three of us have a chat?' Without waiting for an answer Barbara went back into the garden where she could be heard issuing instructions. She reappeared within seconds, Kit and his five friends in tow.

'What have you been up to?' I hissed, as they stood, shamefaced, their earlier adolescent cockiness and high spirits seemingly evaporated into thin air.

'Shall we go into the kitchen, Harriet?' Barbara indicated the door on the right with a simple movement of her head.

'Harriet, what *is* going on? How do you know this woman?' Nick demanded, obviously still bewildered or drunk. Probably both if the alcohol fumes he'd just breathed into my ear were anything to go by.

'It's my good friend, Barbara Richmond, ex school-colleague and now butch basher down of doors,' I hissed back as Barbara led Nick and me into the kitchen and the boys trooped down to the sitting room.

'Right,' Barbara said, folding her arms and making herself

comfortable as she leaned against the fridge. She's been watching too many cop shows, I thought idly, as Nick and I sat down obediently.

'I assume you know what's been going on down in your valley over the past few months?'

'Going on?' Nick asked, looking at me for help. 'As in – what?'

'As in the area around Butterfield woods?'

'I think you're going to have to help us out here, Barbara,' I said. 'We've no idea what you're talking about.'

Barbara shifted her position slightly – I bet it was bloody cold leaning against that fridge – and, pausing as dramatically as any reality show host about to announce a winner, exhaled deeply before announcing, triumphantly, 'Dogging and Piking.'

Chapter 15

'Dogging and Piking?' I looked helplessly from Barbara's animated face to Nick's bewildered one.

'Dogging and Piking.' Barbara repeated. 'Down in your valley. And your son seems very much involved with it all.'

'Well, I know Kit has always wanted a dog of his own – he says having Bertie in the house doesn't count, being just an excuse for a dog – but piking? He's never shown any interest in *fishing* before. Mind you, he's suddenly become interested in watching herons so maybe he *does* want to be involved with nature a little more. Is fishing against the law then? Or is it that it's late at night and I don't suppose he has a fishing licence?' I tailed off, realising that both Barbara and Nick were looking at me in what I could only describe as utter astonishment.

'Harriet, get a grip.' Nick shook my arm, not overly gently. 'Dogging and Piking is a group sexual deviancy carried out in rural places.'

'What do you mean, a group sexual deviancy?' I was suddenly horrified. What had Kit and his mates been up to?

Barbara sighed, raising her eyebrows at Nick before smiling at me. Very patronising, I thought.

'Harriet, I'm amazed you hadn't heard about this,' she said, walking to the table and sitting on the chair opposite.

'Maybe I've just got too many *other* things on my mind at the moment,' I snapped, glaring at Nick.

'Well, it has been hitting the headlines recently. "Dogging" is when couples drive to a rural place – in this case Butterfield woods and the fields around them – and take part in a sexual activity. If

174

they want others to join in they leave the headlights of their cars on which is an invitation for them to either just watch or actually take part. 'Piking' is the actual watching of people involved in their particular activity.' Barbara sniffed disdainfully. 'Usually couples doing the dogging, while the dirty old men are in the bushes getting their rocks off.'

'Really? How fascinating! And down in Butterfield woods, you say?' I shook my head in astonishment. It never ceased to amaze me what people got up to in their spare time. Come to think of it, it never ceased to amaze me that people actually *had* any spare time.

It suddenly hit me. 'Has this been going on down in the woods for a while?' I asked, remembering Ralph-next-door's sudden appearance from the bushes with his binoculars round his neck.

'Yes, quite a while. When a site becomes too well known, residents begin to complain and the police move in.'

'Ralph certainly wasn't doing much complaining the other night,' I muttered and then immediately wished I hadn't.

'Ralph?' Barbara's eyes gleamed. 'Mr Ralph ...?' and here she broke off while consulting the little notebook she whipped out from her purple parka-pocket.

'Ralph?' Nick asked. 'What's Ralph got to do with it?'

I shrugged my shoulders, refusing to be drawn. I reckoned I had enough problems without having Ralph's incarceration in the local nick on my conscience.

'We have reason to believe that a Mr Ralph Ulysses has been joining in with the *fun*,' Barbara said, sounding like something off CSI, squinting as she attempted to decipher her own notes.

Oh shit. Ralph must have been caught in the bushes again, or even worse with his pants down, given his Christian name to the police and then panicked, coming up with the first name that entered his head for his surname.

'Ulysses?' Nick started laughing in great guffaws, unable to stop even when glared at by DI Richmond.

'Ulysses?' Nick repeated, when he was able to catch his breath. 'Ulysses is Ralph's *cock*.'

Barbara looked mystified. 'Mr Westmoreland, I'm really not

interested in your neighbour's name for his *penis*.' She spat the word with contempt. Of course, she was apparently gay. Probably didn't have a great deal of time for penises, named or otherwise. '*Or* why you should happen to have knowledge of it.'

In turn I began to giggle, which set Nick off once more. There we sat, me in my winceyette nightie and Nick, looking like the recovering drunk that he was, giggling helplessly, tears rolling down our cheeks.

'I don't believe either of you are taking this very seriously,' Barbara snapped. 'Your son could be in a great deal of trouble. How come he was out on his own at eleven o'clock at night, a spectator of sexual deviancy, while you two seemed totally unaware of his whereabouts?'

That sobered us both up somewhat. What dreadful parents we were. Both spark out after consuming too much alcohol, while a gang of sexual deviants was seducing our only son. How was I going to explain this to the other boys' parents? They'd allowed their sons to come round, thinking they were partaking in an innocent potted-meat sandwich party, with perhaps a game of Trivial Pursuit thrown in. And then look what happens. While the birthday boy's drink-sodden parents sleep off their excesses, their vulnerable adolescents are abroad, out of control and in extreme moral, if not mortal, danger.

'Where exactly was Kit when you found him, and what was he doing?' Nick now asked.

It was Barbara's turn to look a little uncomfortable. 'They were all in your garden.'

'Our garden?' Nick and I looked at each other.

'Not down in the woods then?' I asked. 'Not actually taking part in any of this – what do you call it – *Dogging?*'

'They had a pair of binoculars,' she said defensively.

'Yes, but how did you know they were in our garden?' Nick asked. '*We* knew they were there because we'd actually given them permission to have a bit of a party in our new potting shed. Granted they were out longer than they should have been, but I don't believe it's a crime for fourteen year olds to be in a garden shed with pizza and a crate of coke when there's no school in the morning because of half term?'

'And a pair of binoculars,' Barbara insisted. 'What do you think they were up to with those?'

'Well, why don't we ask them?' Nick asked, calmly. He'd obviously sobered up and was thinking rationally. 'But before we do, can I just ask again how you knew they were there?'

'Mr Westmoreland, there are occasions, like tonight, when we in the Crime Squad have to find a suitable vantage point to carry out our surveillance operations. We need to be near enough to log number plates. We can then make a very unwelcome visit to these people's homes. It's amazing how many wives are totally unaware of their husband's new hobby of walking in natural beauty spots at ten o'clock at night.'

'So our garden happened to be a natural vantage point? And let me guess, when you staked your claim to our garden – without asking our permission – the last thing you expected to find was a bunch of giggling, teenaged boys?'

'We needed them out of the way. Their flashlights were very distracting.'

'So you frightened them half to death by arresting them?' Nick remained calm, but a muscle was twitching in his cheek, and his fingers were beginning to drum the wooden table.

'Mr Westmoreland, we haven't actually *arrested* them,' Barbara tutted, obviously exasperated by Nick's last comment, 'though maybe we did come on a bit strong. However, I certainly wouldn't want a child of mine anywhere near those perverts.'

'As neither would we,' Nick agreed. 'Let's have them in and see what they have to say for themselves.'

All six boys, looking pale and terribly young, shuffled into the kitchen, lining up in front of us as if summoned to their headmaster's office. All refused to meet our eyes, preferring to look at the floor, which, I noticed, needed a good clean after India's party.

'Kit,' I said, feeling terribly sorry for him, 'did you all know what was going on down in Butterfield woods? Is that why you wanted the binoculars?'

Kit nodded. 'Sam Sheridon at school said he'd heard there was this thing going on in the woods near our house. So we just thought we'd take the binoculars and have a look for ourselves. We didn't really see anything. Just a couple of cars driving up the lane in front of the woods, and some headlights flashing. Then the next thing we knew we were being pounced on by *her*'– Kit acknowledged Barbara's presence with a slight nod of his head – 'and a couple of others. She gave us the right willies sneaking up behind us and jumping on us like she did.'

Hmm. A rather unfortunate turn of phrase, given the circumstances.

'Kit, we were on a surveillance operation. Trying to locate these people without being seen ourselves. Your flashlights and giggling didn't really help.'

'Isn't it trespass going into people's gardens without permission?' I asked.

'No such thing,' snapped Barbara rudely. 'If we'd started knocking on your door, actually asking your permission, you may have been able to warn these people we were trying to watch.'

'Like we know a whole load of people who spend their Sunday evenings shivering in their pants in the woods?'

This was getting silly and I'd had enough. People *we* know tend to spend their Sunday evenings scrubbing mountains of fat-encrusted roasting pans that have been soaking in the sink since lunch time in the hope that someone will eventually get round to actually washing them. People *we* know spend Sunday evenings sewing on the name-tapes that should have been done months ago because there is a kit inspection at their offspring's school the next day, before trying to work out their children's maths' homework that should have been handed in before the weekend.

'You know this Ralph Ulysses,' Barbara said, with some degree of triumph. 'You'd have been able to warn him.'

Nick rubbed his hands over his eyes. They were hollow with tiredness. 'Look, I assume you've finished with the boys? We'd all quite like to get to bed now.'

Barbara glanced at her wristwatch, a huge, very masculine model, and nodded. 'I'll be off then. See what's happening down the road.' Turning to the boys who appeared to be relaxing somewhat, and were even managing to give each other knowing looks and little surreptitious grins she added, 'Make sure you behave yourselves, boys. This really could have turned out very unpleasant.' She turned up the collar of her huge padded coat and headed for the door.

'Well, Harriet, I don't see you for almost twenty-five years and then bump into you twice in one weekend,' Barbara said as I opened the front door for her. It was really quite nippy out there; how anyone could even contemplate flashing their bits and pieces in zero temperatures such as these was beyond me.

'Amazing, isn't it?' I trilled, trying to get her through the door. If I remembered rightly, I hadn't liked her much when we were at school. I certainly wasn't overly enamoured with her now. It wouldn't surprise me if it had been her who had shopped us to Amanda all those years ago in the games shed. Getting in some practice for when she was head of the Crime Squad or whatever it was she was now jack-booting about in.

Barbara laid a leather-gloved hand on my arm. 'You know, Harriet, if you ever need someone to talk to about anything, anything at all, just give me a ring down at the station.' She handed me her card and headed into the night.

'I'll do that Barbara,' I called after her. 'No problem. Off you go, now, and catch some more perverts.'

I closed the door behind her, locked it and leaned heavily against it for several seconds gathering my thoughts and strength before going back to the kitchen to see the boys.

The penitent looks had all but disappeared in the atmosphere of relief and cocky bravado that now permeated the kitchen. Nick and the boys, all suddenly lads together in an accepted male complicity, were drinking hot chocolate and eating the remains of India's birthday cake.

'Why didn't I get a birthday cake this year, Mum?' Kit asked through a mouthful of Bratz-tattooed sugar paste.

Guilt at having forgotten to buy him one, let alone design and actually make one, made my retort sharper than was necessary. 'It's not your actual birthday until tomorrow, Kit, and from what you've been up to this evening, I would have thought you felt yourself far too advanced in years to want a birthday cake.'

'Come on, guys, bed,' Nick said. 'It's all over and done with now. It's up to you what you tell your parents about this – if anything. Harriet and I ...' and here Nick gave me a warning glance, 'won't mention anything to them.'

They all trooped out, making their way to the camp beds and sleeping bags that had been organised in Kit's bedroom earlier in the day. The atmosphere in the morning after six triumphantly flatulent fourteen-year-old boys, together with their assorted trainers and socks, had spent the night in there didn't bear thinking about.

Kit, ensuring he was the last one out of the kitchen, hugged me fiercely. 'Sorry about all this, Mum. Love you,' he whispered before going up to join the others.

Ah! Still my beautiful boy, then!

'I'm off up too,' Nick said, not meeting my eyes, as I made to collect the abandoned hot chocolate mugs. Birthday cake crumbs lay resplendent on the floor as well as on the table. The tiny field mouse that Bones was too fat and idle to even flirt with, let alone play with and kill, would be able to fill its little boots.

'If field mice have boots,' I muttered, skirting past Nick and heading for upstairs.

'Sorry, did you say something?' Nick asked politely.

'No,' I sighed, 'not a word'.

Chapter 16

Both Nick and I were obviously in need of sleep. We politely kept to our own sides of the bed and, despite the rain lashing down outside, slept like babies. I've never understood that turn of phrase – 'slept like a baby': any babies I've ever known have categorically not slept.

The next morning, the first day of the half-term holiday, I woke early out of habit then, realising I didn't need to get up, turned over, luxuriating in the knowledge that I could go back to sleep for an hour or so. Both Liberty and India weren't at home of course, and I doubted whether I'd see any signs of the boys before midday.

Nick emerged from the en-suite bathroom, towelling dry his hair while looking down across the wet garden at something that had obviously caught his eye. His back, towards me, was still tanned and I watched the movement of his muscles as he continued to rub his hair. I don't think there'd ever been a time since that very first morning at his student house when I hadn't desired him, hadn't wanted to be a part of him. A simple, unconscious movement of his broad, toned shoulders was enough to make me want to catch my fingers in the thick hair at the nape of his neck and bury my nose in it.

And I'd thought he'd always want *me*. Never thought there'd come a time when I'd have to feign sleep so as not to risk being turned down by Nick. There was a time – in fact when *wasn't* there a time? – when we couldn't get enough of each other.

Nick was only my third lover. There'd been the quick, disappointing 'thank god I've finally done it, but what was all the fuss about?' fumble in the Upper Sixth with a boy from the boys' grammar school. Then, of course, there was Michael, my boyfriend before Nick. He was quite a few years older than me, gave me my first orgasm, and was more than willing to allow me to practise a variety of techniques Grace had already tried and recommended.

But with Nick it was Martini time –'anytime, anyplace, anywhere' – *all* the time. Each time I was invited down to Surrey to stay with Nick at his parents' house before we were married became a mind-boggling feat of opportunistic sex under Sylvia's ever-watchful eye. I would sit, politely talking to my future mother-in-law at the Westmoreland's dining table, while Nick, lounging opposite me, would inch his foot up my bare leg until his toe made contact with my knickers. He became adept at very gently shifting the flimsy lace of the crotch to one side and, while apparently deep in conversation with other guests, circle the fleshy pad of his toe against me until I almost came under cover of the white, starched tablecloth and the debris of a Sunday lunch abandoned in Sylvia's prized Wedgwood dinner service.

Every morning, once I'd unofficially left my shared student house and moved in with Nick, was a race against time to get to lectures.

'Come *on*.' I'd say, slapping Nick's groping hand and heading for the shower. 'I've been late for lectures every day this week.'

'What about this?' Nick would beseech, his chocolate-brown eyes indicating something standing to attention under the duvet.

'No time for that now. Put it away please.' This in my best teacher's voice.

'But I can't possibly get dressed with *this* in the way. And it *is* your fault, you know. You are soooo gorgeous.'

I would hesitate, weaken, glance at my watch and then reach under the duvet. And I was never disappointed. His penis, thick and silky would be at a one hundred and eighty degree angle (amazing how young rampant males manage such a mathematical feat) against his stomach and I would be lost once more.

When I took Nick home with me to Yorkshire for the first time he insisted on walking the purple moorland that stretches for miles at either side of the highest point of the M62.

'But you said you fancied a hike,' I remonstrated as he immediately tumbled me into the heather, his erection nudging my thigh, eager for release.

Nick had laughed, reaching under my skirt. 'You fell for that one didn't you? The only thing taking a hike is your knickers.' And with one fluid movement they were off and sailing through the air towards the distant sheep. For years after, Nick said he was unable to drive on the M62 past that particular bit of moorland without the stirrings of an erection as he recalled my legs, wrapped around his waist, urging him to go faster and faster.

And now here I was, pretending sleep, continuing to watch him through half-closed eyes while he dressed. I assumed he would don jeans and a sweater prior to his spending another day at his laptop, but he moved to the wardrobe bringing out a navy suit which he lay on a chair before buttoning himself into a shirt the colour of Amanda's eyes. His tie, maroon silk, was one I'd chosen myself for his last birthday.

Curiosity got the better of me and I yawned, shifting slightly before sitting up, not wanting him to know I'd been awake and watching him while he dressed.

'Where are you off to?' I asked.

'Got a meeting with David Henderson and a couple of his financial people in Leeds.'

'You didn't say.'

'You didn't ask.' Nick smiled but his tone was bleak.

'I just did,' I said indignantly. Why was *he* taking his bat home? It was me who'd been left once more to sort out the kids yesterday while he'd hotfooted it upstairs with Little Miss Goodness.

'Whatever,' Nick sighed, distancing himself from further questioning with a single word. 'I've several things to do in Leeds, and I'm probably going to have to drive over to Manchester as well later on, so I don't know what time I'll be back.'

'So is Mandy going with you as well?' I couldn't resist it. The desire to know what she was up to was becoming, I realised, compulsive.

'No, Harriet, Mandy's essential knowledge of Italy and all things Italian won't be needed either in Yorkshire or, if I do go to Manchester, Lancashire. As far as I recall they speak, albeit rather strangely I grant you, English in both those counties.'

Pompous or what? If he didn't like living in the North, he could jolly well sod off back down the M1 where he came from. He was beginning to sound just like his father.

'You do know that Mandy still sees John, don't you?' John had sworn me to secrecy, but I'd already spilled the beans to Di. Damage done, I reckoned.

'Sorry?' Nick adjusted his tie in the mirror, bending slightly to accommodate his upper body and ran his fingers through his hair.

'Mandy? And John? He came round to see me when you were in Italy, absolutely distraught that you were in cahoots with the Hendersons. He's still seeing her, you know.'

'What?' That had obviously got his attention. 'Well, that's all I sodding need. My brother-in-law still having a thing with my boss's wife. What's the matter with him? Is he out to wreck this deal of mine? You just tell him to back off, Harriet, because if you don't, I certainly will' and without a backward glance he turned on his heel, slamming the bedroom door behind him.

I lay there, my stomach churning. Had Nick's reaction been a result of worry over David Henderson throwing in the towel if he were to become aware of Nick's relationship with my brother, or was it the fact that Nick couldn't cope with John's continuing involvement with the woman with whom he himself was now in love?

Sighing loudly, I pulled the covers right up over my head and tried to get back to sleep but I knew I was going to have to face the world sooner or later. And I didn't want to: it was pouring down outside, I had six adolescent boys to sort out, and if I didn't go down to Sainsbury's and buy myself a pregnancy test in order to set my mind at rest that I wasn't up the duff, I'd be unable to enjoy any of the days ahead.

Maybe my period had actually started and I'd be able to save the tenner or however much the little blue packs cost these days.

Jumping out of bed, I had a furtive grope of my bosoms as I made my way to the bathroom. Mmm, still rock hard, but then they were always like that in the days before I actually started bleeding.

Finding no evidence to assure me that a trip to Sainsbury's wasn't necessary, I quickly showered and pulled on jeans and sweatshirt. At least I didn't feel sick any more. Feeling, instead, more confident, I crossed over to Kit's room and opened the door slightly in order to work out the state of play amongst last night's Peeping Toms. Greeted by six inert, sleeping-bagged hummocks and the all-consuming fug of boy combined with enough cheap aftershave to overcome a Parisian whore's bathmat, I hastily withdrew and went downstairs.

Crossing the sitting room and making my way over to Sylvia's flat, I found India already up and breakfasted, but still in pyjamas, intent on making a papier mâché witch's mask in preparation for Hallowe'en. Bertie sat at her side, wheezing asthmatically, surrounded by torn pieces of soggy flour-and-water-pasted newsprint.

'Hi, you two. I'm just dashing down to Sainsbury's before it gets too busy. Do you want anything, Sylvia?'

'That's very kind, dear. Could you get me a couple of packets of Bath Olivers? I seem to have run out. What was all the commotion about last night?' Sylvia peered over her glasses, fixing me with an intent stare.

'Commotion?' I glanced over at India's bent head, her tongue protruding slightly as she concentrated on building up the cohesive layers. The last thing I wanted was her overhearing and then relaying how Mummy and Daddy and *all* of Kit's friends had spent last Sunday evening involved in something called 'Dogging and Piking' when asked to write down the events of the half-term holiday in her Monday Morning Diary.

Looking meaningfully at India and her apparent lack of interest in Sylvia's question, but knowing, from experience, that she was taking it all in, I answered, 'I'll tell you later. Little pigs etc.'

'I'm not a little pig,' India retorted indignantly, looking up from her task and catching Bertie's ear with her glue stick while confirming, by her reaction, my good sense in not telling Sylvia of last night's little debacle just at that moment.

Praying that my latest salary cheque had not only been paid into my account but that its contents were still in situ, I headed for the town centre. At ten in the morning Sainsbury's was already a haven for mothers and childminders harassed by the first few hours of a wet half-term Monday. The florid orange and black glow emanating from the multitudinous Hallowe'en pumpkins and plastic witches displayed in the entrance to the store demonstrated the vulgar commercialism of this heathen celebration. In my day it had been an unyielding swede from Dad's allotment that had had its innards gouged out to make a lantern and which we'd carried round while indulging in nothing more daring than smearing treacle on door handles. Now, influenced as ever by what was happening in the USA, not only had Mischief Night been shoved out of the way by 'Trick or Treating,' the humble swede had been unseated, superseded by the larger, fleshier pumpkin.

I made the decision to do my other shopping before making my way to the pharmacy department, but halfway round the store realised I needed a pee. Oh hell. Was this a result of the butterflies in my tummy that were going into overdrive as I approached the aisle which boasted an amazing, but thoroughly confusing, medley of pregnancy-testing gadgets? Or was it, God forbid, another little sneaky sign of pregnancy?

Parking my trolley outside the ladies' loo, I opened the door to find a woman struggling with a furious toddler as she tried, without much success, to disrobe him of his little blue and white striped OshKosh dungarees in order to change his very stinky nappy.

Under normal circumstances I would have given her a little smile of sympathy, uttered a couple of words of encouragement or even offered a helping hand, but today, faced with what was, in effect, a manifestation of my very worst nightmare, I hastened into the nearest loo without a word.

Shaken, I grabbed the trolley, made my way straight back to the aisle I'd just left and, snatching the nearest package without regard to its cost or percentage reliability, shoved it under the pack of frozen peas I'd picked up earlier. In the checkout queue I had the sudden thought that the Arctic conditions of the peas might possibly hamper the chemical reaction in the test and hastily withdrew it, looking for a more suitable hiding place. This was getting ridiculous. I was acting like a fifteen year old, not a mature, married woman of nearly forty. Mind you, I seemed to be acting less and less like a mature woman of any age these days.

Once on the moving belt, the copy of the *Daily Telegraph* I'd used in place of the frozen peas sailed unhindered towards the checkout guy, leaving the rectangular blue box gaily adrift on an open sea of black rubber. Red-faced, I shoved it once more under the newspaper, meeting the amused, appraising glance of Sam Bolton's mother as I did so. Sam had been in my class last year and, on the few occasions I'd met his mother, had always got on well with her.

'For my neighbour,' I mouthed across to the parallel checkout where both Sam and Angela Bolton waited patiently for their turn with the checkout girl.

'Absolutely,' she mouthed back. Sam, wondering to whom his mother was miming her response, glanced in my direction, before turning the same colour I'd flushed earlier. Strange how children can be perfectly at ease with their teacher in the school environment, but place them in a situation where they don't expect said teacher to be, and they instantly clam up, embarrassed at seeing them in the real world, as real people.

The checkout guy, a young, bored student obviously working off his loans debt, had no interest in either me or my blue box and, thanking God (and the local education authority) that my October salary cheque had obviously gone into my account, I was able to make good my escape while Sam and his mother were still packing their orange plastic carrier bags.

Driving home, my stomach a tight knot, I suddenly remembered Diana and Dad's appointment with Mum's GP later on that day and felt myself tense further. I seemed to have more plots and subplots in my life than an omnibus edition of '*EastEnders*'.

Stuck in a traffic jam, the cause of which I couldn't work out, I drummed my fingers on the steering wheel, making a mental list, in no particular chronological order of what was making me feel so uptight:

1. We're broke and more than likely getting broker.
2. My son is a Peeping Tom.
3. My neighbour is a Peeping Tom. (Do I really care?)
4. My husband is very probably being seduced by another, very glamorous, very rich woman. Will rich woman's husband execute revenge on *my* husband, making him forfeit all of Sylvia's money?
5. Worse still – maybe it's my husband doing the seducing. Oh shit! Double revenge.
6. My best friend is possibly up to no good with my husband's new boss's very young son.
7. Will husband's boss and boss's wife want revenge on best friend and best friend's family for possible deflowering of said son? (Scrub that about the deflowering – no way on this planet was a gorgeous sex god like Sebastian a virgin.)
8. Will resulting revenge mean we have to sell house and live in council-supplied Bed and Breakfast with a geriatric Granny and decrepit dachshund?
9. What about poor old Mum? Who will look after her? And Dad?
10. Is Margaret Walker's daughter pregnant? (No scrap that one too. I really don't *care*. Not my problem even if said daughter was fertilised on my Persian rug.)
11. OK. Let's go for the biggy I've been leaving until last. Never mind Jennifer Walker. Am *I* pregnant and what the fuck do I do if I am?

A sharp but insistent blast of a horn from the car behind brought me out of my preoccupation with unsolved problems and, realising that the gridlock had miraculously sorted itself, I put the car into gear, pulled out into the fast lane and headed for home. The little blue pregnancy-test packet sat innocently in the Sainsbury's bag on the passenger seat next to me, waiting to be opened. Like Pandora's box, it was an inconsequential piece of nothing: an irrelevance until opened and utilised. God knows what it would reveal once I'd plucked up the courage to release its contents.

Once home, I hid the blue box in my handbag and hoisted the rest of the shopping into the kitchen where a mountain of breakfast debris assured me that at least Kit and his friends were up and about even if they had assumed the maid would clear up after them.

A note from Grace on the kitchen table reminded me that she'd collected India from Sylvia's part of the house and taken her, as arranged, for a birthday treat of cinema, shopping at Claire's Accessories, and lunch at McDonald's. Goodness, I'd been so preoccupied with other things I'd totally forgotten what had now become an annual tradition on Grace's part. She took each of my children out for their birthday, letting them choose where they would like to go. Over the years she'd done everything from Manchester United to ice wall climbing. The only time I'd seen her lose her composure was when a pre-pubescent Liberty, obsessed with all things equine, had begged to be taken on a day's pony trekking across the Moors. They'd returned with Libby even more desperate to own a horse of her own while Grace, saddle-sore, bow-legged and sneezing from a newly acquired allergy to horsehair wheezed that she'd never again get on a horse as long as she lived. 'Have you seen how big the bloody things are?' she'd asked. Never again. I tell you now Harriet. Never again!'

The steady thump of a bass guitar, fairly faint but nevertheless as insistent as a Chinese water torture, drifted down from the direction of Kit's room echoing the rhythmic pulse that was beginning just above my right eye. Brilliant! For once I welcomed the headache that monthly proclaimed the imminent arrival of my period. I'd go upstairs right now with Pandora's pregnancy box and put my mind at rest once and for all.

'What's for lunch, Mum?' Kit, racing through the kitchen,

stopped momentarily.

'Lunch? Haven't you just had breakfast?'

Kit looked at his watch. 'That was over an hour ago. We're starving.'

'Well you'll just have to starve. I've got a few things to do before I even think about food. What are you all doing anyway?' I glanced over to where Kit was helping himself to an apple that even I had to admit had seen better days.

'Setting challenges,' he said, through a mouthful of apple.

'Challenges? What sort of challenges?'

'Oh you know, can you "down a bottle of vodka in half an hour?" sort of thing.' And then, seeing my face, laughed, 'Kidd-ing! We haven't got any vodka. So, once I've eaten this –' Kit looked at the apple in his hand – 'prune, I've got to go back in there and do fifty sit-ups in a minute.'

'Bit juvenile isn't it, compared to what you were up to last night?'

Colouring slightly, Kit sighed and said, 'That's tight! I knew you'd go on and on about it.'

'Have I said a word?' I said, throwing up my hands in protest.

'Yeah, you just did.'

Ignoring this, I said, 'Why don't you all go outside for a bit. Kick a ball or something?' 'It's pouring down out there.' Kit nodded towards the garden before tossing his apple core into the bin.

'You big girl's blouse,' I jeered. 'When I was your age I was out chumping during the October half-term holiday whatever the weather. Going off on raiding trips and seeing off the marauding enemy.'

'Sounds like the bloody Vikings. Mind you, I suppose you're old enough to be a Viking.' And he was off.

Clutching my handbag to my chest, I hurried up to our bathroom, locked the door and without further ado attempted to divest the box of its cellophane wrapper. Jesus, I could have given birth and had it potty-trained in the time it took me to wrestle this off. I didn't even bother reading the bumph. I knew the procedure: pants down, pee and pray.

Unlocking the bathroom door, I carried the stick over to our bed, laid it on the bedside table and, with myself prone on top of the duvet, steadfastly refused to acknowledge its presence until the allotted four minutes were up.

'Oh Fuck! Oh Fuck! Oh My Godohmygodohmygod! No! No! No! FUCK!'

Hugh Grant's ranting in the opening scene of *Four Weddings and a Funeral* had nothing on me as I clutched the smug-looking stick in one hand and attempted to beat the living daylights out of Nick's pillow with the other.

Nothing could have prepared me for this. I really *hadn't* expected the blue line of success to be standing smartly to attention in the second little window. I'd only done the test to put my mind at rest so that I could relax and enjoy my half-term holiday. This was a disaster; the worst thing that could have happened, our situation being what it was. There was no way on this planet that I could have another baby even if I'd wanted one, which I most certainly didn't. If *I* didn't work, *we* didn't eat; *we* didn't have a roof over our heads. Nick had thrown in his job, borrowed half of his mother's entire savings to line the pockets of the already loaded Hendersons on a whim. And now this.

Fury at Nick's stupidity welled up in me like a tsunami and came crashing down with another foul-mouthed invective.

'You stupid man. You stupid, fucking, idiotic *man.*'

I think I'd have probably carried on blaspheming and berating my absent husband indefinitely had not a slight scratching movement under the bed brought me up short. Jesus, did we have *rats* now as well?

Cautiously I lifted the edge of the duvet away from its resting place on the floor and peered warily under the bed.

'Hi Mrs Westmoreland.' Richard, the relatively new friend of Kit's whom I'd met for the first time only yesterday, crawled out from the dusty nether regions of my bed. 'I think I must have won the challenge to "disappear for a minute." Is it time for lunch yet?'

Following Richard down the stairs, I suddenly recalled the one thing that was left in   Pandora's Box once she'd unwittingly released the Evils of the World to all four corners of the earth. 'Hope' may have resided in *Pandora's* box, but there was a distinct absence of its presence in the slim, rectangular receptacle now shoved under my knickers at the back of my underwear drawer.

Chapter 17

I know, I know. You're asking, 'How does a thirty-eight-year-old woman whose family is complete and who, because of her financial circumstances, *cannot possibly* have another baby end up pregnant?'

Well the thing is, I'd not used any regular form of contraception since Kit was a young child. Before you all faint clean away, I have to say that I am one of those incredibly lucky women whose body is, and always has been, regular as clockwork. I have my period every twenty-eight days and I know exactly when I'm ovulating. I'm aware of when I'm at my most fertile and just avoid sex on those days of the month. Gynaecology fascinates me – when I was pregnant with India I was actually asked by my consultant if I was 'in the business', I appeared to know so much about my own reproductive bits and pieces.

It wasn't my intention to eschew all forms of contraception, but after years of trying every conceivable – perhaps *in*conceivable would be more appropriate – form of birth control I finally threw in the towel with the goddam lot of it.

I was fine with the pill until after Kit was born and then for some reason my own hormones seemed intent on doing battle with the chemical ones, regardless of the different types of pill my GP prescribed. The resulting acne, mood swings and loss of libido had Nick throwing the lot in the bin, saying he'd rather be celibate for the rest of his life than face this snarling Rottweiler just one more time across the breakfast table.

I went to have a Dutch cap fitted, and the doctor at the Family Planning Clinic – an imposing, and obviously over-worked young woman – offhandedly demonstrated the action needed to insert the appliance and then withdrew from the cubicle in order to let me try it for myself. Squatting on the floor, my skirt hitched up around my backside, I squeezed the cap into the required figure of eight shape whereupon the slippery little sucker flew out of my hand and over the cubicle door landing neatly at the feet of several women whose turn was still to come.

My giggles, as I emerged red-faced from the cubicle, could not be controlled even by a hard look from Dr Patel and, embarrassed by my typically juvenile reaction to anything funny, I beat a hasty retreat out of there, no further on in my quest for the perfect contraception.

The intrauterine coil I wouldn't even entertain after Diana passed out with the sheer pain of having one inserted, and as for the Femidon – well what woman wants to inflate a balloon inside themselves before making love?

Once I'd come to the conclusion that, with a bit of restraint on occasions, I could be a contraception-free zone, it all worked perfectly well. When, with Nick's business doing brilliantly, we decided we'd try for a third child we just reversed our game plan and, hey presto, within a month I was pregnant again. Not with India however. Between Kit and my youngest child there were two more pregnancies – both where the foetus never really got going. Something called 'blighted ovum' on both occasions. The experience of these two, both very early, miscarriages made me desperate for a baby that would go full term. My body didn't let me down again: India was born, perfect, arriving two weeks late as if making up for the babies I'd lost so early in their formation.

Now, after years of playing what I considered to be a foolproof version of Russian Roulette, here I was up the proverbial creek without a paddle, and all I could think of was Grace. Grace, who would give her right arm – probably her left as well – to be pregnant. How could I possibly tell Grace that I was having a baby and that I wasn't going to keep it?

Switching to auto-pilot I fed bread into the toaster and heated up a veritable mountain of baked beans for Kit and his friends hearing, but not listening to, their fourteen-year-old banter as they sat at the kitchen table awaiting food.

'You alright, Mum?' Liberty, home from her sleepover, dropped her bag by the kitchen door and joined me at the hob.

'Umm? Alright? Yes, fine why shouldn't I be?'

'Well those beans will be dizzy if you stir them any longer.'

Beaten almost to a pulp, the beans could have passed for tomato soup. I hastily buttered the last of the toast, added the liquidised beans and handed them to Liberty who, for once, didn't seem averse to serving her brother and his mates.

By the time the boys had eaten, various mothers and grannies had arrived to carry them home and I offloaded them thankfully into the cars parked on the drive. The need to erase every toast crumb, every squashed baked bean, and every smear no matter how tiny from my granite kitchen surfaces was frantic. I swept, washed and polished with increasing circles until I was exhausted. Anything to take my mind off this new problem I'd just added to my apparently ever-increasing repertoire.

Desperate for some peace and quiet, I walked down the garden to the potting shed. Abandoned pizza cartons and coke cans from Kit's little supper party lay in the middle of the floor, but apart from that, the place was neat and welcoming. Bill, the electrician from Wells Trading, had been as good as his word and had spent all morning bringing power to the shed. He nodded, but said nothing as he drove home the final couple of screws into the sole power point on the wall. I didn't dare ask who was paying his bill – I certainly couldn't – and just prayed that it was being covered in the insurance pay out.

Determined to stamp my authority on the place, I went back indoors and up to the attic that Nick had christened Death Row – anything incarcerated up there was fated never to see the light of day again. After much rummaging under the dusty beams, I found what I was looking for: a couple of rugs and a squashy settee that had been booted up there soon after we bought the house. It certainly smelt a bit, and tufts of brown innards resembling the ear of a particularly hairy mammal sprouted from its top corner, but I knew this settee to be one of the most comfortable I'd ever lain down on and I wanted it for my shed.

When pregnant with Liberty, Kit and, particularly after the two miscarriages, with India, I'd studiously avoided doing anything strenuous but, as I certainly hadn't come to terms with the fact that I *was* actually pregnant, and perhaps even subconsciously saw the humping of a settee down the steps single-handed as a means of *not* being pregnant, I manoeuvred it to the top of the flight of steps and blithely launched it downhill.

'I name this sofa, "The Hairy Mammal," I intoned in what I felt to be a particularly good impression of the Queen. 'May God bless her and all who sit on her.'

'For God's sake, Mum. What the hell are you doing?' Both Liberty and Kit dashed from their respective rooms on the first floor as the settee shot down the uncarpeted wooden stairs amazingly quickly.

'Getting in some practice for when I'm Queen,' I said, following the settee down the steps. 'Like greased-lightening,' I added with satisfaction.

'What are you *doing?* Liberty repeated, looking with some disdain at both the 'hairy mammal,' which had lodged itself at an acute angle at the bottom of the attic steps, and my cobweb-embellished hair and clothes.

With both kids press-ganged into service as removal men, I soon had the few bits and pieces I required in situ in the shed. A couple of throws and some rather moth-eaten cushions were draped artistically over the 'hairy mammal' which, in turn, presided over a low table bearing books I'd been meaning to read for ages, and magazines.

I plugged in the old filter-coffee machine I'd had since my student days and which I'd ferreted out from behind the Christmas decorations in the attic, and was delighted when its red light instantly glowed as I flicked the switch.

'So, lass, is this place for t'tools or for thissen?' Bill, gathering his own tools and bits of wire, glanced round doubtfully as I stretched out on the 'hairy mammal' and gazed down the valley at the same view I'd made my own when I was in what was now Sylvia's flat.

'For missen, Bill. Definitely for missen.'

There was no way I dared send our already astronomical electricity bill soaring by bringing down the little electric fire we sometimes used on chilly summer evenings, but wrapped in Nick's old ski jacket and with my Ugg boots keeping my feet cosy, I lay under the bright-green duvet cover, clasped my cup of coffee with gloved hands and closed my eyes on the world.

How did one go about terminating an unwanted pregnancy? I supposed I'd have to throw myself on my doctor's mercy and plead insanity. Wasn't that what Nuala had done when, in the first year of university, she'd found herself pregnant after a one-night stand with the president of the Student Union on the last night of Rag Week?

I tried to look at the problem calmly and logically. Could I have this baby, take maternity leave from school, and then be back earning our daily bread within a couple of months? I'd taken maternity leave after having Liberty, and returning to school after six months had almost killed me. I'd hated leaving her at the nursery, just down the road from my school at the time. I was still breastfeeding and I would dash to feed her in my lunch break, watching the clock in panic and then have to go through the misery of leaving her for the second time as I returned to the particularly large and unruly class I'd inherited from the old dear who had been brought out of mothballs to cover my maternity leave.

Those six months I endured in a no man's land of being neither a good teacher nor good mother shook my naïve belief that a woman was her own person and could have it all. Some women maybe, but I certainly couldn't – and mine was a job, with its relatively short days and long holidays, that was geared to doing both. The one thing that I hadn't realised was, that in having a baby, I was *not* my own person. I was the willing slave of this little bundle of humanity, and I resented every minute I was away from her.

Luckily for me The Pennine Clothing Company had been going from strength to strength, and once Nick, at the age of just twenty-four, was able to get his head round the fact that he was responsible not just for himself but a wife, a baby and a rapidly expanding company, he was more than happy for me to quit work and be a stay-at-home mum. And how I loved it. Liberty went from being a fairly scratchy baby to being a smiley, contented one; the home-made flapjack tin overflowed and all was well with the world.

I felt myself in danger of having a little snivel as I pulled the green duvet cover up to my chin and drained the last of my now cold coffee, and played the dangerous game of 'if only'. If only Nick's company hadn't gone to the wall there would have been no problem in my having another baby. For heaven's sake, a lot of women were just *starting* their family at my age. I allowed myself to think about the option that up until now I had denied myself – that of actually having this baby. My heart gave a little leap and I unconsciously moved my hand further down the duvet to my stomach and stroked it protectively. What would I want: another son like my beautiful boy or a third girl? I really didn't have a preference.

Having grown up with no brothers my own age – John, after all, was seven years older than me – I hadn't known much about boys. Diana and I had done everything together: played hopscotch on the street, dressed up in Mum's ancient 1950s dirndl skirts with their net underskirts, and designed and made clothes for our dolls. We'd sit for hours cutting out and stitching by hand tiny garments for our Barbie and Sindy dolls, always delighted to receive bagfuls of material from Dad's two sisters who were both competent dressmakers. My Uncle Ted, the undertaker husband of Dad's sister Audrey, once dropped off a load of beautiful satin offcuts for Diana and me and we pounced on them with joy, revelling in the sensual silkiness of the fabric as it slipped through our fingers. Granny Morgan wasn't as impressed. We'd taken the satin with us when we were staying round at her house one night and she'd shrieked in horror at the sight of it.

'That's for lining coffins,' she'd shuddered, as if having the stuff in her house meant she was next in line for one of her own. She made us leave it outside the porch at the back, refusing to have it in the house.

My formative years, then, were necessarily girly and I dreamed of one day having a little girl of my own: she'd be called April and have two long, blonde plaits down her back just like the golden-haired doll I'd been given one Christmas and whose hair I was constantly plaiting and braiding.

Pregnant at twenty-three, very happily, I'd crossed my fingers constantly that the baby would be a girl. After all, what did I know of little boys, and the intricacies of Meccano and Lego? Now, fifteen years on and thinking back to those glory days, I closed my eyes, marvelling at the fact that my only worries then were about the child's *gender*.

I took my hand away from its resting place on my tummy where it had been making its first tentative contact with the baby and gave myself a shake, distancing myself from the life that was growing inside me. This would not do. I could not see this pregnancy through to its natural conclusion. Even if Nick hadn't thrown in the towel at Wells Trading to set off on this hare-brained scheme of Henderson's, I still didn't see how we were in any position to have another child. If I were knackered *now* at the end of a day's teaching, what would I be like after having been awake several times in the night with a fretful baby? I'd found it almost impossible to work and bring up a child fifteen years ago. How could I possibly do it now when I was pushing forty, flat broke, and with three other children to look after?

The reality was that we had to have my salary to pay the bills, so maternity benefit, small as it was, just would not be enough to make ends meet. And how much did nurseries cost these days? Once back at work, a hefty portion of my salary would immediately be eaten up in child care – I couldn't countenance this little innocent being left at home with Sylvia and Bertie, even if Sylvia agreed to it which, at the age of almost seventy, I'm sure she wouldn't.

'Look, India, it's Rip Van Winkle, asleep for one hundred years and still counting.' Grace and India, back from her birthday treat, were at the shed window, noses pressed against the glass, peering in to see what I was up to.

I guiltily withdrew my hand away from my belly, terrified that

Grace, her antennae constantly in tune to the subject of babies, might somehow know what was going on, and waved.

'This is so wonderful, Mummy,' India enthused opening the door and gazing round. 'You'll be able to play "Mummies and Daddies" down here.'

'Except we'd need a Daddy,' I muttered to Grace as India went back out into the garden 'and they seem to be a bit thin on the ground at the moment.'

'What do you mean?' Grace asked sharply. 'Where *is* Nick?'

'Oh he's out drumming up business in counties far and near.' My tone, I knew, was cross. In fact I was fast becoming one big crosspatch and I didn't like it.

'Harriet, you have got to start supporting Nick. He's working really hard and he knows he *has* to succeed – he doesn't have a choice in the matter; he *has* to succeed.'

'Yeah, well, he's succeeding a little *too* well with the lovely Amanda, if you ask me,' I said sulkily. I wasn't in any mood to be castigated by Grace.

She sighed in what I supposed to be exasperation, and, as India returned, I rapidly changed the subject, questioning her about her day.

'Why haven't you got any heat on down here?' Grace now asked, rubbing her hands together against the chill and looking round for a solution.

'You're wired for electricity I see.'

'Can't afford it,' I said shortly, still annoyed at what I saw as her ganging up with Nick and Amanda against me.

Grace didn't tell me I was talking rubbish as I thought she might. Instead she said, 'Listen, we've got that Calor gas heater thing that Dan brought home when we were putting in the new electrics and had no heat. I'll bring it up for you. I certainly don't need it so you may as well have it until Nick makes his fortune again and you can afford to heat this place for yourself. I can see that you really do need a place to escape to every now and again and there's almost a full bottle of the gas left.'

She looked at me with some degree of sympathy and, mood that I was in, I couldn't decide which was more galling – Grace's chastisement or her condolence.

'Thanks, I'd appreciate that.' I said, relenting.

'I'm off,' Grace now said. 'I'll call round tomorrow with the heater and you can play at being Greta Garbo to your heart's content.'

'Greta Garbo?' I asked as I emerged from the duvet and gathered up my coffee things to take back up to the house.

'Yeah, you know – "I just vant to be alone". Never understood why anyone wants to be by themselves when they could be out socialising and having a ball.'

'Try living with this lot for a couple of days and you'd soon know,' I replied tartly, and then could have kicked myself. How could I be so insensitive when Grace not only didn't have the children she longed for but whose husband had left her home alone?

India, bored of adult conversation, had already made her way up to the house where she had no doubt joined Kit and Liberty in front of the TV, arguing over who was watching what. We'd cancelled our Sky subscription several months ago after yet another cost-cutting exercise, so at least there was less choice for the kids to fall out over.

'Any news on Dan?' I now asked in an attempt to soften the blow I'd just delivered.

'On holiday, presumably with Camilla,' Grace said shortly. 'I had to ring him at the office this morning. There's a problem with the outside guttering again and I don't have the number of the guy who fixed it last time. His secretary just said he was away on holiday.'

'How do you feel about that?' I asked, wanting to hug her and make it all go away.

'Bad, if you must know. It really does make it all seem a bit final.'

'Has he mentioned divorce?'

'No, but I think I will when he gets back. It's all so messy like this. A bit like living in no man's land. I'm neither married nor a gay divorcee – gay in the original sense of the word of course.'

'Of course,' I smiled and moved to give her the hug. She felt brittle, tense. 'You know, he's only been gone a month. It probably feels like forever, but maybe you shouldn't throw in the towel just yet.'

'Whatever.' Grace obviously wasn't in the mood for opening up. 'By the way, I've got an interview for the deputy headship of Kings Mede Primary. The letter came this morning.'

My heart sank. I felt like a kid whose best friend has just told her she's moving away to another town and won't be going to school with her any more.

I forced a smile. 'Hey that's great. Well done. When's the interview?'

'Not for a couple of weeks. It's what I need, Hat. I can't carry on without some sort of challenge in my life.'

'Maybe you should stick with what you know for a bit while you're going through this thing with Dan,' I said hopefully. 'Too many changes can be very stressful, you know.'

'I'm fed up with what I *know*,' Grace said fiercely. 'What I *know* hasn't got me anywhere.'

'Ok, ok. You're a big girl now. Do what you think's best.' I suddenly felt very tired. And, unfortunately, very sick. Throwing up all over Grace's new tan-coloured Jimmy Choo boots would not, I could guarantee, put her in a better mood. 'I'm going to have a bath,' I said, fighting the nausea that was threatening to overwhelm me.

'Um, you look a bit pale. I should go and catch up with some sleep as well if I were you. I'll pop over tomorrow with that heater.'

Funny state to be in, pregnancy. One minute you're leaning your head against the bathroom mirror trying to find a cool place to put your sweating brow while your stomach makes up its mind whether to put you through yet another bout of heaving. The next you're ravenously hungry and only marmite on toast smothered in peanut butter and Brie will suffice. Or, my other favourite: Hobnobs, with lemon curd and Stilton.

I sat at the kitchen table, licking the peanut butter from my fingers like Nigella Lawson, while keeping an eye on the lane from the window. I'd no idea what time Nick was going to be home, but if he caught sight of the concoction on which I was feasting he would immediately know why. This particular combination – and it had to be *smooth* peanut butter and *Brie* cheese – had been the mainstay of all my previous pregnancies. There was no way I could tell Nick I was pregnant. This really would be putting the boot in. And I did have to take a certain responsibility for getting myself in this situation. I know, I know – one doesn't get oneself pregnant. It takes two to tango and all that. But this was going to have to be one bit of information I would keep to myself. I was going to have to be mature and sensible and sort out the whole sorry mess myself. I was, by my reckoning, less than five weeks pregnant. The sooner I worked out how *not* to be pregnant the better. And no one, but no one, must ever, ever know I had been.

Chapter 18

'I'm pregnant.'

'What?' Diana turned her head to look at me in amazement, seriously jeopardising not only our lives but also those in the car in front of us.

'I'm pregnant,' I repeated, my voice a monotone.

'That's what I thought you said. But how?'

'Well, last night the Angel Gabriel appeared in our front room telling me I was with child. What the fuck do you mean *"how?"* The *usual* fucking way.' I began to giggle, although tears were welling up simultaneously. 'That's quite funny – getting pregnant the fucking way. Is there any other?'

'Stop it, this minute, or I'll have to slap you. You're getting hysterical.' Diana pulled into the almost deserted car park of the Laughing Cavalier, the only place I'd been able to think of when Diana had called in on her way to a client, suggesting we went somewhere nearby to grab a coffee and discuss her appointment with Mum's GP the previous evening. Sylvia had been hovering and we hadn't wanted to talk about Mum in front of her.

Neither of us uttered another word, waiting in what amounted to a constrained silence at the counter until the attendant deigned to leave his copy of *The Daily Express*. Sighing heavily and removing his little finger from its exploratory resting place in his right ear, he wandered over, obviously put out at actually having to attend to us.

'Yes?'

'Black coffee and an Earl Grey tea please.'

'We don't do black coffee.'

'Oh.' Momentarily nonplussed, Diana was silent as she scanned the menu written in 'Ye Olde English' on the plastic beam above our heads.

'We do "Americano",' the guy said, folding his arms over his ample girth and leaning against the counter.

'What's that?' Diana asked irritably.

'Black coffee.'

'Fine.' Diana raised both her eyebrows and hands in acquiescence before looking at her watch. 'I really don't have much time,' she said, turning to look at me. 'God, you look awful. Go and grab a table and I'll bring these over.'

I found seats down at the far end of the coffee bar, away from the couple of tables that were already occupied. An elderly couple, false teeth mumbling enthusiastically on flaky vanilla slices, and a couple of mothers with their offspring were the only others in there, testament to the sheer awfulness of the place. The fluorescent lighting, necessary even in the height of summer, but doubly so on a gloomy November day such as this, cast an unearthly shadow on the moulded plastic statue of the cavalier whose mouth appeared set in a tight grimace rather than laughter.

'Not sure this is Earl Grey,' Diana said, sniffing suspiciously at the orange liquid before setting it down before me.

I took a tentative sip and immediately wanted to heave. It was my previous pregnancies that had given me a lasting horror of any tea stronger than gnat's pee.

'That is disgusting,' I shuddered, slopping the over-stewed brew onto the saucer.

'Good God, this is ridiculous,' Diana snapped, her stress level obviously gone into overdrive by her probable lateness for her next appointment and the bombshell I'd dropped without warning in the car. She grabbed my cup, sloshing even more of the noxious stuff over her hand.

'Don't.' I protested. 'I'm really not bothered about a drink.' But she was off, on a mission.

'Excuse me.'

'Yeah?'

'This tea is disgusting.'

'What's wrong with it?'

'It's cold, stewed and patently *not* Earl Grey.'

Heads turned, craning towards the counter in anticipation of a confrontation.

'This isn't any old *shite*, you know.' The guy paused dramatically. 'It's *PG Tips*.'

'I don't care what it is. It *is* not Earl Grey. Now, I'd like a refund and a glass of water for my pregnant sister.'

Oh Jesus. What was the *matter* with her? I looked round nervously, terrified there might be children or staff from school lurking in Ye Olde Shadows.

I glared at Diana as she sat down. 'Was that really necessary?' I hissed.

'Probably not, but very cathartic all the same. Now, who's going first – you or me?'

'You,' I sighed, taking a sip of the lukewarm water in an attempt to remove the tannin taste of the tea that, compounded with the metallic taste of early pregnancy, was adding to my nausea.

'There's not really much to tell. Dad told Mum he was off for an early drink at the British Legion and then met up with me at the surgery. Apparently she's still muttering about Patricia, and had had another session shouting at Granny Morgan only that morning.'

'What did Dr Armstrong say?' Edward Armstrong, now nearing retirement age, had been our family doctor for what seemed like forever.

'He was great. Got Dad to explain everything, but said there wasn't really much he could do without Mum actually going to see him and admitting there was a problem.'

'Well she's not likely to do that is she?'

'No.' Diana shook her head in agreement. 'What he did say he'd do, though, was to have a word with the practice health visitor and ask her to go round and see Mum on the pretext of an annual health check-up she'll say she's due now that she's seventy-five.'

'Um,' I said doubtfully. 'Can't really see that doing much good unless she opens up to her and tells her what's on her mind.'

'No. Well at the moment there's not much more we can do.'

Diana drained her cup, glanced once more at her watch and said, as if reading the next item on an agenda, 'Right. Pregnancy. How pregnant are you and what do you want to do about it?'

'Very early – not even five weeks. And you know as well as I do that I can't have it.'

Diana raised an eyebrow. 'Do you want another child?'

Did I? In different circumstances, yes, I'd be more than happy to be pregnant, I now realised, but I couldn't admit this to Diana. She'd tell me to throw caution to the wind and just go ahead with it.

'It's a totally hypothetical question, Di. At the moment there's only my salary coming in and, apart from some trust money left by Nick's father for the kids' education, everyone, including Sylvia now, is dependent on me. Interest rates are so low now I don't even know if the trust fund will continue to function.' Tears of self-pity were hovering at the back of my eyes just waiting for the signal to fall.

'Get the kids out of their schools,' Diana said, never a proponent of private education. 'It's absolute madness paying for education if you're struggling to make ends meet. Just think how much money you'd save. What *does* it cost, anyway?'

'You don't want to know,' I breathed.

'Yes, I *do*. This could be the answer to your problem. Come on, how much?'

'About twenty-five thousand a year,' I muttered, knocking off a couple of grand in my embarrassment.

'Earnable?'

'Sorry?'

Diana tutted impatiently. 'If you're forking out that sort of money for education, then obviously a greater amount has had to be earned before tax. Basically *you* are working just so that you can send your kids to an elitist institution.'

Was I? If that was the case, who the hell was paying the mortgage, gas and Sainsbury's bill every month? My brain, already fuddled with worry, was beginning to feel like cotton wool.

'No, it doesn't work like that,' I said, struggling to get my poor old mushed brain around how exactly it did work. 'I told you, the money for education comes from a trust.'

Diana snorted dismissively. 'I bet that money can be used for whatever you want. You need to get Nick to look into it.'

'Nick doesn't know.'

'No, but I'm sure he can find out.' And then seeing my face, she registered what I really meant. 'Oh, Hat, you mean he doesn't know you're pregnant?'

I shook my head miserably. 'No.'

'So when are you going to tell him?' Diana took my hand.

'I'm not. He'd never admit it, but I know Nick so well. I know he's already worried sick that he may have made a mistake in trying to start up this new company. Particularly now, when other well-established companies are going to the wall on a daily basis. He didn't get in until one this morning, fell asleep straight away but was then up wandering around at four. Then he was off again at seven. He's due to go back to Italy tomorrow. You know, Di, Nick's driving me mad at the moment, but I love him sooo much' – here I threatened to break down and sob – 'I can't tell him I'm pregnant and I'm going to have to make the kids leave their schools and go to the local comp which, incidentally, has just been put into Special Measures. I can't put that pressure on him, I just can't.'

Diana squeezed my fingers sympathetically. 'So, if you can't do that, what are you going to do?'

I couldn't say what I was going to have to do because the Herculean sobs that I'd managed to keep at bay during our conversation finally found their release, rendering me inarticulate. There was nothing much else either of us could say after that. The 'A' word hung between us, unsaid and, once I'd used up all of Di's mini pack of tissues, we abandoned our virtually untouched cups and left.

It was well after lunchtime by the time I got home. When I'd left that morning, Liberty and Kit were still, as my mother used to say, stinking in bed. India, now Adriana Saxton's best friend once more, no doubt as a result of the garden party, had been collected by Adriana and her mother to spend the day in their six-bedroom, six-bathroom, plasma-TV-on-every-wall, neo-Georgian box.

A motorbike, presumably Sebastian Henderson's, was parked on the drive. I'd totally forgotten he'd promised to come and spend time on the garden. Anxious that he wouldn't see me red-faced and puffy-eyed, I shot inside and tried to repair the ravages of a good half- hour's protracted sobbing. I really was going to have to get a grip. The sooner I made an appointment to see my doctor the sooner I could sort out the problem.

A note from Libby informed me that she'd gone off to the nearest shopping outlet with Beth, while another, unsigned, but presumably from Kit, read 'Yo me ma. I'se off wiv me muckers skateboarding. Back late.'

And I was worried about putting Kit into the local comp? He'd fit perfectly.

I didn't quite know what to do with myself, but spent the next hour pottering around, watering the plants, making a casserole for our evening meal, even making a list of all the things I needed to do for the new half term.

Once the October holiday was over, I realised, we were into the silly season. Christmas comes early to primary schools: once Bonfire Night is out of the way we're straight into deciding which class will do what for the Nativity. It might only be November, but Baby Jesus is already poised to put in an appearance so that by the time December comes nerves are run ragged, staff are not speaking to one another, Jesus has been lost and found several times, and the kids are thoroughly pissed off with the whole caboodle.

Realising I was putting off the call I had to make, I took a deep breath, grabbed the phone and tried to make an appointment to see my doctor. Tried is the operative word. When I was a little girl, if we needed to see the doctor, we simply walked down to his surgery and took our place in the queue in the waiting room. You eyed up who was in front of you and knew exactly when it was your turn to go in without any help from a frosty-faced receptionist. No problem.

'Hi, this is Harriet Westmoreland. Could I make an appointment to see Dr Chadwick?'

'When were you thinking of?'

'As soon as possible please.'

'Dr Chadwick is away for the week. It *is* half term you know.'

'Yes, I am aware of that. Next week then?'

'I'm afraid she's fully booked. You need to ring at the beginning of the previous week to make an appointment for the next week.'

'I just did.'

'Today is Tuesday, Mrs Westmoreland. You need to ring on a Monday.'

'So, you're telling me that I have to wait until *next* Monday in order to make an appointment for the Monday after that?'

'Yes, really.'

'But I could be dead by then.'

'Are you dying, Mrs Westmoreland?'

'If I say "yes" will that get me an earlier appointment?'

Obviously a receptionist with a sense of humour failure, she ignored my query, shuffling papers importantly before sighing, 'Dr O'Leary could see you tomorrow.'

I bet he could. An ancient, bible-bashing Catholic from Ireland, regularly seen walking to and from early morning mass, his distaste for anyone wanting contraception or advice with anything of a sexual nature was legendary. Not the best person to ask for a termination then.

'I'd rather see Dr Chadwick,' I said. 'She *is* my doctor, not Dr O'Leary.'

'Oh, just a moment, Mrs Westmoreland. There *is* a gap here – next Tuesday morning? At ten?'

'Lovely.' I'd work out what I was going to tell Valerie Westwood later. And Grace. Grace would want to know why I needed to see a doctor.

Relieved that I'd set the ball in motion, I made coffee and set off to find the gorgeous gardener.

After a rather miserable start to the week, the weather had improved and was unseasonably warm once more. I was all for global warming if it meant pleasant days like this in early November. I stopped to admire my little plot which, given all the attention it had received from Dad and his little band of workers on Sunday, was looking pretty damned good. There were now enough bulbs in there to ensure a fabulous display of daffodils and tulips come spring and I made my way down to the banking that Sebastian had said he wanted to get his hands on. I couldn't see him anywhere but could see the fruits of his labour. He must have been here all morning, clearing much of the overgrown creeper, dead grass and brambles, which had been choking the honeysuckle and clematis. A forsythia hedge, which hadn't seen the light of day for years, hidden as it was by a parasitic trail of ivy stems, appeared as shocked and pale as a newly released prisoner, blinking in the weak, autumn sunlight.

Once again I see these hedgerows, hardly hedgerows;
Little lines of sportive wood run wild.

A great surge of pleasure raced through me as I stood there, breathing in the smell of newly turned earth, quoting Wordsworth and surveying this fabulous garden that was becoming more fabulous by the minute. A robin, its breast deepened to a scarlet hue in anticipation of the coming winter, hopped brazenly near my feet, emboldened by my stillness. It moved a short distance as I shifted slightly looking around for Sebastian. His coat, a navy donkey-jacket, was hanging on the amorphous, elongated branch of an ancient apple tree to the left of the new potting shed.

I set off towards it, but stopped short a few metres from the potting shed as the sound of laughter came from within. I stopped in my tracks, straining to listen, but all was quiet. Stopping only to pick up a huge, crumbling flowerpot, I tiptoed to the rear of the shed, positioned the flowerpot underneath the window, climbed on and peered in.

All I could think was how beautiful they both looked together, their dark hair indistinguishable one from the other as they lay entwined on my 'hairy mammal.' Sebastian's bronzed thigh, tightly muscled as only a twenty-three-year-old thigh can be, lay possessively alongside Grace's slender leg. Her eyes were partly closed, her face softened in a way I'd not seen since Daniel's leaving had left it polished with a hard, though still beautiful, veneer.

Sebastian, hooking a strand of Grace's hair, wound it slowly through his fingers before bending his head to her open mouth. Grace's red cami, the straps falling wantonly over her raised arms, was the exact colour not only of her lipstick but of the Remembrance Day poppy which, nestled for some reason in Sebastian's mass of black pubic hair, was totally and utterly inadequate in covering up what was intent on rising from its depths.

Realising I'd been holding my breath, I forced myself to exhale, carefully lowered my Wellington-booted feet from the upturned flowerpot and, picking up the untouched coffee mug threw it, along with its cold, scummy contents, as hard as I could over the banking, down into the newly ploughed field below.

'Are you ok?'

'Fine,' I snapped, not looking up as Grace came into the kitchen, but continuing with the task of polishing the granite work surfaces for the second time that morning.

'I brought you the heater.'

I didn't say a word, just stabbed viciously at a particularly tenacious smear.

'The heater?' Grace repeated, sitting down opposite me at the kitchen table. 'The one I promised you yesterday? Sylvia gave me the key to your potting shed on her way out so I went down there and fixed it up for you. It's lovely and warm, now. You can go and play at being Greta Garbo to your heart's content.' Grace laughed nervously.

I put down the cleaning cloth, folded my arms and glared at Grace. 'Whose potting shed exactly, Grace?'

'Sorry?'

'Whose fucking potting shed is it, Grace?'

'Ah.'

'You might well say "Ah". How dare you use my new shed as a knocking shop? What if it had been Kit or Liberty who'd wandered down there? Or India?'

'It wasn't planned, Hat. I didn't for one moment think Seb would be here. Why should I?'

'Possibly because he'd told you he'd offered to do my garden for me?' I snapped, holding her gaze.

Grace reddened. 'He may have done. But I certainly didn't expect to find you all out. When I arrived, Sylvia was just leaving. She gave me the key and told me you were all gone for the day.'

'The kids, maybe. But not me. Sylvia must have told you I'd only gone for a quick coffee with Diana.'

'She didn't, actually.' Grace walked over to the sink. 'Can I make *myself* a coffee?'

'Help yourself,' I said shortly. 'You usually do.'

Grace turned, stung by my abrasive reply. 'What exactly is it you're objecting to, Harriet? Before all this happened with Nick and the Hendersons you'd have been first in line to hear all the juicy details. You've changed, you know. Lost your softness, your sense of humour. In fact you're fast becoming a miserable old harridan.'

I gasped at the sharp words but before I could reply Grace went on, 'Is it the fact that we've used your precious potting shed? If so, I apologise. I'll make sure that Seb and I keep out of your way in future.'

'The future? There is a future then?'

'Harriet, the minute I saw Sebastian in *"Jimmy's"* last Friday night I fell in love.'

'You fell in lust,' I said nastily. Oh, God, What was the matter with me? This was my best friend I was laying into. Why couldn't I be pleased for her?

'Why can't you be pleased for me?' Grace echoed my thoughts.

'Because it's all too close to home. In case you've forgotten, Sebastian is Little Miss Goodness's only, adored son. You, Grace, are not only years older than him, but also the one person that Amanda could never bring to heel. I hardly think she'll open her arms to you as a prospective daughter-in-law.'

'Harriet, for heaven's sake. I only met him on Friday. Alright, admittedly I've been with him ever since, but …'

'You've been,' I broke off, trying to think of the right word, '*dallying* with him since Friday night, and you never told me?'

'Dallying with him?' Grace chortled. 'I wouldn't exactly call fucking his brains out "dallying" with him.'

'Don't be disgusting,' I hissed.

Grace looked at me curiously. 'You're jealous. For some reason, you're jealous.'

'Oh don't be ridiculous,' I snapped, taking up my frantic polishing once more. 'Why should I be jealous of you having sex in my potting shed with someone just out of school?'

Grace smiled. 'Because he's the most gorgeous specimen you've ever seen? Because he's young and bright and funny and comes unhindered by all the crap that we oldies have in our lives? Because he makes love like a dream – and ten minutes later comes back for more?'

Well, I suppose put like that, maybe she had a point. But there was no way I was going to admit that seeing Grace and Seb together had made me feel middle-aged: bogged down in a seething mess of bills, adolescent kids, work and worries about Nick. Or that seeing Grace and Seb together, totally wrapped up in each other, had reminded me so much of how Nick and I used to be. I missed him so much.

And what was it about my house that induced everyone who came to it to have sex in it? First there was young Jennifer Walker in my sitting room the other night, then the 'doggers' down in the woods, and now Grace carrying out her Lady Chatterley fantasy down in my potting shed. Maybe I should get in on the act – set up a brothel and become a Madam. It would be one way of paying the gas bill, which was surely due any day.

Even after Grace's accusation that I was becoming – what was her phrase, 'a miserable old harridan' – I seemed unable to relax, laugh and concede that she might just have a point. Instead, like an out of control lorry, I blundered on. 'I'm concerned about Amanda's reaction if she knows what you've been up to with her one and only son – and the repercussions it might have on my family,' I said primly.

'Oh don't be such an arse, Hat.' Grace raised her eyes to the ceiling. 'You sound just like my mother. What I'm *up to* with Seb has nothing at all to do with you and Nick. Or Little Miss Goodness come to that.'

'Of course it has. For a start you are *my* friend, and you've been doing the dirty deed on *my* premises.' I paused while Grace laughed out loud at this, infuriating me further. 'An outraged Amanda only needs to tell David to pull the plug on this whole business deal and my family is in the mire.'

'Hattie, Amanda isn't going to do that.' Grace now said placatingly. 'She's into Nick far too much to jeopardise what they've sorted out so far.'

'What do you *mean,* Grace?' I said icily. 'What has Sebastian said to you about Nick?'

Grace reddened again and moved away to fill the kettle so she wouldn't have to meet my eyes. 'Nothing,' she blustered. 'Seb just said she's working really hard with Nick on this project. Wants him to succeed – like we all do.'

'He's said something else hasn't he? Grace, I need to know. What did Seb say about Nick and Amanda?'

'Oh you know Amanda. Always has to be top banana. Wants everyone to love her. Seb adores her, but he knows what she's like.'

'That hasn't told me anything, Grace. You *know* I think Nick is having a thing with Amanda. You've not said anything to put my mind at rest.'

'Harriet, just go with the flow. Nick is a big boy – well capable of looking after himself.'

'Hang on a minute,' I interrupted, 'if I remember correctly it was *you* who said Amanda was ruthless, would get what she wanted in the end. Remember my brother John? Almost had a breakdown over her?'

Refusing to meet my eyes once more, she sighed before changing the subject. 'Sebastian has made me feel good about myself again. It may just be sex, but it's bloody good sex, I'm having fun and it's helping me get over Dan.'

I didn't say anything. I knew I was being a total dog in the manger, but this whole thing with Seb seemed dangerous. He might feel he knew his mother, but we tend to look at our mothers through rose-tinted specs. I remembered Amanda from years back – a week's suspension from school was nothing compared to what I really believed she could muster if she was crossed or thwarted in any way. And Grace having a passionate affair with her son was one hell of a thwart.

Amanda came from a long line of Old Midhope mill owners. They'd built their factories in the heart of the Pennines where the water was soft and plentiful and the sheep that produced the wool grazed for free on the coarse moorland grass. The spinners and weavers who had made their living for centuries, working at home in their cottages, were forced to abandon their looms and work in the mills for the woollen magnates who now ruled the roost, jack-booting over any odd peasant who caused 'trouble at t'mill' or got in the way of their ascent.

Genes would out – Amanda wasn't Frank Goodners' daughter for nothing: she wouldn't think twice about getting rid of anyone she thought might be a fly in the ointment of her game plan. And if we were implicated we'd be in the firing line.

'Look, Grace, you as much as anyone know what Amanda is like. She would absolutely loathe the idea of you having a thing with her precious son. Can't you see what she will do if she finds out? She knows how you and I have always come as a pair, and she won't have anything to do with something that involves you. You are involved with me, you know you are.' Here I drew breath and then went on, my voice rising as I pictured the worst scenario. 'The minute she finds out that Seb is having anything to do with you she'll find a way to persuade David Henderson to pull out of this deal. And much as I didn't want Nick to get involved with him – them – in the first place, he is now up to his neck in it and has to go forward. If this whole thing falls apart my family has had it. Can't you see that?' Frustration and an excess of hormones were in danger of bringing on a crying fit and I banged the tin of polish down hard on the granite worktop.

'I'll make sure Seb keeps this to himself. There's absolutely no reason why Amanda should know anything. It's nothing to do with her. And,' Grace added as she gathered up her things and headed for the door, 'we'll make absolutely sure we keep out of *your* way too. You obviously can't get your head around this at all. It's a shame because I feel like a fifteen year old – I need to talk about Seb, tell you all about him, how he kisses and things. I want to tell you the little things he says and how gorgeous he is and what it's like on the back of his bike going over ninety miles an hour.' She paused before carrying on. 'You know, Hattie, I've always done what other people wanted me to do. I did what my parents said, and I went along with what Daniel wanted. Now I've got to the age of thirty-eight and I'm going to do what *I* want for a change.'

'What?' I looked at Grace incredulously. 'You've always done just what *you* wanted. Your dad wanted you to be a solicitor and join his firm, but *you* insisted on being a teacher. Daniel always did your bidding until recently. *I've* always done what you wanted me to do since the age of eleven.' I paused, racking my brain for other examples of her bossiness. 'You even change Jamie Oliver recipes because you say he hasn't got it quite right.'

She pulled on her leather gloves and then removed them again in order to pin more securely her Remembrance Day poppy, which had fallen drunkenly to one side of her jacket.

'It's just that I'd rather you find somewhere other than my garden to play at being Lady Chatterley,' I added when she didn't respond to my little outburst.

'Lady Chatterley?'

I nodded towards her poppy, last seen through the potting-shed window flagrantly waving at me from the depths of Sebastian's groin.

Grace looked puzzled for a second and then blushed as crimson as the flower in question.

'My goodness, you don't miss a trick do you? What exactly did you see?'

'Enough to realise you were having fantasies about Sebastian being in a D. H. Lawrence novel.'

Grace looked me straight in the eye, shrugged her shoulders and said loftily, 'That's just *poppy-cock*, Harriet. Absolute *poppy-cock!*

Oh, and just one more question, Harriet. How long have you had CGD?'

'CGD?'

'Compulsive Granite Disorder. You've got a *very* nasty dose of it. You're forever cleaning and polishing that bit of granite. I should see someone about it if I were you, before it's too late.' And with that she sailed from my kitchen, slamming the door behind her for good measure.

'Did you know Grace is having a thing with Sebastian?'

Nick turned from where he was folding newly laundered shirts into a case in preparation for another trip to Italy the next morning. 'What sort of thing?'

'What *sort* of thing? The *only* sort of thing. And it includes having rampant sex in our potting shed, and using poppies as sex aids.'

'Really?' Nick laughed what can only be described as a particularly dirty laugh, and then sobered up as he realised just who Grace had been entertaining in my shed.

'Sebastian as in David's son?'

'You know any other Sebastians?'

'For heaven's sake don't let Mandy or David know. They're both incredibly precious when it comes to their only son. I can't see them being over the moon at the idea of his being seduced at *my* house.'

I snorted. 'And by someone old enough to be his mother?'

'This is not going to do my partnership with David Henderson any good at all, Harriet. Bad enough that you say your brother is still involved with Amanda, though to be honest, Hat, I think it's all wishful thinking on John's part. And as for Grace, well this is absolutely not on at all. You are going to have to have a word with her. Warn her off.' Nick was beginning to sound as pompous as I must have sounded when berating Grace earlier that day.

'Me? Why me? I can't tell Grace who she can and who she can't have sex with!' I snapped, remembering I'd spent most of the afternoon doing just that.

'Well for goodness' sake, don't say a word to either David or

Mandy and let's hope it all fizzles out.' I passed Nick a couple of Ralph Lauren polo shirts I'd bought when we were able to afford such luxuries. They'd lasted well, thank goodness.

'Talking of Grace, I actually had a drink with Dan this evening. Bumped into him in the bank as I was getting some more euros and we popped next door into *The Rose and Crown* for a quick one.'

I stared at him. What is it about men that they can have riveting news circulating in their heads but forget to pass it on?

'Nick, you have been home exactly one hour and twenty-five minutes. You have sat opposite me at the table and eaten my chicken casserole, and yet you forget to tell me you have just had a drink with my best friend's errant husband?'

'It was a very quick drink,' Nick protested.

'And?'

'And he wonders if he's made a mistake in leaving Grace.'

'What? He actually said that?'

'Well, not in so many words. But that was the general gist of the conversation. Unfortunately, we'd only been chatting five minutes when his new woman arrived.'

'Camilla?'

'Is that what she's called? She's a cracker isn't she? Gorgeous red hair. I gather they'd been away on holiday for a few days. Actually, there was something about her that reminded me of you.'

'Of me?'

'Yes. Can't pinpoint it exactly.' Nick looked at me intently, searching my face for clues and then laughed. 'Must be that you're both gorgeous!'

'Do you still think so?' I said, snuggling into him. 'That I'm gorgeous, I mean?'

'Absolutely,' he said, slapping my bottom. 'Now let me finish my packing.'

Hmm. Not so gorgeous then that he could forget about his trip to Italy for one minute in order to ravish me there and then? I went downstairs feeling disconsolate once more.

Chapter 19

The first morning of the new half term began badly and carried on in the same vein throughout the day. Granny Morgan's alarm clock which, like its namesake, could behave itself for weeks before unexpectedly, and for no good reason, going off in an indignant sulk, had failed to wake me on time. It was India, shaking me awake, that had me rushing to the loo for a two-minute bout of dry retching.

'Aren't you well either, Mummy?' India's plaintive little voice came from the other side of the bathroom door.

'Me? I'm fine darling,' I yelled cheerfully, between retches. 'Just trying out this super, new, minty mouthwash. Gargle, gargle, spit.' I leaned my sweaty forehead against the cool tiles. 'Out I come. All done now. Mmm. Lovely. And how are you?'

India looked at me doubtfully. 'You don't look as if that was lovely. You look all pale and yucky. And I don't feel well. My throat hurts and I think my ear hurts.'

'You *think* your ear hurts?'

'Yes it does. I know it does – in my ear.'

Was India playing up because she didn't want to go back to school after the holiday? If so, I knew the feeling. The last thing on earth I felt like doing was teaching thirty-two bolshy eleven-year-olds. I wanted my head under a pillow and to have it stay there until all the problems hanging over it were whisked away by my Fairy Godmother.

This was all I needed on the first day back at school. Normally I'd have bundled India back into bed and asked Sylvia to come over, but Sylvia had gone off on one of her jaunts back down South.

Nick, due back from Italy two days ago, was still living La Dolce Vita in Milan.

'Oh darling,' I cajoled, 'just get dressed and let's see how you feel then. Things always seem worse when you've just got up.'

Shouting to Liberty and Kit to sort themselves out, I quickly showered, dressed and, going downstairs, considered making scrambled eggs for everyone. I only considered it. The kitchen clock informed me there was no time; the fridge informed me there were no eggs – and not much else either. I must do a shop, I thought, grabbing a box of All-Bran and a rather suspicious looking carton of low-fat milk.

'Is this all there is for breakfast?' Liberty asked, looking disdainfully at the kitchen table.

'Have some toast and marmite,' I suggested, throwing her the remains of a stale loaf.

'Marmite? You're joking. Marmite is scrapings from the devil's underpants.' She visibly shuddered. 'Bethany's mum always gives *her* warm croissants, and freshly squeezed orange juice.'

'Well bully for Bethany's mum,' I snapped.

I dropped the elder two off at their school bus stop and set off for India's school, planning to leave her in their Early Morning Club – a boon for working mothers.

'My ear still hurts,' India wailed as we pulled up into her school car park.

My heart plummeted. The last thing I wanted to do was to abandon my class to some unknown supply teacher – not only would it go down badly with Valerie Westwood, I'd be catching up all week, getting my class back under control. While I generally take my hat off to supply staff, we seemed to have been landed with a bunch of eclectic, if not downright dangerous, stand-in teachers lately. Margaret Walker – Jennifer-the-baby-sitter-having-sex-on-my-Persian-rug's mother – had, only the other day, given over-the-phone instructions to the supply teacher of her class of six-year-olds.

'I was about to start introducing Sets,' Margaret had informed the newly qualified, and obviously very eager, young man who would be taking her class the next morning. 'Nothing fancy, just the usual stuff, if you wouldn't mind starting that.'

Give the guy his due. He'd gone overboard with diagrams, posters and other visual aids which he'd proudly shown to Margaret on her return at lunchtime. Tony Drummond, our new head teacher, had had to send out a letter of apology to thirty sets of parents as to why their little cherubs were now rather more in touch with human reproduction than when they'd been dropped off at school that morning.

And just before half term Grace had left her class with a supply teacher who, according to the kids, had sat with her coat on all day and, apart from whispering a few basic instructions, had not spoken to the class at all. She'd only removed herself from Grace's chair during the PE session in the hall. Still wearing coat, hat and scarf she had stood, rooted to the spot while almost forty thoroughly overexcited children swung from the ropes shouting 'Geronimo' as they flew past her through the air narrowly missing her woollen-hatted head and those of a set of visiting prospective parents

'Let me have another look, darling,' I now said, praying I wouldn't see anything untoward that would mean I had to stay at home. India proffered her ear, looking at me dolefully with her big brown eyes.

'I really think you'll be fine once you get inside out of the cold,' I said heartily, and bundled her up the drive and into school.

Phew! Three down and one to go. But what sort of mother was I? Oh God, what if there was really something wrong with India? Meningitis? Swine flu? She was only six for heaven's sake and I'd left her – poorly. I had to get back to her. I dithered, did a dangerous U-turn and was greeted by a blast of outraged horns and raised fingers. Heart pounding, I pulled in to the nearest lay-by and scrabbled in my bag until I found my mobile. Shit! No credit. Taking a deep breath I turned once more and, putting my foot down, abandoned the main road in favour of a little known rat run, and was in school with just enough time to leave a message at India's school for them to ring me if she became worse.

How on earth could I do this with a new baby in tow as well? The simple answer was that I couldn't. Trying to get the pictures of dead babies 'plucked untimely from their mother's womb' from my mind, I thanked, as I always did, the guardian angel who had seen fit to give me an hour's free period every Monday morning.

'Ah, Harriet,' said the guardian angel, aka Valerie Westwood, as I took off my coat. 'Just the person I wanted to see. I've a new child for you.'

My heart shifted southwards for the second time in half an hour. There wasn't *room* in my classroom for any more children. And new children often brought baggage with them, whether they'd moved house and school because of a split in the family, or had behaviour or friendship problems at their old school.

'Nice little boy. Something to do with the Duke of Leeds,' Valerie went on. 'I've sent him out into the playground with Daniel Sanderson.'

Oh well, at least he sounded a bit different. The only child I'd ever had with anything amounting to fame attached was a supposedly well-known stand-up comic's illegitimate son. He used to make *me* laugh, so maybe there'd been something in the rumour.

Derek, who'd been standing in for Ray, our usual caretaker whose legendary bad back had now kept him off work for almost a year, was waiting for me in my classroom.

'He's gone again, lass,' Derek said importantly. I bet he'd been there since the early hours awaiting my arrival so that he could be the one to break the news.

'Oh not again.' I sighed. 'I really thought he was on his last legs this time. That's why I didn't send him home with one of the children over half term. The little bugger must have had a new lease of life and made a run for it again.'

'I've popped in every day to look at him and feed him, like you said. He was here yesterday afternoon when I checked on him.'

'Are you sure he's not hiding? You know, having a game with us?'

'He's a bloody 'amster, lass, not Bruce Forsyth.'

I laughed at that. 'You know as well as I do that Humbug is no ordinary hamster, Derek. He is the Houdini of all hamsters.'

And he was. I was actually very attached to him, as were the children who came into my class, but he did have a Colditz approach to life – he was off whenever he got the chance.

'I don't think he can survive another adventure,' I now said to Derek as the bell went and my class began to line up outside the classroom door.

'I think you're right, love. I'll keep an eye out for him while I'm cleaning up.'

Two minutes into the new school half term and I was already fed up. I hadn't seen or heard from Grace since she'd swept out of my kitchen after frolicking in my potting shed with the gorgeous Enrique. I missed her terribly, needed someone to talk to, but she was obviously keeping out of my way. I considered popping down to her classroom, but my kids were barging in, shrill with their news of half-term holiday events and outings. Usually fairly laid-back about my class's behaviour in the cloakroom, I surprised myself as well as the children and Donna, my ETA, who was sorting books, by completely losing it and shouting, 'Out, out. OUT!'

Lady Macbeth was a mere novice compared to my ranting this Monday morning. I was of a mind to take it one step further and shout, 'Out, Damned Class,' as thirty-five bewildered eleven-year-olds backed out of the cloakroom, falling over themselves and each other to escape the madwoman bearing down on them. Catching sight of a row of open-mouthed mothers who'd just delivered their children into what they presumed was my safekeeping, I thought better of it.

'This is *no* way to come into school, especially on a Monday morning,' I stormed as my class lined up outside the cloakroom in what can only be described as gob-smacked silence. 'Any repeat of this morning's *appalling* bun fight in *my* cloakroom and we shall spend break times *and* lunchtimes practising how to proceed in a much more orderly manner. *Do* I make myself clear?'

'Blimey, what's up with her this morning?' I heard Darren Slater mutter from behind his reading book.

'Time of the month probably,' Toby Armitage giggled, totally oblivious to the fact that he was in earshot. 'My dad always says that about my mum when she's in a bad mood.'

Adrian Pettifer shook his head and sniffed in disagreement, for all the world as if discussing the current state of the economy rather than my menstrual cycle. 'Nah. The flying Tampax was only just before the holiday.' All three boys now giggled, but very quickly flushed as, one by one, they became aware of my furious glare in their direction.

In need of my favourite red pen for marking, I'd been scrabbling around in my handbag which, as usual, was awash with all manner of bits and pieces, from the minutes of that week's staff meeting to a desiccated tangerine. After what seemed like several minutes' fruitless searching, my fingers finally found what they were after and I fished my pen from the depths of my bag in triumph. Unfortunately the speed at which I brought it to the surface dislodged an ancient Tampax, which proceeded to launch itself across my desk in a perfect arc. Its near faultless landing, in the middle of Adrian Pettifer's *Abacus Maths 6* text book, warranted a round of applause from Houston, Texas. As it was, Adrian had looked at the Tampax, I'd looked at Adrian, and, like Pluto claiming Persephone for his own in the underworld, I'd smiled sweetly, pocketing the offending object with a simple, 'Mine, I think, Adrian,' and then proceeded to mark his maths with huge and overzealous green ticks.

Right, we have someone new joining us today, everybody. This is Tyson and I want you all to make sure you look after him and make him feel at home.'

I stopped talking and weighed up this new child in front of me. Tyson? Not really an aristocratic name, surely. William, Charles, George maybe. But Tyson? He didn't look as if he had a drop of blue blood in him either, his regulation buzz cut and stud earring more West Yorkshire council estate than North Yorkshire country estate. He was pleasant enough though, and buckled down straight away to the job in hand once I'd returned to the classroom from my half hour's non-contact time. The rest of the class, fresh from a week's break, seemed open to the non-negotiable idea of getting on with some hard work and I began to relax into the routine of being back with the children.

Apart from tender, itchy boobs that were a constant reminder of my present state, I was able to switch off from the problem of being pregnant and concentrate on the intricacies of factors and multiples.

My relaxed state lasted only until break time. Desperate to see Grace, I hurried down towards the staff room but Valerie stepped out, ambushing me into the tiny cupboard she liked to call the deputy head's room.

'A quick word, Harriet?' Valerie trilled, pouncing on me and dragging me into her cupboard in much the same way I'd seen Bones carry off a field mouse.

'Is it important, Valerie? I really could do with a cup of tea.' And a pee. I'd forgotten what pregnancy, even early pregnancy, does to one's bladder.

'Won't take a minute. It's this report, dear.'

I groaned inwardly. 'What report?' I knew I sounded irritable, but I was desperate for the loo.

'This report you wrote on Neil Smith.' She wafted the paper in my face. Neil had left my class a couple of weeks previously and I'd been asked for a fairly detailed report on all aspects of his work by his new school.

'What's wrong with it?' I asked. 'Shouldn't it have gone off by now?'

'Well, yes, and I would have sent it before half term if you'd written it up on the computer. But quite honestly, Harriet, I can't send this.'

'You're not sending it because I wrote it by hand rather than typed it up?'

Valerie peered at me over her glasses. 'I just don't understand why you've written that you feel Neil needs to be much nicer to otters.'

'*Otters?*' I looked at Valerie. Had she been drinking? I took the offending piece of A4 paper and scanned it quickly looking for any evidence regarding river mammals, and then started to giggle. '*Others*, Valerie. I've written that Neil needs to be nicer to *others*, not otters.'

'Oh right, dear, right. It's your handwriting that's caused the other big problem too. You see your "o"s and "r"s look just like "a"s and "n"s,' she paused, 'with rather unfortunate results.'

'What?' I frowned. What was the old bat going on about now?

Valerie moved closer, peering over my shoulder at the one-page but nevertheless quite extensive report I'd written on Neil. The fumes from *Poison*, her perfume, were beginning to have a serious effect on the remains of my breakfast, but she had me up against the filing cabinet and there was no escape.

Admittedly I'd been in a hurry when I wrote the report. My printer had been out of paper and I'd scribbled it off by hand rather than go all the way down to the stock room for new paper, anxious to complete it before the holiday. But I still couldn't see any major problem with it.

'The word "work" appears, as it obviously should in a child's school report, many times.' Valerie said, her tone placating. 'Unfortunately, dear, the word doesn't read as *"work."*'

I scanned the page and began to giggle again as I read: 'Neil has wanked consistently well throughout this half term' 'Neil has wanked his socks off in science' 'Neil has particularly impressed me with his French oral wank' 'Neil has enjoyed wanking with his peer group …' And the *pièce de resistance*: 'I'm sure Neil will continue wanking to the best of his ability at his new school.'

Valerie looked at me sympathetically, but without an ounce of humour in her small grey eyes. 'I think you get my drift, dear? Shall we say tomorrow morning, typed up and on my desk?'

Sniggering to myself, I desperately wanted to recount this little dialogue to Grace, but what had happened last week was a barrier between us. I was missing her so much, felt quite isolated knowing that she was near and yet apparently avoiding me. Besides, the bell had gone to resume lessons, and, if I didn't get to the loo, I was in great danger of delivering my literacy lesson with my hand held tightly between clenched thighs.

I usually made a point of sitting next to Grace during staff meetings

– she would make me laugh by writing little notes and drawing cartoons on her agenda – but this lunchtime was different. She merely nodded at me across the room and went to sit with Margaret Walker and her cronies. Feeling like the kid in the schoolyard with no mates, I was miserable. I decided to suck up to Tony Drummond, our new head, and parked myself next to him. He'd only been with us since September and, while the consensus was that he was a bit wet, I was beginning to like him very much. As with any new head teacher, but especially a very young one who had stepped into the shoes of a much-loved, much older head, he'd had to work hard to establish his authority. Valerie Westwood, whose overlong nose had been put out of joint when she'd been turned down for the job herself, had been particularly deprecating about him, and those in her gang had, like a kitten-heeled bunch of lemmings, followed suit. Both Grace and I, perhaps because we were nearer in age to Tony, or simply to wind up Valerie and her cronies, had made a beeline for him in the past few weeks and, while we still didn't know too much of his personal circumstances, had learnt he was unattached, 'but looking!'

'I've spent all half term trying to buy a sheepskin rug,' Sandra Young, one of our Year 4 teachers, was now saying conversationally to anyone who was listening as we waited for Valerie Westwood to join us from where she was berating a poor unfortunate in the dinner queue.

'House of Fraser does some good ones,' Margaret said. 'Have you been there?'

'They only have single skins. I want a really large one. Maybe two skins sewn together.'

'I've got a huge one,' Tony Drummond joined in, oblivious to the polite smirks from the women in the room. 'In fact it's made from four skins sewn together.'

'Blimey, painful or what?' Grace sniggered, and the entire room collapsed in hysterics, unable to stop even when Valerie finally walked in, glaring at us in much the way she used to keep Year 6 in order.

Even Tony was chortling, seemingly unembarrassed by his

double entendre. I looked at him curiously. He seemed different, confident – glowing almost. I glanced across at Grace, and realised what it was. I bet he'd found himself a woman at last. Both he and Grace had the same 'I'm in love' aura about them and were suffused from sex – and lots of it.

Good on him, I thought, pleased.

Overriding Valerie who had begun to take over the staff meeting as usual, Tony plunged straight in, putting her in her place by suggesting she take the minutes.

Last on the agenda was the announcement that, whilst Ray the caretaker's continuing bad back was preventing his return to work, he was to be congratulated on the fact that his partner had just produced their fifth child during the half-term holiday.

'Ok for sex then?!' I scribbled on Tony's agenda, forgetting for the moment that he was my boss.

'Yes, thanks very much!!' he wrote back, grinning at me.

Maybe Tony Drummond could be my new best friend, I mused, walking back to my classroom in readiness for the afternoon session.

By the end of the first session of the afternoon I was exhausted. I just wanted to close my eyes and go to sleep. When I'd been pregnant with Kit I'd regularly put Liberty down for her afternoon nap and put myself down for one as well. What luxury! Here I was, pregnant again, but this time my brain and body thirteen years older, trying to remember the 'My very eccentric mother just shot uncle Norman's pig' mnemonic for the solar system, when I was barely able to remember my own name.

The science lesson had gone down really well though, and the kids had asked if they could make up their own mnemonics after break, so at least I could get some marking done and try to make a quick getaway when school finished for the day. I had to pick India up from school as Sylvia wouldn't be back until that evening.

Fighting sleep, I was desperately trying to concentrate on the digits in Darren Slater's maths book. They seemed to have a life of their own, moving out of focus or jumping around the page so that I couldn't quite work out what they were or where they were supposed to be. The children, working in pairs on their planet mnemonics, would occasionally give a hoot of laughter as they came up with something rude or absurd, but on the whole their voices were as low and soporific as a night-time lullaby. So it was that I was unaware of my classroom door opening until Valerie Westwood announced, 'You have a visitor, Mrs Westmoreland.'

Thirty-six pairs of eyes, including mine, turned as one. For a few seconds I couldn't get my befuddled brain into gear to work out who it was standing in the doorway with Valerie. I knew I'd seen her before, and fairly recently too, but it was only when she spoke that I realised who she was.

'Hello children. Mrs Westmoreland very kindly invited me to your school to meet you all. It's *such* a long time since I've been to school. What *are* you all up to?' All eyes, including Valerie Westwood's raised ones, turned back to me. What the hell was her name? I couldn't introduce her as 'the inebriated Lollipop-head' from Amanda's dinner party.

I needn't have worried. Suzy totally took over the classroom, introducing herself in her clipped tones and networking the room as if she were at one of her drinks' parties. She sat with the children, apparently genuinely interested in what they were up to and reading out some of the funnier mnemonics in an accent the kids had only ever heard on the BBC. Even Darren Slater and his cronies, obviously impressed by her designer gear, made an effort to be civil (Darren, bless him, telling her that he was particularly interested in Uranus rather than 'yer anus' as he'd repeated constantly to the rest of the class before her arrival).

With the rest of the class enraptured by Suzy's voice and presence, and with ten minutes to go before the end of the day, I beckoned Tyson over to my desk in order to sort out the admin work that goes hand in hand with a new arrival.

'Blimey, Miss, you've got big tits!' Tyson stared at me in wonder. Horrified not only that my pregnancy-inflated chest should evoke such a comment from an eleven-year-old, but that he had the audacity to utter it in my presence, I looked him full in the face and hissed,

'I beg your pardon!'

'Yer tits, Miss. My teacher at my last school only had little ones. And she only ever did 'em in red ink, never in green.'

Fighting the hysterical cackle that was about to be released not only on young Tyson and the rest of the class but also on Suzy's swinging, perfectly streaked bob, I patted Tyson's hand repeatedly and with great affection.

'So, Tyson,' I breathed, once I'd got myself and my patting under control, 'Mrs Westwood tells me you have something to do with The Duke of Leeds.' I looked him over at close range to see if I could decipher a noble brow perhaps, or an aristocratic nose.

'S'right, Miss.'

'So should we call you, "Your Grace",' I laughed, trying to ferret out just what his position was in the Royal line.

'Grace?' Tyson looked at me in surprise. 'That's a girl's name, Miss. Me name's Tyson. You know, like the boxer.'

Realising I'd better stop being nosey and get on with the task of filling in his details, I said, 'So, Tyson, where are you living now that you've moved to Farsley.'

Tyson looked at me as if I was a mad woman. 'At the Duke of Leeds, Miss.'

'You're *living* with the Duke of Leeds?' He was going further up in my estimation. Christine, my sister-in-law, would be very impressed.

'Yeah, well *at* the Duke of Leeds, Miss. Me mum's moved in with the landlord and she's working behind the bar.'

Suzy hung around while the children were dismissed and then joined me at my desk.

'It's really good of you to make time to come over, Suzy,' I smiled, and meant it. 'The kids always enjoy the diversion of having someone new in the classroom.'

'I've really enjoyed it,' she barked. 'I bet you never thought I'd take you up on your word.'

'No, I didn't,' I admitted, 'but I'm really glad you did.'

'Well, at a bit of a loose end at the moment.' Suzy retrieved her Chloe bag from where she'd left it under Darren Slater's table.

'I'm surprised you say that. I thought you'd have a constant round of lunches and charity dos and girly things ....' I trailed off, I wasn't quite sure what women like Suzy *did* do with their lives.

'Well, I do normally, but my partner in crime is off again.'

Warning bells began to ring.

'Your partner in crime?' I asked, smiling pleasantly.

'Yes, Mandy.' Suzy leaned towards me, smiling confidentially. I could smell cigarettes and Chanel No. 5. 'Entre nous and the doorpost, she's got the hots for some chap. Rather gorgeous-looking chap he is too. Actually, I think he was at the Hendersons' for dinner the night that you were there.' Suzy screwed up her face, as she searched her memory for details of that particular evening. ' Do you remember him? Tall, chunky and blonde with devastating brown eyes? I know we were all rather spiffy that night – well at least I was. Spent quite a bit of the evening in the loo in fact.' Suzy giggled, nudging me in the ribs as she did so. 'And I couldn't for the life of me work out for ages what the name and address you'd given me on the envelope was all about. Anyway,' she went on, 'you *must* have noticed him. Even though Mandy made sure she kept him to herself all evening. None of the rest of us got a look in. I'm amazed David puts up with it.'

'So where is she then?' I asked, trying to be nonchalant. Nonchalance is actually very hard when your stomach is churning and your heart going ten to the dozen. If I'd been half asleep an hour ago, I was most certainly very awake now.

Suzy sighed theatrically. 'Italy of all places. Can you imagine? Wouldn't you just *love* to be in Milan at the moment with some gorgeous, illicit hunk?' She poked me playfully in the ribs once again. I wanted to poke her, not so playfully, in the eye with a rusty nail. 'Hang on a minute, I've got a photo of him! Ginny Fairweather – do you know Ginny? Lovely girl, but a bit of a monkey, like Mandy. Well, Ginny happened to bump into them in Milan – she was there for the new spring collection, lucky girl, and caught them red-handed. What a scream she is! Anyway, caught them on her

BlackBerry and emailed the photos to me this morning. Did I recognise Mandy's new man? Who was he? Well, for once, I was one up on Ginny. Recognised him immediately from that dinner party. I mean, how can you forget those devastating eyes? Hang on, here we are. What do you think of that? Do you remember him now?'

Suzy thrust her mobile phone under my nose. Nick was sitting at what looked to be a café table, both arms wrapped tightly round Mandy. Her head was buried into his chest and he appeared to be kissing her hair, his eyes almost closed.

Suzy drew breath for a nano-second before going on, 'We'd actually got two days at The Sanctuary booked as well. Thought we'd treat ourselves to a bit of pampering. But then she tells me that Mick has rung her up from Italy. Says he desperately needs her in Milan. Can't be there without her.'

'Nick,' I said through gritted teeth.

'Sorry? Oh yes, Nick.' Suzy looked at me, eyebrows raised. 'Ah, you do know who I mean, then. Gorgeous isn't he? Anyway, there goes our little treat. Don't suppose you're available? I do so hate going off (she pronounced it 'orff') on my jollies *tout seul*.' Suzy turned to look at me, saw the pile of unmarked books that was threatening to fall off my desk, and sighed, 'No, I think not.'

'I need to get off, Suzy,' I said, wanting to be away from her. 'I have my younger daughter to pick up. She wasn't too well this morning.' I looked directly at her before adding meaningfully, 'And she's missing her daddy terribly.'

Suzy reached for her bag, searching for her car keys, totally oblivious to my last comment. Turning her lollipop-head to me, eyes wide with horror she squeaked, 'There's something in there. Something that certainly wasn't there an hour ago.'

'What do you mean, "something"? What kind of something?'

Gingerly, Suzy opened the bag fully before dropping it in fright. 'Good God, Harriet, there's a rat in there.'

I picked up her bag and held it at arm's length. Nothing seemed to be moving. Was she having some sort of hallucination? Perhaps she was an alcoholic and regularly saw elephants coming out of the wall and rats in her bag. Putting the bag onto my desk, I peered in. There, supine on top of soft, black leather gloves and an expensive-looking wallet, at the climax of his very last adventure, was a peaceful, but obviously very dead, Humbug.

Chapter 20

'Mummy, why are you crying?' India caught my eye in the driving mirror from her back seat vantage point in the rear of the car.

'Oh, I was just thinking about poor little Humbug,' I lied, trying to stem the tears that were flowing insistently, despite my best attempts to hold them in. 'He was such a brave little thing, and now he's dead.'

'Will he find Granny Morgan?' she asked anxiously, although her only knowledge of her great-grandmother was through the stories I'd told of her.

'I'm sure he will,' I assured her, smiling in spite of the fact that Suzy's carelessly spoken words and the photographic evidence of Nick's infidelity were crashing through my head like unstoppable waves on a pebbled shore. Nick's face had had such a look of peace in that photo. And what was it he'd said when he'd rung Amanda? He desperately needed her in Milan? When had he rung her? When had she gone out there? And why hadn't he told me she was there with him when he'd rung home a couple of nights ago?

'My throat still hurts, Mummy,' India whined, curling herself into a ball – as much as she was able, within the confines of her child seat.

'Granny Sylvia will be back this evening,' I soothed. 'If you're still feeling bad tomorrow then you don't need to go to school. Granny will tuck you up and bring you lovely things on a tray in bed.' Whatever Sylvia's faults, she was kindness personified when dealing with anyone not feeling one hundred percent. What wouldn't I give not to have to go to school tomorrow; to stay in bed and have lovely things that wouldn't make me throw up brought up to me on a tray?

'When's Daddy coming home?' India said plaintively, continuing to move restlessly in her car seat. I glanced in the mirror. India's previous pallor had been replaced by a red flush that stretched from her throat right up to her left ear. Oh my God! What if it was meningitis? Nick would just *have* to come home now, Italian contract or no.

'He won't be long now, darling. He may even be home tonight.' I spoke with a confidence I certainly didn't feel. 'Anyway, look, we're almost home now. Liberty and Kit shouldn't be too long. We'll have tea and then tuck you up in bed with Calpol and a lovely hot-water bottle.'

The house, once I'd managed to persuade a fretful India to leave the warmth of the car and go into it, was in darkness, and felt cold and unwelcoming. The kitchen table was still laid with the remains of the morning's breakfast and, in our hurry to be out of the house that morning, the door to the utility room – Bones' only means of access to the rest of the house – had been left open. He could be anywhere, revelling in the fact that the entire house was his kingdom until our return. He'd acquired a nasty habit lately of peeing in dark corners of the house – anywhere where he could find a nice soft place to park his backside – and he needed watching like a hawk.

I settled India in front of her favourite cartoon programme and, wrapping a duvet around her against the almost damp cold which had settled in the sitting room like a melancholic maiden aunt who has outstayed her welcome, I went back through the hall to ring the doctor's surgery. Their line was constantly engaged so I returned to the kitchen to think about food. Realising I'd have to unload the dishwasher in order to reload it with the breakfast things, I sighed and pulled on the handle. Cold, greasy water, afloat with the remains of last night's shepherd's pie, poured over the edges of the door, soaking my feet and the kitchen floor.

Right, I told myself, you can either be grown-up about this or scream. Swallowing every possible expletive I could think of in the knowledge that India would not only hear them but also store them up for future reference, I went to find the mop and bucket.

Bones, looking incredibly guilty, was in the process of sneaking out of the dining room, standing stock still when he saw me, before making an undignified dash to the utility room and his cat flap.

He'd certainly found somewhere to park his furry bottom. The basket of clean clothes, which I'd left in the dining room in an 'out of sight, out of mind' attempt to fool myself I didn't need to do a week's ironing, was now scented with a particularly pungent aroma of tomcat pee.

And that's when I did shout, and holler, and stamp my feet and throw the tainted washing at the dining-room door. And carried on shouting when Liberty, home from school, and, giving me a look of absolute astonishment, handed me the phone and told me Nick was ringing from Italy.

'Harriet, what *is* the matter?'

'What's the *matter*, you moron? You ring me from fucking Italy to ask what is the *matter?* I'll tell you what's the matter. While you're whooping it up in Italy with your fancy woman – and don't tell me she's not there because the lollipop-lady told me you'd begged her to go out there to be with you – while you're with the … *the magnificent Mandy*, I, single-handed, by myself, all alone am bringing up your three children – one, I might add, who is very poorly, am wading thigh-high in floodwater vomited from an antiquated dishwasher that has *finally* decided to lay down and *die* and am, even as I speak, throwing cat-pee stained clothes at the dining-room door. *And* I found Humbug, dead, in the … in the … in the lollipop-lady's handbag.'

Great big sobs rent the air as I ended my monologue by throwing the phone in the same direction as the ironing.

A hand, holding a glass of white wine, appeared round the door.

'Here, Mum, drink this,' said a disembodied, anxious voice. 'You always say, "if in doubt, put on your lippy," but I didn't know where to find your lipstick and I *did* know where the wine was.' Kit peered round the door. I took a sip of the wine, unable to speak. 'Libby has cleaned up the flood and she's making some tuna pasta.'

Oh God, how much of that little outburst had the kids heard? Had they heard me shouting about Nick's fancy woman?

I'd never known Liberty to do anything for anyone that didn't involve bribery, blackmail or threat, but here she was, in charge of the kitchen, sitting me down at the table and forcing me to eat pasta. She'd even persuaded India to leave her little cocoon in the sitting room and, with warm Lucozade inside her, India was managing to eat a morsel of food. I looked closely at her. She did seem slightly better, thank goodness.

No one quite met anyone else's eye; an undercurrent of politeness bordering on forced jollity ensured that we skirt around the subject that was uppermost in all our minds, but which none of us dared vocalise.

I thought we were home and dry until Kit, without looking up from his plate, where he was in the process of chasing a lone pea across it with his fork, suddenly blurted out, 'Is Dad having an affair with that Mandy woman?'

'Mandy? Daddy? Having an affair? Ha ha ha! Whatever next? What on earth gave you that idea?'

'The fact that you called her his fancy woman on the phone? And that you threw the phone at the door? The batteries have come out and it's all cracked down one side, you know. It's totally broken.'

I was starting to feel nauseous: Liberty, bless her, hadn't drained off any of the oil before adding the canned tuna to the pasta and it was beginning to churn uneasily in my stomach.

'Just need the loo,' I said brightly. 'Won't be a sec.'

I'd never been as sick as this with my previous pregnancies. Rinsing my mouth with cold water I tried desperately to make up excuses for my actions both in the dining room, and now, here in the downstairs' loo, where, I was sure, my retching sounds would have carried down to the kitchen.

'Mum?' Libby was hovering outside the loo door.

'Mmmm?'

'Are you ok?'

'I'm fine. Several children were sent home from school today and I think I must have caught their bug.'

'Dad's on the phone again.'

'I thought the phone was broken?'

'It is. He's ringing on my mobile. He says he can't get through on our landline or your mobile.'

Very likely. I'd not had any spare cash to top up my mobile for weeks.

'Can you hurry up? It's a really bad line and my mobile desperately needs recharging.' Libby thrust her phone round the door, her squeamishness, like that of any fifteen-year-old girl, rendering her unable to bring herself to actually enter the loo while her mother was in it.

'Hello, Nick.' I sat on the loo seat feeling tired, defeated and still very sick.

'Are you there, Harriet? Can you hear me? This is an awful line. Look, I'm really sorry about all this. I just can't leave here for quite a while yet.'

'Nick, why didn't you tell me Amanda was out there in Italy with you?'

The ensuing pause seemed to go on forever. And then Nick said, 'Because I knew I'd get just this reaction from you. I cannot do this without Mandy, Harriet. You're going to have to just put up with it. I can't afford to rock the boat at this stage.'

When I remained impassively silent, Nick carried on speaking, blurting out, 'Things aren't going well, Harriet. The Italian legal stuff is beyond me, and Mandy is the only one who knows how to sort it.'

'Is she coming on to you?' I asked, almost politely.

'Oh for fuck's sake, Harriet. Give me a break will you? I have to do what I have to do.'

'And does that include Mandy?'

'Harriet, you're breaking up. I can hardly hear you. Listen, I need you to tell Grace to lay off Sebastian. It's essential that she does.'

'Lay off him?' I laughed mirthlessly. 'Lay off him? You make it sound like she's on a diet and Sebastian is a box of chocolates. Why don't *you* try *laying off* Mandy?'

'Look, Mandy is acting very strangely over something at the

moment. It's all to do with Grace but she won't tell me what it's all about. She was quite hysterical last night. I've told her she's being silly – that what happened when you were all at school is all in the past. Even lied and told her Grace was back with Dan. I can't afford anything, and I mean anything, Harriet, to mess this all up ... .' Nick was beginning to sound desperate.

'What, Nick? What do you think she will do?'

'She'll be back on the next flight to Manchester for some bloody reason I can't quite fathom and I can kiss goodbye to fifty thousand pounds and any hope of this contract.'

And then he was gone, cut off as Libby's out of credit and out of power mobile finally gave up the ghost.

Automaton like, I patted cold water on my forehead, washed my hands and reached for the lipstick I kept in the downstairs loo cupboard in case anyone should knock at the front door. As I painted the vivid colour onto my bloodless lips with a trembling hand, I knew, without any doubt, I could not have this baby. Taking the children out of their private schools in order to release cash; managing to jiggle a new baby with a full-time job – I just couldn't do it all. Mandy was as much a force to be reckoned with now as she was when I was fourteen. If she wanted to get at Grace – Grace who had never shown her the respect her huge ego demanded and who had now had the temerity to fall in love with her only son – well, that was one sure way of doing it. Through Nick and me. Was Nick having to keep her sweet over there so that she wouldn't come back before things were sorted, leaving him high and dry? Or was he keeping her sweet because he wanted to? I thought again of the photo. That surely was a picture of a man who was more than happy to have the lovely Mandy in his arms. And in his bed? I felt sick again at the very thought. But really, who could blame him, when it came down to it? I mean, a cross, hormonal wife at home in a Yorkshire November or the gorgeous Mandy in glamorous Italy? No contest.

I went through to the sitting room where India was once more ensconced in Nick's grandfather's old chair. I picked her up, stroking her brow, which, thankfully, seemed a lot cooler. 'Let's get you to bed, sweetie,' I murmured, holding her close. 'Some more Calpol and a good night's sleep and you'll be fine. And if not, well, Granny will be here tomorrow to look after you.' I glanced at my watch – it was nearly seven o'clock. No sign of Sylvia yet.

India was asleep as soon as her head touched the pillow. Forcing a smile onto my face, I went downstairs to face Kit and Liberty. The supper table had been cleared, the dishes washed, and the kitchen brought to some semblance of order. Libby had even sorted the cat-pee tainted washing and the first lot was already halfway through its wash cycle. My two eldest children now sat at either end of the kitchen table, arms folded, wanting explanations. Avoiding their questioning eyes I went to fill the kettle for the ginger tea my stomach was craving.

'Mum, what's going on?' Liberty's tone was that of an indignant parent impatiently questioning its offspring.

'Are you poorly, Mum? Have you got cancer?' Kit was frightened. 'Only, Josh Barker said his mum kept being sick when she had cancer …'

'No, no, Kit. Of course not,' I interrupted him. 'Josh's mum was sick because of the chemotherapy treatment she had to cure the cancer. And she's fine now isn't she?'

'Well, she's a bit bald.' Kit, still doubtful, glanced at my hair for any further signs that I might not be being quite honest with him.

Liberty was staring at me.

'What?' I asked, taken aback by the look of sheer horror on her face.

'Oh-my-God!' she enunciated, each syllable raising a semitone as she spat them out.

'What?' I repeated, nervously.

'You're not – *pregnant* are you?'

'Pregnant?' I twittered. '*Pregnant*? Oh ha ha ha. At my age? Don't be so daft. Pregnant! Duh!'

'Well thank God for that. That would have been, like, so *gross*. I thought for one terrible moment you were up the duff without a husband.' And she chortled at her own ridiculous notion.

'Dad *is* coming back isn't he?' Kit was almost in tears. 'Has he gone off with that Mandy woman?'

I was saved from answering by a banging on the front door which, in our present state, made all three of us jump.

'Jesus, who on earth is that at *this* time of night?' I exclaimed, jumping up from the table. It was only seven-thirty, but by making a song and dance of the knocking I was able to divert attention away from Kit's last question.

I shot off through the hall to open the door. Standing on the step, bottle of wine in hand, was a rather apprehensive-looking Dan.

'Hi.' He gave me a rueful grin and brandished the bottle. 'I need to talk to you, Harriet. Can I come in, or have *you* given up on me as well?'

'Why, who else has given up on you?' I asked, taking him down to the sitting room after collecting a couple of glasses from the kitchen and suggesting Kit and Liberty go do their homework.

'Grace, of course.'

'I rather thought it was the other way round.'

'I've been to see her, Harriet. Several times. I've been a real idiot, I know, but I want her back. I want to go back home and sort all this mess out.'

'Right.' I didn't know what else to say.

'What's she said to you, Hattie? She always tells you everything.'

Not any more, Buster. Not after I found her frolicking, with her pants down, with young Enrique in my potting shed.

'Um, well, she hasn't said much, really.'

Suddenly I was angry. All the fury that should have been directed at my own husband came tumbling out in an unleashed torrent and hit Grace's husband squarely where I hoped it would hurt.

'What *is* the matter with you men? Why do you need some little floozy to bolster your flagging ego? It's not all about sex, is it? That's part of the appeal, obviously, but really you are all little boys. You've never grown out of wanting what Mummy says you can't have. You get bored with the wife and want to move on to the next toy. Because the wife represents the mortgage, the bills, the ritual of sex once a week on a Saturday night in the familiar bedroom, the developing paunch, the loss of hair.' I paused for breath while Dan looked down in surprise at his still very flat stomach as though expecting a layer of fat to have appeared around his torso. 'Whereas the floozy represents danger, sex wherever and whenever you can get it, not being nagged about the wallpaper peeling off in the bathroom. Fun!'

'Right' Daniel cleared his throat nervously and loosened his tie. 'Well, yes, Harriet, I think you're very right. We men are, as you say, mere pond life compared to you women.'

Pond life? I didn't recall lowering myself into calling him names. I was just about to protest that he was putting words into my mouth when a second, even louder, knocking at the front door, rent the air.

'My God, this is getting like Piccadilly Circus! Who the hell is this, now?'

I moved over to the window so that I could peer out onto whoever might be standing there.

'I think it's Camilla,' I hissed. 'What the hell's she doing here? How does she know where I live?'

'Probably because I told her.' Daniel looked at me steadily.

'What? Why would you need to tell her where *I* live?'

'That's why I needed to talk to you. I didn't expect her so soon. Would you just go and let her in?'

I opened my front door for the second time in twenty minutes. Standing there, even more stunning close up, was the auburn-haired beauty I recognised from the Friday evening, weeks ago, when I'd seen both her and Dan going into her flat.

'Hi, Harriet,' she said in that nasal twang common to all Australians. 'I really hope you don't mind me turning up like this but, the fact is, Patricia sent me.'

Chapter 21

I stared at Camilla, unable to speak.

'Look, can I come in?' she said, her voice tense. 'I assume Dan's told you?'

Daniel had followed me from the sitting room and was now standing beside me, shaking his head and glaring at Camilla who had one foot over the threshold. She was wearing faded Levis tucked into soft tan leather boots, and the brown cashmere jumper complemented both her hair and complexion beautifully. She really was stunning and, even though Grace was my best friend, I could totally understand how Dan had fallen under her spell.

'I told you to give me a good half-hour before you arrived,' he hissed at Camilla as I led them both back down to the warmth of the sitting room which was now snug and comforting after the unwelcoming chill of a few hours ago. The thick, tapestry curtains were drawn against the cold November evening and the lamps were dimmed, sending warm shadows across the room.

'Is someone going to tell me what's going on?' I asked, motioning them to sit down. I reached for the untouched glass of wine that Dan had poured earlier and took a sip. Even though my heart was pounding, and a huge swig was what was really needed, I was mindful of my present state and carefully placed the glass back on the coffee table.

'Well?' I demanded, when both of them remained silent. 'Aren't either of you going to say anything? Maybe you could just tell me who the hell Patricia is?'

Camilla had stood up and walked over to where she'd left her bag on the floor, made to open it, but then obviously thought better of it.

244

She glanced at Dan and then said quietly, 'Patricia is my mother.'

'Right. Ok. So, why would your mother send you, presumably all the way from Australia, to see me?'

Camilla took a deep breath before saying, 'Because I think she's your sister.'

'My sister? Why would *your* mother be *my* sister? Camilla, I really don't know what you're talking about.' I looked helplessly towards Dan but he just raised his eyebrows towards Camilla, indicating that I should listen to her.

'My mum was born in the UK – her birth certificate says that *her* mother was from Midhope in West Yorkshire. When I knew I was coming to work in England – I was supposed to be spending the two years secondment in London – Mum asked me to try and visit her mother's place of birth. I hated living in London – it really was too big – so when I was given the choice of transferring to Manchester or Leeds I jumped at the chance of coming here to see if I could dig up any family history.'

Camilla paused as Liberty came into the sitting room.

'Libby, I need you to do me a big favour,' I said, urgently. 'I want you to ring Auntie Diana, now, and tell her she *must* come up here this minute. If she argues with you, tell her she has to come, right now, because I think I've found Patricia.'

'Blimey, what's going on? And who's Patricia? Hi, Uncle Dan. Is this your new girlfriend? I thought she was called Camilla, not Patricia?'

'Libby,' I said, through gritted teeth, 'please just go and do as you're told. Tell her it's urgent.'

'Problem, Mum – there's not one phone working in this house.'

'Here, use mine.' Dan proffered his mobile and I grabbed it, pressing the buttons of Diana's home number.

'Diana,' I said, trying to speak calmly, 'can you get down here straight away? Don't ask any questions. Just grab your coat and come over. I think we've found Patricia.'

I handed the phone back to Dan and said, 'Go on, Camilla.'

'Well, when I arrived in Midhope last January I had no clues as to who my mum's mum might have been. Mum had been adopted at birth and been taken to Canberra by her new parents when they emigrated back in the early 1950s – they went out to Australia on one of those £10 assisted passages, loved it in Canberra and never came back to the UK. Mum had known from being a tiny girl that she was adopted, and to be quite honest had never had any interest in finding her real parents.'

'Mum, can I have one of those posh chocolate biscuits you keep hidden in Bones' biscuit tin?' Kit paused at the door, surprised to see so many people in the sitting room. He glanced across at Camilla and then did a double take, colouring furiously as his adolescent brain frantically tried to deal with the images sent out from the beautiful redhead sitting in his usual chair by the window.

'Shh,' hissed Liberty. 'Listen to this, it's really interesting.'

'Go on, Camilla,' I said again, pouring her some more wine. She took a good slug of it before continuing, occasionally looking at Dan as if for help. She must only be about twenty-four, I guessed. She really was very young to be so far away from her home, her family and friends.

'All that Mum knew was what her adoptive parents had told her – that she'd been born on the Isle of Man – I don't even know where that is – but that her birth mother was actually from Midhope in the North of England, and that she'd been named Patricia. She's called Joy now, by the way. Over the months, while I've been here in Midhope, Mum has become much more curious about her past. She's been in touch with various adoption agencies and she rang me last week to tell me what she'd found out.' Camilla stopped in mid-flow as we heard the front door bang and, five seconds later, Diana bustled into the sitting room.

'And?' I asked as Diana stared agog at the assembled company.

'And my mother's real mother was Keturah Morgan from Midhope in West Yorkshire.'

'Bloody hell,' Kit whistled. 'I think I'd better have some of that wine to make sense of all this,' and he grabbed my virtually untouched glass.

'What I don't understand is how you realised the name Keturah Morgan had anything to do with Harriet?' Diana asked after shoving Kit off the settee and catching up with the bits she'd missed.

'I wouldn't have had any idea if it hadn't been for Dan.' Camilla had the grace to look a little embarrassed: at the end of the day she *had* run off with my best friend's husband. 'When Mum rang me last week to tell me she'd now found out her birth mother's name, I obviously told Dan ...'

'Well, how many Keturah Morgans can there be in one small town?' Dan spoke for the first time since Camilla had started her tale. 'I mean, if your mum had been called Betty or ... Dorothy or something *usual* we'd have been none the wiser. But knowing your mum was called Keturah, and having met your Granny *Morgan* at various family dos – and you don't forget Granny Morgan in a hurry – well, I just put two and two together.'

'Bit of a coincidence, isn't it, Camilla? You shacked up with Harriet's best friend's husband, I mean?' Diana could be very cutting when she wanted.

'Well, yes, incredible coincidence.' Camilla stood her ground, holding Diana's stare. 'I've a couple of photographs of Mum here.' She went over to her bag and brought out a large, buff-coloured envelope.

One was of Patricia as a toddler with very fair hair and big blue eyes, holding onto an oversized ice cream with one hand and a rather plump, but kindly-looking woman's hand with the other. I turned the photograph over. It just said, 'Joy, Canberra 1957.'

'I don't think my Nan ever got over ending up with such a beautiful daughter. Nan and Grandpa were very ordinary people – from Liverpool originally – and they suddenly found themselves with this very bright, very pretty daughter. I know she's my mum, and perhaps I shouldn't say it, but she was, and still is, a very attractive and very *gifted* woman.' Camilla looked very sad. 'I've really missed her while I've been in England.'

'Beautiful and gifted?' Kit screwed up his nose. 'I wouldn't say any of your family are "beautiful and gifted" would you, Mum? Apart from me of course. I know Granny Keturah is a whiz at making stew and dumplings, but gifted ...?'

Ignoring Kit, I had a good look at the other three photographs Camilla had brought with her. Patricia/Joy was certainly a very beautiful woman. The last photograph was the most up to date, having been taken, apparently, last year when she was fifty-six. I couldn't stop looking at it. This was my sister, for heaven's sake. My *sister*.

'Have you got brothers or sisters?' I suddenly realised I might have nephews and nieces I knew nothing about.

Camilla smiled. 'Yep. There's Patrick. He's the eldest. He's twenty-nine and a pilot with Quantas. My sister, Saskia, is three years older than me. She's twenty-seven and runs her own consultancy business. Mum always hoped one of us would follow in her footsteps.'

'What does she do?' Diana asked.

'Mum? She's a consultant obstetrician. One of the best in the country actually.'

'So, how do we tell Mum that we've found Patricia?' Diana demanded once all this information was beginning to sink in. 'I mean,' she went on, turning to Camilla, 'I am assuming your mum is only our *half*-sister. Dad doesn't seem to know anything about any baby. If he'd known Mum had had a baby when she was, what … eighteen? he'd have known all about Patricia and, of course – it's all falling into place now – the Isle of Man. Why the Isle of Man, I wonder? Why didn't she just have the baby here in Midhope?'

'And if Grandad wasn't the father,' Liberty burst in excitedly, 'who was?'

Libby's excitement about Patricia was contagious. I had a new sister. A new sister for heaven's sake! Diana and I just looked at each other, silly grins on our faces, unable to say a word.

I looked at my watch. Too late now to start introducing Mum to the idea that not only had we found Patricia but that, in doing so, we all knew that she'd committed that most heinous of all crimes – having sex out of wedlock!

Chapter 22

Tuesday morning and there was no way I could go to work. I had an appointment with my GP, India was still running a temperature, and Sylvia appeared to have disappeared into thin air. As far as I knew, Sylvia had been spending the weekend in Surrey with some people she'd apparently known for years, but she'd been expected back yesterday. We'd tried to persuade Sylvia to get a mobile, even offered to buy her one for Christmas, but she was adamant she didn't need one. Maybe she'd already got wind of Nick's defection and had made the decision to throw her lot in with Little Miss Goodness and her camp. Wouldn't blame her if she had – Italy with her son and his lover would, I'm sure, seem an infinitely more promising prospect than West Yorkshire in November with an increasingly cantankerous daughter-in-law with Compulsive Granite Disorder, and her strange relations.

Despite being so utterly tired – I felt as if I'd been squeezed and left out to dry, a bit like one of my mother's dishcloths which she would regularly make from Dad's ageing Y-fronts: bleached, boiled and hung out on the line – I'd been unable to sleep, and had tossed and turned all night until, at four o'clock, I'd gone downstairs and made myself some hot milk and given the worktop a bit of a polish. The double realisation, that within a few hours I'd quite possibly lost my husband, my house and security but gained a half-sister and a whole new family in Australia, had done nothing to help me nod off, but everything to bolster my compulsion to clean the granite.

Tony Drummond, our new head and my new best friend, had been fine about my missing the first half of the morning when I'd approached him at school yesterday. He'd promised to hold the fort with my class until my return, but I hadn't envisaged not having Sylvia as back-up if India was unable to go to school – which by the look of her she wasn't. My sensible head assured me that India had nothing more than an ear infection, but my neurotic head – taking over, it seemed, at an alarming rate – insisted that she had something more serious.

Once I'd got Kit and Liberty off to the school bus, I decided to take India to the surgery with me and, if she was well enough, drive her over to Mum and Dad's so that I could at least have the afternoon at school. I'd also be able to casually explain that Diana and I were going to pop in that evening with a friend of ours who we thought they'd both like to meet. Before she'd left last night, Diana and I had arranged to meet up with Camilla so that we could take her round to our parents' house. Beyond that we didn't have a plan.

I'd assumed that Daniel and Camilla had left together, going back to her flat in Netherfields, but now, thinking back to Dan's pleading that he wanted Grace back, I wasn't so sure. I was determined to find out, though. Grace, I presumed, would want to know and, even if we were being pretty cool with each other, I just had to tell her that the woman her husband was hitched up with was, in actual fact, my niece!

Where was Sylvia? I actually felt a bit miffed she hadn't been in touch – just left me high and dry, wondering where she was. I did hope she hadn't been mugged and was lying in a gutter somewhere. Mind you, I suppose it would be a bit difficult for her to tell me what she was up to when all our phones appeared to be on strike. I'd made the decision, during last night's fight with insomnia, not to do anything about the phone problem for the moment: ostrich-like I was actually terrified of speaking to Nick and of him telling me things I was terrified of hearing. Also, the lack of a phone would stop the kids spending more of my hard- earned cash on interminable and, I felt, unnecessary, phone calls to their mates.

Leaving India in the surgery play area, where she'd not only pass on her own bugs but no doubt collect several others from the snot-encrusted toddler who was leaving a viscous trail of green goo on the books and toys, I made my way to the far end of the surgery from where my name had been called by Dr Chadwick.

'Right, Harriet, what can I do for you?' she asked without looking up from her computer.

'I'm pregnant.'

'That good or bad?'

'Bad. Most definitely bad.'

This had obviously attracted her attention for she deigned to glance up. 'Why?'

'I'm working full time now – we can't do without my wage. My children are all at private school. I'm constantly tired and bad-tempered. I've just discovered that my poor mother who, in addition to going a bit, you know, ga-ga, has another child which means I've got a new sister, not to mention a *niece* who, unfortunately is shacked up with my best friend's *husband*. This best friend *isn't* my best friend anymore because I was really horrid to her when I found her having sex in my potting shed with Enrique Iglesias. My husband seems to have moved permanently to *Italy,* living La Dolce Vita with Enrique's mother who I adored when I was eleven, hated when I was fourteen, and with whom my whole security now hangs in the balance. Oh, and India has got something horrible.'

Like an unstoppable geyser, the torrent of words spewed out, landing in an undignified, but invisible heap on my doctor's neatly bobbed head.

'Harriet, whoa, whoa, slow down. Take your time. Tell me everything.' The good doctor had now taken off her glasses, poured both of us a plastic cup of water from the water cooler outside her room, and settled herself for the duration.

'Harriet, you are in no state to make any decision about this baby,' Dr Chadwick said ten minutes later, handing me a tissue to mop up the tears that had begun in earnest as soon as she started being sympathetic. 'For a start, Nick isn't here. It must surely be a joint decision as to what conclusion you come to. The other thing is, there is no certainty that this pregnancy will be viable.'

'Viable? What do you mean, viable?' I sniffed.

Dr Chadwick had been scrolling down through her computer. She'd obviously found what she'd been searching for because she now said, 'The two babies you lost, several years ago, were both caused by a blighted ovum. Your chances of other pregnancies going the same way increase greatly once you've experienced one of these. You've had two – *and* you're now seven years older. What I want you to do is what you did when you were first pregnant with India. I want you to make an appointment at the hospital for an early scan. It's no good doing it before you are six weeks' pregnant – the heart of a healthy baby can't always be seen until then. If there is no heartbeat, then the amniotic sac has carried on forming but the baby itself hasn't. In effect, the baby never got going. What I also suggest you do, once you've let me have a quick look at India, is go home, put both of you to bed and stay there for the rest of the day. Things might look a bit better after that.'

And so we did. On the way home I popped in to Ralph-Next-Door's to use their phone and rang school to say I couldn't leave India as the doctor had confirmed she had an ear infection, rang Dad to say we were coming round to see him and Mum that evening, and rang the hospital consultant's secretary to arrange a scan in a week's time. I was about to ask Ralph's wife, Deirdre, if I could possibly ring Italy, but then thought better of it. I really didn't want to face up to anything Nick might be going to tell me about his business – or Mandy.

India and I then snuggled, like nocturnal hamsters, into my bed, her with Calpol and me with toast, marmite and peanut butter, and stayed there until Liberty and Kit were due home from school.

By seven o'clock that evening I was ready to face Mum. Actually, after catching up with several hours sleep and feasting on a huge home-cooked lasagne I'd found lurking in the depths of the freezer, I was beginning to feel I could perhaps face the world as well. There was absolutely nothing I could do about this pregnancy until after my scan, and I also felt I'd done a fairly good job in convincing the two elder children that everything was absolutely fine and dandy. Kit in particular seemed to have been affected by recent events, and spent a lot of time keeping me in his sight – something he hadn't needed to do since he was a little boy and frightened of the wolf on the landing. There seemed to be little else I could do about the state of my marriage while I was deliberately remaining out of contact with the perpetrator responsible.

I left Liberty in charge and set off with Camilla to pick up Diana, making a quick detour via the village co-op so that at least we'd have milk, bread, juice and fruit in the fridge the following morning.

'Sorry about that,' I said to Camilla, throwing the bulging carrier bags on to the back seat. 'It's chaotic enough at our house in the morning *with* breakfast. Without it, it's sheer hell.'

'Yes,' she said almost wistfully. 'I never thought I'd miss the breakfast arguments back home, but I do.'

'How much longer are you here in England?' I asked, heading for the next village where Diana lived in the tiny cottage she shared with her overindulged cat.

'I'm supposed to do another year, really.' Camilla paused, her next words unspoken.

'But?' I prompted.

'But, I think I'm going to go home. I miss everyone, I don't think I can stand another English winter and, besides, there's really nothing here for me now.'

I glanced across at her. 'What about Dan?'

'I think both Dan and I know that it's over. He hasn't said, but I guess he's as homesick for his wife as I am for Mum and Dad. You know, Harriet, I feel really bad about Grace. Going off with someone else's husband was never on my agenda. He actually told me he and Grace were separated.'

Bastard!!

'Anyway,' Camilla continued, as we drew up outside Diana's cottage, 'I really need you to tell her from me how sorry I am. She was so welcoming when she invited me round to their house when I first arrived in Midhope – and then I went and did this to her.'

'Not by yourself you didn't,' I said grimly. 'Daniel played his part, you know.'

'I'm so nervous about seeing your mum. I really don't want to open a can of worms.'

'Camilla,' I sighed. 'I think this is one can that has well and truly been opened already. And if it makes you feel any better, I'm actually *terrified* of facing her with this.'

I sounded the horn and Diana came out, almost tripping over the cat as he wove himself round her legs while she locked her door.

'We were just saying, Di,' I said, as she fought her way through the co-op shopping to find a seat in the back, 'are we doing the right thing in telling Mum about Joy? Do you not think we might be better letting sleeping dogs lie? At least we now know Patricia actually exists, so Mum isn't going completely bonkers. Being confronted with the result of what she got up to all those years ago could tip her completely over the edge, you know.'

'No,' Diana said firmly. 'I really feel she needs to meet Camilla. I rang Dad this afternoon and met him up at his allotment. I hope you don't mind, both of you, but Dad now knows that Patricia is a real person, not some figment of mum's brain.'

'Blimey,' I breathed. 'What did you tell him? What did he say?'

'He actually had tears in his eyes after I'd told him about Camilla coming round last night,' Diana said. 'He said thank goodness Patricia actually exists. He really thought Mum was going completely round the bend.'

I hesitated before saying, 'Well maybe a *bit* round the bend? Don't forget she's been talking to Granny Morgan, too.'

'Granny Morgan?' Camilla raised an eyebrow.

'Mum's mum. Mum has been having very one-sided conversations with her despite the fact that she's been dead these last four or five years.'

Dad opened the door to the three of us and ushered us into the tiny lounge that still carried the faint odour of their midday meal, and where Mum was watching the end of *Emmerdale*. She peered over her glasses, staring intently at Camilla who had gone very pale.

Her hands, clasped around the mug that Liberty had brought back for her from a school trip to Haworth, were brown with the liver spots of old age. Putting the mug down on to the table next to her armchair, Mum placed her slippered feet squarely in front of her and sat bolt upright, never once taking her gaze from Camilla's face.

'Now then, Keturah, Diana and Harriet have brought someone to see you,' Dad said, his breezy manner unable to hide the trepidation he was obviously feeling. 'This is Camilla.'

'Oh aye? And who might Camilla be then?'

'Come and sit down, love.' Dad motioned for Camilla to come forward and she sat down on the sofa. 'Get yourself warm. It's cold out there tonight.'

Diana crossed over to the scratched leather pouffe that had been a feature of my parents' lounge for as long as I could remember, pulling it up so that she was sitting at Mum's feet. 'Mum, Camilla has come from Patricia. She's Patricia's daughter.'

'Patricia? My Patricia?'

'Yes, Mum, that's right.' Diana took Mum's hand which had been fingering the chintz fabric of her armchair and held it tightly to stop the trembling which had started the second Patricia's name was mentioned. 'You've never told us about her before. Will you tell us now?'

Mum looked at Dad, real fear in her eyes.

'Nay, lass, why didn't you ever tell me about her? I wouldn't have minded. You know that.' Dad stood there shaking his head.

'Your Granny Morgan said I must never tell *anyone*.' Mum looked first at Diana and then at me. 'She said I was a dirty little trollop and if anyone knew what I'd been up to I'd never get anyone to marry me. Oh, but I didn't want to give her away – she were so lovely. But they made me. Your Granny Morgan said I couldn't come home if I kept her. I had no money, you see, and nowhere else to go. I couldn't look after Patricia, could I?'

'Why did you go to the Isle of Man?' I asked.

'Well, I went looking for her, you know, but I couldn't find her.'

'No, Mum, I mean why did you go to the Isle of Man to have the baby? Why didn't you stay here and have her?'

Mum looked a bit bewildered for a moment, but then became

quite lucid, taking her hand from Diana's and folding her arms crossly.

'When I found out I was carrying, I had to tell your Granny Morgan. I didn't know what else to do. Ooh, she was cross. Wild she was. I thought she was going to kill me. She went and had a word with the parson of Leygate Baptist and together they shipped me off to the Isle of Man to one of them mother and baby places there. Run by t'church it were. It were a dreadful place. I thought I were going to die on that ferry going across the sea. It was winter – so cold and I was so sick all the way there. Ooh and homesick I were too. I'd never been away from your Granny Morgan before.'

'Where did Granny tell people you were?' I asked, curiously. 'Surely they wondered where you'd gone?'

Mum shrugged. 'Said I'd got a job in one of the bed and breakfast places on the Isle of Man. In the years after the war a lot of young girls were restless and moved about a bit. The war changed everything, you know.'

Mum leaned forward in her chair. 'You're very bonny, love,' she said, scrutinising Camilla once more. 'Is your mum pretty too?'

'She's really beautiful,' Camilla gushed, desperate for Mum to know more about the baby she gave away. 'Look, I've some photos of her.'

Mum took them with shaking hands, silently staring at the black-and-white images. 'And is she still on the Isle of Man? You've got a bit of a funny accent, love, if you don't mind me saying so – is it an Isle of Man accent? I did look for her, you know. I made Kenneth take me there when we got married. Of course, I never told him why I wanted to go there.'

'Mum emigrated to Australia when she was adopted,' Camilla smiled. 'We live near Canberra.'

'*Australia*?' Camilla might as well have said 'Mars.' 'Eeh, that is a long way away. Fancy. Australia. No wonder I never found her.'

I went to stand behind Mum, looking once more at the photographs Camilla had shown for the first time the previous evening.

'She is pretty, isn't she?' I smiled.

'Like her dad, love. She looks just like her dad.'

'Mum,' Diana asked quietly, 'who *was* Patricia's dad?'

'Her dad? Well, it were Young Mr Frank, of course.'

'Young Mr Frank?' We all stared, especially Dad, who'd been straining to hear what Mum was saying.

Mum chuckled. 'Well it certainly wasn't *Old* Mr Frank. *He* must have been nearing seventy by then. Eeh', she said almost dreamily, 'We all fancied Frank in them days.'

'Frank who, Mum?'

'Frank Goodners of course. From Goodners and Sons Mills.'

'This is getting more like a Barbara Taylor Bradford novel every minute,' Diana hissed, closing the kitchen door so Mum wouldn't hear us discussing her past as we made tea.

'You mean, "trouble at t'mill" again?'

'You're not kidding. Do you reckon she had to tug her forelock before dropping her knickers for *Young Mr Frank*?'

'Diana, that's awful!' I gasped, shocked by her flippant words. 'You can't talk about Mum like that.' Despite the shock brought on by Mum's completely unexpected disclosure, Diana's remark was in danger of setting off a fit of nervous and inappropriate cackling. It was the same as at Granny Morgan's funeral: one glance at Great Aunt Edna's disconcertingly phallic hat had rendered both Diana and me speechless with uncontrollable chortling. It really was about time we both grew up.

'You do know who Frank Goodners is, don't you?' I asked, sobering up. 'Well *was*. He's dead now.'

'Don't be stupid! Of course I know who Frank Goodners is. I can't hear the fucking Goodners' name or pass their mill without thinking of John and how he reckons his life was ruined by Frank Goodners' daughter.' Diana poured milk into a jug before glancing at me. 'And now she's got her claws into Nick.'

When I didn't say anything, she sighed and went on, 'What on earth is it that has made our family such a target for the Goodners family? Because that's what it seems like, don't you think? First Mum, then you – yes, Hat, I knew all about your schoolgirl passion for Amanda – and then poor old John and now Nick.' Diana shook her head in disbelief.

'Frank Goodners was actually very nice when I met him all those years ago. He once gave me a lift home in his Roller or his Bentley or whatever it was.'

'So nice that he abandoned Mum when she was pregnant,' Di pointed out crossly.

'I can't work this out any more,' I said, when she didn't say anything further. 'Does this mean that I'm now related to my husband's possible mistress?' My brain, befuddled by pregnancy hormones, general tiredness and the shock of all these relatives crawling out of the woodwork, was heading for meltdown.

I was trying to cast my mind back to that day, so many moons ago now, when we'd performed in the school play at Midhope Grammar and then been invited back to the Goodners' mansion. Back in the other room, I passed a cup to Mum and said casually, 'Mum, do you remember that time when you came to my school to watch me in a play? I was Ratty in *Toad of Toad Hall*?'

'Aye, and you went back to Frank Goodners' for tea. And he brought you back home in his fancy car.'

'Gosh, you remember?' I felt humbled. My mother had kept this secret all her life and told no one, so ashamed she'd been of having a baby as a young unmarried girl. She must have gone through such a lot without telling a soul.

''Course I remember.' Mum sounded bitter. 'I'd no idea his daughter were at your school until that day. I knew he'd married some woman from down South, but I'd heard his wife hadn't been able to have children. Like me and your dad, I reckon they must have been married for a long time before they actually had any children, and I think she was the only one they had. So, aye, it were a bit of a shock, like, seeing him sitting across from me at that school of yours.'

'Didn't he say anything to you?' Camilla asked. 'Did he see you?'

'Oh aye, he saw me alright. You have to remember, I hadn't clapped eyes on him for nigh on thirty years – our paths never crossed, him being such a bigwig, an all. Seen him in t' local paper of course – he were a magistrate and Tory councillor, even tried to become an MP at one point – but I'd not seen him in the flesh as it were, until that afternoon at your school.'

'And? Did he speak to you, lass?' Dad was getting a bit agitated.

'Just came over and said "How are you doing, Keturah?" and asked which was my daughter.' Mum cackled. 'I reckon it must have been a bit of a shock, his old mill-worker's daughter being at the same posh school as *his* daughter. And that was it. I seem to remember then he spent a lot of time talking to Grace's mother – I think he must have known her socially.'

'But didn't he ask you about the baby?' Camilla was clearly upset now.

'He never knew about Patricia!' Mum spat angrily.

'What, you never told him?' Diana, Camilla and I spoke as one.

'No. Your Granny said it'd do no good. They'd probably deny it were anything to do with t' boss's son. It wasn't just me who worked there – had done since I were fourteen – but your Granny and Grandad worked there too. We all worked there, and your Granny didn't want any boats rocking.'

'Oh bugger me,' Diana shouted angrily. 'Sorry, Mum, excuse the language, but you weren't living in the dark ages. There'd been a war. It was the 1950s for heaven's sake.'

'Your Granny knew there were no way the Goodners family would have let him marry one of his workers – even if he'd wanted to, which I don't suppose for one minute he did. She didn't want anybody to know what I'd been up to – like I said, she told me I was disgusting, called me a whore, used goods. As soon as she found out, she virtually threw me out. I had to go somewhere where no one knew me, where "t'consequences", as she called it, could be dealt with.' The line of Mum's mouth hardened. 'I never forgave her for making me give my little girl away.'

'You know, Mum, Camilla says Joy – Patricia – has done really well in Australia. She's a doctor,' I said, wanting my mother to know that things weren't all bad. That by giving up her daughter she'd allowed her to have a good and very productive life.

'I think Patricia will want to come over and see you, Keturah.

Would you let her do that?' Camilla was beginning to relax.

Mum's face softened. 'Ay, love, I'd like that more than anything. So I could just tell her how much I'd loved her. How I've thought about her every single day since she was born.'

Mum paused and then looked at all three of us girls before saying fiercely, 'Never, never give your baby away. You look after it, love it, and care for it. No matter what happens, it's your baby, your flesh and blood, and you *keep* it.'

And then she began to cry.

And, once I was in my own bed, so did I. I cried for my poor mum, for my marriage, for my husband who wasn't there and probably wouldn't be again, for my lovely house that we might have to leave and for my bewildered children. But most of all I cried for *my* baby. *My* baby that I simply could *not* keep.

Chapter 23

After an incredibly mild start to the month, the latter part of November sought its revenge, plunging the whole country, but particularly the North, into a sudden and premature winter. While no snow had fallen, the local weathermen, anxious to avoid being caught unawares, were being absolute drama queens, behaving totally over the top as they warned of icy Arctic blasts heading our way.

After watching Paul Hudson – *Look North*'s jocular resident weatherman – on the early evening news, Kit suggested it might be a good idea if we battened down the hatches and not go to school for a few days, 'just in case.'

'Just in case, what?' I asked, clearing the kitchen table so I could catch up with a pile of marking and preparation.

'Just in case he has a French test,' Liberty intervened, throwing Kit's exercise book at him.

'When am I going to ever *need* French?' Kit groaned. 'I don't get it. How do you *know* if a ruler is feminine or a book masculine?'

'Those magazines at the back of your wardrobe have got enough bare bosoms in them for you to know *they* most certainly are feminine,' said Liberty, neatly dodging the missile's returned flight.

Kit reddened. 'Back off, Birdbrain. Anyway, if I *have* to learn a strange language, it ought to be Italian.' Kit had his head down, avoiding my eyes.

'Why's that, Kit?' I asked softly, finishing one pile of books and reaching for another.

'Well, if I'm to be the victim of a broken home, and Dad is going to be living in Italy with his fancy woman, I really ought to know the Italian for "You bastard.""

In the week since Camilla had become part of our family, very little had happened apart from the day-to-day ritual of everyday life. Sylvia had turned up a couple of days later and unpacked her bags before setting off again with a huge case and a similar-sized grin on her face.

'Now, dear, I hope I'm not letting you down,' she'd chirruped, 'especially with Nick away so long, but I've been invited to join a house party in Barbados.'

House party? Blimey, when did anyone still call them *house* parties? And who had invited her? Lucky old Sylvia. What wouldn't I give to be lying on a hot, tropical beach for two weeks, my every need attended to by a bevy of drink-carrying waiters.

With the house phone still in casualty and all the mobiles out of credit because of a lack of funds, there'd been very little contact with Nick. He'd tried to ring me once at school, but when I was finally able to leave my class and had dashed, breathless, to the office in order to take the call, Valerie Westwood had replaced the receiver, unaware that my recalcitrant husband was on the other end. There'd been one postcard, addressed to the children, saying how much he loved them all, but wouldn't be seeing them for a while as he was unable to leave Italy just at the moment.

Oh Nick, come home, I'd whispered to myself turning the card over to reveal Milan, at night, in all its splendour. Your children need you. I need you.

I'd managed to get Grace alone one morning before school in order to tell her about Dan's visit, but she'd been very cool with me, said she knew all about it: Dan had spent the previous evening round at her place and they were 'in discussion.'

With the phone out of order, my day's absence from work, and Grace away from school on a course, as well as being interviewed for that deputy headship she'd applied for, there had been little opportunity to tackle the cold war that had sprung up between us since the potting-shed incident.

I suppose I was also keeping my distance because there was no way I could tell her that I was pregnant with a baby that I was not going to keep. That would crucify her, and more than likely put an end to our friendship for good.

On the morning of my hospital scan, we woke to a world made white by a dusting of snow. Like the sprinkling of icing sugar on the butterfly buns India had begged me to make with her the previous evening, the snow was fine and powdery, already melting in exposed places.

I hadn't told my class that Tony Drummond had agreed to cover my games lesson that afternoon while I was at the hospital. He'd really grown on the kids in the three months he'd been head teacher but I knew he was planning to take them out for a cross-country run and, particularly for the girls – whose idea of exercise was imitating Beyonce's dance routines – the idea of stripping off to their pink Lycra, before careering round several boggy fields, was anathema.

Seeing Tony disappear into the staff room just before the bell sounded for the start of morning school, I put my head round the door shouting, 'Where's that six inches you promised me last night, Tony?'

Three prospective candidates for the position of Parent Governor (available due to the present incumbent's child defecting to a school that was higher in the league tables), looked at me aghast.

'Snow, I meant the snow, ha, ha, ha,' I trilled, backing out of the staff room, while my new best friend was left to explain that he liked to think he knew a bit about weather forecasting.

Six hours later, full to saturation point with the water I'd obediently forced down, I was waiting nervously for my name to be called. Desperate for a pee, I tried to take my mind off my bladder by delving into the dated, tatty magazines that littered the surrounding seats. Not an upmarket read among them. I was back to twiddling my thumbs, crossing my legs and musing about which of my fellow outpatients were actually happy to be pregnant. Surely not the little girl opposite who couldn't have been much older than Liberty? She was alone, not even her mother for company, intent on snapping off the split ends from her mass of unkempt hair. My gaze went to the couple opposite: they were sat holding hands, occasionally stroking the stout, solid bump that protruded from beneath their entwined fingers.

Desperately held-in tears began to sting my nose as I remembered how excited Nick and I had been, sitting in this same room, waiting our turn to be called for my twenty-week scan when I was pregnant with Liberty. Nick had been very unsure about becoming a father at the age of twenty-four – Sylvia had said we were quite mad – but we were married, desperately in love, and, as far as I could see, that was all that mattered.

A sudden and total need for Nick threatened to overpower me. I had to speak to him, tell him where I was and what was going on. I scrabbled in my bag, hunting for my mobile phone amongst the Sainsbury's till receipts and redundant car park tickets before remembering it was still out of credit. Cursing myself for my pig-headedness in staying deliberately out of touch with Nick, I sat back, miserably conscious that my panic-stricken fumbling had been watched with interest by the rest of the waiting room.

Like a mantra I began to repeat to myself, *'please let there not be a heartbeat, please let there not be a heartbeat.'* If, as Dr Chadwick had warned, there was a high chance that this pregnancy could also be the result of a blighted ovum, then there wasn't an actual baby developing. I would be given a quick D and C to remove the material that was, even now, developing into the absent baby's life-support system, and the decision about what to do about a baby I couldn't afford would not have to be made.

How ironic that I'd sat here, almost seven years ago, a few weeks pregnant with India, my nails digging into Nick's hand, waiting as I was waiting now, but chanting in my head, *'please let there be a heartbeat, please let there be a heartbeat.'*

'Harriet Westmoreland?' A motherly looking, white-coated doctor with a very ample bosom ushered me in to a side room, introduced herself as my consultant's registrar and pulled my hospital file towards her.

'Your GP wants you to have an early scan because of previous pregnancies that have been a result of blighted ova. Is that right?'

When I just nodded miserably, she patted my hand saying, 'Come along then, dear, let's get you up to X-ray and put your mind at rest.'

The walk along the sludge-green painted corridors up to the hospital's X-ray department where the IntraUterine scans were carried out seemed interminable. Clutching my forms in sweaty hands, I moved along, my legs battling their way, it seemed, through a vat of treacle.

Ten minutes later I was up on a paper-covered bed having cold gel smeared onto my stomach.

'Is there a heartbeat?' I asked nervously. The radiographer had been swishing around with the wand for a good minute, moving it around my naval, glancing at the screen as she zoomed in and out, but not saying a word apart from, 'Just relax, please.'

'Is there one?' I asked again. My own heartbeat seemed to be pounding in my ears as well as my chest.

The girl paused, pushed an escaped lock of blonde hair behind her ear, but still remained totally non-committal. The clock on the wall ticked steadily, its beat seemingly in rhythm with the pain-staking movement of the radiographer's wand. I counted another thirty seconds until, in desperation, I almost cried, 'Is there a heartbeat? Please can you tell me? It's really important that I know.'

Without looking at me, the girl said quietly, 'No, there isn't one.'

Relief coursed through my whole body and I felt my shoulders relax.

'No,' she went on. 'There isn't one. There are two!'

'Two? It's a baby with two hearts?' I screeched.

She laughed. 'No! It's two babies with one heart each! Look!'

The girl clicked her wand first on one and then on a second area of the screen, pointing out the tiny, but very quick, pulse of two tiny heartbeats.

These were my babies. Two of them.

Numbly I used the proffered tissue to wipe away the colourless jelly, slid off the bed, dressed and made my way back to the registrar.

Chapter 24

It was dusk by the time I left the hospital. A penetrating damp fog had wrapped itself almost seductively around the shabby hospital buildings, softening their facade and dimming the orange lights that shone out from the multitude of windows. A few snowflakes, tiny but tenacious, were starting to fall from a mustard-coloured sky and attempting to settle on my hair and coat as I made my way across the car park.

Removing the slight build-up of snowflakes from my windscreen, I put the car into gear and headed for home. By the time I reached the exit the snow was no longer playful, flirting with my windscreen wipers, but coming down in huge, gobstopper-sized flakes.

The quickest way home was down the motorway: if I attempted to go into Midhope town centre and out again there was a big chance I'd get stuck in the early rush-hour traffic that was already beginning to build up around me. With Sylvia partying in sunny Barbados, I'd had to pull in some favours and arrange for all three children to have tea with friends, but they would all need picking up at some stage later that evening.

The dual carriageway that led onto the motorway had obviously been well gritted, allowing the traffic to move easily, and within twenty minutes I was approaching the slip road onto the M62. The snowflakes, dancing on my windscreen, were hypnotic and I had to concentrate hard on getting into the appropriate lane. There was a huge amount of traffic in all three lanes but it was flowing freely, unhampered by the atrocious weather that was becoming steadily worse as the motorway followed its course, climbing into the heart of the Pennines.

With only a few miles to go before my exit from the motorway, brake lights began to gleam through the white of the still falling snow; the flow of traffic in all three lanes began to slow and within a few minutes came to a total standstill.

Shit! A blanket of snow began almost immediately to settle on the car bonnet and I had to turn the wipers up to deal with the snow on the windscreen. Without the constant movement of vehicles which had been destroying the snowflakes as they fell, turning them to wet mush, the snow, like an advancing army, began to invade the motorway itself and, finding no resistance from the now immobile traffic, swiftly and thoroughly began to take control.

I'd no real experience of motorway driving in conditions such as these. Not the most confident of drivers at the best of times, I had to force myself to take deep breaths, make myself relax in order to stave off the panic that was threatening to overwhelm me. I tried to open the window to see exactly what was happening ahead, but the build-up of snow on the glass immediately fell on to my lap and I hastily closed it again.

I switched from the Mozart CD that I'd been listening to in an effort to calm myself after the bombshell from the hospital, and tuned into the local radio in the hope of finding out what was going on. After ten minutes of inane chat from the teatime DJ, jingles advertising local conservatory dealers, and solicitors more than willing to sue on anyone's behalf, an update on 'the weather and travel near you' was broadcast.

> *'A four-car pile up has brought westbound traffic on the M62 to a standstill. The build-up of rush hour traffic and atrocious weather conditions are hampering the emergency services. Drivers are advised to stay in their vehicles and listen for further news bulletins.'*

And that was it. No advice on what to do if you were shit-scared and in need of a pee. Without my mobile phone I had no one to call. I wanted Nick. I wanted him to tell me what to do – about everything. A big fat tear rolled down my cheek and then another one. Sniffing, I opened the car door braving the snow that fell in on me. Drivers around me were beginning to turn off their engines and headlights; some, like me, were getting out of their vehicles, even walking a few yards up the hard shoulder, in an attempt to see what was going on, mobiles clamped to snow-covered hair and ears.

I got back in, rummaging about in the glove compartment for the half-eaten Mars bar I was sure I'd abandoned in there the week before. Only in pregnancy would I ever leave half a bar of chocolate – I'd started eating it feeling ravenous and ended, halfway through it, feeling thoroughly sick.

Comfort eating, I made another attempt to assess my life and the mess it was in. Twins! Where the hell had they come from? As far as I knew, there were no twins on either my side or on Nick's side of the family. I'd always wanted twins. One of each of course; or maybe identical boys who would adore their mother, as well as each other. God, I had to stop this. One new addition to the family would be a disaster; two would be an impossibility.

A wild thought went through my brain: maybe I could have these babies and let Grace bring one of them up? Grace would have the baby she so desperately wanted while perhaps I could, *somehow,* manage the other?

Nope, I'd seen *Blood Brothers* and look how that ended up. I didn't want my twin growing up only to be shot by Grace's twin. Or was it the other way round? Which twin shot which twin? Knowing Grace, it would *have* to be her twin that did mine in.

I thought back to last New Year when the five of us, even India, had gone to see the production at the Phoenix Theatre in London. Sylvia had treated us for our family Christmas present and we'd had a totally brilliant time. It had been a real family outing, seeing the play before having a meal and walking down towards Trafalgar Square to wait with the crowds for the fireworks at midnight. It had been India's first trip to London and she was ecstatic, insistent that her little legs could keep up with us until she eventually tired and Nick had lifted her on to his shoulders. We'd found a good vantage point with a jolly – probably boozed-up – crowd around us and waited for the display to begin. More and more revellers had come, squeezing into every available space, smelling of perfume and garlic and drink. I'd begun to feel uncomfortable, and then claustrophobic, and as the masses swelled and swayed, downright panicky.

'Nick, I've got to get out,' I'd said.

'Out? Out where?' Nick and the kids turned from the conversation they'd been having with another family, India gazing down at me from her vantage point on Nick's shoulders.

'I've just got to get out of this crowd,' I'd hissed, beginning to push my way back against the mass of bodies.

'Hat, you can't. You can't get out.'

'Nick, I have to. I can't *breathe.*'

And my wonderful husband came to the rescue, pushing back the crowd, easing me through the pressing, heaving mass of humanity with a 'Can we pass please? We have a child who needs to get through.' The relief, the utter relief I felt when I eventually reached the metal railing and hoisted myself over was immeasurable.

'You're a big Jessie, Mum,' my kids had jeered, but Nick had stroked my hair, calmed me and then winked at me as he set off back through the crowd once more, kids in tow.

If I hadn't been recollecting my claustrophobia, it would probably never have occurred to me to start feeling that I was trapped in my car, but the mind plays funny tricks, and pretty soon the mounting snow, now that the windscreen wipers were turned off, was beginning to make me feel hemmed in. I got out of the car again, took some deep breaths, had a bit of a walk round, even had a conversation with the guy in front and began to feel better. The snow flurries actually began to ease, and several flashing blue lights hurtling the wrong way up the other side of the motorway meant something was being done to get the traffic moving again.

I really was desperate for a pee: my whole abdomen seemed swollen and pulsating with the need to find a loo. Obviously I wasn't going to find one here. Could I just crouch down on the hard shoulder? God no. Not only was there half of West Yorkshire as audience, I'd probably freeze my tush off into the bargain.

The snowstorm seemed to be abating as I got back into the car and found what I was looking for under the passenger seat. I took the lid from the antifreeze container that had rolled there a couple of frosty mornings ago, pushed back my seat as far as it would go, hoisted up my skirt and, with my woolly tights and knickers at half-mast thanked God I was a whiz at pelvic-floor exercises. With the utmost control, I filled the lid, opened the window and threw its steaming contents out into the snow. Oh the relief as the pain began to recede with each filled lid.

I was just about to start on my six or seventh lidful, and was congratulating myself on my inventiveness, when there was a tap on the snow-covered window. I froze momentarily and then, galvanised into action, pulled up my knickers and tights and wound down the window.

'Harriet, it *is* you. I wasn't sure, but when you stepped out of the car a few minutes ago, I knew I recognised you.' David Henderson, buttoned up against the cold in a navy Crombie coat, snowflakes in his dark hair, was peering into the car.

The relief of seeing someone I knew was almost as tangible as the relief at having emptied my overstretched, indignant bladder.

'Oh, David, I'm so glad there's someone here that I know. I'm really terrified of this weather. And I'm frozen.' I hadn't realised just how cold I was, but the effort of grasping the antifreeze container lid, and then continually opening the window, had left my fingers numb.

'Come and get into my car,' David ordered. 'It's about four back from yours and much warmer.'

I locked my own car and followed David to the Porsche Cayenne that stood big, solid, and utterly dependable a few yards back up the motorway. Inside it was warm and smelled of Hugo Boss aftershave.

'You poor little thing,' David said noticing my white hands. 'Haven't you got any gloves?'

'I've lost them somewhere in the car.' I didn't like to tell him I'd abandoned them in order to pee better into an antifreeze tin lid. I rubbed my hands together, wincing as the blood began to return.

'Come here, my hands are warm.' David took my hands in his much warmer and larger ones and rubbed them gently. 'I've a hip flask somewhere,' he said. 'I use it occasionally when I'm playing golf.' Releasing my hands, he reached over to the glove compartment and brought out a small silver flask. 'It's got some brandy in it – here have some, it will warm you up a little.'

Handing it back after a swig of brandy that seemed to reach even my frozen toes, I couldn't help but read the inscription engraved in copperplate on the back of the silver flask:

To darling David. Love always, Mandy.

'Were you on your way home from work?' David asked. 'I thought you taught over in Farsley?'

'I had a hospital appointment at St Mark's and thought this would be the quickest route home. Obviously not,' I grimaced, looking at my watch. It was going up to six o'clock.

'Well, at least it's stopped snowing. Your exit is the next one isn't it?'

'Yes, but I'm absolutely terrified of driving once we do get going. I'm no good in snow. I know that you're supposed to steer into a skid, but I just close my eyes, jam on the brakes and pray the minute I feel the wheels going.'

David laughed. 'Typical woman. Look, once we get going, I'll get in front of you and you can follow me. If there's a problem we'll abandon your car somewhere safe and I'll drive you home.'

'Oh would you? That is *so* kind.' The relief at knowing I didn't have to battle my way home alone, together with the calming effects of the brandy made me almost light-headed. 'You're not a bit like I thought you were,' I said, almost shyly.

David laughed again. 'And what did you think I was like?'

'*The Godfather*. You know, like in the Mafia?'

'The Mafia?' David looked at me incredulously.

'Well, The Great White Shark at your dinner party more or less told me that if Nick didn't come up to scratch with your little dealings, you know, double-crossed you somehow, we'd probably find a horse's head in our bed.'

'Sharks? Horses' heads? Harriet, what in God's name are you

271

talking about?' David gave the silver flask a slight shake, obviously trying to work out if I'd had more than my fair share of the brandy.

I took a deep breath. I decided I might as well lay all my cards on the table. What had I to lose?

'David, I did *not* want Nick to go into any sort of partnership with you. After his first business went into liquidation we struggled to get ourselves back upright. But we did. We managed. Only just, mind you, but we did it.' I must have sounded very fierce because David sat back in his seat a little. 'I went back to teaching and, with what Nick earned at Wells Trading, we managed to keep our heads above water. And then *you* came along, with your fancy ideas, and your even fancier wife, and totally upset the equilibrium we'd managed to achieve. We were poor, but happy.' I could feel tears beginning to well.

'Bloody hell, Harriet, you sound like some B-rated movie. Poor but happy, for God's sake? When I met Nick he most certainly was *not* happy. He was utterly frustrated at being in a third-rate job, knowing, as did I once I'd researched his past history, just what a brilliantly clever man he is when it comes to the textile industry.'

'Well, why was that man at your house so obnoxious about you?' I said peevishly, feeling as if I was being well and truly told off.

'Which man?'

I struggled to recall his name. 'Got big white teeth – Mike somebody.'

'Mike Rawlinson? Oh, no wonder you think I'm a gangster if you'd been talking to Mike. He's desperate to do business with my company, but I wouldn't touch him with a bargepole – or, perhaps, according to you, a fishing rod.' David laughed to himself. 'As I say, Harriet, I only work with people who I can almost guarantee will come up trumps. Nick is one such person.'

'But what about the fifty thousand pounds you made Nick put up as surety? Where the hell do you think that came from?' I felt angry again, remembering that we still owed Sylvia the money.

'I've no idea, Harriet – that's really not my problem. But you don't think I was going to set Nick up with all my financial contacts without some sort of surety do you? I'll be honest with you, all business is bloody hard work at the moment and the eurozone problem isn't helping. It had made me think twice about investing in a new business, particularly in Europe.' David looked glum for a moment, but then smiled. 'I don't take risks, you know, I'm not really a gambling man, but this whole opportunity – as long as I could find the right man – was just too good to miss.' He laughed out loud. 'And Richard was very put out that I got in there before him.'

'Richard?'

'Mm? Richard? Oh, Richard Branson. Had lunch with him a couple of weeks back and told him all about it.'

Was this man for real? I stole a sideways glance at him, but he seemed genuine enough, chuckling away to himself and quite unaware that he'd been name-dropping. Not that I was particularly interested in the great bearded one. What I was more interested in was the whereabouts of Sylvia's fifty thousand pounds.

'Where is that money now?' I asked, looking David Henderson straight in the face. I pride myself on always being able to spot a fraud.

'In the bank, untouched, and ready to give back to Nick now that he's accomplished what we set out to do.'

I looked at David. 'What do you mean?'

David looked back at me, equally surprised. 'Well, he's taken the first step in achieving what we set out to do together. What I was backing him to do. I've very little knowledge of the textile industry, but Nick has masses of experience.'

'And what exactly *has* he achieved?' I asked slowly.

'Harriet, haven't you spoken to Nick lately?'

'Err no, not exactly.'

'Jesus, woman! Listen, Harriet, your husband has just pulled off one of the best deals ever in Italy. Even in the middle of this bloody recession he has managed to sign watertight contracts that have cornered the Italian market. It's obviously very early days, but with Nick's knowledge of the men's clothing industry and my company behind him, we are one step nearer in making a real go of this.' David sighed contentedly.

'We are?'

'Absolutely.'

So why wasn't I feeling overwhelmed with relief? Well, obviously there was still the little problem of Nick being out there with Amanda. What was the point of having a much-lauded husband if said husband was possibly about to push off with the wife of the very man who was singing his praises? And what about Grace and Sebastian? And my brother, John? I couldn't see David Henderson being too pleased about them. Would he think Nick and I were to blame for that?

I squirmed in my seat trying to work out what, if anything, to say to David about Nick and Amanda. He might not actually be a hood, but I couldn't see him being anything but pretty narked at my telling him what my husband and his wife had been up to in Milan.

'David, there is a slight problem,' I eventually said.

'What's that Harriet? You going to tell me my fancy wife, as you so succinctly put it, has got the hots for your husband?'

I stared at him. 'Err, well yes, I was actually. In fact, I was going to say that they've probably got the hots for each other.'

David sighed. 'Harriet, you have to know something about Mandy. She comes from a long line of serial philanderers. You wouldn't have known her father, Frank,' (Oh wouldn't I??) 'but he was a randy old goat. Chased anything in a skirt. While I truly believe that Mandy doesn't actually have affairs like her father did, she constantly needs the approval of other men. Blame her upbringing, if you like. While Frank did spoil her rotten, there was a lot of time when he wasn't there; when he was off like a dog on heat sniffing out his latest conquest. It was all in the chase, I'm sure. Once they'd submitted to his charms he tired of the whole thing and hotfooted it back home to Mandy's mother. Mandy, I'm sure you've noticed, wants to be admired, actually needs men to be enthralled with her and spends a lot of time and effort making sure that men fall in love with her.'

Was now the time to tell him about my brother John? Glancing once more at this man who'd rescued me from the snow, I had a feeling that, not only was John just one of many men at the beck and call of Little Miss Goodness, but that David Henderson would more than likely know everything about every one of them.

'But how does that make you feel?' I said indignantly, thinking of my poor silly brother and the hopelessness of the whole situation. I couldn't see that he'd ever be able to cut loose from her while she was allowed to play her games whenever, and with whom, she was allowed.

'Well, in a way, I'm partly to blame. I don't always give her the attention she craves – I'm away a lot and she gets bored. Her letting me know that other men fancy her is, I think she feels, a way of keeping me on my toes.'

'But don't you ever worry that she might actually go off with one of these men one day?'

'No. She'll always come back to me.' He said this without any arrogance. 'It's just the way we are. We understand each other. There's an unwritten rule that it never goes further than flirtation. I know that if I know about it I don't need to worry. And I know about her and Nick and exactly how far the flirtation goes. You really don't need to worry.'

It all sounded pretty weird to me. What a funny way to be married, having to play games all the time.

'Mandy craves affection,' David went on. 'I think it's something to do with being a Daddy's girl. Frank Goodners doted on her, but that didn't stop him having affairs with half the women in Midhope and beyond. With me, she has security. She knows I'll never leave her.'

'That's all very well and good, but what if my husband is in love with *her*? Where does that leave me?'

David sighed again and took my hand. 'Listen Harriet, when I'd done my homework and Nick's name came up over and over again as the man to headhunt for the Italian Job, as I called it, I approached Brian Thornton to get the low-down on him and arrange an introduction. You know who I mean by Brian?'

'Yes, of course I know Brian. He did a lot of work with Nick when he was running The Pennine Clothing Company.'

'Brian's known Mandy all his life. He's been in the textile trade for years – actually used to work for her father. When I said I'd probably have to send Mandy out to Italy with Nick because of her legal knowledge and because she's fluent in Italian, Brian laughed, saying at least Mandy wouldn't be able to get up to her old tricks with Nick Westmoreland.'

'Oh?'

David smiled. 'Brian said to me, "Nick Westmoreland is a one-woman man. Has the most gorgeous, if at times scatty, wife whom he absolutely adores. You need have no qualms about him being distracted by Mandy."'

'Really?' I felt myself go red with pleasure. 'Is that what Brian said?'

'Yep.'

'Would you mind just repeating that?'

'What?'

'The bit about having a wife whom he absolutely adores.'

David laughed again and ruffled my hair. 'If you've fallen out with Nick I don't suppose you know he was due to fly in to Manchester Airport this afternoon? I spoke to him last night and again this morning just before he left. If this snow hasn't held him up, he should be at home by now. Do you want to speak to him on my mobile? Tell him where you are?'

'No,' I said slowly, 'I'll surprise him.'

'Up to you. Come on then, it looks like the traffic might be moving. Let's get you home.'

Chapter 25

Once off the motorway I followed David Henderson down into the valley where we lived, the amount of fallen snow decreasing steadily as we got to the lower levels. It was still pretty treacherous, but nothing like the conditions caused by the freak blizzard on the motorway.

By the time we were a mile or so from home, sleet was already turning what snow there was to a wet slush and David indicated before stopping at the side of the road. He jumped out of his car and came back to where I'd pulled up behind him.

'Do you think you'll be OK from here?' he asked as I wound down the window. 'I'll go all the way with you if you'd rather, but I think the roads are pretty clear now and Mandy has just rung wondering where I am.'

'What, she's rung from Italy?'

'Italy?' David asked, frowning. 'Mandy's been back from Italy for almost a week. She flew out for a couple of days to ensure the legal documents were all in order before Nick signed on the dotted line, but she didn't need to stay out any longer than that. I have to say I was surprised when she didn't stay longer – Milan is her favourite city – but she said she had to do some sorting out with that nice friend of yours – Grace is she called? Don't ask me what. She was very cagey about it.'

Seeing the expression on my face, David reached into the car and, tying my scarf more securely round my neck, kissed my cheek. 'Look, lovey, I don't know what's going on between you and Nick,' he said, 'but you need to get home and sort it out. Take it from me, your husband is one man Mandy didn't manage to play games with.

I always know when she's not got her own way with whoever she's been dallying with – she comes home, stays home and makes my dinner every night. Which is where I'm going now, with a bottle of champagne and some flowers if I can find any.'

David squeezed my still cold hand before saying, 'And I can quite understand why Nick will always be a one-woman man when it comes to you: you *are* gorgeous, even with a cold nose and mascara that's run.' He reached into the car, kissed me, almost politely, and was off.

I realised I was smiling. No, grinning. In fact very soon I reckoned I'd be laughing out loud. My euphoria lasted as long as it took me to reverse off the pavement and skid into the road, missing a lamp post by inches.

I drove slowly home, trying to remember the exact words Nick had used in that last telephone conversation we'd had over a week ago – and of course there was Suzy's photo to take in to consideration – but nothing made sense any more.

I finally pulled, or rather skidded, into our drive at seven o'clock. It had taken almost three hours from leaving the hospital to getting home. Nick's car was parked up by the front door – he'd obviously made it home before the snow had started to come down.

I realised I felt horribly nervous, my euphoria draining away again with each mile that brought me closer to home. What if David was being incredibly naïve about Nick and Amanda's relationship and Nick was, even at this moment, packing his bags to move out while desperately thinking of the best way to break the news to me?

I sat in the car, unwilling to actually walk up the path and face Nick. Then I shook myself, reached into my handbag for my reddest lipstick, replaced my run mascara and combed my fingers through my hair. A good squirt of 'Aromatics' and I was ready for action.

There was no evidence of any packing having been done: no bags, suitcases or suits in their protective hangers slung over the banisters in the hall waiting only for my return before being bundled into Nick's car. Bones appeared, weaving comfortingly through my legs as I made my way down to the sitting room; someone had obviously let him out of the utility room.

There was no television noise, no CD playing. Silence prevailed.

Nick lay on the settee, a half-empty glass of whiskey on the floor beside him. His eyes were closed, blue shadows of utter exhaustion smudged beneath them. I walked right up to him, gazing down at his beloved face, but still he didn't stir, one arm thrown up above his head, the dark-blue pinstriped material of his suit jacket nestling carelessly in his tousled dark-blonde hair.

'Hi,' he said sleepily, his velvety chocolate eyes opening as he yawned. 'Where on earth have you been? What time is it?'

'Past seven o'clock. I need to fetch the children – they're all out at friends.''

'How're you doing?' That's all he said, but his gaze never left my face, and he took my arm pulling me down to him. He was warm, and the faint tang of lemon, Nick's beloved smell, filled my senses.

We lay there for a good half a minute, Nick's arms clamped tightly around me. This surely wasn't the action of a husband about to leave home for another woman?

'Are you home for good?' I whispered into his neck, holding my breath until he spoke.

'For good?' Nick struggled to sit up, releasing his hold on me only to push his hair back and reach for his whiskey.

'Are you staying?'

'Staying?'

'Nick, will you stop repeating what I've just said?' I needed to take the bull by the horns, but seeing as there was nothing remotely bovine in the sitting room, I did the next best thing and grasped Nick by his suit lapels instead. 'Are you staying here with me and your children or are you leaving us for Amanda?'

'No, Harriet, I am not leaving you for Mandy or anyone else,' Nick said wearily.

'But you said you needed her, couldn't be without her.'

'Did I? When?' Nick looked at me in genuine surprise.

'When you rang home last week.'

'Ah, well, yes, I probably *did* say that. I *did* need her. Bloody hell, Harriet, it really was touch and go at one point. We had two evenings when Mandy was supposed to be going over the legal stuff with the Italians and on the first evening I couldn't find her in the hotel. We had an appointment that we almost ended up missing because she'd had a phone call from a friend telling her she'd seen Sebastian wrapped around some woman old enough to be his mother. I eventually found her down in one of the street cafes on her mobile desperately trying to get in touch with Sebastian and, I think, Grace.'

'Grace? How the hell did she know the woman was Grace?'

'Apparently the friend was one of her prefect cronies from school and knows Grace as well as Mandy does. She knew Mandy had some sort of issue from the past with Grace and couldn't wait to get on the blower and spill the beans.'

'Blimey.' I could see how close Nick had been to losing the contract. With Amanda so distracted over the knowledge that her beautiful son was throwing himself away on Grace she wouldn't have been able to concentrate on anything else.

'I had to calm her down, soothe her and get her back up to the hotel ...'

'Hang on a minute,' I interrupted. '*Soothe* her? Just exactly how did you go about *soothing* her?'

Nick hesitated. 'Look, Hat,' he said finally, 'I had to calm her down, alright? I had to hold her, physically wrap my arms around her to keep her sitting there. If I hadn't she'd have been off in a taxi to the airport. I'd never seen her like that before. She has got real issues with Grace, you know.'

A light seemed to go on in my brain as Nick spoke of having his arms around Amanda. *He* didn't know I'd seen photographic evidence of his apparent infidelity, so why would he bother to tell me all this unless it was as he said? I tried to recapture the image on Suzy's Blackberry. He *had* had his arms round her, but I suppose, like he said, they could have been there to *restrain* her rather than as an indication of any *passion* for her.

'Yes, you don't have to tell me about Amanda and Grace.' I now said. 'Amanda's been like this about Grace ever since we were young but, I have to say, since we've got to know her again, she seems to have got worse rather than better, even before she found out about her and Seb. She's totally over the top about it, don't you think? I mean, for heaven's sake, why can't she just laugh about what happened when we were kids? But that's Amanda for you, I suppose.' I shook my head at the thought. 'So what happened then?'

'I *had* to get her back up to the hotel. I knew there were at least three others, including some Germans and another lot from near Leeds, who were pitching for the contract. If we didn't turn up to sign the first set of papers that evening there were others who would. And that would have meant the end of everything.' Nick ran his hand through his hair distractedly. 'That was Sunday evening, I think. By two in the morning we still hadn't sorted everything out and we had to have another round of talks on the Monday and Tuesday. I tell you, it was nerve-racking keeping everything going when I could see Mandy was getting more and more distracted.'

'I bet she was all over you wasn't she?' I said crossly. Even though I really was beginning to see Nick's point of view and understand the position he'd been in, I still couldn't bear the thought of Amanda in his arms. It might have been a restraining hug to Nick, but I didn't for one minute believe that Amanda didn't relish both the embrace and the whole drama of it all.

'I bet she loved every minute of it,' I said. 'Don't forget, Nicholas – I know just what she's like.'

'Does it matter if she did love it?' Nick sighed again and drained his glass of whiskey. 'What does matter is that it worked – I got her back up to the hotel on that first evening and kept her on course for the next two days. If she hadn't been there as interpreter – she really is fluent in Italian, Russian and German you know – or as my lawyer – she's amazingly on the ball with the legal jargon – I would not have been able to pull off the deal that means, my darling Harriet, we are going to be fine. OK, it's still going to be a hell of a lot of hard work, I'm not saying it isn't, but you really don't have to worry any more. I promise you, Hat, it is going to be FINE!'

I wasn't convinced. He was still speaking about Amanda with reverence.

When I didn't say anything, just looked at him, Nick took my hand saying, 'Didn't you hear what I just said? I've done it! I've got the contract! David and I are going to be managing the most fabulous Italian menswear you've ever seen. Eventually womenswear as well. There's a huge market for top Italian designer brands particularly in London but also in Germany and, apparently Russia, which are the places to be at the moment. The Italians want to sell it and the Germans and the Russians want to buy it. David's company – with me in the hot seat – has the ability to bring all interested parties together. Yes, Harriet, I will have to travel back to Italy and also to Germany and probably Russia as well but it will be worth it.'

'Russia? Are you mad? It's all snow and The Mafia isn't it?'

Nick laughed as he stroked my hair. 'And vodka. And of course there's no bloody Mafia involved, you moron. I tell you, Hat, David Henderson is not only one of the most astute business people I've ever come across, he's also the most law-abiding and scrupulously honest guy I've ever worked with. He's got far too much to lose to ever cosy up with any dirty dealing. Would you be happy if it was Richard Branson who was behind all this? Yes? Well, David is the Richard Branson of the North!'

'Mmm,' I still had my doubts, particularly where Amanda was concerned, although the time spent with David that afternoon had given him a hell of a lot of Brownie points. 'Carry on,' I said, 'tell me more. Oh and keep on with the hair-stroking too!'

'Let me put it in a nutshell,' Nick went on. 'Italy produces some of the most beautifully designed and manufactured clothing. Right? And people can't get enough of it. Even China and India, now that they are on the up and up, want this stuff. David realised all this, had the money and contacts to set the ball rolling but needed someone in the textile trade to source the best stuff. That's where I come in. David will back me to the hilt, Harriet. He's invested a lot of time and money in this venture – he's actually been working on it for years – and waterproof contracts have been signed.'

'But are you sure people are still wanting these expensive clothes?'

Nick smiled. 'Absolutely. Look, this is a global economy. There will always be people somewhere with money who are prepared to pay money for quality. Look at Mulberry handbags. Even when there's not as much money about, people still can't get enough of them. They're opening factories in Turkey and China to cope with the demand. What you have to remember is that this is *beautiful* Italian clothing and that David had already got the contacts here, but needed me, with my knowledge of the textile trade, to be the middle man.'

'And Amanda? Nick, you know I have to ask.' I looked into his face, searching for anything that might confirm my suspicions that Nick's 'soothing' of Amanda might have involved a lot more than just a comforting, restraining hug, but all I saw was love. Love for *me*.

'Harriet, my darling, I love you.' Nick leaned forward, simultaneously untying the scarf that was wrapped around my neck and kissing me gently on my lower lip. 'There's never been anyone else for me since the moment my eye caught yours in the union bar,' he went on, his mouth still soft against mine. 'I know you've had a rough time this last couple of years but you never once complained even when Mum moved in with us.'

'Oh Nick,' I said, ashamed. 'I've done nothing *but* complain from the moment you signed up with David Henderson.'

'Understandable. I know how hard it's been for you especially with Mandy in the equation. I'd have been just the same if you'd swanned off to Italy with some hunk of a man leaving me to work full time, share the house with *your* mother as well as bring up three kids.'

Put like that I felt much better. Maybe I wasn't such an old harridan after all.

'Talking of my mother, Nick, there's ever such a lot I need to tell you …' I never got any further. His mouth, more insistent now, cut me off, mid-sentence.

Nick loosened his tie, his eyes never leaving mine, his fingers slowly stroking the inside of my thigh.

'What time did you say you had to pick the kids up?' Nick asked, unbuttoning my white shirt at the neck before kissing my collarbone.

'Half an hour ago,' I said, as I loosened his tie further, undid his buttons slowly and licked my way down his chest. 'Wow,' I whispered, as I descended further, 'Is that a present from Italy, or are you just pleased to see me?'

An hour later, sated with sex and love, I sat up, looking round for the remains of my clothes.

'There is something you need to know.' We both spoke at the same time.

I knew *I* certainly had something that I couldn't keep from Nick for much longer. I hadn't quite picked my moment until then – was actually a bit nervous now about coming out with the news that he was not only going to be a daddy again but this time of twins. Blimey, five kids! But I reckoned after the mind-blowing sex we'd just had, I could get away with anything.

'Go on, you first,' I smiled, hoping he was going to tell me again how much he loved and adored me. I'm a sucker for declarations like that.

'Well, I promised I wouldn't tell you ...'. Nick hesitated, not meeting my eyes.

'Tell me what?' I was alert now. 'Tell me *what*, Nicholas!'

Nick still hesitated and then said, 'I promised Mandy I wouldn't tell you ...'. And then, 'Mind you, she's probably told her herself by now.'

'Told who what, for God's sake?'

'Well, you're not going to believe this.' Nick sighed and stopped speaking as he refilled his glass from the decanter on the nearby table.

'Believe what? *What?*'

'Well, the real reason Mandy was so desperate to get back to England and why I had to literally hang on to her or she'd have been off, was that she's got it into her head that Grace is her half-sister. And if so, then Sebastian is having sex with his aunt!'

I just stared at Nick. Was I missing something here? Hadn't I spent the last week getting used to the idea that *I* had a new half-sister? Of course Mandy would have to be told about Patricia being *her* half-sister too, but where the hell did Grace come into all this? Before I could tell him about Mum and Patricia, Nick went on, 'It seems Mandy's father, Frank Goodners, was a bit of a poet on the side. Also kept diaries. When he died, five years ago, Mandy had the job of going through all his things. She found diaries going back years. Apparently one of the entries logged that he'd been to see a play at your old school.'

'Yes, he did,' I interrupted, 'I told you all about that.'

'Well apparently he wrote something along the lines of, "I saw my beautiful Kat today. I'd no idea her daughter was at school with Amanda. She was in the play Amanda has been directing, and I suggested to Amanda that she brought the daughter and a couple of her friends back to the house for tea. I've never forgiven myself for not doing anything to help Kat when I heard she'd had my baby all these years ago, and I wanted to have a good look at the girl – see if she was anything like Kat."'

'Nick, none of this is making any sense.' I continued staring at him, my mind reeling.

'Mandy recalled having seen Grace's mother talking to Frank constantly during the play's interval and, after reading the diary entry, made some enquiries as to Grace's mother's name.'

'Katherine,' I said automatically. 'Grace's mum is called Katherine'

'Exactly!' Nick said with some degree of triumph. 'Katherine – Kat. There you go. Sounds to me like Grace's mum had a fling with Frank while he was married to Mandy's mum and Grace was the result. Katherine must have got pregnant and then almost immediately married Grace's father – presumably told him the baby was his. Bloody hell, Hat, no wonder Mandy was in such a state when she got that phone call from her friend in Italy.' He suddenly became serious. 'Mandy *must* have told Sebastian by now. Hasn't Grace said anything to you?'

I shook my head, as much in response to Nick's question as to try and clear my head. 'I've not seen Grace all week. She's been away on a course. And anyway, she's not really speaking to me.'

'Well, someone's going to have to tell Grace, you know. I'm sure there's a law against having sex with your nephew, half or otherwise.'

I suddenly began to laugh. Great big, almost hysterical guffaws that went on and on and then, before I realised it, turned into sobs. All this emotion was too much for me. I was tired out, exhausted by the events of the last few hours.

'Wrong Kat, Sherlock,' I eventually hiccupped. 'Kat is Keturah.'

'*Your* mother! Oh, my God, Frank Goodners was *your* father and *you're* Mandy's sister?' Nick looked aghast and I started to cry again. Frank Goodners had known all along that my mum had had his baby and he'd done nothing about it.

'No, Nick, I'm not and Grace certainly isn't. But Patricia is.'

Six months on …

It's a hot Friday afternoon and I'm stretched out on a sunbed in the garden, soaking up the late May sunshine and rubbing oil into my already tanned bump. The daffodils, planted in my little plot by Dad and his bevy of six year olds at India's 'garden party', have already been doubled over and tied back with rubber bands, but the tulips are still a riot of colour.

Lying next to me, resting her nicely browning arms on a just-oiled bump of her own, is Mrs Pregnancy-Expert herself – my best friend Grace. Seems she had no problem getting pregnant after being ditched by Daniel and taking up with the lovely Sebastian.

'Inferior swimmers, obviously,' Grace had sniffed, referring to Daniel's sperm. And, secure in her own fecundity, had gone even further, suggesting that had Daniel been a prize pig (which of course, in all our minds, was just what he was – the adulterous swine) then his lack of breeding ability would soon have had him on a breakfast plate together with an egg and a nice piece of fried bread!

Coming from a long line of philanderers, and being hardly more than a baby himself, one might have imagined that Sebastian, on learning the news, would have been off, roaring down the M1 on his motorbike, leaving Grace to her fate as a single parent. But no, rather than disappearing off to London to do his law course, he switched to one at Leeds University and moved both himself and his Harley-Davidson in with Grace.

As soon as Amanda had helped Nick clinch the Italian Job last November, she had flown home and (quite hysterically, I gather) told Sebastian that he must have nothing more to do with Grace, that if they'd been even *thinking* about it, they must certainly not *attempt to* – in Amanda's words – consummate their relationship, because Grace was, in all reality, quite probably his aunt.

'A bit late for that, Mum,' Sebastian had said grimly and gone round to break the news to Grace. Whereupon Grace had gone straight round to *her* mum's to have it out with her.

Katherine Greenwood, Grace's mother, had (allegedly) raised herself up to her full height (she's five foot nothing in her stockinged feet) and said, how dare she? There had only ever been one man in her life and that was Grace's father. And, she would have Grace know, she had walked down that aisle to Grace's father unsullied, untouched by any man, a true bride!

Grace and Sebastian are hoping that their offer on a dilapidated farmhouse with a huge overgrown garden – Sebastian apparently is itching to get his hands on it – will be accepted later on today.

Daniel is still hanging around hoping that Grace will, as he puts it, come to her senses and 'ditch the little toe-rag' so that he can move back home and take care of his wife and her baby. He's assured her that he won't hold it against her that the baby isn't his (good of him) and he'll bring it up as if it were his own if only she'd see sense and let them start over.

Grace reckons he'll get the message soon that, even if she didn't have Sebastian at home, she's more than capable of bringing up this much-wanted babe on her own. Her parents are overjoyed that they're going to be grandparents at last and will be happy to help her financially if needs be. Considering that Grace's baby will have the legacy of the Henderson millions as well as the Goodners' fortune at its fingertips, I hardly think that will be necessary.

Patricia came over from Australia last month to meet her natural mother for the first time since being given up for adoption almost sixty years earlier. She stayed with us for some of the time and also with Diana. Both Diana and I were with her when she and Mum came face to face. It was an amazingly emotional reunion and we all wept buckets.

Of course we can't forget that Little Miss Goodness is just as much a sister to Patricia as we are. When I first broke the news to Amanda that her beloved father had seduced and impregnated *my* mother all those years ago she'd coloured slightly but coolly retorted that she wasn't a bit surprised that her father might have sired other offspring. She was already aware of one half-brother in Midhope and another half-sister in London. I think the real disappointment for Amanda was that her father had had an affair with one of his mill girls – rather slumming it, after all. It also meant that there was absolutely no reason why Sebastian shouldn't move in with Grace.

Patricia (I find it difficult to think of her as Joy) and Amanda are very alike both in looks and bearing, but Diana and I reckon she's more like our side of the family in temperament. For a start, she has a brilliant sense of humour, and although she's way up in her chosen field of medicine – the power thing, admittedly, must be in her Goodners' genes – she's seriously scatty in a lot of other ways.

I'd love to report that, once she'd been reunited with Patricia, Mum's eccentric behaviour became a thing of the past, but unfortunately that's not really the case. Having found her long-lost baby she doesn't need to go looking for her anymore, but she still has blazing rows with Granny Morgan. Luckily, these appear to be confined to Mum and Dad's kitchen rather than amongst the baked beans in Sainsbury's. Dad is really brilliant with her, and we are hoping that the medication she's on will help to slow down her illness.

Amanda is still doing what she does best – reigning supreme and looking a million dollars while doing so. She would like me to think, I'm sure, that Nick fell passionately in love with her in Italy but that she sent him packing. Back to the little wife in Yorkshire. And who knows? Maybe there *was* a bit of unconfessed dallying between the pair of them in Milan. Would *I* have admitted to a quick snog with George Michael had I ever found myself alone with him? (On meeting me in Milan, George, of course, would have suddenly realised just what he'd been missing all these years with regards his sexual orientation!)

Amanda had a huge rant once she was told of Grace's pregnancy.

Not only was she going to be a granny at the age of forty-four, there was every chance she'd end up as Grace's mother-in-law. I reckon that David, whose first meeting with Grace in her German Officer get-up had left him impressed and happy to have Grace as a prospective daughter-in-law, had serious words with Amanda. After all, the new Italian Clothing Company – Luomo – would need a company lawyer and what better way of keeping it all in the family than by giving the job to Sebastian once his training was complete?

I don't delve too deeply into what I assume to be my brother John's ongoing relationship with Amanda. Any time he tries to discuss her with me, I just tell him I don't want to know – to keep me out of it. I think she'll probably always be a part of his life and, as the song goes, 'he'd rather live in her world than live without her in his.' Perhaps I'm being simplistic, but she's his drug and I guess he has to see her every now and again for a fix. It probably makes living with poor Caring Christine bearable and, while Hollie, John and Christine's only child, is my niece, she's a grown woman and I don't feel the need to fight any corners on her behalf. As I said, it really isn't my problem. I'm *almost* convinced that David was absolutely right about Amanda and her flirting – that it's just that and nothing more. I say 'almost' convinced because, at the end of the day, the main player in these little dramas is Amanda. And who knows with Amanda?

We're still nowhere near being millionaires – but I'm happy to say we're getting there. I still can't believe that Nick has managed to pull this off when this country, and much of the world, is riding such economic turbulence. But he has. He is working incredibly hard, but loving every minute. He knows he's not alone with this company; he has David Henderson's business expertise and money behind him this time round.

I quit work at Easter. I didn't dare give up until then – still couldn't believe we would be able to manage without my wage. I miss the buzz of working, and my new best friend Tony Drummond has promised me some part-time work if I want it, much to the disdain of Valerie Westwood who doesn't believe in working mothers *or* part-time teachers.

Sylvia is back living in the South, her little flat being converted back to the main part of the house by bronzed-bodied lovelies as we speak. Unbeknown to Nick she'd kept in touch with his ex-girlfriend's parents in Surrey – she probably hoped I was a flash in the pan and that once Nick had come to his senses she'd be able to orchestrate his reunion with the District Judge's daughter.

Which, if it were to happen now, would result in a relationship with his future step-sister because Sylvia has done the next best thing and got herself engaged to, and moved in with (the hussy), the widowed District Judge himself!

My garden is looking fantastic. Armed with rubber gloves and protective clothing (one can't be too careful when pregnant – there might be some nasty Toxoplasmosis just ready to jump out from the soil) I've harvested my first lettuces and leeks. Kit's been helping, for mercenary rather than altruistic reasons of course, and I've spent many a happy weekend down here with Dad and India in tow.

And Nick and me? Well, once he'd got over the shock of me being not just pregnant but pregnant with twins, Nick took me out for a celebratory meal to a cosy little restaurant we'd always wanted to visit but couldn't afford. As I sipped my (non-alcoholic) wine, his eyes never once left mine.

And there we were once more, but twenty years on. Playing that glorious game which has only two players. And which ignores everything around it, but concentrates solely on the meeting of eyes, again and again.

'Lust,' Grace laughed when I told her all about it the following day. 'Pure, unadulterated, no other word for it, Lust.'

'The One,' I laughed back, secure in the knowledge that indeed he was, and always would be, The One.

Printed in Great Britain
by Amazon.co.uk, Ltd.,
Marston Gate.